The Diva's Daughter

The Diva's Daughter

Heather Walrath

The
Book
Guild

First published in Great Britain in 2025 by
The Book Guild Ltd
Unit E2 Airfield Business Park,
Harrison Road, Market Harborough,
Leicestershire. LE16 7UL
Tel: 0116 2792299
www.bookguild.co.uk
Email: info@bookguild.co.uk

The manufacturer's authorised representative in the EU
for product safety is Authorised Rep Compliance Ltd,
71 Lower Baggot Street, Dublin D02 P593 Ireland (www.arccompliance.com)

This work is entirely fictitious and bears no resemblance to any persons living or dead.

Typeset in 11pt Minion Pro

Printed and bound by CPI Group (UK) Ltd, Croydon, CR0 4YY

ISBN 9781835743324

British Library Cataloguing in Publication Data.
A catalogue record for this book is available from the British Library.

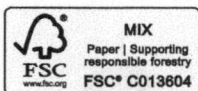

MIX
Paper | Supporting
responsible forestry
FSC® C013604

For Nana and Mom, whose love helped me soar

One

*A*ngelika wasn't supposed to be singing. She wasn't supposed to be visiting Viktor Bauer's beer garden at all. Yet there she stood – a Viennese immigrant bleeding Bavarian patriotism while wearing a blue-and-white striped peasant dress reminiscent of the state flag flapping high above the brewery.

"Ein Prosit, ein Prosit!"

Angelika's words slurred, and the notes stretched sharp as she led a crowd of sweaty middle-aged men and boisterous brown-shirted boys in a rendition of the traditional German drinking song. How simple this sort of superficial performance seemed. Much simpler than singing long legato lines and finessing Italian phrasing with her overbearing voice teacher.

"A toast to friendliness!"

Warmed by the *Biergarten*'s strands of shimmering

lights, plus a couple too many steins of *Märzen* lager, Angelika attempted to ignore the gaping, ever-present gash that eviscerated her heart. As usual, the chaotic ugliness surrounding her was a far cry from the elegant Vienna State Opera and marvellous memories she and her mother had made there.

"One, two, three…"

Nevertheless, for these few fleeting moments, she could smile and laugh, pretending she felt every bit the carefree, spellbinding eighteen-year-old young woman Herr Bauer and his followers believed her to be.

"…drink!"

Angelika carried the song to its end, the courtyard seeming to spin as pairs of arms and wandering hands lifted her down from the rickety table upon which she teetered.

"Kiss me, beautiful," a sausage-breathed boy all but demanded, his frenetic fingertips tangling in Angelika's auburn hair.

"No, kiss me," said another.

"*Nein*, boys, that's enough." Angelika's pulse quickened, and she squirmed beneath the brownshirts' grasp. "Not so tight, now." The young men's odorous musk mixed together with the unsettling stink of other patrons' cigarette smoke. "Please, I need some air."

Angelika searched the crowd for the faithful friend who'd remained by her side all evening long until his father – the brewery owner – had called him away. She hated asking a man, friend or not, to rescue her. But at the moment, Angelika believed she had little choice.

"Erich," Angelika said.

She kept hollering his name, but her cries evaporated amidst a rollicking sea of beige.

"For the Fatherland!" The Hitler Youth and *Sturmabteilung* recruits pummelled the air with their saluting palms. "*Sieg Heil!*"

Angelika's prior giddiness gave way to impending nausea.

"Come on, gorgeous, cheer with us."

If only a meeting hadn't kept her sweetheart working late at the office. Then she'd have spent an evening dining and dancing instead of whiling away the hours at Bauerbräu alongside hypocritical men who on one hand spouted drivel about feminine virtue and domesticity, yet also fell like flies while ogling dazzling socialites, models and actresses, including the fiery red-headed Swedish songstress Zarah Leander and sultry German screen star Marlene Dietrich. Heaven only knew why they'd condoned Angelika's silly serenade. Nor could she be certain how long their bewitchment might last.

"Are you all right, Angelika?"

A muffled shout met her ears.

"Erich?"

Her friend was still nowhere to be seen. Uniformed Johann Schmitt, however, elbowed his way through the crowd and enveloped her in a vice-like embrace.

"Do you know where Erich is?" Angelika asked.

In spite of the warm August evening, Johann's hands felt like ice.

"His father sent him to see whether a group of

conniving communists tossed rocks through one of the festival hall's windows," Johann replied, pimply cheeks dimpling as he smiled at Angelika. "But don't worry. I've got you."

The quad continued to sway, and she had no choice but to lean against Johann's stiff, scratchy shirt.

"You shouldn't drink so much, though." The seventeen-year-old Hitler Youth devotee attempted to feather nubby strands of his recently cropped blond hair. "I don't drink, and neither do most of my friends. You'd feel a lot better that way."

Angelika wasn't so certain. For as dreadful as she always felt afterward, the burning alcoholic brews never failed to dilute her pain, at least temporarily.

"Sorry I spilled mustard all over your regular dress," Johann went on. "But you look lovely wearing that old *Dirndl* Erich dug up. Your voice sounds sensational, too. How about coming to sing at some of our National Socialist concerts?"

Another male voice cut through the cacophony before Angelika could answer.

"Let go, Johann." Angelika recognised Erich's vocal rhythm, and she willed her hazy eyes to focus upon the well-built, nineteen-year-old former classmate standing on the cobblestones. "If she'd wanted to surround herself with wild boars, she'd have headed to the Black Forest to join a hunting party. Are you all right, Anni? I came running back as soon as I saw those overeager octopuses grabbing ahold of you."

"I'm fine," Angelika said.

She moved away from Johann, then leant forward to clutch Erich's muscled arm, which was covered by soft, cerulean-coloured cotton rather than a rough brown shirtsleeve.

"Why don't I walk you home?" he asked.

Angelika took a stumbling step, dreading the one-and-a-half-kilometre journey.

"You don't have to escort me."

But she continued holding onto Erich while Johann and his friends inundated the pathway.

"Sing for us," they said, along with something else unintelligible.

"No more singing tonight," Erich answered.

"Sing for us. Come sing for us."

"Yes," Angelika said with a dismissive wave of the hand, the boys fading into the background as Erich propelled her forward. "Very well. Next time."

"She said yes. She'll do it. She'll sing for us."

Angelika gripped Erich's bicep all the way back to her quiet residential neighbourhood, where she stumbled across a canal bridge and caught glimpses of the ornate Nymphenburg Palace looming in the distance.

"At this rate, I'll never become a famous opera singer," she whispered as the two of them passed beneath lush chestnut trees and approached a three-storey dwelling quite smaller than her family's forsaken villa in Vienna. "So much for my mother's legacy."

Angelika often wondered what might have happened if she'd remained alone in Vienna the previous summer, pursuing her dream and continuing to work with the talented teachers she loved. But that would have meant facing the backlash from her mother's scandalous death and being chaperoned by hateful relatives, all while enduring the sharp tongues and vicious stares of people she'd once trusted. Instead, Angelika had followed her father and twin brother to Munich in search of a safe haven, leaving her beloved mother – her dearest friend – buried in Vienna's Central Cemetery alongside an irreplaceable piece of her heart.

"I was only having fun tonight," Angelika muttered. "Trying to set aside my troubles."

"I know," Erich said. "We overdid it with the alcohol."

Angelika's gaze had steadied enough to take in his lamplit hazel eyes and sloppy, sand-coloured hair. She'd never forget the way he used to rake frustrated fingers through messy curls after bungling every last French vocabulary exam at the secondary school they'd attended. Nor the way he'd gifted her a jaunty beret during their July graduation festivities at the brewery, as thanks for her tutoring efforts. When they'd first met the previous year, she as a new arrival in Munich and he as a struggling student upon whom she'd taken pity, Angelika had hardly expected they would form a lasting friendship.

"I'll collect my regular dress and return this *Dirndl* tomorrow," she told Erich.

"I can ask my housekeeper to deliver the dress." Erich handed Angelika her peacock-embroidered pocketbook, which he'd mercifully remembered to grab before leaving the beer garden. "As for the *Dirndl*, you may as well keep it."

"I can't. Not after Johann Schmitt said I looked lovely in it."

"Johann is a *Dummkopf*, but this is one time he's right."

Even though Erich wasn't a singer, Angelika could imagine his voice ringing out as a rich and chocolatey baritone.

"You can forget the flattery," she said, heat rising into her cheeks. "Save that for your sweethearts."

"Last time I checked, the only girl I want for a sweetheart is taken."

Angelika's thoughts flickered back to the blustery October day when he'd asked her to forgo studying French and instead see a film adaptation of *The Threepenny Opera*. But after suffering the loss of her mother, Angelika hadn't felt ready to begin courting again, much less open her heart to someone she'd just recently met. And now, many months later, her heart belonged to an accomplished and far more suitable young man.

"I'm going inside now, before I get sick," she said.

"Fine, but I stand by what I said before."

"That I look 'lovely' in this *Dirndl*?"

"You look lovely because you *are* lovely. And not just because of a certain outfit or the way you danced on top of a table."

Angelika started to answer back, but found that her stomach had other plans. The nausea resurging, she rushed inside, then spent the following hour huddled upon the bathroom floor in a house that would never feel like home.

Tomorrow would be better, she promised herself as relentless grief crashed all around. Tomorrow, she would douse her regrets in coffee and chocolate, then forget this invigorating and infuriating night had ever happened.

And by the following afternoon, Angelika remained determined to do exactly that.

*

Though lacking the familiar world-class teachers Angelika had studied with in Vienna, Böhm's School of Music and Dance was well-regarded, and she headed there almost every day for private or group voice lessons, an occasional waltz class and sessions with the school's recently hired expression adviser.

Given the steady rise of cinema, I predict that in the coming decades, there'll be more emphasis placed on singers' acting ability. Angelika could hear Viennese opera director Daniel Weiss's astute advice playing out inside her head and pulling at her heart. So many months – more than a year – had passed since Angelika, her mother and Daniel had last made music together while gathered about his heirloom upright piano, hope still alive.

Angelika continued reflecting upon Daniel's kind voice and thoughtful nature as she made her way down a chandelier-lined corridor past other secondary school- and university-aged students toting everything from sheet music and violin cases to pointe shoes and librettos. She'd squandered so much time at her favourite café, sipping away the previous night's regrets, that she had missed her group voice lesson and was late for dance class.

"Are my eyes deceiving me, or is your form getting

worse by the minute?" Even before rounding the corner, Angelika could hear her teacher's reprimanding words carry beyond the partially open ballroom door. "What sort of a finish was that?"

Angelika peeked inside just as the final piano notes were fading and a gaggle of exhausted dancers went limp.

"Fine, I suppose that's enough for today," Margarete went on, her small stature and immaculate appearance belying the roughness of her tone. "But thanks to that lazy closing, we're going to add an extra ten minutes next time."

Agitated whisperings filled the room, and the would-be-waltzers began gathering their belongings while Margarete Böhm vanished out of one of the side doors right ahead of the pianist. Angelika had apparently arrived even later than expected, and she quickly turned to go, hoping that, for once, she'd manage to elude Margarete unnoticed.

"Why, if it isn't Angelika Eder."

No such luck.

"I knew I'd seen you peering through the doorway." Margarete's petite figure appeared alongside her slinking student. Though she'd never spoken extensively about her past, word in the artistic circles said that fifty-year-old Margarete had once been the toast of Belle Époque Paris in the decade preceding the Great War. "It's so good of you to grace us with your presence, although it is a pity you couldn't do us that honour while class was still in session. A word, please."

A frown marring her fastidiously made-up face, Margarete gripped Angelika's arm and ushered her into the emptying ballroom, where a couple of lingering students scurried away, afraid of getting caught in the crossfire. Angelika could hardly blame them, her own heartbeat echoing in her ears as she waited for Margarete to start in with what was sure to be a very impassioned, or at least very loud, scolding.

"So, to what do I owe the privilege of seeing you this afternoon?" the instructor began, shaking her head but sounding slightly less harsh in tone than she had when addressing all of the other students. "It appears you took the liberty of skipping class again."

Angelika didn't respond.

"I know you're far too advanced for some of these group sessions, but your absence sets a poor example for the other pupils. Do you understand?"

"Yes." Angelika hoped Margarete couldn't smell the coffee and chocolate on her breath. As the voice teacher and Angelika's mother had imparted, she should only enjoy them in moderation, and never before lessons or performances. "I'm sorry, Frau Böhm."

"You certainly are not sorry, and anyway, that's hardly what I wanted to speak with you about. Have you given any more thought to the discussion we had last week about the young singers training programme in Vienna?"

"I have," Angelika said, striving to sound calm and confident. "And I think you'd be better off asking someone else to attend."

"Unconscionable. What in heaven's name is the matter with you? Don't you realise what a grand opportunity you're throwing away?"

"Yes, I do, but… my father's forbidden it." A lie, but one Angelika hoped might work. "He says it's too expensive in light of the economic collapse."

"Nonsense. Do you really expect me to believe that falsehood?"

Once again, no such luck.

"Why, your father still has so much money, he probably eats it for breakfast," Margarete said. "He's also a wretched fool, bringing you here in the first place when you already had the world at your fingertips in Vienna."

"Frau Böhm, please. Moving to Munich last summer after… our loss… wasn't easy, but it was the best decision we could make at the time."

"Silence." The teacher paused to compose herself, and when she continued, her voice was once again less acerbic. "Now, that's not to say we aren't quite proud of our own music culture and school, but nevertheless, when our founder – my father-in-law – and I travelled to Vienna five years ago to see your mother as the Queen of the Night in *The Magic Flute*, I'd never before seen anything like it. I was mesmerised. And to think I'd someday have her own daughter standing here before me, passing up a marvellous opportunity we all know you're ready for."

Chest tight and head spinning, Angelika turned away.

Yes, her mother had been mesmerising, every time and always, confidently commanding the stage in an ethereal black gown and gossamer headdress while flawless, infallible high notes soared through the air.

"Honestly, young lady, what do you plan to do with your life? I realise it's none of my concern, but ever since you started visiting that blasted beer garden everyone's gossiping about, not to mention stepping out with your stinking-rich sweetheart, you've become utterly unfocused. Here you are, the most talented soprano of your age at this school, and yet I sometimes wonder why you even bother if you aren't the least bit willing to challenge yourself. This opportunity would allow you to reach beyond what we can offer here, and to push yourself toward becoming a truly remarkable singer, just like…"

Angelika's mesmerising mother. The tall, auburn-haired, azure-eyed diva who could have passed for a glamourous older sister. A woman unmatched and, up until now, untouchable.

"Yes, I know my mother was remarkable." Angelika whirled back around and faced her teacher. "I also know that at my age, she was already immensely talented, far more so than me. You and the other instructors say I'm one of the best here, and perhaps I am, but believe me, there is no comparison between my mother's talent and my own."

"You are right," Margarete said, lowering her voice. "There is no comparison, yet. And with that attitude, there never will be."

Angelika looked down at the floor, recognising the truth in Margarete's words and feeling helpless in their wake.

"Very well, so be it," the woman went on. "I have wasted enough time trying to make you see the error of your ways. Instead of returning to Vienna for a month as you so wisely should, you may remain here."

"Fine," Angelika said, trying to convey a sense of composure and strength, even though she was too distraught to look her instructor in the eye.

"I'm certain we can find a far more willing student to go in your stead. As your mother often used to say during interviews, advisers can offer guidance, but…"

The singer chooses which roles she will play.

"Good day, Fräulein Eder."

Margarete then stalked out of the room, extinguishing the lights so that only the sun's glare from westward-facing windows remained. Alone in the quiet stillness, Angelika sat for what felt like more than a few minutes, gazing about at the gilded walls, the buffed floor, the lone pair of abandoned dance shoes surreptitiously peeking out from behind the piano.

Although in one respect she felt an incredible sense of relief, from deep within she could also feel her heart break little by little as she thought back upon the countless times she'd dared to imagine herself a famously respected performer of her mother's calibre, uniquely gracing the stage at the Vienna State Opera.

It wasn't until the ballroom's golden grandfather clock chimed four that Angelika at last made her way outside into the late afternoon sunshine and hesitated alongside the music school's neoclassical, columned entrance. A slow stream of automobiles – motley combinations of everything from expensive Horches to beat-up Opels – travelled down Prinz Ludwigstrasse, one of the young drivers having the audacity to tip his cap after catching sight of Angelika standing there in sapphires and silk.

Her sweetheart had promised he'd try his best to come for her after class that week, just as he so often had during the infancy of their courtship the preceding winter and spring. Back when he used to see her most every evening, before the pristine winter snows had turned to muddy slush, and all the maple blossoms had died. Before so much of his time had become consumed with business merger meetings.

When his chauffeured car failed to materialise, Angelika instead began trudging toward the nearby Barerstrasse streetcar stop. Although it would mean a longer trek, she purposely wove through Karolinenplatz in a direction opposite the imposing Brown House mansion, headquarters for the National Socialists, or as opponents colloquially called them, Nazis. Gauche, ignorant peasants.

It wasn't that Angelika was afraid the men who traversed its harried hallways might harm her. On the contrary, just as she'd witnessed at the beer garden, it was their attentiveness and purported kindness that made her uneasy – the way cold-fingered, mustard-spilling Johann Schmitt always offered to walk her places and introduce her to people, never hesitating to pepper her with curious questions and tell her how lovely she looked.

"Angelika!"

A young man's familiar voice, though hardly the one she'd wanted to hear, resounded.

Palms going clammy, Angelika sidestepped two roller-skating schoolgirls, glanced to the right and found herself face-to-face with the very brown-shirted, crop-haired boy she'd hoped to avoid.

Two

"**W**hy'd you pass by without saying hello?"

Johann Schmitt's tone sounded innocent enough, but there was something about the question that made Angelika's heart beat faster. She drew a sharp breath and came to a halt in the middle of Karolinenplatz, where a group of summer-session university students sat studying on the nearby obelisk steps as noisy automobiles whipped through a roundabout encircling the plaza.

"I didn't see you," she said. The swastika-emblazoned sword on Johann's bronze breast pin, something he'd claimed to have won during a racing competition, caught the sunlight and made her squint. "Anyway, I'd better be going, before I miss my streetcar."

"Let me first give you one of these terrific new pamphlets Herr Bauer had printed." Johann's pale blue eyes darted up and down, sweeping across Angelika's tall, hourglass physique before homing in on her daisy-dotted skirt. "You can carry a couple of extras in your pocket, too."

"No, really, that's quite all right," Angelika said. She wished that Viktor Bauer – her friend Erich's father – would stick to running his brewery and beer garden rather than involving himself in Nazi politics. "I've heard enough about National Socialism. I don't need to read any more."

"You do need to." Johann took hold of Angelika's arm and pressed three copies into her hand, voice as commanding as she'd ever before heard it. "Everyone does. It concerns the future of our country."

But Angelika was Viennese. Austrian. Germany wasn't her country.

"We can't allow corrupt communists and Jews to get the better of us," Johann continued. "We have to rise up. I'm doing my part by handing out these leaflets. You should see how many I've passed around this afternoon."

His messenger bag – black, just like his tie, shorts and boots – did seem rather empty.

"And soon enough, you'll be doing your part," he said, sounding, as he usually did, like a walking, talking propaganda piece. "Herr Bauer was thrilled when we told him you'd agreed to sing the national anthem, plus a couple of other songs, during our next big concert this October." The lad paused to adjust his swastika pin, lips twisting into a smile of wretched reverence. "Celebrating German music helps unite our people and attract more supporters to our cause. It shows the world how superior we are when it comes to music and art."

Angelika, however, was still processing the first part of his statement.

"The... concert in October?" she asked.

"*Ja.* The one we told you about last night, when you were leaving Herr Bauer's beer garden. When we asked you to come sing for us, and you said 'yes'. There'll be folk dances, lute songs, performances by the National Socialist Symphony Orchestra, appearances by famous singers… everything you can imagine. The Hitler Youth and League of German Girls will be performing there, too. Herr von Schirach, our youth leader, says that with the correct grooming and guidance, a beautiful young singer like you will be the perfect finishing touch. The party will make an official announcement next month."

Angelika's heart lurched against her larynx, and she averted her eyes to stare at the towering, twenty-nine-metre Karolinenplatz obelisk, a dark and silent memorial to the Bavarians who'd perished while fighting a Napoleonic War in the early-1800s. Thirty thousand young men slain far from home in pursuit of someone else's glory.

"Do you know any songs by Richard Wagner?" Johann said. "Adolf Hitler will of course be attending the concert and giving a speech. He loves Wagner. And because you're an opera singer—"

"I'm not an opera singer." Angelika forced her gaze back to Johann and away from the rams-head statues adorning the memorial's base. "Not yet. That's my dream, but it'll take time."

Angelika couldn't possibly have agreed to sing at the Nazis' propaganda concert. It must all be some sort of misunderstanding.

"Poor Herr Hitler," Johann continued. "I can't believe it's been almost a year since his beloved niece Geli died by…"

The cement sidewalk seemed unsteady, and bitter bile rose into Angelika's throat. She knew which wicked word was coming next.

"...suicide."

Its sound reverberated with the force of a one-hundred-piece orchestra, and yet somehow, Angelika willed herself not to react. After all, she was fine. Everything was fine. She must find a way to convince him of it. Just as she must find a way to convince herself.

"Geli was a singer, too," Johann went on, while Angelika used a diaphragmatic breathing technique to keep herself from retching all over the memorial's pristinely manicured lawn and marigold beds. "Herr Bauer told me she used to be one of your mother's biggest fans. Didn't your mama also die by..."

A car horn sounded from behind, and Angelika turned to see a chauffeured, cream-coloured Rolls-Royce Phantom pulling up to the kerb just as its attractive backseat passenger, a familiar twenty-one-year-old man with chestnut-brown hair and royal blue eyes, rolled down the window and leant out.

"Hurry up, Angelika," her sweetheart called, his tall and slender frame clad in a custom-tailored tan suit. "As soon as I've finished seeing you home, I'm due at another appointment."

"I'd better be on my way," Angelika told Johann, a flood of relief replacing the dread.

As always, she had no desire to discuss the horrific details surrounding her mother's death. And as far as the concert was concerned, Johann must simply have gotten his wires crossed. Partly because he was a *Dummkopf*, but mostly because it was inconceivable that Erich's father or his confidant Baldur von Schirach – the National Socialists' youth leader – would ever want her to sing at a marquee event.

"All right, but come by the brewery tomorrow," Johann replied. "You can sing a few more songs then."

"Come on, the clock is fighting us," Kurt said.

"*Tschüss.*" Angelika offered a hurried farewell, slipping away without giving Johann an answer. She then rushed over to the car, where Kurt's chauffeur had gotten out to hold open the door.

"I can't stand seeing any of them talk to you," Kurt muttered as she slid across sleek leather seating. "It's bad enough the Nazis won so many seats in last Sunday's election. Do they have to loiter all around town?"

"They're everywhere," she agreed. "And still not satisfied, either. Now that they're the largest party in parliament, they say Hitler ought to be the one leading the government as chancellor."

"That'll never happen. President von Hindenburg doesn't trust him. He won't agree to it."

Angelika told the chauffeur where to go, then looked down at the copies of Johann's handbill, its slanted letters and ugly cartoons leering back at her. As if anyone needed more propaganda falsely claiming that the Jewish community had orchestrated the global economic collapse of the past three years. The Nazis used the Depression as a means of drumming up hatred that drowned out the voices of brilliant businessmen like Kurt, who had identified the real causes, including American stock market speculation and people taking out loans they could never hope to repay.

"I should have given Johann a piece of my mind," Angelika said. "I always want to, but every time he talks to me, I lose my nerve. It's cowardly."

"It is not cowardly." Kurt tugged her closer as the steadily humming vehicle pulled back out into traffic with Johann watching it go. "Those boys have hurt people. I don't want anyone hurting you."

He tilted Angelika's face toward his, but she turned away before he could kiss her.

"Why, dearest, I believe you're trembling," Kurt said. "What's the matter? Did he upset you?"

"No, I'm… fine." If only repeating it time and time again could somehow make it true. "Luckily, we weren't talking very long. You pulled up at the perfect time. So perfect that I'm a little less cross with you about cancelling our dinner plans last night."

Kurt's handsome brow furrowed.

"You've been working yourself to the bone these past couple of weeks," Angelika added before he could cut in with the usual apologies. "And you've been working my poor brother to the bone, too."

"Is that what he's been telling you?" Kurt said, voice lilting upward, just as it always did whenever he believed he could make a winning argument. "That I'm working him too hard at the office? As you know, I'm supposed to be training him. If Andreas ever wants to move higher up in our company and help manage the chocolate factories, he'll need to be comfortable handling difficult tasks. This is precisely the same way I learnt."

"Of course it is," Angelika quipped. While Kurt von Hügel may have been respected as an intelligent and masterful young businessman, he wasn't the only one who prided himself on being persuasive. "Whatever you say."

She stared out of the window at a passing park, arms folded across her chest, waiting for him to relent.

"Fine, listen," Kurt said after a short pause. "I have to go meet with a new accountant across town right now, but why don't I let you out at my office instead of your house? You can tell your brother he's free to leave for the day."

Angelika remained silent, pretending to feign great interest in the stately red-brick buildings that lined the thoroughfare.

"And if it'll make you happy…" Kurt sighed loudly enough that, had he been a performer onstage, the sound would have surely carried all the way to the back row of the balcony. "I suppose I can try lightening his load. But only a bit, mind you."

At that, Angelika allowed herself a guarded smile. She'd gotten her way, and with nary a simper or pout – two tactics she'd seen far too many other women employ.

"Will you also come meet us at the Wolpertinger Kaffeehaus after your appointment?" she asked. "We can spoil our supper with coffee and pastries."

Kurt sighed a second time, then pursed his lips.

"You know I can't stand that tacky little place," he said. "Besides, I have another late night ahead of me. Why don't you let me take you to Schwarz tomorrow evening?"

"The specialty restaurant?" Angelika chuckled. "Again? We just went there Saturday."

"I thought you liked it."

"I did." Those precious couple of hours, spent dining on roast goose and sipping overpriced *Grauburgunder* wine, had been the only uninterrupted stretch of time he'd been able to devote to her as of late. "But do we have to eat at formal restaurants all the time?"

"Those formal restaurants are quite expensive. Eating there as often as we do is a great privilege."

"I know, but—"

"No 'buts'. I want my girl to have the best of everything. Now stop being silly, and give me a kiss."

The next thing Angelika knew, she was on Kurt's lap and in his arms, her resolve diminishing the same way it had during last year's Christmas recital, when she'd glimpsed him in the audience and felt her heart soar nearly as high as the notes she sang. Kurt's attendance had made it abundantly clear that, after six years of acquaintance as family friends, he and Angelika were destined to forge a more intimate path.

"You look so pretty today," Kurt whispered, lightly tousling the ends of Angelika's thick auburn hair and reminding her once more of that snowy December evening after the performance, when they'd first become a couple. "I missed you last night."

At those whispered words, Angelika leant in and gave him a gentle kiss, just firm enough to leave behind the faintest glimmer of pale pink lipstick. All summer long, busybodies in the business circles had begun spreading rumours that Kurt might be planning to propose sometime soon. Of course, the idle gossip was undoubtedly just that – gossip – and yet, when Kurt held her like this, and spoke so tenderly, Angelika wondered about his intentions.

"I missed you, too," Angelika said. She made no mention of her drunken serenade at Viktor Bauer's *Biergarten*, nor the ensuing confusion regarding the National Socialist concert. "We've hardly spent any time together lately."

"I know, *mein Schatz*, but there's still so much to do before our families' business merger officially goes through. What with trying to please your father, and mine, and all of the investors."

"Yes, yes, of course," Angelika agreed, giving him a harder, longer kiss. "You just look so tired all the time."

"If I do, I'm not the only one." Kurt fingered a dark circle beneath one of Angelika's eyes. "Haven't you been sleeping?"

"Not very well."

"Is it the usual nightmares?"

Angelika shook her head and let her cheek fall against Kurt's shoulder, the safe, familiar scent of amber cologne comforting her.

"It isn't nightmares this time," she said. "It's other thoughts. Remembrances and stories. I've started writing them down in the memory book Doctor Hoffmann gave me for graduation. He figured it might help."

"You can always talk to me, you know." Kurt's arms tightened across her back. "I'm sorry I've been so busy."

The thoughts Angelika was talking about – memories of her mother – weren't things she liked to discuss with anyone, except perhaps her brother, once in a while, when she and he could bear it. The best thing about the memory book was that she could write as if she were speaking to a stranger who knew nothing about her family and held no prior judgements. Someone who would listen, indefinitely, without ever answering back or trying to say the right thing. But Angelika, at the moment, didn't feel like explaining any of this.

"Won't you please come to the coffee-house after your appointment?" she asked instead. "Have a bit of spontaneous fun for once?"

No sooner had the words left Angelika's mouth than she regretted having said them.

"For once, you say?" Kurt laughed and patted Angelika's head. Why, oh why, had she used that foolish phrase? So much for being persuasive. "Yes, I may work hard, and don't care to go running around to second-rate bakeries like some of your childish friends. But that does not mean I don't know how to have a nice time."

Angelika sat up straight.

"That's not at all what I meant. And what do you mean, my 'childish friends'?"

"You know who I'm talking about."

"Yes, I do. And I think you're being very unfair about Erich."

"I hardly think it's unfair to…"

But then, to Angelika's relief, Kurt stopped.

"You're right," he said. "I was, and I apologise. I'm merely frustrated thinking about all of the reports I still have to review. Forgive me?"

Angelika nodded in silent agreement as the chauffeur pulled to a stop close to Kurt's office building and the bustling Rotkreuzplatz newsstand. Everyone in Munich remained hungry for information about the recent parliamentary elections.

"Here," Angelika said, taking a monogrammed lace handkerchief out of her bag and placing it in Kurt's hand. "Be sure to wipe your mouth before you waltz into the accountant's office."

She planted a peace-brokering kiss on his now rose-stained lips.

"And remember what you promised, about lightening Andreas's load," she added.

Kurt rolled his eyes. If he did someday, though hopefully not anytime soon, ask for Angelika's hand, she wondered whether he would continue condoning her opinions, or simply expect docile obedience if she agreed to become his wife.

"I'll remember," Kurt answered.

"And get rid of that ridiculous rubbish, will you?"

Angelika gestured toward Johann's Nazi leaflets, discarded on the seat alongside Kurt's wide-brimmed Homburg hat.

"Consider it gone, my sweet."

Kurt gave Angelika's hand a final squeeze before she stepped out onto the kerb.

"Thank you, Otto," Angelika said to the chauffeur as he closed the car door behind her.

"My pleasure, Fräulein."

Angelika wove her way past the newsstand, a

hodgepodge of papers and glaring political headlines greeting her eyes.

National Socialists On Top In Parliament... Bolstered By Election Gains, National Hitler Youth Membership Continues to Climb; May Reach One Hundred Thousand By Year's End

One of the headlines in particular, stretching across the front of a local business paper, struck a very familiar chord.

Eder-von Hügel Merger Nears Completion; Board Elections Forthcoming

"Afternoon, Fräulein Eder."

A group of workmen toting ladders and approaching the same seven-storey refurbished brick office building as Angelika tipped their tweed caps and paused to let her pass. They'd been there practically every day throughout the past few months, tirelessly toiling in order to satisfy Kurt's expectations.

"Look what we have here," one of the men proclaimed, gesturing toward a large rectangular object sticking out of the back of a rusted delivery truck. "An eventful day, that's for sure."

Angelika smiled politely and thanked them, watching as two of the four labourers revealed a sign bearing the name "Eder, von Hügel and Sons" in loud, large lettering. The official sign declaring Angelika's and Kurt's families to be business partners.

She then passed through a revolving glass door, the office's luxurious ceiling fans raising a series of goosebumps upon her skin as she headed toward a lift that would carry her to the fourth floor and her twin brother. All the while, Angelika tried her best to push aside thoughts of Margarete Böhm and the Vienna young singers programme, plus Johann Schmitt and the upcoming propaganda concert.

It had indeed been an eventful day. Just not for the reason the workmen had stated.

Three

$\mathcal{S}$ounds of the company's new sign being installed reverberated throughout the building as Angelika left behind a smoky hallway and entered her sweetheart's cologne-scented office suite. The new workspace, formerly home to a pharmacy, was spacious on the inside and seemed to have been pulled straight from a fairytale on the outside. The castle-like, romantic red-brick building featured turrets and balconets that reminded Angelika of scenery from Gounod's opera *Roméo et Juliette*.

A marvellous new space for our marvellous new enterprise, Kurt had said.

Angelika wished he could have been with her right then and there, instead of heading across town for yet another meeting. His secretary must have also been out on an errand, and although Andreas's desk was empty, Angelika could sense her twin brother's presence nearby.

"Can you repeat that, sir?" An angry voice resounded, and Angelika peeked into Kurt's private office, surprised to find her brother slumped in the swivel chair and shouting into the telephone. "What? Yes, I'll hold on."

"What are you doing in here?" Angelika said, slipping inside and sliding onto a familiar leather sofa as Andreas spun slowly around to face her, frowning. He appeared every bit as out of sorts as he had the previous night, when he'd given his sister an earful about arriving home intoxicated. "Since when do you make telephone calls using Kurt's line?"

"I came in here because Kurt asked me to. He thought the quiet might help me work faster." Andreas glanced toward the street-facing windows and grimaced. "Not that it is very quiet at the moment, what with the new sign going up."

"I know. Kurt told me the first one had to be returned after his father and ours got into a ridiculous argument over whose name ought to be listed first."

A laugh bubbled up, and Angelika stifled a snicker. Thank goodness the men had finally decided to call the company Eder, von Hügel and Sons after bickering about it ever since the Eders moved to Munich the previous August. She could hardly believe it had taken an entire year to finalise the families' business merger.

"And who, may I ask, are you speaking with right now?" Angelika said.

"The publicity director. He's working from his house this afternoon."

"You mean Werner Hertz?"

"Yes. One of the business papers heard that our summer chocolate sales are down. Werner's trying to deflect by getting the press to run another 'uplifting' story about our families' camaraderie, plus your and Kurt's romance. He also needs the sales figures from spring, which were better. But I can't make sense of these balance sheets."

Kurt could report those numbers backward and forward in his sleep, and Angelika believed he should have taken care of the matter himself. Luckily, she knew of another person who might be able to assist.

"Let me speak to Herr Hertz," Angelika said, hurrying across the room and perusing the balance sheets.

"What? No. I can handle this myself."

"But I can help you."

"Fräulein Eder?" The publicity director's booming voice carried through the earpiece as Angelika wrested it away from her brother and took a seat atop an antique, meticulously organised cherrywood desk. "Why, is that you, my dear?"

"*Ja*," she answered while Andreas scowled. "How are you today, sir, and how are your daughters? Kurt and I had a splendid time attending your eldest's wedding last month. We danced so much, I felt as if my knees had turned to pudding."

Andreas snorted, and Angelika swatted his arm, rolling her eyes.

"Ah, yes, what a joyous day that was," Werner said. "Of course, my wife is still upset about the floral arrangements being far too..."

Angelika half-listened to the man's rambling reply while staring out of the window at dozens of leftover political posters plastering a nearby streetcar station.

"And who knows?" Werner droned on. "Perhaps before too long, we'll be celebrating another wonderful young couple's wedding."

A thinly veiled insinuation about Angelika and Kurt – one that required her to deliver a well-rehearsed demure laugh.

"The good Lord knows you deserve some happiness after so tragically losing your mother last summer," he added, speaking as if he were reciting a press statement to a reporter unfamiliar with the story, rather than addressing a young woman intimately familiar with every gruesome detail. "Not to mention enduring the vicious rumours that ravaged Vienna before and after her passing. Imagine, accusing a lovely, upstanding young lady like yourself of being the product of an illicit affair."

"I... um..."

Words failed Angelika as her confidence wavered. She must regain her composure, and quickly.

"Honestly, sir, those rumours... are a thing of the past." Angelika forced herself to draw a breath and level her voice. For as much as she might wish it to be so, the scandals weren't a thing of the past. Yes, she may have escaped the backlash for the time being, but the hurtful memories remained very much alive inside her heart and mind. "And, actually, speaking of the past, Andreas says you need sales figures from the spring?"

She reexamined the balance sheets and, just as she'd seen Kurt do dozens of times, provided the precise information Werner needed. After exchanging a few more half-hearted pleasantries, she said her goodbyes and braced herself for Andreas's questioning.

"I couldn't hear the entire conversation," her brother began, "but why did he mention rumours? Don't tell me he brought up the ridiculous gossip about Kurt planning to propose."

"Uh… yes," Angelika said. Not entirely a lie, since Werner had indeed referenced their romance. "That's what we were discussing when he mentioned the rumours."

She watched as her brother's gaze wandered to the edge of the desk, where a gold-framed picture of her and Kurt – Andreas's prodigious boss – gazed back.

"What an absurd idea," Andreas mumbled. "You're so young. And how you've managed tolerating Kurt for eight long months is beyond me. Let alone being married to him."

The statement came out low and halting, but was more than enough to make Angelika's head snap to the side, a sharp glare narrowing her eyes.

"You just couldn't resist, could you?" she said. "A lot of thanks I get for doing you a favour."

"A favour I didn't even ask for."

"Yes, because you were doing so well when I first walked in."

"Fine, I'm sorry," Andreas said.

"If only I believed you."

Angelika sighed and picked up a long, unfinished checklist that lay on the desk, reading it over while listening to the sounds outside – the workmen hammering out a rhythmic melody that intermingled with the typical echo of rumbling streetcars, paper-peddling news vendors and the rallying National Socialist protesters who occasionally traversed the neighbourhood.

"Did Kurt really expect you to get through all of this today?" she asked.

"I'm supposed to. But I probably won't, especially with you here, talking my ear off."

He was teasing her now, and Angelika couldn't help but smile.

"As a matter of fact, you're in luck," she said. "Kurt drove me here from music school, and he says you're free to leave for the day. What do you say we telephone Erich and Gretchen, then all go to the Wolpertinger Kaffeehaus for a while?"

Angelika expected to see her brother's sapphire eyes brighten at the mention of Gretchen Hoffmann, another former classmate and a girl she'd long suspected he fancied. But Andreas was busy searching his sister's similarly deep blue eyes, a concerned expression brewing.

"What?" Angelika nervously swept long, red waves of hair, as thick and unbridled as her mother's used to be, away from her shoulders. "Why are you looking at me that way?"

Angelika already knew the answer. For better or worse, that was the way it had always been between the two of them. At each other's throats one minute, reading one another's minds the next.

"Something happened to you today," Andreas said, raking a hand through his own thick auburn mane. "Something you're upset about."

"I'm not upset," Angelika fibbed. "I'm fine. Now, come on. Let's go have some fun."

Andreas didn't seem ready to give up so easily.

"What was it?" he pressed, stiffening in the cushioned swivel chair. "Was it Kurt? You had an argument with him?"

"*Nein.* It wasn't Kurt, all right? Now, stop."

"You're not the only one who wants to help, you know."

Angelika did know, all too well. Andreas had done his best to protect her, and she him, ever since they were children, even when their mutual efforts had often ended up making things ten times worse.

You may not understand or appreciate it now, but having a twin is a tremendous gift.

Angelika could recall their mother saying as much after Andreas had tried to stop his sister from wandering too close to the edge of a lakeside dock. When he'd attempted to grab for her, they'd both toppled in, gotten soaked to the skin and been subsequently banished to their rooms by a disgruntled governess.

Being little more than eight years old at the time, Angelika had shrugged away her mother's wisdom, declaring that she no longer liked having a better-behaved brother. But as with so many things, time had wrought perspective, and she'd eventually come to acknowledge the truth in their mother's words. If only she were still alive, and Angelika could tell her so.

"I realise you want to help me," Angelika at last answered her brother, a combination of annoyance and gratitude filling her voice, "but I don't care to talk about it. Now, let's telephone our friends and go to the coffee-house so I can devour a tray of *Krapfen* filled with jelly even sweeter than the kiss you'd get from a certain girl you really ought to work up the courage to ask to the cinema."

Angelika continued tossing out flippant remarks and keeping a jovial spirit all the way to her beloved

Wolpertinger Kaffeehaus, a small but eclectic café where the owners indulged her coffee compulsion. Gretchen had unfortunately been helping her mother prepare supper, and said she wouldn't be able to join them. Erich, however, managed to slip away from the brewery long enough to consume half a tray of jelly doughnuts and chatter so much about a recent reshowing of Marlene Dietrich's 1930 film, *The Blue Angel*, Angelika was surprised he didn't develop laryngitis.

"I know you want to be an opera singer, but perhaps you could consider starting an acting career on the side," he teased her while munching on what must have been his fourth apricot-filled doughnut. "I think Marlene Dietrich's pretty and all…"

"Oh, really? I'd have never guessed that from the way you bring her up every chance you get."

"…but only half as pretty as Angelika Eder."

Fortified by more sugar and caffeine than she ought to have allowed herself, Angelika responded by donning Erich's plaid cap and performing an impromptu, over-the-top rendition of "They Call Me Naughty Lola", one of the film's signature numbers, right there in her seat. Kurt would have been appalled, but Erich, and even Andreas, laughed so hard, they were practically crying.

"I'll send Josef von Sternberg a letter telling him you're available for the next picture he's directing," Erich said as they were leaving. "But only if you'll promise to give me your autograph after you make it big."

Angelika grinned all the way home, the pervasive hole in her heart feeling a little less empty than usual. It wasn't until much later, in the midst of another sleepless night, that the pain came creeping back. She considered telephoning Kurt, but he was surely sound asleep after working long hours again. She could always wake Andreas, or perhaps even try phoning Erich, who might make her chuckle with more of his preposterous jokes.

Instead, Angelika opened her nightstand drawer and pulled out the journal a doctor friend had suggested she use to write down her memories. She'd only added a handful of entries thus far. Starting it off were her vivid remembrances of travelling the continent with her famous mother, the two of them making merry mischief while enjoying everything from flavourful fondue in Zürich to Josephine Baker's intoxicating jazz revues in Paris. Followed by the simpler, but no less poignant, descriptions of shared secrets over coffee, mother-daughter clothing exchanges, Christmas sledding excursions and endless late-night chatter about a cunning yet useless boy who'd once captured Angelika's attention.

But there were other memories that ought to be written, too. More memories of her mother, yes, but also of a man they'd known. Someone special, and someone they'd both dearly loved.

Someone Angelika had left behind in Vienna.

With a steadying breath, she flipped to a blank page, lifted her fountain pen, and – wounded heart notwithstanding – allowed the words to come.

Angelika's Memory Book

November 1920 – Twelve Years Ago
Vienna State Opera

I was seven years old the first time I saw my mother die – and then come back to life – onstage as Gilda, Verdi's tragic operatic heroine from *Rigoletto*.

I wasn't supposed to be watching. I was supposed to be in Mama's dressing room reading *Hänsel und Gretel* with Andreas and our temperamental governess, Fräulein Helga.

But then, as if on cue, the invisible ribbon connecting Mama's heart and my own exerted its magical tug. After Helga excused herself to the powder room, I crept stealthily out into the costume-lined hallway, ducking behind the racks and crawling as I made my way toward the stage, eager to observe the dress rehearsal from one of the wings. I found myself captivated by the imaginative costumes and scenery, romantic swells of the orchestra, bright lights and grand ivory-toned tiers, but mostly by the extraordinary coloratura voice of the inimitable Clara Eder, only twenty-eight, a rising prodigy among Viennese singers.

"Where are you this time, you naughty girl?" I froze and held my breath as Helga's angry voice and marching footsteps approached the spot where I sat hidden behind a collection of voluminous courtier gowns. "Aha!"

The frilly dresses parted, and Helga's fiery eyes met my own.

"This is the last straw," she hissed while forcing me out. "I don't care how upset it makes your mother – when we get back to that room, I'm going to—"

But before she could finish, a familiar pair of arms reached out from behind and scooped me up.

"Here you are, silly goose." It wasn't Mama, but Daniel Weiss, a director's assistant and one of her friends, a former music academy classmate. "I was just coming by to get you."

"Get her?" Helga asked. "For what?"

"To come out front," he said, setting me down but keeping an arm wrapped protectively about my shoulders. "I told her she could watch."

Of course, he'd told me nothing of the kind, but since Daniel said it was so, the governess had no choice but to give in.

"Fine, you look after her, then," she muttered before storming away. "Just as long as she's out of my sight."

Daniel scowled behind her back, then knelt down and smiled, the same way he did each time he gave me raspberry jam-filled cookies or little wooden trinkets he'd selected at the toy shop. Sharing stolen moments with him, in one of our favourite places, always made my soul sing.

"That was close," he whispered after I'd given him a grateful hug. "Come on. We'll sit in the first row, and you can help me keep track of what happens onstage, all right?"

I eagerly agreed, and from that moment on, as long as I didn't get in the way and wasn't noisy, Daniel allowed me to observe the rehearsal like a member of the still non-existent audience, taking in the sights and sounds of the opera right on through to the final scene. The famous finale in which Gilda, having been stabbed by assassin Sparafucile, dies in her father's arms.

"Mama, no!"

The childish scream burst from my throat and carried throughout the cavernous hall while Vienna State Opera directors Richard Strauss and Franz Schalk, plus others, glanced over with annoyance, amusement or both.

"It's only pretend," Daniel reminded me in a gentle murmur. "She's fine. I promise."

But I cried anyway, terrified – knowing it was fake yet still finding it lifelike – until, after what felt like ages, Mama was thankfully alive again, rising to take a bow, to dry my tears, to comfort me with kisses, to smile and tell me, "Don't be afraid, Angelika, *mein Liebling*. Everything's going to be all right."

If only she had been correct.

Four

*A*ngelika heaved a disappointed sigh and forced her attention back to her mother's old songbook, its weathered pages streaked with sunlight as midafternoon rays filled the empty classroom.

"E quel primiero sorso per sempre benedì…"

Although Angelika possessed a strong understanding of the Italian language, her diction had been dreadful all day.

What type of slovenly performance was that? Margarete Böhm's latest scolding flooded Angelika's conscience. *Furchtbar.*

Yes, she had sounded awful during lessons, which had mercifully ended, and then afterward, as she'd continued practising an opening song from Donizetti's *L'elisir d'amore* only to botch the breathing and spoil the high notes. At this rate, Angelika figured she might as well give up and keep to singing "Ave Maria" and other familiar pieces.

Or, if Johann Schmitt had his way, "Deutschlandlied", the German national anthem.

But Angelika had thankfully heard nothing more

about the propaganda concert in the two days since he'd mentioned it, and she could only hope the matter would soon be forgotten.

Besides, she was Viennese.

The National Socialists, however, believed Austrians to be Germanic, and also part of the purported Aryan master race. As a result, they believed the two nations should unite, and that the peace treaties preventing such a union were a travesty. To Angelika's dismay, an alarming number of her countrymen appeared to agree. Even her own father, as well as Kurt's, could see the practical benefit from a business standpoint, especially now that their two enterprises were merging. Kurt, on the other hand, opposed bringing another struggling economy and burgeoning extremist population under Germany's control.

As for Angelika, although she remained too troubled to fathom returning to Vienna, the musical city was still her beloved home and a source of unshakable pride, its very heartbeat woven into her soul. An independent Austria seemed the best way to preserve Vienna's unique, eclectic identity. If only Adolf Hitler, who was ironically Austrian-born himself, saw it that way. But, as everyone knew, he and his followers did not.

"Germany, Germany above all..." Angelika's voice trembled as she murmured the straightforward, easy-to-master song Johann wanted her to sing. "Above all in the world!"

She'd heard rumours about offers the National Socialists had been making to other performers, including the chance to be seen and recognised by thousands, then set on a path to stardom as the increasingly powerful party devised plans to mount concerts, operas and films.

But Angelika was no Nazi. Nor had her mother been one. In the last couple of years of her life, Clara had been hesitant to sing in Munich or Berlin on account of the growing Nazi presence. And yet, Clara was now dead, and the menacing Nazis still there.

Angelika rifled through the songbook, a dried daisy falling from its pages and drifting to the marble floor as if to further taunt her – a bittersweet reminder of many a hike near her family's summer estate outside Salzburg. It was the one place she and her mother had felt forever joyous and free, where the outer world could never harm them.

"*Ach*, what's the use?" Angelika shut the book so forcefully, it fell from the music stand, settling alongside the flower in a far less graceful pose. "I'll never become a famous singer or have one thimbleful of the talent she did. I may as well give up on my dream."

"Give up, huh?"

Angelika hadn't meant to speak aloud, and certainly hadn't expected anyone else to overhear and respond. She whirled toward a ground-floor window, stunned to discover it was open and that a familiar face peered back.

"Erich." Angelika gaped as though he were an apparition. "I... How... What in the name of Mozart and Donizetti are you doing here?"

"I'm as surprised as you are," he replied with a nonchalant shrug. "I delivered lager to Osteria Bavaria a few blocks over, and as I was driving back, I saw and heard you practising through this open window. So, I decided to pay you a visit."

Angelika frowned as the sound of honking automobile horns and chittering passersby filtered in from the street. In her distraught state, she hadn't acknowledged that the practice room window was open, which had surely allowed all of Munich to overhear her putrid performance. She at least hoped that between parking his truck and walking over, Erich hadn't heard her muttering the German national anthem.

"What is this, Heinrich Heine's 'Die Lorelei'?" she asked while approaching the suspendered, smiling friend who stood sheltered in the music school's shadow, a light afternoon breeze tussling his floppy blond curls. "Or perhaps Homer's *Odyssey*? I'm your siren, and you couldn't resist the call?"

"If those Greek sirens had sounded as nice as you, Odysseus never would have survived to tell the tale." A mischievous grin flooded Erich's round, boyish face. "And given how much I detested reading that book, I wish he hadn't."

"Oh, you're insufferable." Yet even as she said as much, Angelika's tense shoulders unknotted, and she extended a hand to help Erich inside. "How can you possibly say I sounded nice? I'm off-key, my pronunciation's pitiful and my breathing is all wrong."

Erich's scuffed work boots squeaked across the floor as he perused the gold-leafed practice space, and he let out a low whistle while taking in floral tapestries, filigreed wall sconces and a shining silver chandelier.

"Look, I don't know much about any of this and probably don't belong within ten kilometres of this fancy school," Erich said. "But you were slouching while singing. If I slouch like that when I go for a run, it collapses my lungs and makes it harder to breathe."

Angelika stared in astonishment, and not only because uncouth Erich looked entirely out of place flopping down upon a velvet-lined piano bench while wearing scruffy slacks and a sweat-streaked shirt. Of all the conversations she'd never expected to have with him, this one topped the list.

"I'm sure you can get better advice from your teachers than from a nobody like me," he continued, "but when I run, I imagine there's a string attached to the top of my head, pulling me upward. It helps keep my body aligned. Think you could try it?"

Of course, Angelika already knew the importance of good posture when singing and had long ago learnt the technique he'd described. If her form had been poor that afternoon, it was because she hadn't been diligent enough. But Erich seemed so eager to help, she didn't have the heart to disappoint him.

"Thanks," she said, genuinely smiling for what felt like the first time all day. "I'll give it a try next time."

"Does that mean you're done practising?"

Angelika nodded, longing to leave and ready for a distraction.

"I'm due to meet Kurt at the office."

He'd promised to take Angelika to dinner at Schwarz the previous night, but had ended up having to work late for the thousandth time. As penance, he'd agreed to get coffee at the Wolpertinger Kaffeehaus after Angelika had finished her Thursday studies.

"Oh, I see." Erich's upbeat demeanour wilted, and he stared at the floor, an unreadable expression clouding his face. "Say, is that your daisy?"

"Yes." Angelika tried to keep her voice from wavering. "Mama and I used to pick them together, in the hills surrounding Lake Fuschl, outside Salzburg. This must be one of the final flowers we pressed and saved before…"

An unforgiving flurry of tears smarted Angelika's eyes, and she turned away in embarrassment, shoulders beginning to shake. If not for Erich crossing the room and placing a steadying hand upon her arm, she'd have surely lost control of her senses.

"Come on," he said, voice low. Erich retrieved the delicate flower and tucked it into Angelika's hair bun, fingers lingering a couple of seconds too long. "I'll give you a ride."

Angelika paused for a beat. It was one thing to continue spending time with Erich when Andreas was present, as was typically the case. But if Kurt saw them riding together or found out she'd visited the beer garden earlier that week, he'd be furious. Even though there was no reason to be, since Angelika considered Erich a friend and Kurt her steadfast sweetheart.

"I can let you off down the street from the office," Erich said, as if reading her mind. "We wouldn't want Kurt blowing up like an over-carbonated bottle of beer."

"Stop that."

But Angelika had chuckled in spite of herself. She set about gathering her things, and instead of donning the berry-hued beret she'd brought – the one Erich had given her for graduation – Angelika left it tucked away inside her bookbag. That way, she wouldn't have to remove the daisy from her hair.

"Is this a new delivery truck?" Angelika asked a few minutes later as she took her seat inside a green Opel Blitz with the word *Bauerbräu* painted in scrolling white script on the side. She had no doubt that within a couple of days' time, Erich would have littered its interior with papers and rags, stray pocketknives and snapped shoelaces. His messiness meshed with her own, and Angelika found it a refreshing respite from Kurt's nagging neatness. "I assume your father's business is booming?"

"It sure is." Erich fired up the engine and rolled his shirtsleeves, revealing well-developed forearms. "When times get tough, people drink too much."

Angelika understood that predicament all too well.

"How about your family?" Erich asked. "Andreas doesn't seem too tickled to have joined the family business, or to be merging companies with Kurt's clan."

"You know the way Andreas acts. He pretends he's fine with it, even though any fool can see he isn't. And even though he ought to be attending a conservatory. He used to love composing tone poems and studying music before…" Angelika stopped herself again. "I'm a real treat today, aren't I? I'll bet you wish you'd never appeared outside my window."

"You're my siren, remember?" Erich answered without

missing a measure, sincerity blending together with his usual teasing tone. "I had no choice."

Angelika fished about for a witty response, noticing as she did that Erich was taking a longer route around, avoiding a trip past National Socialist headquarters. Not that the alternative sight of shabbily dressed folks lining up outside a Catholic church in anticipation of receiving an evening meal made her feel any better. Life was bad for so many people, and yet, Kurt never stopped trumpeting the fact that his father and Angelika's had such a diverse array of holdings, including real estate, candy and chocolate enterprises, salt mines and telephone manufacturing. He also said the larger the new company grew, the more jobs it would help create, and that once people were reemployed and no longer suffering, radical political groups like the Nazis would see their influence and power disappear.

But when Angelika tried relaying as much to Erich, he gripped the wheel so tightly, his knuckles turned white.

"I don't expect the National Socialists to disappear anytime soon," Erich told her. "In fact, it's other people who are doing the disappearing these days."

With Erich's sleeves turned up, Angelika couldn't help but notice a faint string of bruises darkening his arms. She'd noticed similar marks on other occasions, and had tried convincing herself they were merely the result of a too-heavy beer barrel or some other innocent mishap. Anything but the horrible, abusive reality she feared.

"Your father still wants you to join the Nazi party, doesn't he?" Angelika asked.

"Uh-huh."

Erich's response was curt and matter-of-fact, no further explanations offered.

"But you won't?"

"I'd rather read *The Odyssey* every day for the rest of my life than join them."

Angelika had seen plenty of others change their minds, though – the promise of power providing too strong a pull. Plus, as everyone knew, when the fascist Nazis wished for someone to do something, they weren't keen to take no for an answer.

"Here we are," Erich said after they'd driven in silence a short while longer. "But before you leave…" He stopped the truck and slid closer to Angelika, a deep gaze boring straight into her soul. "All those things you were saying earlier, about giving up. You didn't really mean that, right?"

Angelika averted her eyes, albeit only for a moment. She knew she ought to move farther away from Erich, but found herself unable to budge, her focus trained upon him as if drawn by a magnetic force.

"Because I can hardly believe that you – the girl who drilled me in French vocabulary day in and day out to the point I thought my ears had turned to mush – would so easily give up on your dream. You wouldn't let me give up, and there is no way you can give up on yourself, either, all right? Now, come on. Promise."

Angelika had half a mind to tease him. To ask who he was and what he'd done with her pal Erich, the jokester. But instead, what she heard herself say was, yes, all right, she did promise. And then, a minute or two later, she'd said goodbye and Erich was gone, making the brief drive back to the brewery and a father she felt certain must mistreat him.

A noisy streetcar rumbled past, mostly empty ahead of the evening rush. At one of the distant corners, Angelika recognised Johann with a couple of his friends. Quickly, before they could turn around and see her, Angelika walked toward Rotkreuzplatz and made her way inside the familiar red-brick office building, veering past apprentices busy unpacking chocolate crates and candy cartons. A usual group of labourers stood huddled about an unused stairwell, the men in fervent discussion about installing a revolving paternoster lift as a complement to the other, operator-controlled elevator Angelika always rode to the fourth level.

"Good afternoon," she soon greeted Kurt's secretary, who sat fiddling with jammed typewriter keys. "Is Herr von Hügel in?"

The startled young woman, perhaps a year or so older than Angelika, snapped to attention, her golden-brown bob having escaped its pins and her faded red lipstick begging to be reapplied. She'd been working there since early May, when Kurt's father had flown into a hiring frenzy, assigning younger and prettier "apprentice typists" to the more seasoned secretaries. But Kurt's no-nonsense older secretary had wanted none of it, relinquishing her position and leaving younger Ilse to manage Kurt's matters herself.

"Good afternoon, Fräulein Eder," she replied, speaking even more quickly than she usually did. "Please have a seat, and I will see whether he's tied up on the telephone."

There was no need, however, because a nearby door burst open, and Kurt sauntered in on a cloud of musky cologne.

"Ilse, are those revised contracts ready for my signature?" he asked. "I needed them on my desk the second I returned from... Oh, hello, Angelika."

His tone softened, and the scowl on his face vanished.

"I'm glad you're here," he said while rubbing his temples. A sure sign a headache was coming on. "I know we'd planned to get coffee, but might you have time to carry out a couple of quick errands for me instead? I hate to trouble you with this, but Ilse is busy with contracts, your brother's taking far too long retrieving a bundle of archived catalogues..." Kurt glanced toward Andreas's empty desk with a frown. "...and my housekeeper had to take the day off to nurse an ill child."

Angelika considered saying no. Almost every time she and Kurt had made plans to spend time together as of late, he'd cancelled their outings. She'd wanted to get coffee with her sweetheart, not become his Girl Friday, as the Americans might say. Kurt looked so tired and strained, though, that Angelika couldn't help but pity him.

"What can I do to help?" she asked.

"I need a new headache powder collected from Doctor Hoffmann's office, plus two suits and silk neckties fetched from the tailor. After you drop all of those at my house, I'll need you to stop by the *parfumerie* and buy a fresh bottle of cologne. And then, finally, gather some sandwich fixings at the market. I know it's a lot to ask, but everything must be positively perfect for my trip tomorrow."

Angelika's eyes narrowed, and she folded her arms, bracing herself against the impending disappointment.

"You didn't mention a business trip this week," she said.

"Discussions have been in the works for quite some time," Kurt explained, "but the travel plans only came together today. I'll be meeting with a group of German-American businessmen in Stuttgart tomorrow afternoon through Saturday. My father and yours are going, too."

And with that, any pity Angelika had felt flew straight out of the window.

"Through Saturday?" Her heart thumped wildly inside her chest. "So, you're going to miss my birthday? When we discussed it last month, you promised you'd make time for me."

Kurt rubbed his hands across his face, a scarcely audible curse escaping his lips. The man could recite countless columns of numbers by heart and rattle off memorised strategy speeches as though he were a Reichstag politician. But something as simple and important as Angelika's birthday? How could he have possibly forgotten?

"I'm sorry," he said, palms raised as if offering a truce, "but my father's asked me to go, and I can't conceivably say no. This is one of the most important business opportunities we've ever had."

"You always say that," Angelika threw back. "I assumed you'd at least be able to come by the house Saturday evening. My friend Gretchen will be there, too, and Andreas invited Erich."

Kurt grimaced, and Angelika absentmindedly reached

up to touch the delicate daisy that remained in her hair, her own fingers lingering upon it just as Erich's had when placing it there. If Kurt asked, she'd tell him she had put it there herself. No one else need know the truth, nor understand how much Erich's encouragement had bolstered her. If only she were still riding in the truck and talking with him instead of arguing with Kurt.

"You mean 'brewery boy' Bauer?" Kurt said, his scowl returning tenfold. "I've no interest in spending an evening with a glib young man whose father is a Nazi." Kurt's voice had risen a full octave, and he rubbed his temples all the more fervently. "I'd hoped you wouldn't be hanging about with him as often anymore," he continued. "Is there something going on that I should know about?"

"Of course not." Angelika didn't wish to strain her voice by shouting, but when faced with such an audacious accusation, she couldn't resist. "We've been over this a thousand times."

"I know we have, and yet..." Kurt stopped himself, another faint curse falling. "Fine, I apologise. Never mind the errands. Let's go to the coffee-house as we'd planned."

But his lukewarm repentance had come too late. After losing her mother, Angelika's birthday had become a difficult day to stomach. And now, her own beau wouldn't be there to help soften the blow. A beau who seemed more in want of a second housekeeper and business notoriety than the chance to deepen his relationship with a sweetheart.

"Forget the coffee-house," Angelika said. "You asked me to be your errand girl, so that's what I will be. Perhaps I'll tell everyone at the shops what a heel you've been."

"Angelika, enough. You're behaving like a petulant child."

"You said I have childish friends, right? I suppose it's a fitting title."

She stormed into Kurt's office and rummaged through a couple of desk drawers until she'd found an extra house key. Angelika then headed back to the suite's reception area and locked eyes with Ilse, who had stopped work on the errant typewriter and stared at Angelika in what appeared to be a state of awe. Surely, no woman in the building had ever spoken to Kurt in such a forceful manner.

"I understand you're upset," Kurt began again, "but please, I…"

He couldn't finish the thought, however, because at that moment, an even louder and angrier voice rang out. One that could only belong to Rudolf Eder.

"Kurt von Hügel!" Angelika's father appeared ever tall and stout before them, as intimidating in voice as he was in stature. He'd made a similar impression for as long as Angelika could remember, whether he was about to issue a scolding or announce the start of Christmas dinner. "Why are you condoning this deplorable outburst from my daughter when we've got mountains of work to complete?"

"I apologise, sir," Kurt replied, straightening his stance.

It was little wonder Angelika's warm, vivacious mother had suffered a fraught relationship with domineering, philandering Rudolf. Yet when he strayed, it was considered natural. When his unloved wife did the same, it had damaged her reputation and ultimately destroyed her life.

"As for you, young lady," he said, unrelenting as he shifted focus to Angelika, "who do you suppose I met with this morning? Werner Hertz. He said you spoke with him on the telephone two days ago regarding sales figures."

Oh, good grief. Leave it to the publicity director to put his foot in his mouth and make everything worse.

"How many times have I told you that it is not your place to discuss business matters?" Rudolf thundered on. "That while I typically couldn't care less where you go or what you do, when it comes to this company and our reputation, I am not about to let you make fools out of us?"

Angelika didn't respond, afraid that if she did, she'd either dissolve into tears or tell Rudolf he was the only fool in question. Or, to reveal an altogether deeper truth – that while the purported rumours had supposedly been left behind in Vienna, she didn't consider him her real father.

"I'm waiting for an answer," Rudolf said. "After all the damage that was done concerning your mother and her scandalous impropriety, I—"

"Actually, sir, I was the one who suggested it."

Rudolf pivoted his head toward Kurt so quickly, Angelika felt certain it would snap.

"Why would you do a senseless thing like that?" Rudolf asked.

"He wouldn't," Angelika interjected. Angry as she might be with Kurt, she wasn't about to let him shoulder the blame. "It wasn't his fault. He didn't know about it."

But when Kurt had decided to take the reins on something, there was little hope in holding him back.

"I did know," Kurt fibbed. "I was quite busy, and

since Angelika has a splendid rapport with Werner and his family – not to mention a sharp, intelligent mind – I trusted her to speak with him instead."

Angelika opened her mouth to argue, but Kurt, this time with nothing more than a barely perceptible shake of the head, silenced her.

"I still don't understand it, but fortunately for you both, I'm too busy to care," Rudolf said. "All right, then, enough of this nonsense. Angelika, I'll thank you to bite your tongue and make yourself scarce. Kurt, come along. We should sit down with your father and finish devising our meeting strategy."

"Actually, sir, about the trip," Kurt said, briefly meeting Angelika's eyes, "I'm not quite certain I should—"

"I know how concerned you and your father are about the long-term implications of entering into such a serious business deal. That's why it's imperative we have a clear, prudent plan in place."

Rudolf swung an arm around Kurt's shoulders and led him away, leaving Ilse and Angelika alone in a deafening silence.

"Um, Fräulein Eder?" A combination of shock and pity pooling in her eyes, Ilse looked to Angelika as though in that moment, the two of them were no longer Kurt's secretary and sweetheart, defined and divided by status or class. No, then and there, they'd become peers. Two women trying their best to navigate a man's wretched world. "Are you all right?"

Angelika prepared to utter her usual lie, but this time, couldn't form the words.

"No," she admitted. "I will be, though. I always am."

And so, saving her tears, Angelika made her way to Ilse's desk, where the two of them, together, set about repairing the broken typewriter.

Five

*I*f only broken spirits were as easily repairable as Ilse's malfunctioning typewriter, which Angelika had helped set to rights little more than an hour earlier. Her heart, however, remained in pieces thanks to Kurt's carelessness and Rudolf's cruelty.

She hesitated outside Doctor Hoffmann's medical clinic as a middle-aged man dressed in a tattered suit and battling a croup-like cough entered ahead of her. After Kurt had defended her in front of Rudolf, Angelika had felt it only fair to carry out at least one of his requested errands. No matter how angry she might have been, she didn't want Kurt to spend his business trip suffering from head pain.

"Hello," Angelika murmured, acknowledging the sick while she walked into the waiting room – an aging, weathered space replete with cracked paint, stained hardwood and tarnished seating.

"*Hallo.*"

"Good afternoon, Fräulein."

Two ladies returned Angelika's greeting, but several

others stared back with vacant eyes as sick, malnourished children cried in their arms. The parish volunteer work Angelika often performed, plus her repeated petitioning of Kurt to increase the company's charitable contributions, seemed entirely inadequate in the face of such grim realities.

"Angelika?" Stefan Hoffmann – her friend Gretchen's father and the clinic's head physician – approached the reception area, a prescription pad in hand. He wore a crisp white doctor's coat far cleaner than many of the patients' ragged garments. "*Grüss Gott*, my dear. What in the world brings you here today?"

"Good afternoon, *Herr Doktor*," she said. "I've come to collect a new headache powder for Kurt. I dropped by your other practice first, but the sign on the door said you were here."

For as long as Angelika had known him, Stefan had chosen to split his time between a private practice in the Neuhausen neighbourhood, not far from Kurt's office, and this other clinic in the working-class neighbourhood of Sendling. In Kurt's harried state, he must have gotten his days crossed, because had he known Angelika would be travelling across the railroad tracks into what he considered to be a less desirable community, he'd have become overprotective and never condoned the errand.

"Ah, yes, headache powder." Stefan hesitated and searched Angelika's eyes, a hint of concern marring his gaze, as though he could see the day's earlier events reflected there. "Come, I'll fetch it for you right away. I told that mad-minded lad of yours these powders are merely a temporary fix. He ought to slow down and get some rest."

"Kurt always promises he will, but never follows through," Angelika said, the hint of a hard edge creeping into her voice. Perhaps the hectic schedule and frequent headaches had made him forget her birthday, and a fresh dose of powder would improve matters. Or so Angelika had tried convincing herself. "But that's Kurt for you, I suppose. He insists he feels his best when busy."

Stefan led the way into a windowless, closet-like workspace cluttered with copies of the anti-Nazi *Munich Post* newspaper, plus medical journals and a disjointed jumble of decade-old records. He then opened a rusted cabinet and retrieved a small metal canister, which he handed off to Angelika. Kurt could have purchased new headache tablets or powders at a pharmacy, but as usual, he remained set in his ways and insisted this particular, older formula worked best.

"What about you, *Liebling*?" Though surely needing to get back to work, Stefan took the time to share a curious and kind smile, his grin appearing slightly lopsided from scars he'd obtained while serving as a battlefield physician during the Great War. "How have you been feeling? Still having nightmares?"

"Yes, sometimes." As Angelika replied, she glanced at the framed portrait positioned upon his chipped oak desk. There, frozen on film, were Stefan, Gretchen, and their dear wife and mother Adelheid. All three of them were happy and smiling, a loving, unbroken family. "But I'm all right. I mean, I can manage."

"Are you certain? Remember what I said after giving you that memory book. I believe sound health involves the mind every bit as much as it does the body." Stefan's calm voice and gentle green eyes soothed Angelika while other, truly suffering people awaited his assistance. "Should you ever need someone to talk with, my colleagues and I are always available."

A rogue tear trickled across Angelika's cheek, and Stefan stepped forward, offering her a clean handkerchief that smelled of peppermint and antiseptic. She hated to cry in front of anyone, be they friend or foe. But the past few days' events had proven to be too much.

"Actually, there are a few things I'd like to talk about," she admitted. "May I stay until you've finished for the day?"

Angelika trusted Stefan and was prepared to tell him all about her abhorrent behaviour at the beer garden, the confusion regarding the Nazis' propaganda concert, the publicity director's rehashing of past scandals and even the Vienna singing programme Margarete Böhm had continued pestering her about the past two days. Before Stefan could answer, however, a shout erupted from the waiting room, and a nurse flew into the tiny office, shoving Angelika aside.

"*Herr Doktor,*" she cried. The canister of headache powder fell from Angelika's hands and spilled open, a million white granules speckling her stockings and the floorboards like miniature snowflakes. "Come quick!"

Angelika raced behind as Stefan hurried to the reception area, where a young woman strained to prop up a slumping young man with torn clothing, black eyes and a torrent of blood gushing down his forehead. It took

Angelika but a second to realise that the two of them must be brother and sister.

"There's no time to waste," Stefan said, springing into action. He whisked the boy toward an exam room and issued instructions to the nurse. "Fetch me bandages and thread, then telephone for an ambulance."

After the young man had disappeared, a trail of bloodspots lingering in his wake, Angelika trained her eyes upon his dumbstruck sister – petite and frail, with shocks of dark hair peeking out from beneath a kerchief.

"Dmitry," the young woman murmured, teetering on her feet as Angelika rushed forward and caught her by the arm.

"Sit," Angelika said softly, easing her onto a rickety bench as the girl wiped bloody hands against a faded grey cotton dress, a series of sobs wracking her body. "Let me get you some water."

But the young woman, perhaps a couple of years younger than Angelika, reached out to grasp her hand.

"They called us communists," she choked, speaking in a heavy Russian accent. "Told us to go back to our own country."

"Who did?" Angelika whispered, although she feared she already knew the answer.

"The brownshirts out on the street."

Visions of Johann, with his swastika pin and sickening smile, flickered across Angelika's brain, as did memories of his Hitler Youth friends and the slightly older storm troopers who had groped her at the beer garden.

"We should have ignored them and gone right on

returning customers' laundry," the young lady continued. "But Dmitry was stupid enough to answer back. He said our family left Russia and came here to escape the communists. The men started beating him, and I screamed, but they threw the laundry basket into the gutter and pushed me to the ground."

She muttered something else in Russian, and Angelika regretted that, of the four languages she'd mastered, this wasn't one of them. Still, the girl's German was serviceable, and Angelika could tell she'd put a great deal of effort into learning the language.

"Dear God, what if my brother dies?"

"He's not going to die." Angelika squeezed the girl's trembling, blood-stained hand. "Stefan Hoffmann is a wonderful physician, and once your brother gets to the Allgemeines Krankenhaus, he'll be perfectly fine."

But the head wound had looked bad, and Angelika wasn't certain.

"My parents work hard," the girl said. "We are good people."

She started coughing then, and Angelika went to fetch water for the young woman whose name she didn't yet know.

"I'm Angelika," she said after returning. "My friends call me Anni. May I call you by your name?"

"*Ja*," the girl answered. "I'm Tatyana."

Like the heroine in Tchaikovsky's *Eugene Onegin*, a masterful opera based on the classic Alexander Pushkin novel. Angelika tried saying as much, and distracting Tatyana with chatter, but there was little use. In the end, the two young women sat in precarious silence until the screech of ambulance tyres carried through an open window and Dmitry – unconscious but breathing – was borne from the clinic upon a stretcher, both Tatyana and Stefan planning to accompany him. Meanwhile, an assistant doctor and nurse would remain behind, doing what they could to help the waiting patients.

"I'll try my best to stop by your house later this evening, Angelika," Stefan said while rushing out of the door in a hurry, his medical bag, fedora and trench coat dangling in hand. "We can discuss everything then."

Angelika scarcely heard him, however, the sight of immobile Dmitry having reignited horrific memories of her mother's body lying motionless upon the bathroom floor a summer ago, her vocal cords forever stilled, and the diva's last aria having sadly been sung. By the time Angelika had discovered her lifeless form, it was too late. She prayed it wouldn't be too late for the boy named Dmitry.

If only wishing hard enough might somehow make it so.

Saliva suddenly flooding her mouth, Angelika ran to a hallway lavatory and vomited, heaving and retching until she felt as if her insides might erupt. At least, through it all, the dried daisy remained dutifully embedded in her hair, right where Erich had placed it – a small comfort amidst the day's chaos.

After the waves of nausea had passed, Angelika scrubbed dried blood from her hands and splashed cold water across her splotched face, preparing to head to the nearby streetcar stop and start for home. Though he might not like it, Kurt would have to find himself a different type of headache powder.

By the time Angelika stepped outside, the street had begun filling with people. Lower-level office workers and day labourers were returning home, while factory and printing press employees prepared to begin their evening and night shifts. Her family's own chocolate factory was located near the railyard, a short drive northwest, and Angelika wondered whether any of the people before her might be making their way back from the facility, their clothing drenched in the cloying scent of pricey sweets they could help create but not afford to buy.

"What's the matter, sweetheart?"

Angelika had been so lost in thought, she'd missed seeing the cadre of brownshirts loitering near the corner streetcar stop.

"You look as if you've seen a ghost." The tallest of the five flashed her an easy smile, and Angelika glanced behind her to see whether he happened to be addressing someone else. One of the heavily made-up women heading to nighttime jobs at men's clubs or cabarets, perhaps. "Is someone giving you trouble?"

He'd been speaking to no other unwitting woman but Angelika. With her floral-print silk dress, diamond earrings, violet-scented perfume and tooled-leather bookbag, she stood out like a sore thumb. In hindsight, she ought to have asked Kurt's chauffeur to drive her to Sendling. But if everyone else, including Doctor Hoffmann, could travel by streetcar, why couldn't she? If there was one thing Angelika's mother and opera director

Daniel Weiss had taught her, it was that money didn't make someone better or more important than others.

"Um…"

Angelika's voice caught in her throat, and no words came. Were these the same men who'd attacked Dmitry?

"Cat got your tongue?" the brownshirt asked. It was hard to believe this twenty-year-old storm trooper was merely one of four hundred thousand across Germany, most of them unemployed young men who'd been recruited to Hitler's paramilitary organisation. "Let's go someplace else. Whatever it is, you can tell me all about it over coffee."

The only thing Angelika wished to tell these men was how horrible they were. But what would they do? Beat her? Drag her into an alleyway and assault her? Take their anger out on Erich, Andreas or someone else she cared about?

"I… have to go," she managed, eliciting a series of laughs from her amused companions.

"Would you listen to that, boys?" The tall one – blond-haired, blue-eyed and athletic – stepped closer to her, Angelika's heart jumping a jig as the stinking scent of sweat and sauerkraut curled her nose. "She says she has to go."

Angelika looked him up and down, searching for any sign of bloodspots upon his tan shirt and slacks, black boots, swastika armband, two-toned cap and the plain blue collar patch of a low-ranking storm trooper.

"Why do you have to go, beautiful? Tell me the reason, and I'm sure I can find a way out of it for you."

A way out… Angelika wracked her brain.

"What's a girl like you doing here, anyway?" he went on. "Did you miss your streetcar stop and get lost? Feeling a little loopy after drinking too much schnaps last night?"

The young man was teasing her, but the question ignited a series of interconnected thoughts in Angelika's mind. Too much to drink... The beer garden... Viktor Bauer...

"Why, yes, I did get lost." The words flew out in a flurry, and Angelika rose up to her full height of 1.7 metres, plus another few centimetres in heels. "Quite silly of me, really. I never could keep straight a streetcar map." She hated playing dumb. "But I'm on my way to meet with Viktor Bauer. Do you know him? Baldur von Schirach's friend? I sometimes sing at his beer garden. The one called Bauerbräu, across the tracks in Neuhausen."

"Viktor Bauer?" The brownshirt's calculating eyes widened. "Oh, I remember you now. We were there the other night." Hoots and hollers rippled through the cohort, while the throng of people waiting for the streetcar began to thin, a few passengers moving discreetly away to seek out another nearby stop. Each departing person kept his or her head down, pretending to be invisible. "You're the girl who's going to sing at the National Socialist concert."

Angelika feared she might throw up again, but forced herself to continue speaking, sounding far more confident than she felt.

"If Herr Bauer asks why I'm late, I suppose I'll have to tell him it's because I went to get coffee with you."

The slightest flicker of fear blemished the man's smug face.

"No," he said quickly. "No, we can't have that. You'd best be going. Wouldn't want to keep Herr Bauer waiting. I've heard he has an awful temper."

Angelika could see the sky-blue and bone-white electric streetcar approaching from down the lane, zipping along on its overhead line as passengers gazed out of glass windows at the spookily serene Sendling Cemetery.

"In that case, I must say goodbye," she said. Angelika began turning away, a flood of relief passing through, when suddenly, a tiny tug on her hair made her stop and spin back around. Whatever relief she'd felt instantly evaporated, because there, in the Nazi's hand, was the dried daisy Erich had placed in her bun.

"Something for me to remember you by," the man said with a wink, three of the flower's delicate petals having already met an unceremonious end between his too-rough fingertips. "That is, as long as you consider me worthy of it."

Angelika bit down upon her lower lip as behind her, the streetcar pulled to a stop – the door opening and passengers hopping off, everyday life bustling on by as one of the final remnants of her mother now lay in Nazi hands.

"It's…"

She met the man's eyes, finding a hint of a challenge reflected within, his body still and solid while awaiting her response. And that was when she noticed the flecks of dried blood buried beneath his fingernails. Dmitry's? Someone else's? It didn't matter. All Angelika knew was that she had to leave, and fast.

"Consider it yours," she said, keeping her head high and voice steady.

It was only a foolish flower. Not a human life. Not anything that mattered.

"Say, Fräulein, are you getting on or not?"

The streetcar operator called to her through the open door, and with that, Angelika clambered into the vehicle, paying the requisite toll and doing her best to ignore the disapproving looks several other passengers threw her way.

"Uppity rich girl," they whispered. "Flirtatious tramp."

The daisy had been a material possession. A foolish flower and nothing more.

Nevertheless, Angelika squeezed onto a long wooden bench between two scowling housewives, her back to the window so that she wouldn't have to watch the smitten storm trooper stuff the daisy's lovely remains inside his pocket.

*

How the Wolpertinger Kaffeehaus's patrons managed to enjoy their elderberry tea and cream cake over Angelika's thunderous "Ride of the Valkyries" rendition, she wasn't certain. Yet on she played, sloppily pounding out notes while seated before an out-of-tune upright piano the café's owners kept tucked away in a corner beneath a taxidermy *Wolpertinger* – part rabbit, part squirrel, part deer and part pheasant – a mainstay of Bavarian folklore.

After circumventing the Nazis in Sendling, Angelika had considered returning to Kurt's office in the hope of making amends. Perhaps she should have been more understanding about the business trip. In light of the serious problems occurring throughout the world, and in spite of the tragic loss she had suffered, Angelika knew she should be grateful for the many comforts available to her. Just as she must also do more to help others.

"Here you are." A voice sounded from behind, and Angelika sighed in relief as her brother sank down beside her on the piano bench. "Kurt's been tied up in meetings, but he said you were upset and sent me to find you."

Angelika forgot all about playing the piano and flung her arms around Andreas, her twin, the boy who had tattled on her for sliding down the banister as a child; whose thick auburn hair and blue eyes so closely mirrored her own; whose annoying knuckle-cracking habit never ceased to drive her mad; and whose exceptional musical talent was unfortunately going unused.

"What happened?" he asked as Angelika's tears dotted his smart blue suit jacket and pin-striped tie. "Are you all right?"

"It was awful," she sputtered, no longer caring who might catch her crying. "That poor boy."

Angelika told her brother about Dmitry and his brutal attack at the hands of the brownshirts a couple of hours earlier. To Angelika's surprise, however, Andreas didn't appear nearly as distraught as she'd expected him to be.

"You say his name was Dmitry?" Andreas said. "Probably a Russian communist."

"His sister said he wasn't a communist. Even if he was, do you think that means he deserved to be beaten bloody?"

"No," Andreas replied, forcefully enough that Angelika believed him. "But you only heard one side of the story. You don't know what really happened."

"I know enough."

"All I'm saying is that we need to be careful who we trust." Andreas used his free hand to brush away several small teardrops that had settled upon Angelika's cheek. "The communists have hurt people. Remember the story in the papers last January? How the communists murdered a Hitler Youth boy in Berlin?" He shook his head. "Immigrants like this Dmitry also take jobs away from Germans."

Immigrants, Andreas had said. Had he forgotten that he and Angelika just so happened to be immigrants themselves?

Angelika thought as much but didn't ask the question. Her mind had grown weary, and she had no strength left to argue. She already knew the answer anyway – that many people considered Austrians like her and Andreas to be "good" immigrants, who ought to be part of German society. Russians and Poles, on the other hand, were considered "bad" immigrants. Still, hearing the words on her own brother's tongue unsettled Angelika.

"But that's not all that's troubling you, is it?" Andreas asked.

Angelika squeezed her brother's arm and let her head come to rest against his shoulder.

"How could Mama abandon us like this?" The painful memories flared again. "Didn't she know we loved her? Didn't she care?"

Angelika's tears soaked Andreas's lapels, and he hugged her tightly, shielding her from others' view.

"I care," he told her. "And so do Gretchen, Erich and Doctor Hoffmann. We're all here, and we all love you. We just have to keep taking things one day at a time."

Angelika nodded against his jacket, and then, tears subsiding, sat up and stared at *The Valkyrie* sheet music spread open before her.

"One day at a time," she repeated. "Even if today, I ended up offending everyone's ears with my horrible piano playing."

Andreas took a clean linen handkerchief out of his breast pocket and handed it to her.

"It's not always horrible," he said. "Only when you try to play Wagner. Or Mozart. Or Bach."

"All right, all right." Angelika allowed herself a quavering laugh, then swallowed down the last of her espresso. "Go audition for a cabaret act, won't you?"

She gathered her things and walked with Andreas to the streetcar stop near Rotkreuzplatz, heading past a couple of recently shuttered businesses and the ubiquitous banks of political posters left over from the parliamentary elections.

Only the German People's Party can free us from Red chains!... For work and food, vote Adolf Hitler and National Socialism!... Vote Communist – down with the system!

"Did you and Kurt have another argument today?" Andreas dared to ask after they'd ridden the streetcar and gotten off a couple of stops later, the two of them traversing the Nymphenburger Kanal's nearest bridge on foot. Had Angelika been in better spirits, she'd have suggested travelling the two additional kilometres to Nymphenburg Palace, where serene lakes and a botanical garden beckoned. But after all that had happened, even the promise of singing frogs, circling swans and darting dragonflies didn't appeal.

"Yes," she admitted. "He and I have been utterly off-key with one another lately. I suppose that must make you happy."

"Seeing you hurting could never make me happy. You should know that."

They soon turned onto Malsenstrasse, ambling past familiar chestnut trees before entering a three-level, canary-coloured house with geraniums in its window boxes. After stopping to give their long-haired dachshund, Mokka, a quick snuggle, the twins set about retrieving a polished copper tea kettle and box of spices. The hot water and ginger would help soothe Angelika's voice.

"Do you want me to reheat the rest of this *Schnitzel*?" Andreas asked, opening the icebox. "Father must have given the cook the night off again. He never eats at home anymore. Too busy visiting his brothels."

Angelika placed the water-filled kettle on the stove and shrugged. She had little appetite, and the meat was two days old. Nevertheless, her brother – a bottomless pit when it came to meals – switched on the electric oven.

One day at a time, Andreas had said.

Angelika monitored the tea kettle, a litre of water silently simmering beneath its surface.

And one more day without their mother.

Six

As promised, Doctor Hoffmann dropped by later that evening. Though Stefan's face was sallow and his eyes weary, he assured Angelika that with the proper care, Dmitry was expected to recover from the injuries he'd suffered at the hands of the Nazis. Stefan asked Angelika if she still cared to discuss her troubles, but the diligent doctor appeared so exhausted, she insisted they speak another time. She did, however, send him away with a bundle of clothing, jewellery and necessities he could either give to the families at the medical clinic or sell to raise money for those who needed help.

Not an hour after he'd left, Kurt also arrived, hat in hand and profusely apologetic about his and Angelika's row at the office. He wanted to talk, but Angelika decided she'd had enough with words for the time being. Instead, she took him by the hand and led him to her favourite spot in the house – the music room – a spacious yet intimate chamber boasting tall windows, a grand piano, colourful Turkish carpets, and French impressionist paintings by Claude Monet and Pierre-Auguste Renoir.

There, she locked the doors, drew the curtains and spent the next two hours sprawled across a velvet chaise lounge, going further with Kurt than she ever had with him or anyone else. If he'd had protection available, she probably would have gone even further still, but he didn't, and besides, Kurt said he wanted to do things properly.

Angelika pointed out that they'd already gone octaves beyond what would be considered proper, though she felt too euphoric to ask much more about what he meant. She instead used her influence to secure Kurt's promise that he would push for an increase in workers' wages and an expansion of the company's charitable endeavours. Things may not have been perfect between the two of them, but if they could only reestablish rhythm and harmony in the relationship, everything would be fine.

Angelika continued telling herself as much two days later, while spending Saturday afternoon – the day of her dreaded nineteenth birthday – exploring the Hellabrunn Zoo with her close friend Gretchen and trying not to feel Kurt's absence too keenly. If not for a series of ill-timed business meetings in Stuttgart, he'd surely have been right there by her side. As indicated by the flood of courier-delivered presents that had been waiting at the house when Angelika and Gretchen returned from the zoo, he also felt guilty about being away.

"Oh, Anni, how romantic." With Angelika's permission, Gretchen had read the stylish notecard accompanying the gifts. "I'd be thrilled to have a young man to tell me I set his heart aflame."

Angelika averted her eyes, glancing about her airy

bedroom at the antique armoire, built-in ceiling-high bookcases, cushioned window seat and hand-carved, photo-adorned bureau. Anything to help mask the small, unexpected swell of disappointment that rippled through her core.

"I'm sure Kurt's 'flaming heart' was in the right place," Angelika replied, the words wobbling unsteadily, as if she didn't quite believe them. "But he must have been rushed when he wrote it. That's why it sounds like a form letter a man could send to any old sweetheart. Just like in the opera *Falstaff.*"

"Well, I think it's delightful."

Angelika couldn't help but smile, her friend and fellow singer's good-natured enthusiasm proving to be infectious. Not a day went by that Angelika didn't thank her lucky stars she and nineteen-year-old Gretchen had met and become kindred spirits the previous year. Unlike Angelika's former friends in Vienna who had forsaken her – whether as a result of the scandals, her mother's death or the competitiveness that often existed among young singers – Gretchen was different. Angelika had noticed it immediately, and so had Andreas, although he'd yet to admit it.

"These gifts are marvellous, too," Gretchen added.

Angelika sank onto the bed beside her friend and took in the vast collection of items littering her nightstand. First, in the middle, was a crystal vase bursting with two dozen red roses. Beside it lay a diamond bracelet, two bottles of lavender-scented Provençal perfume, three cashmere scarves and one monogrammed stationery set. Peeking out of the jewellery box on her vanity were also two enormous, glistening sapphire earrings, which matched the bluebird-shaped necklace Kurt had given Angelika last Christmas.

"Pick your favourite scarf," she told Gretchen. "We can donate the other two, plus the perfume and bracelet. Kurt certainly outdid himself."

Gretchen remained so caught up in the romance of it all that she didn't appear to notice the other small present and notecard lying on the eiderdown quilt amidst Angelika's messy medley of old newspapers, half-studied song sheets and discarded candy wrappers. The gift from a special person in Vienna. Someone who, despite all that had happened, had still remembered to send Angelika and Andreas raspberry jam-filled cookies on their birthday. Someone she'd written about in her memory book a couple of nights earlier – Daniel Weiss.

"Now, hurry up, you starry-eyed girl," Angelika teased Gretchen after her friend had settled upon a cocoa-coloured scarf. "We've got to get ready to go to the cinema."

Despite Angelika's initial desire to have a simple celebration at home that evening, Erich had offered to treat her, Andreas and Gretchen to a night at the pictures, where a recently released Brigitte Helm film, *The Countess of Monte Cristo*, was showing.

I'll buy the tickets if you can smuggle in some of your family's famous chocolate, he'd said while Angelika laughed. He'd then winked and smiled his characteristic mischievous grin, making it impossible for her to say no.

"Did I tell you Frau Böhm telephoned me yesterday

evening?" Gretchen asked as she and Angelika fixed their hair before the vanity table mirror. "I can hardly believe she's invited me to go to Vienna for that young singers programme at the Tonkunst Conservatory. But last night, she also said that a student from another music school dropped out. So, if you're interested, there's still a spot for you."

The voice teacher had telephoned Angelika, too, as had the conservatory's headmaster, who'd conveyed what an honour it would be to have the daughter of renowned opera singer Clara Eder attend. In other words, he'd love the chance to exploit Angelika's name, as well as her departed mother's complicated legacy, for publicity purposes. It seemed no matter what Angelika did, she couldn't escape the pull of the past.

"I do wish you would come," Gretchen added. She gathered her long blonde hair into an elegant bun as Angelika finished dragging a brush through her own wavy auburn locks. "We could spend the entire next month together in Vienna. I've never been there, and you could show me everything."

While Gretchen continued chattering about the singing programme, Angelika shimmied out of her burnt-orange silk day dress and into a knee-length, sleeveless black frock she'd acquired on Paris's Champs-Élysées a couple of years prior. She adored it, as had her mother, who'd believed the V-neckline, sparkling sequins and beaded gold flowers made Angelika appear as glamourous as Coco Chanel. Kurt, however, had been less than enthused the first time she'd worn it during one of their outings. He considered its hemline too daring and the dropped-waist style less than ideal, saying the entire getup made Angelika look like an American flapper girl. She'd stood for none of that nonsense, though, telling him she would continue wearing what she pleased, when she pleased.

"What do you say we have some fun with make-up tonight?" Angelika next asked Gretchen, changing the subject. "Let's get you all dolled up. When my brother sees you, his eyes are sure to pop straight out of his head."

Gretchen blushed as red as one of the cherry candy sticks socked away in Angelika's sweet stash, but nevertheless allowed her friend to experiment.

"Are you sure it isn't too much?" she asked, scrutinising her reflection after Angelika had finished. "You know I don't usually wear cosmetics unless I'm performing."

"I purposely went light with the rouge, and the pink lipstick looks pretty with your blonde bun and sky-blue dress."

Angelika handed Gretchen an aquamarine hairclip and earring set that matched her eyes.

"Put these on, and *voilà* – look out, Brigitte Helm," she said. "You'll be as irresistible as a film star."

"Oh no, I won't." Gretchen giggled, but went ahead and affixed them. "You are, though. Why'd you get so dressed up? Kurt isn't here, and we're only going to the pictures with Erich."

Angelika shrugged, but caught a sideways glance of her own face flushing in the mirror. Perhaps her sunburn from the zoo was getting worse, and she ought to reapply more powder.

Bring-bring. The doorbell chimed, and Angelika made haste with the powder puff. She also applied a thick layer of blood-red Coty lipstick and dabbed on Frau Tonis No. 37, a violet-scented perfume actress Marlene Dietrich fancied.

"Erich must be here," she said. Angelika opened the bedroom door so that her year-old miniature dachshund, Mokka, who'd been asleep on the cushioned window seat, could bolt from the room, happily barking and wagging her tail. "Let's go say hello."

Angelika led the way down the curved, carpeted staircase, heading past what had once been her mother's prized collection of Italian tapestries, African pottery and antique Persian vases. Angelika's father had wanted to sell the pieces, but after she'd begged Kurt to intervene, Rudolf had given in and agreed to let her keep them.

"Who's that pretty girl I see?" A familiar, strapping young man with curly, sand-coloured hair stood in the foyer, addressing not Angelika, but the adorable dachshund who zigzagged between his legs and danced about his boots. "Hello there, Mokka. I brought you a special surprise today. Think you can find it?"

Erich tossed his plaid cap and dark leather jacket onto the marble floor, then dropped to his knees, petting Mokka while she sniffed his pockets as though she were hunting a badger.

"Oh no, not that," he said. Erich shifted a folded envelope from his trouser pocket to a nearby jacket flap before Mokka could extract its contents. "Here's what you're looking for."

Angelika shook her head as he produced a handkerchief filled with several thick slices of sausage. Such a silly spectacle, and yet, she couldn't stop a huge grin from splitting her cheeks.

"You like *Bratwurst*, right?" Erich made a big show of getting Mokka to stand and take four pieces out of his hand. "Next time, I'll bring you some *Weisswurst*, too. Perhaps even a little..."

He then trailed off, mouth falling agape as he glanced up and caught sight of Angelika standing there smiling in her beaded dress and bold red lipstick.

"Holy smoke!" Erich rose, brushing fur from his taupe trousers, pin-striped suspenders and cobalt-coloured sport shirt. "You look like you're ready to go dancing at the Odeon Casino nightclub. Should I have worn a tuxedo? Or at the very least, a tie? I feel like an underdressed slob."

Erich was joking, but his hazel eyes remained so intently locked upon Angelika, it took her several beats to devise a witty response.

"You're hardly a slob," she said at last. "More like a dashing Don Giovanni, sweeping my innocent dachshund off her feet with your charm."

Mokka, who'd remained by Erich's side, gave an approving bark, while Gretchen, who'd been watching and laughing, finally said hello.

"Hello, Gretchen," Erich answered. Though Angelika didn't know the entire history, the two of them had been acquaintances since childhood, both growing up in the Neuhausen neighbourhood and attending the same mixed-gender schools. "You look awfully pretty tonight." His eyes travelled back to Angelika. "You both do."

Erich came a couple of steps closer, and Angelika – standing a mere hair shorter than him when wearing her heels – discerned the tiniest of wobbles in her knees.

"So, um, anyway… your housekeeper let me in and said she'd try to find Andreas," Erich told her. "Any idea where he is?"

"Probably sneaking a smoke in the potting shed outside." Angelika detested the smell of cigarettes, not to mention the way smoke affected her singing voice. "He's been slipping packs of Eckstein's into the house behind my back. Gretchen, why don't you go ask him to come inside? We can have a bite to eat before heading to the pictures."

"You want me to be the one to tell him?" Gretchen asked, flushing.

"Why not?" Angelika and Erich exchanged a knowing glance. "If I go, he'll only get mad. And if Erich goes, I'm afraid he might start smoking, too."

She knew he wouldn't. Erich had made it quite clear he didn't care for it either, but Angelika couldn't pass up the chance to get her brother and Gretchen alone together.

"Uh… all right." Gretchen straightened up, a resolute look glinting in her sea-blue eyes. "I suppose he might like hearing my good news."

"What good news?" Erich asked.

Gretchen explained that every year, the Tonkunst Conservatory in Vienna invited an elite group of eighteen- and nineteen-year-old voice students to participate in a month-long, late-summer singing programme. Working with an esteemed team of professors, the students studied everything from expression and diction to ear training and opera history. And this year, Gretchen would be one of the lucky programme participants.

"Best of all, we'll get to take lessons with Lotte Lehmann," she said, practically squealing. "Do you know who she is, Erich? The famous opera singer?"

Erich didn't know, but Angelika certainly did. Madame Lehmann, as she liked to be addressed, had sung at the opera house with Angelika's mother. Angelika had spoken with her on several occasions and been awed by her talent, especially when she'd seen Lotte appear as the Marschallin in Richard Strauss's *Der Rosenkavalier*. Yet even if Angelika lived to be as old as fairytale villain Rumpelstiltskin, she'd never find another singer who measured up to – or awed her as much as – her own departed mother. Truth be told, she didn't want to.

"Angelika was invited to join the programme, too," Gretchen said. "I'm trying to convince her to come with me, but she keeps saying no."

Oh, bother.

The conversation lasted a couple of minutes more before Gretchen went out back and Angelika gestured toward the music room, where the housekeeper had laid out coffee, sweet mustard, salted breadsticks, *Pfennigmuckerln* rye rolls and a potato, onion and cream spread called *Kartoffelkäse*.

"Come on." She avoided Erich's eyes as he hung his jacket and hat on an oaken rack. The housekeeper had surely offered to do it for him, but Erich never liked being fussed over. "Let's eat."

"I'm not hungry," he mumbled, following her through the gold-leafed double doors, then plopping onto a velvet sofa alongside Angelika's well-worn copy of Thomas Mann's *The Magic Mountain*. She'd been re-reading it a couple of nights earlier, trying to steady herself after the red-letter rendezvous with Kurt.

"I know why you're disappointed," she said while pouring herself a brimming cup of straight black coffee and watching Erich stroke Mokka at his feet. "But there's no use trying to convince me. Do you have any idea what it would be like for me to go back to Vienna?"

"No." Erich's baritone voice sounded particularly deep. "But I do know what it'll be like if you don't even try."

Angelika stared at the red-and-blue Turkish rug cushioning her patent-leather pumps.

"I also know you made me a promise the other day," he continued. "A promise you're breaking."

"I am not breaking my promise." Angelika smacked down the porcelain cup, a few stray droplets of hot coffee speckling her skin. "Just because I don't want to be a part of this singing programme, it doesn't mean I'm giving up."

"It sure sounds that way to me."

"You're being impossible."

"I'm the one being impossible?" Erich rose and crossed the room, standing face-to-face with Angelika, so close that if she took so much as a single step forward, she'd have fallen into his muscular arms. "Not you? The girl with a special talent and a once-in-a-lifetime chance to use it? A chance a thousand other singers would give anything for?"

"It isn't your decision to make, Erich."

"I never said it was." Angelika wished he would avert his all-consuming gaze and retreat, but Erich didn't make a habit of running away from difficulties. "I don't understand how you – the strongest, smartest, most talented and dazzling girl I've ever met – could so badly underestimate yourself. I don't know everything that happened to you in Vienna, and I can't imagine how awful it must have been losing your mother the way you did. But I know you can do this."

The heat of a hundred electric spotlights shot through Angelika's veins as Erich's warm fingers reached out and gripped her bare shoulders. In spite of the passionate exasperation filling his voice, his coarse hands felt gentle, kind and calming.

"If you don't face the past, it'll gnaw away at you forever," he said. "And you'll always wonder what might have been."

Erich Bauer. Angelika's silly, goofy friend turned suddenly serious and standing so incredibly close. One single step – a mere single, shuddering breath – away. Just like Kurt, the night of the Christmas recital. And just like Paul, her former sweetheart from Vienna. The boy she'd once entrusted with her heart, only to have him smash it to pieces as rumours of the scandals spread. The boy who'd responded by calling Angelika vicious names, then never speaking to her again. Kurt may not have been perfect, but at least she knew what to expect with a longtime family friend like him. At least he knew the truth about her past, and had chosen to stand by her.

"Does Kurt know about the singing programme?" Erich asked, as if reading Angelika's mind.

He dropped his hands but remained in place.

"No. I didn't tell Kurt. But he'd agree that if it's too upsetting for me, I ought to stay here in Munich."

Erich huffed a frustrated, peppermint-scented breath. He seemed so invested in the matter, Angelika had half a mind to ask whether he was receiving a cut of the Vienna conservatory's tuition. The reality was perhaps even more shocking. He obviously cared for Angelika, and believed in her, far more than she'd dared to admit.

"Of course Kurt would tell you to stay here," he said, making little effort to hide his grimace. "And if that's what you want, it's your decision to make. But I think you're letting fear hold you back, when really, you have the strength to do anything you set your mind to."

Erich raked a palm across his face, and when he removed it, the tiniest of grins had popped up, crinkling his distracting dimples.

"I also think you're about to call me a louse and toss me out of your house," he said. "Either that or pull a whip and handcuffs out of the front of that heart-stopping dress."

Angelika wanted to laugh, but couldn't. Not with horrible visions of Erich's father, who had likely used a real whip more than once, flashing across her brain.

"I'm not going to toss you out," she murmured. "Or curse, or shout, or anything else. How can I when everything you've said is right?"

Erich reared back in surprise, as if she'd just told him Marlene Dietrich was at the door.

"There must be something wrong with my hearing," he mumbled, snapping his fingers alongside each ear. "I'd better telephone Doctor Hoffmann and schedule a visit."

"There's no need to waste Doctor Hoffmann's time." Angelika allowed a teasing note to enter her voice, even as it quavered a bit. "Because shocking as it is, you heard me correctly. If I really do want to become a famous opera singer, I have to take advantage of every opportunity available to me. And that means…"

Her tongue tripped up as if confronting a tough libretto passage penned in an unfamiliar language. Angelika could scarcely believe the words she was about to utter, and yet, as difficult as it would be to face the past and weather painful memories, pursuing her dreams required it. Angelika could never change what had happened, nor bring back her beloved mother, but perhaps she could summon the strength to carry forth Clara's legacy and try living the life her mother would want her to have.

"It means going back to Vienna for the young singers programme," Angelika said, quickly, before losing her nerve.

She lifted her cup of coffee with a trembling hand, which Erich reached out and steadied. She'd considered going to the liquor cabinet and procuring something stronger, but with someone as supportive as Erich helping to bolster her spirit, Angelika didn't need to rely upon alcohol.

"What happened to you in Vienna?" he asked, voice low and solemn. "Will you tell me?"

Could she? What would Erich say if he knew? Yes, he'd been a reliable friend thus far, but he didn't know the half of it. Angelika wanted to believe he wouldn't say the horrible things that Paul and others had. But what if she was wrong? Hadn't she been hurt enough?

"Perhaps." Angelika decided to stall, buying herself a little extra time to decide. "I'll consider telling you if… you'll also tell me why you just so happened to have a young woman's peasant-dress folk costume lying about at the beer garden. You know, that *Dirndl* you let me borrow the other night."

"Let's just say you're not the only one with secrets."

"Was it Barbara?" Angelika pressed. "The girl you met in the English Garden and brought to the coffee-house a couple of weeks back? The one who ended up being more interested in asking questions about your father and his National Socialist friends?"

"Good grief, no."

"What happened with her, then?"

"The same thing that happens with every girl," Erich said, frowning. "I stepped out with her once and felt sorely disappointed."

His large, warm hand remained wrapped around Angelika's knuckles, and although she knew she ought to, she didn't pull away.

"I don't want those indoctrinated girls, anyway," Erich added. "I hear enough Nazi nonsense from my father. He remembers struggling and being poor as a boy, and thinks Adolf Hitler is the answer to all of Germany's woes."

"And here I thought Hitler was making everything worse."

"Not according to my father."

Angelika finally slipped away her hand, downed the coffee in a single gulp and went to the settee, beckoning for Erich to follow.

"All right," she said as he took a seat beside her, close to the marble fireplace, this time keeping a respectable distance. "I'll tell you the story about my mother and family. But you have to promise not to say anything to your father."

"That'll be an easy promise to keep."

Angelika nodded and drew a breath so deep, she seemed ready to sing a Wagnerian aria.

"When my mother was a voice student in Vienna, she attended an avant-garde music academy," Angelika began. "One that allowed young men and women to attend together. There, she met a brilliant, wonderful boy named…"

A sudden commotion erupted in the hallway, and Angelika stopped speaking. She looked toward the music room's open double doors, heart catapulting into her throat. For there, toting a Zeiss-Ikon collapsible camera and carrying a notebook in his pocket, stood an unfamiliar man with beady eyes, ink-stained fingers and a suspicious stare.

"I tried stopping him, Fräulein Angelika, but he pushed his way past me." Helene, the housekeeper – a kindly, middle-aged woman with greying hair and a stout physique – came rushing into the room, hysterical. "He says he's a…"

Angelika already knew the rest, and could hardly hear Helene's words over the pounding pulse in her ears.

The unwelcome intruder had the same look about him as countless others who'd once hounded Angelika's mother in Vienna.

The man was a newspaper reporter. And he did not appear pleased.

Seven

Angelika sprang to her feet and tried to remain unruffled. Not an easy feat with an intruder – a newspaper reporter, no less – staring her down.

"Who are you?" she said. "And what are you doing inside my house?"

The man, visibly swaying and reeking of schnaps, took a staggering step closer.

"Oh no, you don't." Erich positioned himself in front of Angelika and Mokka, who'd left her warm spot on the rug and taken refuge behind her owner's legs. "Stay where you are."

His voice sounded commanding yet calm, and it soothed Angelika in spite of her thundering heart.

"Are you all right, Helene?" Erich asked the housekeeper, who stood trembling in the doorway. "Did this man hurt you?"

"I'm fine," she choked out. "I told him Herr Eder was away in Stuttgart for business meetings and that Andreas was nowhere to be found. I even threatened to send for the police, but he still forced his way inside."

Erich nodded, never having turned his head away from the drunken, dazed interloper. The newspaperman was of medium height, perhaps a few centimetres shorter than Erich, and nowhere near as well-built.

"I don't know who you are," Erich said, addressing the reporter. "And I don't care. I suggest you turn around and leave. Now."

Erich hated physical violence, but Angelika knew he wouldn't hesitate if he feared her, Helene's or Mokka's safety was at risk. She could only hope Andreas and Gretchen would remain occupied in the potting shed out back, and not yet come inside.

"I'm not leaving until I ask Fräulein Angelika Eder a few questions." The bearded, twig-like man slurred his words, voice emitting as a guttural bark. He appeared to be in his mid-twenties, with greasy blond sideburns and a sneer that could startle a lion. "I'm with the German National People's Party newspaper. We heard rumours she's going to sing at a Nazi concert this October."

His words seemed to resonate like a high F in an empty opera house. Like the Nazis, the German National People's Party was nationalistic and antisemitic. Another group Angelika despised.

"I don't know what you're talking about, and like I said, I don't care." Erich maintained his cool demeanour, but Angelika felt her heart beat all the more rapidly, every last hair on her arms standing on end. "Now, turn around and leave. This is the last time I'll ask nicely."

For the briefest of moments, Angelika almost believed the reporter might comply. Then, with a fitful jerk and determined grunt, he bolted toward the grand piano, his lopsided fedora tumbling to the floral-patterned Turkish carpet as he tried to get past Erich.

"Look at me, Fräulein, and don't blink," the man said, grey eyes wild and menacing. The accordion-like camera snapped a quick photograph. "And get ready to start explaining."

Fortunately, there was no need for Angelika to run. In the mere blink of an eye, Erich had restrained the reporter, pinning the man's arms behind his back and throwing the camera onto a chaise lounge.

"Seems strange the National Socialists would want the likes of her to sing for them," the reporter yelled as Erich hauled him toward the hallway. "Seeing as she's…"

The coffee Angelika had guzzled threatened to come back up, and she reeled as if slapped. She knew the precise words that were coming. The same words her former sweetheart Paul and countless others had once hurled at her.

"…the illegitimate, bastard daughter of a good-for-nothing Jew," the reporter said, spittle flying from the corners of his lips. "Don't they realise her blood is mixed? Impure? Don't they know she's a *Mischling*?"

Helene gasped, and for the next few horrible moments, the room became so silent, one could have heard a pin drop. Angelika stole a glance at Erich's face and saw a disdainful look appear. But the anger wasn't directed at her. It was aimed, fully and completely, at the man who had made the statements.

"What did you just—"

Erich started to ask the question, fire in his voice, but didn't get the chance to finish.

"*Hilfe!*" The reporter cried out as he slipped from Erich's grasp, the man's body suddenly pummelled with kicks and punches by another unwanted visitor who must have shown himself in through the open front door. A boy in a crisp Hitler Youth uniform with a gleaming swastika pin. A boy named Johann Schmitt. "Stop hitting me."

"How dare you spread an ugly lie about Angelika?" Johann said. He seemed bigger, and more powerful, than Angelika remembered. Still, he was no match for Erich, who'd been thrown off balance but recovered quickly, yanking Johann away before he could knock the groaning reporter unconscious. "Do you think our youth leader would want her to sing at the concert if he believed she had impure Jewish blood running through her veins? Would Viktor Bauer let her sing at his beer garden if he thought she was a—"

"Enough!" Angelika shrieked so loudly, she felt certain her cry must have been heard all the way in Vienna. Poor Mokka definitely heard it far too well, because the next thing Angelika knew, the pooch had let loose a likeminded, uncharacteristic growl. "Get out of my house."

Angelika should have gone further, telling off both Johann and the reporter, plus revealing the secret she'd long believed to be true – what she'd been about to tell Erich seconds before the reporter had stormed in. That she and Andreas's real father was not cold-hearted businessman Rudolf Eder, but rather a kind and brilliant Viennese opera director named Daniel Weiss. A man the

Nazis, plus plenty of others, hated simply for the fact that he happened to be Jewish. And yet, in the present moment, Angelika didn't know what was worse – the hatred others spewed or her own cowardly silence.

"You heard her," Johann told the reporter. "Get out of here, before I flatten you."

The reporter, nose bloody and eyes blackened, stumbled to his feet, scooping up his fedora and camera before backing toward the doorway. Angelika wished Johann would leave, as well, but the boy's boots remained firmly planted in place.

"You'll be sorry," the reporter said. He tripped over his own feet and wingtip shoes, barely missing the art deco grandfather clock and a pile of gramophone records balancing upon a decorative, vine-inspired wooden side table. "You'll read about this in tomorrow's paper. You hypocrite National Socialists and your *Mischling* friend."

He gave Angelika a nasty glare before turning and running, as fast as his spindly legs could carry him, out of the music room.

"Fräulein Angelika, are you all right?" Helene asked, regaining her composure after Erich had verified the man's departure. "May I bring you anything?"

Angelika couldn't answer, her legs feeling like liquid as Erich wrapped a sturdy arm around her shoulders. She didn't want to think what might have happened had he not been there when the reporter arrived.

"Let's give her a few minutes, Helene," Erich said, pulling Angelika closer. "And Johann, I'm sure my father told you where I was, and that you dropped in to say happy birthday, but Angelika's been through a lot tonight. I think you'd better leave."

Angelika expected Johann to protest, but to her surprise, he immediately agreed.

"I have to be somewhere," he said, anger about the reporter still flashing in his narrow blue eyes. "But don't you worry, Angelika. We know the things he said weren't true."

Helene gave a curt nod of agreement, and Angelika felt her stomach turn a second time. When the rumours had spread in Vienna the previous year, there had been two primary groups of people. First were those who believed the news was true and hated Angelika, whether for being an illegitimate child or having a Jewish father. Second were those who believed it was all a big lie orchestrated by her family's business rivals or her mother's competitors. Few and far between were those who believed it was true, but had continued supporting her, regardless.

"But before I leave, here." To Angelika's horror, Johann removed his prized swastika-and-sword pin. "Take this. If you ever find yourself in trouble, just present this pin, and it'll prove what a proud and loyal German you are."

"Oh no, I…" Angelika, suspended somewhere between fright and fury, struggled to respond. "I could never…"

He grabbed her clenched fist, unfolded it and pressed the bronze trinket inside.

"This pin means a lot to me, but not as much as you do," he said, looking as if he half expected Angelika to kiss him out of gratitude. "And I want you to know we're on your side. I promise we won't let you down."

How foolish she'd been to ever consider Munich a safe haven. Of course, powerful men like Viktor Bauer and his Nazi friends must have already uncovered the past stories about her paternity. And, for whatever reason, they'd joined the ranks of those who refused to believe any of it was true.

"Go, Johann," Erich said, tone sharpening. "You've said enough."

With a quick wink and pat of Angelika's hand, the boy did at last leave, disappearing right as Andreas and Gretchen came rushing inside.

"What happened, Anni?" Andreas asked. He appeared breathless and distraught, a faint smear of pink lipstick staining his cheek. "I had a terrible feeling you needed help."

Angelika opened her mouth, but no words came. Only silence as she beheld her brother's troubled expression. Whether he'd heard the shouting or not, Andreas had sensed his twin sister was in trouble. And if she told him what had happened, he'd be as flabbergasted about the reporter's intrusion as she was. He'd also be furious when she revealed she'd accidentally agreed to sing at a Nazi propaganda concert.

"I'm all right," Angelika murmured. She left Erich's side and flew into the foyer, swiping her peacock-embroidered pocketbook off the hallway credenza and hastening toward the front door. "I just need some air. I'll be back in a little while."

They could go to the cinema some other night.

"Angelika, wait," Erich said, appearing alongside

with Mokka hot on his heels. He knelt down to give the dachshund comforting ear scratches and a kiss to the head, affection shimmering in his eyes as the then satisfied hound trotted away to check on Andreas. "It's not a good idea to be wandering around outside by yourself right now."

"Coming with me, then?"

Angelika stared at Erich a moment, a challenge in her gaze, before hurrying outside and leaving the housekeeper to explain things to Andreas and Gretchen. She felt guilty for abandoning her brother, and not being the one to impart the news, but an urge to flee overpowered her.

"What a fool I am." Angelika marched down the sidewalk, heading in the direction of Nymphenburg Palace, the Baroque residence of Bavarian royals across the centuries. "For thinking that after I left Vienna last summer, I'd no longer have to read articles calling me an illegitimate bastard and, thanks to the Nazis and their sickening racial beliefs, a *Mischling* – a supposed half-blood."

Angelika continued condemning her foolishness as Erich's footsteps echoed from behind, her friend approaching in fast, wide strides.

"Come here, all right?" He caught Angelika by the arm and turned her around to face him. "All this talk about pure blood and mixed blood is made-up nonsense. That's what Doctor Hoffmann says, and I believe he's right."

Angelika nodded, then looked down at her fist, where Johann's pin remained ensconced. She considered flinging it to the pavement and crushing it beneath her heel. But fearing he might enquire about it later, she instead popped open her pocketbook and stuffed it deep inside an interior pocket.

"You'd already heard whisperings about my family, hadn't you?" she said. "About my mother's longtime affair and my own paternity?"

"Only bits and pieces. My father and the Nazi youth leader, Baldur von Schirach, were talking about it a few weeks back. They said they didn't believe the rumours were true."

Angelika shook her head, shoulders sagging as Erich stood dangerously close in the diminishing daylight. As much as she might have liked to remain frozen that way for the rest of the evening, Angelika felt a compulsive need to continue trudging onward.

"Rudolf Eder – the man you know as my father – has always denied the rumours, too," she said while passing alongside a meandering canal that led to the palace gardens. "But I don't believe he's our real father. I know in my heart that Daniel Weiss, the incomparable Viennese opera director, is our real father. He and my mother loved each other since they were teenagers, but her parents didn't approve of the match. They pushed her into marrying Rudolf, but I could tell she and Daniel never stopped caring about one another."

"And did your mother believe Daniel is your real father?" Erich asked.

"When the rumours started spreading, she tried telling us she didn't know for certain, probably because she wanted to protect Andreas and me from ignorant people's hatred. But I think she knew we were Daniel's. I think she knew all along, but just never told us. And then she died by…"

"You don't have to say it," Erich whispered.

After moving to Munich, Angelika had never wanted to speak about her mother's cause of death. But Andreas, driven by anger and resentment, had been uncharacteristically blunt about the fact that she had died by suicide. Given the overly detailed obituaries that had run in the Bavarian arts papers, plus the rumours Angelika now realised had always been lingering in the background, the information was hardly a secret.

"Andreas refuses to believe Daniel is our father," Angelika said after reaching the two-hundred-hectare palace park, where swans swayed in the water, mist from a geyser fountain dusted her face and the setting sun illuminated the castle's white limestone façade. "He says it's Daniel's fault Mama is gone."

Without thinking, Angelika briefly wrapped an arm around Erich as the evening air cooled. Though Erich didn't discuss it much, Angelika knew he had lost his own mother, too, when she'd passed away a couple of hours after giving birth to him.

"And now, once that news article runs tomorrow, everyone will be gossiping about my family, plus the horrendous concert," Angelika continued. A cloying scent of roses carried on the breeze and made her want to gag. "Did you already know about that, too? That when we were leaving the beer garden earlier this week, I apparently agreed to sing at a Nazi event? It's a show they're putting on in October. Propaganda and lies masquerading as culture and art."

"I heard a couple of things in the last day or so," Erich admitted. He followed Angelika as she ambled about a crescent-shaped *cour d'honneur* pathway and approached the palace's reflecting pool, its edges dotted with snuggling sweethearts. "I didn't want to say anything to you until I was sure, and could come up with some sort of plan. They want to make the official announcement closer to the concert, to maximise publicity."

"Why do they want me so badly?" Angelika's voice rose, and she wished the gilded walls of the palace – birthplace of famed "Fairytale King" Ludwig II in 1845 – would open up and swallow her whole. "Baldur von Schirach's sister Rosalind is an opera singer in Berlin, and I believe my mother met her a couple of times, but that's as far as any connection goes."

"Schirach said he saw you singing at the beer garden last month, when we were there for our graduation party," Erich explained. "He thinks you're beautiful and talented, and that with a 'little guidance' from party leaders, you'll be a sensation. He also says..." Erich sank onto the damp manicured lawn, appearing so sickened, he could hardly continue. "...that you remind him of Adolf Hitler's niece, Geli. The one who died last year."

Angelika sat and shivered, prompting Erich to remove his leather jacket and wrap it around her. From what she recalled reading in the newspaper, Hitler's twenty-three-year-old niece Angela Raubal had been an aspiring singer who'd studied in Vienna and was rumoured to have had a relationship with her Jewish music teacher there. The Nazis maintained that she'd died by suicide in September 1931, but Angelika didn't believe it. She, plus others, believed Hitler and his henchmen had likely ordered her murdered.

"This is my fault," Erich said. "I should have asked you to stay away from the beer garden. Hell, I shouldn't even be living and working there myself. We both always drank too much, and didn't think about what we were really doing. We were complicit and stupid. I wanted to be with you – to hear you sing, and see you smile, and listen to you laugh at my dumb jokes. Even though you'd probably be better off if I'd never let my shadow darken your French books at school last autumn. Then, you'd have never gotten tangled up in this fiasco."

Erich hung his head, avoiding her eyes, and Angelika slid closer, resting her petite palm against his large bicep.

"Don't say that," she replied. "This isn't your fault. It's mine. What I did – getting drunk and singing at the beer garden those couple of times – was abhorrent. Mama and Daniel would be disgusted, and rightfully so. But if we'd never met, I don't know what I would have done this past year. Yes, you've driven me mad at times, and my attempt at teaching you French was a catastrophe. But you've been a good friend and… well… the truth is, I'm going to miss you while I'm away in Vienna."

She thought Erich might respond by teasing, but he only raised his head and nodded.

"I'll miss you, too," he answered. "And don't worry, all right? About the concert. I'll think of something."

"We'd better think fast, because once that article comes out tomorrow, Kurt and Rudolf are going to be furious about the concert, plus all of the family stories recirculating. Kurt already knows the truth about my past, thank goodness. He knows I believe Daniel is my real father. He's been supportive so far, but if anyone asked him publicly, he'd probably pretend the stories aren't true."

"And have you ever denied it? Publicly? To the press?"

No, Angelika hadn't denied it. That said, she hadn't confirmed it, either.

"I've never answered one way or the other," she admitted, ashamed. "I don't make a habit of speaking to newspapermen."

But if Angelika hoped to become a famous opera singer, she would someday have to face members of the press and answer their questions.

"Well, just so we're clear about things," Erich said, "I'm not like my father, or my grandfather before him. That miserable old geezer wasted so much time hating and judging people, it ended up killing him. For all I care, you and your parents could be Jewish or Catholic, princes or paupers, railroad barons or circus clowns. Your parents could have been lovers for a day or married one hundred years. It wouldn't matter. You'd still be my siren, no matter what."

Angelika's heart swelled, and there were many things she wanted to say. Before she could utter a word, however, Erich reached inside his trouser pocket and extracted a tiny box.

"Before I forget, here," he said, handing it to her. "It

isn't much. Just a little something I picked out at a second-hand shop the other day, after I saw you at the music school. I wanted to give you something for your birthday."

Angelika tore the plain brown paper and opened the package, tears brimming as she beheld a daisy-shaped dress clip and, beneath it, an accompanying scrap of paper.

Don't give up, the note said in Erich's dreadful, chicken-scratch handwriting.

"I know it's a cheap hunk of metal with chipped paint," he said, a mischievous lilt at last returning, "but you don't have to cry over it."

Angelika laughed and wiped her eyes, affixing the clip to the front of her V-neck dress and slipping the note inside her purse.

"Thank you, Erich," she said, sparing a smile. "It's perfect."

She wondered what he might utter in response, and what she'd say when he did. But, as luck would have it, her hungry belly decided to spoil the moment.

"We should get you something to eat," Erich said upon hearing the gurgling growl. He stuffed the discarded paper and giftbox into his pocket. "Want to go back to the house?"

Angelika couldn't yet bear the thought of facing Andreas. Besides, judging from the pink lipstick she'd spotted upon her brother's cheek, he and Gretchen had seemed to be getting along quite nicely on their own. It was about time, too, after they'd been making eyes at one another for nearly a year.

"Let's go to the Wolpertinger Kaffeehaus," Angelika

said. "Watching you consume an ungodly number of jelly doughnuts will help me forget my troubles."

Dining alone with Erich while Kurt was away would be considered inappropriate, but Angelika didn't care. She felt her spirit lift ever so slightly as she and Erich left the palace park and boarded a streetcar together, his jacket still slung about her shoulders. By the time they'd exited at Rotkreuzplatz, Angelika was so engrossed in sharing more details about the young singers programme that she almost missed spotting a batch of bright flames rising into the sky and intermingling with the pink-orange glow of sunset.

"Erich, look," she said as an open-topped red fire truck rumbled down one of the side streets. "A large building must be burning."

They raced down Schulstrasse toward the blaze, gasping in shock at the sight of broken glass, smashed typewriters, crushed camera bulbs and reams of paper littering the walkway. A sizable crowd had gathered across the street and at the corner. Some of the onlookers stared in horror while others hooted and hollered in apparent celebration.

"There you are." Andreas's familiar voice rang out, and Angelika turned to find her brother and Gretchen standing beneath an Italian restaurant's awning, the two of them practically hidden amidst the crowd and chaos. "We were worried and wanted to come find you. I figured you might go to the Wolpertinger Kaffeehaus."

"Never mind about me." Angelika shifted her gaze back to the four-storey brick building, every last window having been blown out as the flames leapt higher and a team of firemen futilely sprayed water. "What the devil happened here?"

"They're saying it was the Hitler Youth and *Sturmabteilung*'s handiwork," Gretchen explained, her usual sweet smile having been replaced by a scowl. She pointed at a green-uniformed, disinterested-looking Bavarian State police officer who stood amidst a sea of scattered typewriter keys, plus splattered ink that seeped across the sidewalk like a river of blackened blood. "I overheard him saying it's a wonder everyone working there got out alive."

Angelika's heart seized, and she moved toward the officer, her brother and friends following.

"Excuse me, sir," Angelika said. "Do you know whose building is burning?"

The man appeared agitated, but delivered a matter-of-fact reply.

"There was a secret newspaper office located in the basement," he told her. "Home to the German National People's Party. There were other offices in the building, too. Mostly law and accounting firms. The owners will have to try salvaging whatever they can afterward."

"No," Angelika said, the word a mere whisper in the melee. "Oh, God, no."

A loud bang reverberated as the building's triangular roof caved in, the heat from the blaze reaching Angelika's face as smoke filled the air and the smell of burning paper made her cough.

There would be no news article reporting about the

concert or Angelika's paternity. When Johann said he had to leave, this was the reason why. He and his friends had set fire to the newspaper office in a twisted attempt at defending Angelika's honour. To teach the intruding reporter a lesson, and to issue a dire warning.

"It's all right, Fräulein," the police officer told Angelika. "These types of disturbances are becoming all the more prevalent as of late." He waved his hand dismissively in the direction of the blaze. "The National Socialists are becoming so powerful now, the things they do are beyond anyone's control."

Erich and Andreas tugged Angelika's arms, trying to pull her away. Several other police officers also began pushing back the crowd while firemen struggled to contain the blaze, its sparks threatening to ignite the grocery shop next door.

"What do you mean, beyond anyone's control?" Angelika said, as angry at the police as she was with herself. "You're the police. You're supposed to be protecting this city."

"Protecting this city means protecting my own loved ones, too," the officer spat back. "Going up against the National Socialists is a losing proposition." He again gestured toward the burning building. "As you can see with those big blue eyes of yours."

"Come on, Angelika." Erich gave her hand a tight squeeze, then looped an arm around her waist. "Let's go back to your house."

"Yes, get your sass-mouthed girl out of here," the officer grumbled. "And teach her to watch her tongue. I've got enough problems without dopey women poking their noses where they don't belong."

At the moment, Angelika didn't know where she belonged or who she truly was. All she knew for certain was the unrelenting grip of Erich's fingers as the two of them, plus Gretchen and Andreas, retreated westward, racing through Munich's resplendent neighbourhoods and toward the setting sun.

Eight

*T*he last time Angelika had stepped foot on the Tonkunst Conservatory's well-manicured grounds two summers earlier, she'd been a precocious sixteen-year-old eager to see her famous mother lead lessons at the acclaimed Vienna university. Angelika remembered not only the lessons themselves, during which students had fawned over her mother and improved their technique as if by magic, but the smaller, more intimate moments afterward.

With a bittersweet stab, she recalled a surprise summer storm and warm soak of rain, her mother's melodious laughter filling the air as the two of them skittered across the mud-splotched courtyard and past a flooding fountain. Giggling like best friends, they'd sought refuge by an entrance to the adjacent women's residence and mused about whether a rainbow might appear once the deluge subsided.

Remember the time our canoe capsized at Lake Fuschl? Clara had said, referencing the family's summer estate outside Salzburg. *When the handsome young groundskeeper*

you fancied jumped into the water to "rescue" us? At least
you got to see him wearing a wet sport shirt. This time, we're
the only ones who are wet.

Finally, when the rainstorm had ended, they'd walked
beneath a rainbowed sky to nearby Café Sperl, where they
had shared stories and secrets over piping-hot, cream-
topped mochas while their dampened dresses dried.

Now, poised beneath the conservatory's limestone
archway a couple of years later, Angelika half expected to
see her mother's tall, regal figure appear by her side. What
a thrill it would be to hear her melodic voice, as lovely
speaking as when she was singing, utter something sweetly
sarcastic and bitingly witty. Clara's sparkling charm was a
mere memory, however, and the young man who stood in
her stead had been driving Angelika mad.

"You're certain you'll be all right after I leave?" Kurt
asked for what felt like the thousandth time. "Do you have
enough money on hand? Austrian schillings, plus German
Reichsmarks for returning to Munich next month?"
Although Kurt still opposed the unification of Austria
and Germany, he often complained that the differing
currencies complicated business relations. "Just don't carry
all of your money at once, and watch out for pickpockets. I
hate leaving you here on your own, unchaperoned."

Angelika had told Kurt he didn't need to help her get
settled in Vienna. She and Gretchen would have been
perfectly fine taking the train, reaching the conservatory
and checking into the women's residence by themselves.
But Kurt hadn't listened to reason, and neither had
Andreas.

Angelika supposed she couldn't blame her brother for wanting to see off both his twin sister and newly proclaimed sweetheart. After a whirlwind week-long romance comprised of cinema outings and stolen kisses, he and Gretchen now stood several yards away, enthusiastically embracing and whispering heartfelt goodbyes. Not that Angelika was watching too closely. As happy as she was for the two of them, seeing her brother kiss her closest friend was about as appealing as trying to sing a song while battling bronchitis. Though Angelika hated to admit it, she also envied their joviality.

"I have everything I need," she told Kurt, weary from repeating herself ever since the four of them had arrived in Vienna the previous afternoon. "I spent nearly eighteen years of my life in this city. I'll be fine."

Seeking tenacity and solace, Angelika touched the lace collar of her dark-green day dress, where the daisy-shaped clip from Erich was attached. She must remain strong and behave as confidently as her self-assured words made her sound. It was hard to believe eight days had passed since Erich had given Angelika the clip on her birthday. The same dreadful evening a reporter had forcibly entered her home and the Nazis had subsequently burnt the newspaper office. Kurt and others assumed the arson had been the result of a political disagreement. They didn't realise it had also been a heinous attempt at defending Angelika, and that the fire had prevented a news article discussing the Nazi propaganda concert and her paternity. Only Angelika and Erich, plus Andreas and Gretchen, knew the full truth.

"Where did you say you got that pathetic piece of tin?" Kurt asked, interrupting Angelika's thoughts and frowning as he eyed the daisy clip.

"At a second-hand shop in Neuhausen," she answered without missing a beat. "It isn't pathetic, either. It's pretty."

Once Angelika had relayed how important an opportunity the singing programme was, Kurt had supported her decision to attend. And thankfully so, since Rudolf Eder had said he wanted nothing to do with the matter, and that it was Kurt's decision whether or not to grant his sweetheart permission. Kurt had then insisted upon speaking with the conservatory's headmaster and making all of the travel arrangements. He had also demanded a telephone be installed inside the women's residence where Angelika and Gretchen would be staying. Well-intentioned efforts, albeit a bit overbearing.

"You deserve better, darling," Kurt said, practically pouting. "When you're seen wearing a cheap trinket like that, it reflects poorly upon me. In case you'd forgotten, I've purchased you plenty of real jewellery."

The clip *was* real, though. True, it didn't contain expensive emeralds or rubies, but Erich had put a tremendous amount of thought into choosing something special and personally meaningful. The clip served as a poignant reminder of the pressed daisies Angelika and her mother had created as keepsakes, and wearing it helped Angelika feel close to her.

"How could I forget when you've reminded me half a dozen times?" Angelika said. "I never realised you had such strong opinions about women's accessories. Perhaps you ought to quit the chocolate and telephone industries, and begin a new occupation as a fashion adviser."

She strived to sound playful but could hear a sharp edge creeping into her voice. She at least wished that when she made mischievous remarks, Kurt would respond in kind. Then they might turn the discussion into a game of sorts and find a little something to laugh about.

"I'm quite well-suited in my current profession," Kurt said. Unfortunately, he'd never been the playful type. "I have enough new opportunities coming my way as it is."

Had Erich been there in Kurt's place, Angelika would have made another joke, telling him that in English – one of the four languages she'd mastered – the word "suit" was used to describe clothing. Of course, had Erich been there, they'd never be having an argument about Angelika's appearance in the first place.

Gretchen and Andreas's light-hearted laughter carried over from beneath a nearby maple tree, and Angelika felt an unexpected sting of sadness. She'd been so busy getting ready to leave for Vienna the past week that she'd only been able to see Erich for a brief goodbye at the coffee-house. She had no doubt he would write to her, though, and continue believing in her, come what may. Perhaps Angelika could write him a letter that very evening, after her first day of classes had concluded. She'd tell him about the conservatory, and her professors, and…

"What are you smiling about, dearest?"

Guilt replaced the sadness, and Angelika's grin vanished when she looked up to meet Kurt's confounded blue eyes. Though his overwhelming attentiveness was indeed annoying, Kurt had gone to great lengths ensuring Angelika's first trip back to Vienna went smoothly. He had also insisted upon footing the tuition and boarding bills himself, rather than letting Angelika use some of her mother's leftover money. Rudolf allowed the twins access to the leftover funds out of pity, but Kurt had told Angelika that seeing to her needs gave him great pleasure. In his own way, Kurt had been a thoughtful, caring sweetheart, and for that, Angelika ought to be grateful.

Perhaps it was also unfair to flaunt the daisy clip another young man had given her. While Erich certainly cared about Angelika, and she about him, he was still a friend and nothing more. And yet, if that was true, why had she been wearing the dress clip every day since he'd given it to her? Why did visions of his hazel eyes and velvety voice taunt her at night? Why did she long to see his dimpled smile and laugh at his droll humour again?

"It's nothing," Angelika told Kurt, face flushing as if it were a hot mid-afternoon instead of a cool early morning. "I was just remembering a funny story I read in the newspaper."

"As much as I'd love to hear about it, I'm afraid Andreas and I must be going. We're due at the train station. But if you need anything at all, telephone me or visit our company's Vienna headquarters. I want you to be comfortable and well taken care of, especially since you're a few hours away from Munich." Kurt's stern expression diminished his otherwise attractive features. "And be careful. No going out after dark by yourselves or with strange young men. If you need a chaperone, I can arrange for a business acquaintance to be of service."

He gave Angelika a chaste public kiss.

"Goodbye, *mein Schatz*," Kurt said. "I hope the next month passes quickly, and that we'll soon be reunited."

Angelika said she wished the same, though deep inside, a confused muddle of emotions swirled like whirling dervish dancers. Even the memory of her and Kurt's almost-love-making on the chaise lounge a couple of days before her birthday no longer heated Angelika through in the same way it had at the time. Honestly, that night – little more than a week earlier – already felt like a lifetime ago. A proverbial eternity throughout which she'd had time to consider what sort of life she wanted and who she wanted in it. If only the correct answers could materialise as easily as the commendatore's ghost in *Don Giovanni*.

With a self-deprecating sigh, Angelika turned her attention away from Kurt, who had climbed into the backseat of a chauffeured Austro-Daimler automobile with all the panache of an emperor ascending his throne. Angelika knew the time had come to focus on the next tough task at hand – saying goodbye to her twin.

"I know it's hard being back here," Andreas said, sapphire eyes brimming with long-suppressed sentiment. "But if there's anyone who can take this singing programme by storm, it's my feisty 'older' sister." He'd always teased Angelika for having elbowed her way out of the womb first. "Don't forget it, all right?"

Temporarily parting ways with her brother seemed more unbearable than expected, and Angelika's throat tightened as she embraced him. Their entire lives, the twins had scarcely been apart, and certainly not for a month's time.

"I won't," she promised, telling herself that even while physically separated, the two of them would always remain connected. Angelika then lowered her voice to a whisper before muttering the next line. "And you and Erich be careful in Munich."

Erich and Andreas had insisted they would find a solution regarding the National Socialist concert before Angelika returned in mid-September.

"We will," he answered, giving her the biggest of brotherly hugs before joining Kurt in the open-topped, periwinkle-coloured car.

Angelika summoned a smile, watching and waving while the two already bickering young men rode away. She had no idea how they'd managed staying on the same floor at Hotel Sacher the night before whilst she and Gretchen made themselves at home in the women's residence – a dormitory occupied by university students and single working women. Still, for better or worse, the two female friends were finally alone in Vienna, ready to begin their new adventure.

"This certainly is a lot bigger than the Böhms' school," Gretchen said as she and Angelika traversed the dahlia-filled courtyard, preparing to attend their first day of lessons.

While much about the conservatory remained the same – a handful of columned nineteenth-century, Renaissance-style buildings clustered around a central quad – the grounds did seem larger and more imposing than Angelika remembered, the maple trees having grown taller and the cobbled walkways more worn since she'd last encountered them in the summer of 1930. A year before her mother's horrific death and the subsequent move to Munich.

"Was I wrong to be excited, and to ask my parents to spend so much money letting me enrol?" Gretchen asked as a group of fellow students sped by on bicycles, nearly bowling over a couple of young musicians carrying violin cases. With regular classes out for the summer, the university seemed relatively quiet, though far from deserted. "What if I sing off-key and forget everything I've learnt?"

"You sounded wonderful during our practice session yesterday, and you're going to be perfect. Now, let's see where we're supposed to go." Soothing Gretchen's shaky nerves helped Angelika forget that she, too, was becoming a bit anxious. "Our welcome papers say we should head to the Gallery Terrace in Linden Hall."

According to the paperwork, the conservatory's headmaster would give an introductory speech at half past eight. After that, students would attend courses in expression, diction and ear training before lunch. Then, in the afternoon, there would be an opera history course, plus private instruction and practice. Throughout the programme, they'd also enjoy special lessons with Lotte Lehmann, the renowned soprano Angelika fondly recalled meeting.

"I miss Andreas already," Gretchen whispered, halting in front of the entrance steps. The five-storey building's arches and verandas mimicked the architecture of the nearby

Vienna State Opera, home to the statue-flanked grand staircase, lovely loggia and whimsical *Magic Flute* frescos that had forever enchanted Angelika. "Don't you miss Kurt?"

Angelika didn't answer. She gave her friend a quick hug, then found herself distracted as she and Gretchen snaked through a labyrinth of white marble hallways and up several flights of stairs. She purposely avoided the stairwell showcasing pictures of her mother and other opera singers, opting instead for the one bearing images or artwork that depicted Gaetano Donizetti, Gustav Mahler, Wolfgang Amadeus Mozart, Johann Strauss II and other influential composers.

"My goodness," Gretchen said while taking in elegant, coffered ceilings and woven tapestries portraying Vienna across the centuries. "It's like attending school inside a castle."

Several twists and turns later, and after passing a small theatre specifically designed for recitals, the two young women at last stepped out onto a sunlit wraparound terrace. Although the morning sun glared brightly, from five storeys up, Angelika could make out the tops of familiar landmarks. There, clustered about the famed "ring street" that encircled the city's centre, lay the Burggarten park, Rathaus government building and Hofburg palace to the northwest, plus the Vienna State Opera and Musikverein concert hall to the east.

While she couldn't see it from her present vantage point, Angelika also knew that the Academy of Fine Arts – the very school that had twice rejected Adolf Hitler twenty-five years earlier – sat a couple of blocks away. In spite of the ongoing unrest in Germany, it seemed Kurt had been right about President von Hindenburg distrusting Hitler. A couple of days prior, the elderly statesman had refused to meet Hitler's post-election demands, denying him the German chancellorship, at least for the time being.

"I'm going to find the 'palatial' powder room," Gretchen said after setting her things on a velvet-backed chair close to the exit.

Meanwhile, two fair-haired young men who were seated up front, alongside a podium, turned their heads and stole a quick peek at Angelika. Though it mercifully wasn't him, the taller of the pair reminded Angelika of her former sweetheart Paul Ritter, a boy she'd once fatefully caught staring during a performance of Bach's *Christmas Oratorio* her last winter in Vienna.

The son of a wealthy textile manufacturer, Paul had shared her passion for music and languages, and had treated Angelika respectfully throughout the first couple of months of their courtship. It was only after stories about Angelika's mother and Daniel Weiss began circulating that Paul and his family had revealed their true, hateful nature. Oh, how he, and many others, had managed to fool Angelika.

She mustn't dwell upon Paul and his wretched behaviour, however. If Angelika allowed the past to constantly permeate her thoughts, she'd never make it through the young singers programme. But being back home in the city of her birth, and at a familiar conservatory where she could already feel Vienna's poetic music keeping time with her heart, made it impossible to hold the bygone memories at bay. Perhaps she'd been wrong to come back. How would she cope with the pain, especially once everyone learnt she was Clara Eder's daughter? Perhaps it wasn't too late to race to the train station, catching Kurt and Andreas before they left.

"Um, excuse me. Fräulein?"

Mind racing, Angelika turned to find a short, bespectacled young man standing nearby.

"Is this the Gallery Terrace?" he asked in a bashful, breathy voice. "I'm here for the young singers programme."

"You're in the proper place." Angelika nodded politely and, pushing aside her inner panic, pointed out an identifying sign that had been strung from the podium. "This building's a maze, isn't it?"

The fellow nodded, puffing a small sigh of relief yet remaining paralysed in place. Like all of the students in the programme, he must have been eighteen or nineteen years old, though his slight stature made him appear younger.

"Are you a tenor?" Angelika asked.

Another nod.

"Where from?" she said.

"Linz."

"Ah, Linz is beautiful."

Once upon a time, in honour of Angelika and Andreas's thirteenth birthday, their mother had chartered a boat that sailed the Danube from Vienna to Linz for a week-long holiday. They'd visited the market square at Hauptplatz, consumed ungodly amounts of raspberry *Linzer Torte* and enjoyed a scenic electric train ride to the top of Pöstlingberg hill. Several friends had come along, too, but they'd all eventually turned their backs several years later as a result of the scandals.

"Uh, pardon me, Fräulein," the still nameless young man murmured, "but have we been introduced before?"

"I don't believe so."

"You appear oddly familiar."

In Angelika's opinion, their entire conversation was becoming rather odd.

"Why don't you have a seat?" she asked, lowering herself into one of the velvet-lined chairs and gesturing toward an empty spot beside her.

But the boy didn't seem to hear, instead glancing sheepishly about the veranda, then back at Angelika, a slight, though hardly complete, realisation flickering in his caramel-brown eyes.

"I know what it is," he said at last. "You remind me of someone. My favourite opera singer. The late Clara Eder. I assume you've heard of her?"

The terrace was growing noisier with sounds of fellow students arriving, meeting and greeting, laughing and chattering. Angelika, however, could suddenly hear little of it as she focused on the boy and waited for the sensation to come – the familiar jolting gut punch that typically followed public mentions of her mother.

Only, to her surprise, it wasn't there this time.

"Yes," Angelika told him. She laid the word out gently, carefully. "Of course I have. Clara Eder…" It had been ages since she'd stated her mother's name aloud. "…was incomparable. She was the most talented singer and teacher I've ever known."

"You studied with Madame Eder?" The young man spoke in low, almost reverent tones. "Before she…"

He didn't finish the sentence, but Angelika felt her throat constrict and wondered whether she ought to continue. All of the other students, even if they didn't recognise her outright, would eventually discover who she was. But that didn't mean she had to elaborate or talk at length about her mother. Unless... Unless, of course, she wanted to.

"Yes, I studied with her." The words flew out, and Angelika, for once emboldened rather than overwhelmed by the memories, could feel the twinge of a smile tugging at her lips. "I knew her quite well, as a matter of fact. Clara Eder was... I mean, she still is... and always will be... my mother."

"Your mother?" The boy let out a gasp and flung himself into a seat so forcefully, it almost toppled. "Why, yes, of course. You're Angelika Eder. What a pleasure it is to meet you. My name is Georg Schneider."

"It's nice to meet you, too, Georg."

"I remember the way your mother used to speak about you during her press interviews," he continued while sliding lopsided, wire-rimmed round glasses up the bridge of his nose. "She said hearing you sing 'Caro mio ben' in recital was one of the proudest moments of her life."

"I remember, too." The smile that had tickled Angelika's mouth fully freed itself. "That recital happened a couple of years ago. Mama always helped and encouraged me, no matter what. I learnt so much from her."

"Well, gosh, I hope we can work together." Georg ran his fingers through windswept dark brown hair. "In this programme, I mean. If you're, uh, interested."

"Certainly."

Angelika was about to ask what sorts of songs he was studying when Gretchen reappeared, and Georg, excusing himself, rose and hurried away in the opposite direction.

"What was that about?" Gretchen asked. "Did I miss something?"

Angelika considered sharing the discussion about her mother, but decided to keep it tucked away inside her own heart, at least for a little while.

"I was talking with a new friend," she said. "His name is Georg Schneider."

Angelika stole another glance at Georg, who stood awkwardly off to the side in baggy trousers and a misbuttoned shirt, quietly observing his surroundings.

"He's probably sweet on you," Gretchen answered with a chuckle. "Those two blond-haired boys up front keep staring at you, too. I'll bet they'd like to be your friends."

"*Ach*, enough," Angelika said, teasingly, before standing and smoothing her pleated silk dress, exhilaration replacing her prior uncertainty.

Yes, this was only the beginning, and yes, there were sure to be plenty of difficult moments during her time in Vienna. But perhaps revisiting the past could foster joy, and not only pain.

"Now, come on," she told Gretchen, pulling at her friend's paisley-print sleeve, then easing a thumb across the unburnished daisy clip. "Let's say hello to everyone else."

Nine

he headmaster's welcome speech blurred by more quickly than the Orient Express as it whisked passengers through Vienna on the way to Paris. Before Angelika knew it, she and Gretchen were leaving the sunlit terrace and heading to their first lesson of the day, a movement and expression class.

Much like the music school in Munich, Vienna's Tonkunst Conservatory had in recent years started offering movement and expression courses in addition to classical training. In fact, it was Daniel Weiss, who believed the rise of cinema would eventually foster changes within the opera world, who had been a leading voice in advocating for the avant-garde additions.

A flutter of emotion rippled through Angelika's core as she imagined the possibility of reuniting with Daniel for the first time since leaving Vienna. Childhood memories surged from within, and a smile passed across Angelika's lips as she envisioned his tall, lanky frame clad in colourful, free-spirited clothing. She remembered thick walnut-brown hair that had belied his age, and bold blue eyes that had twinkled whenever he caught sight of her beautiful, clever mother. Even more clearly, Angelika could hear his high, light voice passionately conversing with colleagues as he staged operas at festivals or worked at the nearby Theater an der Wien – a Viennese operetta venue, and the place where Daniel served as a co-director. And of course, she'd never forget the saccharine scent of sugar on his breath from consuming far too many sweets.

Angelika had been so busy preparing for the singing programme, she hadn't had the chance to write to him and say she'd be returning to Vienna. Or perhaps she hadn't written to Daniel because, irrational as it might be, she feared he might not wish to see her in person. Although they'd exchanged kindly, cordial letters during Angelika's time in Munich, the scandals and loss of Clara had taken their toll on Daniel, too. He'd suffered an unbearable amount of pain, and his relationship with Angelika had changed, the two of them becoming distant in both a geographical and emotional sense.

Not that they'd ever possessed a genuine father-daughter relationship. Theirs had always been strictly a friendship, or rather a close advisership, two opera lovers joyously discussing scores and composers while munching jam-filled cookies, but hardly connecting on a deeply personal level. Angelika had long ago accepted the fact that, close as she had been with her mother, she'd never experience the same special bond with a father. If only accepting as much could help wash the lingering sadness from her soul.

"Thank goodness we were given identical schedules,"

Gretchen said to Angelika as the two friends walked to class behind Georg Schneider and several others they'd spoken with briefly, whether on the terrace or at the women's residence the previous night. "Especially since we're the largest summer class they've ever had."

There were thirty-five students attending the young singers programme that year, most of them from Austria, but some from southern Germany. Respected music schools in both countries applied every spring for the opportunity to send one or two voice students for the summer session. And while a larger class would mean more competition amongst the singers, it also meant more opportunities to learn from one another.

"I'm glad it's a large class," Angelika told Gretchen. "More friends to make that way."

With a nostalgic pang, she recalled her mother and Daniel having started, but never getting the chance to complete, discussions with the conservatory's headmaster about expanding the programme to host students from England, France, Turkey and any number of other nations. Perhaps their dream of an international singing programme might someday become a reality, even though Clara was gone.

"I envy your confidence," Gretchen muttered.

After talking with Georg on the terrace, Angelika had grown more genuinely self-assured. She'd remained in good spirits, too, greeting her fellow students and welcoming polite attention from those who'd recognised her face or last name. As of yet, there had been no mention of plans to use Angelika's personage for publicity. She also dared to hope that Vienna's obsession with the past scandals and her mother's death had waned.

"Oh, bother." Angelika rifled through her tooled-leather bookbag as she and Gretchen approached their fourth-floor classroom. "I must have left my notepad upstairs on the terrace."

She'd used it to jot down a few helpful notes during the headmaster's speech.

"Go on ahead and save me a seat, will you?" she said. "I'll be back in a few minutes."

Angelika wove her way up the marble stairwell past a few stragglers, and when she returned, notepad securely in hand, she was surprised to find Gretchen and nine fellow students not seated inside the classroom, but filing back out into the hallway.

"What are you doing?" Angelika asked, hesitating alongside a picture window that offered a view of the courtyard below. In the past hour, the grounds had grown more crowded with other pupils playing ball on the lawn, reading beneath lush maple trees and chattering by the fountain. "Isn't our lesson about to start?"

"Yes, but the professor's asked us to walk around a bit first," Gretchen explained. "He could tell we were anxious, and said that sitting still is one of the worst things to do when you're nervous. He thinks being idle will only intensify it."

Angelika's heart tapped out an unexpected symphony, and her gaze darted toward the slightly ajar classroom door. She'd heard the same advice before, from someone she used to know quite well.

"He said that instead of controlling our nerves, we were letting them control us," Gretchen added. "But he also said not to worry, because initial nervousness is often…"

One of the best signs of eventual greatness.

The words played out inside Angelika's head, along with vivid images of the brilliant man who'd uttered them. A man who was apparently present at the university, right then and there, only a few short steps away.

You're nervous because you care, Anni. He'd given the guidance two years earlier, after Angelika had found herself unexpectedly anxious the night of her 'Caro mio ben' recital. *And you'll have to work that much harder to control the fear. But believe me, you will learn to control it, and ultimately use it to your advantage.*

He'd then told her to stand up and walk around backstage. To pace back and forth about the passageways, swinging her arms and breathing deeply. Envisioning that with every step, she was leaving the fear behind and replacing it with a far more productive energy. To Angelika's delight, the strategy had worked, and her big recital had been a rousing success.

"There was something familiar about the way he spoke," Gretchen continued. "Almost as if… Oh, I don't know."

But Gretchen obviously did know, albeit without fully realising it.

"I assume he didn't give his name?" Angelika asked.

"Not yet. He said the professor who was supposed to teach the course had to quit because of a family emergency. This man was only asked to fill in a couple of days ago. He hasn't even been given a roster with students' names yet."

Angelika nodded, her breath wavering like the Danube's rippling current.

"Go catch up with the rest of the class," she said to Gretchen. "Have a brisk walk around the corridor, just as the professor suggested. I'll set these things down, then join you if there's time."

Gretchen agreed, and after she'd left, Angelika lingered outside the hand-carved wooden doorway, gathering her wits. So, this was it. The moment she'd been imagining was about to occur that very moment, whether she or the man in question were ready or not. Focusing upon the steadying weight of the daisy clip at her collar, Angelika eased her way into the classroom as if stepping into an alpine lake that had yet to be kissed by warm summer sunshine.

"*Vorstellung*," the forty-year-old professor was muttering, his back to Angelika as he scribbled information onto a rollaway blackboard. Thankfully, all of the other students were out of the room, performing the relaxation exercise. "V-o-r-s-t-e-l-u…"

"Two l's," she instinctively corrected.

How can someone with such a creative, brilliant mind be so abysmal a speller? Angelika would never forget her mother's good-natured teasing about the matter.

"I knew it had to be you," she went on, putting her belongings down and ambling forward, moving as if in a dream-like trance, while the professor simultaneously dropped the chalk and pivoted to face her. "Unless I'm remembering incorrectly, and it was another opera director whose advice kept me from cowering behind the curtain during my 'Caro mio ben' recital."

The joke slipped from Angelika's mouth, and for the briefest of moments, she could almost imagine nothing had changed.

"Anni?" A combination of joy and bewilderment shone in Daniel Weiss's eyes. Much as Angelika had imagined, he wore an artistic ensemble of mismatched sport coat and pants, plus a multicoloured necktie. His hair had thinned and receded a bit, however, and his face bore a sad weariness that had never been present before Clara died. "I... wasn't expecting to see you here today."

"Likewise." Angelika forced herself to look away, staring at the floor, the desks, the Bösendorfer piano – anywhere but into the face of the man she believed to be her true father. For if she allowed herself to really look at him, and feel everything she'd kept bottled inside the past year, tears would overwhelm her eyes. She'd forget all about the singing programme and want nothing more than to rush forward into Daniel's arms as if she were once again a little girl sneaking about backstage at the opera house. "I haven't seen you in... Well, it feels like a very long time."

"I wanted to visit," Daniel said. Angelika met his gaze a second time, discovering that Daniel's own eyes were brimming. "I'd have loved seeing one of your recitals in Munich. *Scheisse*, I'd have loved just getting coffee together."

His caring words and customary colourful language warmed Angelika, and she felt herself relax a bit. Despite the past year of pain, loss and separation, Daniel's heart was still as big.

"But I knew that your... father... would never allow it," he continued, lowering his voice in case any of the other students returned. "With so many awful things happening in Germany, I was also afraid our being seen together might start people gossiping about you again. Or worse, I was terrified a hateful *Arschloch* might harm you."

A tear streaked across Angelika's cheek before she could brush it away. As unfair as it was, she knew Daniel blamed himself for Clara's death, and for others calling Angelika and her brother illegitimate children.

"You and Andreas received my most recent letters, I hope?" Daniel asked. He took a step forward, but stopped before fully closing the distance. "And the cookies on your birthday? I was worried Rudolf might intervene before your housekeeper could give them to you."

Though Daniel tried to hide it, his disdain for Rudolf Eder had always been apparent.

"We got them," Angelika said. "*Danke schön.*"

Angelika didn't tell him that while she kept every last one of his letters, Andreas threw the greetings away, unopened. Andreas had forever been shy and aloof around Daniel, never connecting with him in the same way Angelika had. And sadly, after Clara's death, Andreas had become downright acrimonious toward him.

Mama wouldn't want you to hate him, Angelika had once tried arguing. *Our losing her wasn't Daniel's fault.*

Mama is dead, Andreas had answered, his normally measured tone rising to a fever pitch. *As far as I'm concerned, Daniel Weiss might as well be, too.*

"Sorry I'm late, professor." A flaxen-haired university

student a couple of years older than Angelika interrupted the conversation, bustling into the room just as Gretchen, Georg and others began to return. "I'm Oskar Huber, the pianist you requested. I was in the front office collecting a class roster, along with a stage direction textbook. We thought you might care to refer to it while preparing your lessons."

"Set it down on the desk, please," Daniel said, still focusing on Angelika. There were so many things she wanted him to know, to ask, to say, but that he clearly couldn't. Not then and there. "I neither need nor care to rely upon a dry, uninspired textbook."

At that, Angelika copped a tiny grin, well aware of several students staring and whispering in the background while she, meanwhile, felt overwhelmed yet glad all at once – concurrently distant from and connected to the unexpected scene in which she was starring. She longed to say so much more to Daniel, but it would have to wait until later.

"In this class," Daniel was saying, "we will learn the best way we know how. The only way anyone truly learns anything."

"And how is that, sir?" the pianist asked, listening intently as the renowned stage master began to answer, his words resounding inside Angelika's memory.

"By trying our best, failing, and trying again. Now, sit down, everyone. We've a lot to accomplish and hardly any time in which to do it."

Daniel gave Angelika a look that said they would speak more later. She nodded, then sat down next to Gretchen, whose eyes widened like saucers as other students' whispers circulated.

"Ah, I recognise him now! That's Daniel Weiss. He's Angelika Eder's real father."

"No, he isn't. Those are all just rumours."

Daniel paid the mutterings no mind, taking his place before the class with a small smile upon his face. Only someone who knew him as well as Angelika did could discern the way his blue eyes burnt with unspoken sentiment.

"Good morning," he said to the eleven students assembled about the classroom. "As some of you already seem to know, my name is Herr Daniel Weiss. I'm a co-director at the Theater an der Wien, but first and foremost, I am a lover of music, song and creativity, just like all of you. I'm not a traditional professor, and this will not be a traditional course. I already listen to myself talk too much while directing operas, and I have no desire to do that now. Throughout the next four weeks, I would much rather listen to, and learn from, all of you."

A few students eyed one another curiously, but Angelika beamed more brightly than she had in ages.

"Every day, two of you will sing for the rest of the class," Daniel explained. "After each performance, we'll share our thoughts and work together to help the singer improve. A special guest – someone who also admires this teaching method – should be joining us in a little while. I have a feeling many of you will recognise her."

Daniel stopped speaking and looked around, his own smile broadening after he caught sight of Angelika's grin.

"Now that you know who I am," he said, "I'd like to get to know you. Let's go around the room, and when it's your turn, please stand. Tell us your name, voice type, where you're from and why you sing. You first, miss."

Allowing no time for preparation, Daniel pointed at Gretchen. The desks had been pushed into a semicircle, and Angelika gave her friend a reassuring wink as the uncertain singer rose to face a rapt cadre of classmates.

"Um, hello," Gretchen said, her voice a near whisper. She looked timidly at Daniel, as if afraid he might scold her for speaking too softly. But Daniel continued listening. "My name is Fräulein Gretchen Hoffmann. I'm a soprano from Munich, and I sing because..." She hesitated. "Honestly, I've never thought much about it before."

"That's all right," Daniel said. "There are no wrong answers. Just tell us the first reason that comes to mind, and speak to us from your heart."

"I sing because... I've loved it since I was a child. I started singing in church with my parents when I was little, and people told me I had a nice voice. I've been doing it ever since."

"Splendid," Daniel replied.

He then pointed at Angelika, who stood to take her turn.

"Good morning," she said. "I am Fräulein Angelika Eder, soprano." Hushed murmurings again filled the room, and Angelika tried her best to push them out of mind. "I grew up in Vienna, but currently live in Munich. And I sing because it's my dream to one day become a famous opera singer."

Though Daniel nodded his acknowledgement, Angelika couldn't help but notice his smile wavering a bit. Was it because, for some reason, he didn't approve of her answer? Or because he didn't believe she had the talent to achieve her objective? There was no time to ask, since the next two students – a full-figured mezzo-soprano named Marta, plus the timid tenor Georg Schneider – were already taking their turns.

"I sing because it's the best way I can express myself," Georg said. "I'm not always articulate when I… uh… talk, but singing helps me show what I feel."

"Good," Daniel said. "An excellent reason to sing."

He then pointed to the next young man, one of the blond-haired boys who had been staring at Angelika on the terrace.

"My name is Herr Thomas Schuster," he said, standing at attention as if he were a member of the armed forces. "I'm a baritone from Salzburg, and I sing to honour the German language, culture and people. I hope Germany and Austria will someday find a way to unify, so that I can call myself a German citizen, too. *Heil* Hitler!"

The boy saluted, and several students gasped, while a couple of others, including his stocky friend from the terrace and a willowy girl in pigtail braids, nodded approvingly. Although there were plenty of Austrians who supported unification with Germany, they weren't all advocates for Adolf Hitler and the Nazis. But the more time that passed, the more Hitler succeeded in making himself the face of the unification movement. Too many of Angelika's fellow Austrians either condoned or turned a blind eye to antisemitism and fervent nationalism, whether it was being propagated by Hitler or radical Austrian politicians.

Thomas plopped back into his seat, and Angelika, horrified but silent, looked to Daniel. She wondered whether he might give the boy a piece of his mind. But in all the years Angelika had known him, Daniel had never raised his voice or belittled anyone, even those who had hurt him and clearly deserved it. Instead of engaging in an argument, Daniel pursed his lips and clenched his jaw, a flicker of pain flashing in his eyes.

Had Angelika's mother been alive and present, she certainly would have spoken up. She always had, whenever someone she loved was being disrespected or disparaged, though it often meant she'd ended up being verbally abused in return. With a shudder of shame, Angelika thought back to her own complicit behaviour at the Bauers' beer garden in Munich. She felt more awful than ever that, as of now, she was still expected to sing at the Nazis' propaganda concert once the young singers programme concluded. She couldn't imagine what Daniel might think if he knew. How could Angelika hope to reestablish her relationship with him when she didn't deserve his kindness?

"May I say something?"

Angelika's voice echoed throughout the classroom as she impulsively rose to her feet, hands clenched in fists at her sides. Though it might do little good, she wanted to tell Thomas that there was more to music and artistry than honouring one culture or language. And that Adolf Hitler's vision was narrow-minded, ignorant and bigoted.

But in Thomas's icy eyes, she saw her former sweetheart Paul's hateful stare. The same monstrous glare that had preceded an angry diatribe of vicious words and name calling.

"I… It's…"

Bastard… Trash… Worthless… Better off dead…

Angelika faltered, sinking back into her seat as a regally poised, middle-aged brunette appeared in the classroom's doorway.

"Madame Lehmann," Daniel said.

Seeming glad of the distraction, he stepped forward to greet the renowned soprano. Lotte's sudden appearance helped obliterate Angelika's bitter memories of Paul, at least temporarily. Her anger at Thomas, however, as well as her hatred of Hitler, continued to fester.

"We're honoured to have you join us today, especially since you're busy getting ready to leave town and sing at the Salzburg Festival," Daniel told Lotte. "Would you like to say a few words? Perhaps tell the students where you're from and why you sing?"

Lotte Lehmann wound her way to the front, and when her perceptive eyes landed upon Angelika, the diva's mouth fell open a bit. She appeared every bit as sophisticated as Angelika remembered, making an elegant impression in a high-collared blouse, midi skirt and belted grey jacket that modestly yet stylishly accentuated a curvaceous figure.

"Good morning." Her cheerful tone was a welcome departure from Thomas's rabble rousing. "I am Madame Lotte Lehmann. I was born in Perleberg, Germany, but have spent the past sixteen years singing at the Vienna

State Opera. Why do I sing? To serve God and fulfil my calling as an artist."

She paused, gaze lingering fondly upon Angelika. For as long as Angelika could remember, Lotte and Clara had mutually admired one another and gotten along well, which wasn't always the case among divas.

"I'm thrilled to be here, and I hope to have the chance to work with each and every one of you," Lotte continued, her youthful face alight with passion for her craft. "As you can imagine, I once walked in your shoes myself. And just as I once did, I encourage you to make the most of a wonderful opportunity to learn, create and share your gifts." She paused dramatically, adjusting the two silver barrettes holding back her hair. "And share them, you will, both in the classroom and during our end-of-term competition at the Vienna State Opera."

"A competition at the opera house?"

Angelika had spoken out of turn again, but Daniel and Lotte didn't seem to mind.

"Yes, Fräulein Eder," she answered. "And what a pleasure it is to see you again. It's a new tradition the conservatory started last summer. I will be judging the contest, along with soprano Elisabeth Schumann and a couple of professors. You'll each work on preparing a song to sing in recital inside the opera house's illustrious Emperor's Room."

Now it was Angelika's turn to stare agape. Winning such a competition would be considered a great honour, and something that would help put her on the path toward one day becoming a famous opera singer. Lotte went on to explain that the winning student would be offered a scholarship to continue attending the Tonkunst Conservatory once regular classes resumed at the end of September. The second- and third-place finishers would also be given the option of enrolling, albeit as paying students. And if the first-place winner chose not to accept the scholarship, that was perfectly fine. In that event, it would simply be awarded to one of the others.

"Can you imagine?" Gretchen leant over and whispered in Angelika's ear after Lotte had finished speaking. "Studying here for the next four years? What an adventure that would be."

An adventure indeed, and an upheaval Angelika felt was out of the question, at least as far as her own life was concerned. Returning to Vienna for the young singers programme was one thing, but to remain there the next four years would be a horse of a different colour. Still, Angelika hoped that if she put her mind to it, she might win the competition and carry forth her mother's legacy while also making Daniel, Lotte, and most importantly, herself, proud. The scholarship could simply go to another student.

I know you can do this.

The encouraging words Erich Bauer had spoken the night of Angelika's birthday skipped across her psyche. Yes, she could do it. And she would. Angelika would get to work choosing her competition song that very evening. Right after penning a letter to her hazel-eyed, doughnut-devouring, sorely missed friend.

Ten

I f the beginning of the day had blurred past like the Orient Express, the second part whizzed by like an aeroplane streaking across a cloud-speckled sky. There had been no time for Angelika to speak more with Daniel after class, but she hoped the following day might be less frenetic. After finishing unpacking – which for Angelika meant haphazardly strewing things about her side of the room at the women's residence – she and Gretchen felt exhausted yet exhilarated. They decided to have a quick dinner of fried catfish at nearby Café Sperl, then buy a few postcards before returning to their room to study.

"This one's amusing," Angelika said while thumbing through a shop's selection. "Erich will like it."

The postcard featured a picture of Vienna's famous Prater amusement park, home to the world's tallest existing Ferris wheel. Each year, to celebrate the coming of summer, Angelika had loved taking a spin with her mother and Andreas. Just like Clara, the park had been lively and vibrant, dazzling and exciting. Erich would surely enjoy the rides and atmosphere, too, if he someday had the chance to visit Vienna.

In spite of a couple of difficult moments, our singing programme is off to a good start, Angelika wrote him in messy cursive once she'd returned to the residence. *For the first time in ages, I feel as if my dream of becoming a famous opera singer might really be possible. If only you were here to ride the Ferris wheel with me. I'll write more as soon as I can. Write back to me? (Unless it's to say you've seen* The Blue Angel *ten more times since I left.) Your Friend, Anni*

Once the postcard was ready, Angelika decided to have a long-overdue talk with Gretchen, finally explaining the full story about Daniel and Clara's past. Like Erich, Gretchen had heard only bits and pieces throughout the previous year, and Angelika felt both relieved and comforted to confide in her friend.

"Do you think Andreas will ever open his heart to Professor Weiss?" Gretchen asked once Angelika had finished. "He's such a nice man, and God teaches us forgiveness."

Gretchen was more religious than Angelika, and had been bothered by the discussion about Daniel and Clara's infidelity. But while Angelika didn't condone adultery, she acknowledged that in her mother and Daniel's case, there had been complicated, extenuating circumstances. Including the sad reality that their families, adherents of two faiths that railed against infidelity, had forbidden the relationship due to religious differences.

It was hardly as if Rudolf Eder or Daniel's former wife, Hedwig, had been faithful, either. As Angelika had gleaned over the years, Rudolf had been a philanderer long before he and Clara married. As for Hedwig, a family friend of Daniel's, she had married him at their families' behest, although neither of them loved the other.

"Perhaps Andreas would consider coming back to Vienna one day," Gretchen added. "He could study music and start composing again. If he wanted to, he could even work at your family's office here."

Angelika wished she could say Andreas might open his heart and consider returning, but she feared he never would. She couldn't bear to tell Gretchen, though, and had prepared to change the subject when a sharp knock sounded at the bedroom door.

"Another telegram for you, Fräulein Eder." The housemother's barking voice rattled Angelika's eardrums. "This sweetheart of yours sure is smitten."

Angelika sighed, rising from the polychrome quilt that covered her twin bed in the clean and cozy room. She'd been staying at the women's residence only one full day, and already, the housemother hated her. Not that Angelika could blame the woman.

From the very minute Angelika had decided to enrol in the singing programme, Kurt had gone mad, sending a building inspector to examine the residence, then nitpicking over where to install a telephone. While the dormitory was known for being reputable and comfortable, he'd felt uneasy about Angelika staying there, and had gone so far as to request an interview with the housemother. A request which, despite Kurt's money and influence, had been boldly denied.

"*Danke*, Frau Fuchs," Angelika mumbled while opening the bedroom door.

But the housemother – a no-nonsense, middle-aged widow who'd lost her husband during the Great War – had already set the telegram on the sanded hardwood floor and left.

Sorry telephone call disconnected. Angelika read the wire after shutting the door, wandering past Gretchen's well-organised desk and re-entering her own messy minefield of clothing, books and discarded candy wrappers. *Hope everything still all right. Speak tomorrow. Kurt*

He'd sent an earlier cable after arriving back in Munich, and had also telephoned Angelika once before dinner. She'd wanted to tell him about Daniel, Lotte Lehmann and the upcoming competition, but Kurt had spent every precious moment asking unwarranted questions about her well-being. After the discussion had dissolved due to a bad connection, Angelika hadn't expected to hear from him again that night.

"Such a wretched waste of time and money," Angelika muttered, balling up the telegram.

She tossed it onto a nightstand, where the crumpled cable joined her memory book, a series of song sheets and the daisy clip she planned to wear again the following day. By the time Angelika went to bed, however, her irritation had softened. Perhaps she was being too harsh, and ought to give Kurt the benefit of the doubt. Determined to do exactly that, Angelika drifted into a peaceful, long-lasting sleep. A sleep that ended at the crack of dawn, when she was rudely awakened by another loud rapping upon the bedroom door.

"Fräulein Eder," the housemother croaked. "There's a man here to see you. He says he's one of your family's employees. Your fellow sent him to check on you."

Angelika's face flamed hotter than a fire poker.

"Tell the gentleman he can go jump in the Danube," she snapped, throwing open the door after stumbling out of bed and donning her lace-trimmed dressing gown. "And if my 'fellow' dares bother me again this morning, he can follow suit."

The stout, eagle-eyed housemother, her blonde hair heavy with curlers and her body wrapped in a grey cotton bathrobe, stared at Angelika in shock, then allowed the tiny twitching of a smile to upturn her lips. She wordlessly nodded and left as Angelika shut the door.

"Who does Kurt think he is?" she said through gritted teeth. "My lord and master? How dare he send someone over here to spy on me? And at this time of the morning."

"You're overreacting." Gretchen's sleepy, garbled voice was muffled by her striped cotton pillowcase. "I'm sure Kurt had a good reason for sending the man."

"A good reason, my foot. What did he think this employee would find? That I was sneaking back in after a sordid night out on the town? Perhaps Kurt misunderstood that I'm here to work toward someday becoming the Queen of the Night in *The Magic Flute*, not a queen of the night at a brothel."

Angelika huffed a sigh and flopped onto her bed, staring at the room's cream-coloured ceiling for another hour before rising to dress and repack her bookbag for the day ahead.

"I know you're mad about Kurt," Gretchen said. She removed sheet music from the nightstand separating the two beds, then walked past matching maple desks to the shared armoire. "But are you still happy about the song you're going to sing in class today, then use for the competition?"

"*Ja*," Angelika answered, a steadying sense of joy coursing through her. "I thought I might be nervous, but I'm excited instead."

She fastened the buttons on her purple-and-black plaid day dress, then gently affixed the daisy clip. Angelika had spent the previous evening vacillating between a couple of different songs, but had finally settled upon the perfect one. It was a good thing, too, because when Daniel had asked for second-day volunteers to sing, Angelika's hand had shot up before she could stop it.

"You'll be perfect," Gretchen said with an encouraging smile.

After readying their bookbags, the two friends made their way downstairs into the dormitory's wood-panelled dining room, where a generous breakfast spread of black bread rolls, honey, apricot jam, boiled eggs and cold cuts awaited. Such a delicious feast, and yet, Angelika was almost too eager to eat.

Given the unconventional way Daniel planned to manage the expression course, he had compelled the headmaster to move the class to a later time of day, when students' voices would be better warmed up. While

Angelika knew it was a wise decision, she hated having to wait. By the time afternoon arrived, and she'd had a chance to run through her song in private with the pianist, she was all but ready to burst.

"Madame Lehmann should be arriving in a few minutes." Daniel, wearing another avant-garde ensemble of a sunny yellow vest and lightweight scarlet scarf, greeted the class. "Angelika and Hermann, are you ready to sing for us today?"

Angelika nodded, but the young man named Hermann, who'd said he planned to sing 'Mack the Knife' from *The Threepenny Opera*, appeared more frightened than a supernumerary who had stepped on a diva's train backstage.

"Professor Weiss, do you think..." The towheaded boy stared at his hands. "May I have an extra day to prepare?"

"Since it's only the second day of class, and everyone's adjusting, I'll give you the extra time," Daniel told him. "But be ready to sing first thing tomorrow, all right?"

Heaving a huge sigh of relief, the young man gladly agreed.

"All right, then." Daniel clapped his hands together, an enthusiastic grin spreading across his face. "Starting things off today, we have... Anni."

Several students giggled, and a couple of them started in with the usual whispers.

"Fräulein Eder, I mean," Daniel said, face reddening.

Angelika felt not the slightest waver in confidence, however, even as Lotte Lehmann strode into the room looking radiant as ever in a rose-patterned dress with a scalloped neckline and golden brooch. After Daniel and the diva had exchanged hellos, Angelika rose to her feet, face set and body composed as she handed her sheet music to the pianist. In all the years Clara and Lotte had been acquainted, the latter had yet to hear Angelika sing.

"My music is marked," she reminded the accompanist, indicating spots where she'd added notations about breathing, dynamics and other fundamentals.

Angelika then walked to the centre of the room – the seats having again been pushed into a loose horseshoe-shape – while Daniel sat at an empty desk and Lotte sank into a velvet-backed chair slightly off to the side.

"Good afternoon," Angelika said. "My name is Fräulein Angelika Eder, and I will be singing 'Evening Prayer' from *Hänsel und Gretel*."

One of her favourite songs, and a perfect choice for the upcoming competition.

"At this point in the story," Angelika explained, "Gretel and her brother Hänsel find themselves lost in the woods at nightfall. They know they won't be able to make it home before dark, so they prepare to spend the night in the forest. They're frightened yet also comforted by one another's presence, and Gretel believes that saying their evening prayer, as they usually do, may help elicit divine protection."

Most recently, Angelika had performed this song in recital in Munich, and she could still recall the positive reception, including from domineering voice teacher Margarete Böhm. The woman had all but gushed over how skilfully Angelika managed to project both fearful vulnerability and unwavering faith; how she'd added visual interest by singing while kneeling down instead of standing up; and how she'd portrayed the character well while hitting her notes, controlling her breath and demonstrating strong clarity in German diction.

This time would surely be no different, and Angelika could hardly wait to impress Daniel, Lotte and her classmates.

"*Abends, will ich schlafen gehn...*"

Angelika's clear, melodious soprano floated on air, and her self-assuredness surged with every note she successfully executed. Although there was no one kneeling beside her – no Hänsel singing in unison – Angelika behaved as if there were, turning her body slightly inward, toward him, while also directing her words upward, at God.

"In the evening, when I go to sleep..."

After singing the verse once through, Angelika began repeating it a second time, a sense of hope and optimism now tempering Gretel's fear.

"Fourteen angels stand around me,

Two at my head,

Two at my feet,

Two to my right,

Two to my left,

Two who cover me,

Two who wake me up,

Two who point me to paradise in heaven."

She finished the song by closing her eyes, lying down upon the classroom floor as if to sleep, and then, after a pause, standing back up to receive applause.

"*Brava*," said Lotte, a pensive look pervading her eyes.

"Thank you, Angelika," Daniel added. "What did you think, students?"

"Powerful character portrayal," offered a friendly alto named Ruth.

"I truly believed she was lost in the woods," said Georg. "And that she was glad to have her brother by her side."

"You could sense that the prayer was comforting her as she went along," Gretchen remarked. "She sang the second verse differently than the first."

"Yes," Daniel agreed. He and Lotte exchanged a look Angelika couldn't read. "That's all true. It's a beautiful piece, and you, Angelika, are a talented singer. That's why you're here. However…"

Angelika stiffened.

"How many times have you performed that piece in recital?" Daniel asked.

"Twice. Once in Munich, and another time before that, here in Vienna."

"That's what I thought. And you chose it today for that reason, correct? Because you knew you had already mastered it, both vocally and interpretively."

And just like that, all the confidence Angelika had built up over the past day came tumbling down, much like the houses of cards she and Andreas used to build together as children.

"I, um…" Angelika faltered, surprised and wounded by Daniel's disapproval. "I chose this song because I love it, and because I wanted to demonstrate my knowledge about expression. That's our objective, isn't it?"

"Our objective is to learn and improve," Daniel countered. His tone came across as constructive and concerned rather than harsh or unkind, but the words nevertheless stung. "But you decided to perform that piece again, to great praise, rather than take your chances with something less familiar that needs work and would challenge you. Is this the song you were planning to sing during the competition?"

"Daniel…" Angelika flushed crimson, no longer comforted by the daisy clip at her collar. It seemed Erich had been wrong after all. Angelika couldn't do this, and should never have returned to Vienna. "I mean, Professor Weiss…"

At his insistence, she'd always called Daniel by his first name in private, ever since she was little. This conversation was hardly private, however. In fact, she felt humiliated in front of the entire class.

"Of course you're a gifted singer," Daniel continued after Angelika had trailed off. "As I said, that's why you're here. You also have a marvellous gift for understanding a character and playing off that emotion. That's why I can't help but feel disappointed you chose to sing something familiar and safe."

Angelika remained silent until Lotte spoke up.

"Perhaps you and I can meet privately once I return from the Salzburg Festival," she offered, sounding far more optimistic than Angelika felt. "I can help you study a different song for the competition."

"That's a good idea," Daniel said. "What other pieces are you working on, Angelika? Please don't tell me Giordani's 'Caro mio ben' or Schubert's 'Ave Maria', because I know you've already sung both in recital. Which pieces do you feel we could help you with?"

With fingers trembling ever so slightly, Angelika reached for her music folder.

"I have 'Ch'io mai vi possa' and 'Care selve' by Handel."

"Do you have any other, more challenging material?" Lotte asked. "An aria like 'Mein Herr Marquis' from *Die Fledermaus*, perhaps?"

"Well, now that you mention it, Madame Lehmann, I was recently studying Adina's opening song from *L'elisir d'amore*."

It was the piece she'd been struggling with the day Erich appeared outside the music school window in Munich.

"Excellent." Daniel's grin returned, as did Lotte's. "That's the *cavatina* I think you should sing for the competition. There are a good number of things you can do with the song dramatically, and it's also an excellent fit for your voice."

"But it isn't…" Angelika's tongue felt like sandpaper. "I mean, I haven't been able to…"

"It's all right if it isn't perfect. We aren't here to be perfect, as there is, in fact, no such thing. We're here to grow and learn from one another."

Daniel approached and looked Angelika gently in the eye.

"Madame Lehmann and I can both help you," he said. "If you're willing to try, that is. We can offer our best advice, but…"

The singer chooses which roles she will play. Clara's words had once again come flooding back.

"All right," Angelika at last replied. "I'll start running through it with a voice teacher during my practice session." She hesitated and swallowed her pride. "And I'd of course be honoured to study with you, Madame Lehmann. And you, Professor Weiss."

"*Wunderbar.*" Daniel gave Angelika a small smile. "And even though I said you ought to have chosen something different, we appreciate you singing 'Evening Prayer' for us. You took a simple piece and turned it into something stirring and emotionally moving. You should keep it in mind for future auditions."

Angelika thanked him but didn't smile back, remaining uncharacteristically quiet as Lotte took her leave and the class wore on, the students forming small groups to work on staging exercises with Daniel's help. Her heart aching as if pricked by a seamstress's misplaced pin, Angelika watched from across the room as Daniel fashioned a makeshift dagger out of a paper aeroplane and laughed alongside his students while they sketched out a scene for Pamina's lament aria in *The Magic Flute.*

Angelika knew she shouldn't let a little honest criticism hurt her. She'd always known Daniel to be an exemplary teacher and director – someone collaborative and open-minded, yet not afraid to tell people what he truly thought. They were qualities Clara had respected and admired, and ones Angelika did, as well. And if she hoped to become a famous singer, accepting criticism was all in a day's work.

Still, deep inside, she couldn't help but feel wounded by Daniel's response, not because she didn't believe he was knowledgeable, or because she didn't respect his judgement, but because she wished their relationship could be about so much more than singing. If only she could find a way to make him proud of her, not only as a singer, but as a daughter.

"You like Professor Weiss, don't you?" Angelika asked Gretchen, low, as they headed to their practice session after class.

"Of course. He's intense but inspiring."

Angelika nodded in agreement.

"He's also charismatic, sharp and creative," Gretchen said. "Honestly, the more I see of him, the more he reminds me of…"

Gretchen stopped, appearing unsure as to whether she ought to continue.

"Who?" Angelika pressed, well-known Austrian stage directors' names running through her brain. "Max Reinhardt, perhaps?"

"No." Gretchen shook her head. She seemed stunned that her friend couldn't see what she herself so clearly did. "I was going to say that Professor Weiss reminds me of you."

Eleven

"*Hallo*? Kurt?" Static and cacophony assailed Angelika's ears as she sat slumped in a telephone alcove outside the housemother's office, evening shadows spilling into the hallway from a nearby window. After her humiliating experience in Daniel's class and a difficult practice session, the last thing she'd wanted was to arrive back at the women's residence to another flood of telegrams and telephone messages. But as fate would have it, she found precisely that. "Kurt, are you there?"

"*Ja*," he answered, the response crackling across the wire. "Thank goodness you finally rang me back and were able to get through. Where have you been?"

"I've been practising. In case you'd forgotten, I came here to sing."

A scent of apricot dumplings wafted in from the nearby dining room, and Angelika, who'd lost track of time and skipped dinner, felt her stomach rumble. She was hungry and tired, overwhelmed and vexed. The last thing she needed was an interrogation regarding her whereabouts.

"I understand that, but I was getting worried." Kurt harrumphed so loudly, Angelika had to hold the telephone receiver away from her ear. "Especially after I found out you refused to speak with my business colleague this morning."

"Your spy, you mean?" Angelika's voice ascended to a higher pitch, and she twirled the telephone cord in frustration. "What in Mozart's name were you thinking, sending someone over here at sunrise?"

"I'm sorry he arrived so early." The telephone connection had stabilised, and Angelika could hear Kurt's excuses more clearly. "I asked him to visit you on his way to the office, but I had no idea what time it would be."

"You shouldn't have asked him to visit me at all. I'm not a child, and I have enough to worry about without you sending private eyes to track my every movement."

"What are you so worried about, dearest?" Kurt asked.

Drat. Why had Angelika said that? The day's stresses must have stolen her good sense.

"It's nothing." She pressed a free hand to her furrowing brow and sank deeper into the cushioned stool upon which she sat. "I'm… fine."

But Angelika's voice had wavered while a sudden swarm of tears welled in her eyes. After having disappointed Daniel, she felt all the more certain that, when all was said and done, he viewed her first and foremost as merely another student. She'd been foolish to think their friendship could survive without her mother being alive. And all the more foolish to imagine, even for a second, that he could ever come to love her as a daughter.

"You hardly sound fine." Kurt harrumphed again. "Perhaps this was all a terrible mistake. My father told me I should never have allowed you to return to Vienna, but I insisted that with the proper precautions, everything would be all right."

At that, Angelika's tears evaporated like raindrops on hot pavement, and flickers of fury arose in their wake. Theoretically, Kurt was indeed the one who had allowed Angelika to attend the singing programme. Rudolf Eder had told Kurt it was her sweetheart's decision to make. But the more Angelika had thought about that, the more it set her teeth on edge. Up until this moment, she'd also believed that seeking Kurt's permission had been a foolish formality. She'd never feared he might actually consider stopping her.

"You wish you'd told me I couldn't come back to Vienna?" Angelika's grip on the receiver tightened, the telephone cord becoming so taut, she feared it might separate from the rotary base that had been mounted to a wood-panelled wall. "To the city of my birth? To pursue my lifelong dream?"

In the past few hours, Angelika had also started wondering whether coming back to Vienna had been a mistake. She was the only one who had any right to make that sort of assessment, however. No one else, sweetheart or not.

"You're misconstruing my words," Kurt replied, his own temper rising. "But I can already see that your being in this programme isn't working out. I don't want you becoming hurt or upset."

A strange thing to say, since Kurt himself was presently doing the hurting. Kurt von Hügel, the family friend Angelika had known for seven years, ever since she'd met him one glorious, sun-kissed day at her family's summer estate outside Salzburg. He was the young man who'd offered her a spare handkerchief and caring shoulder during her mother's funeral after her former sweetheart Paul had forsaken her. Kurt was the handsome suitor who'd kissed her after the Christmas recital in Munich, then lavished her with exquisite baubles, silk dresses and lush floral bouquets tied with purple satin ribbon. He was also a sweetheart who, in spite of his ill-advised good intentions, had finally gone too far, behaving as if he could, and perhaps should, try to control her.

"You must return to Munich immediately," Kurt continued. "I'll make the arrangements tonight."

"*Nein.* You'll do nothing of the kind." As if a photographer's flashbulb had exploded inside her heart, Angelika's decision became strikingly clear, and she knew for certain what she must say to Kurt. Difficult as it would be, she'd been thinking of saying it ever since his spy had turned up that morning. She'd also been secretly pondering it since they'd argued at his office a couple of weeks earlier, right before her disastrous nineteenth birthday. "In fact, I…" The words warped inside her mouth, as though she were speaking an unfamiliar language. "I think it might be best if we…"

"If we what?" Kurt pressed, a hint of suspicion tripping across his tongue.

"Spend some time apart." Angelika spat out the

statement before she lost her nerve. "Not only apart in two different cities, but apart as in… no longer sweethearts. I'm just… I feel so confused about everything."

Angelika's throat constricted, but she refused to allow herself to cry.

"I need some time to think," she told him. "And perhaps you do, too."

For a few fleeting moments, Kurt's roughened breathing was the only sound emitting from the telephone receiver. While awaiting his dreaded reply, Angelika used her free fingers to wipe away a tear that had skittered across her cheek, much like the first leak seeping from a dam that seemed ready to burst. A dam that had been in disrepair far too long.

"I don't need any time to think," Kurt said, sounding as if she'd told him the sky were green instead of blue. "What's going on, here? Have you lost your mind?"

"No." With a jolt of adrenaline, Angelika rose to stand inside the small, closet-like space. "But you have. Sending that man over here? Expecting me to report where I've been at any given hour of the day? You've gone from hardly making any time for me this summer to giving me little space to breathe. Don't you realise you're smothering me?"

Kurt's incredulous laugh echoed across the distance.

"How could I have smothered you when I only wanted to make sure you were all right?" he said. "To look out for my girl, seeing to your financial needs and providing for your safety, just as a proper sweetheart should?"

Of course, he would decide to mention the money.

"I asked you to use the money my mother left me,"

Angelika reminded him. "I have enough to last at least another year or so."

A crackling curse escaped Kurt's lips.

"This is about him, isn't it?" he said, deftly switching tactics. "Erich Bauer. He's the one who really gave you that daisy-shaped dress clip? The one that looks like something a pitiful peasant would wear."

"Stop insulting my appearance."

Angelika peered through an opening in the accordion-like divider that served as a door to the alcove, and was unsurprised to find a couple of fellow students eavesdropping outside the nearby dormitory den. On any other occasion, she'd have uttered something sarcastic and sent them scattering. Fortunately for the eavesdroppers, a couple of snoopers were the least of Angelika's cares.

"And stop insulting Erich," she said. "He had nothing to do with this."

Angelika's decision to split from Kurt had come about thanks to his being overbearing and distrustful, pompous and pig-headed. Not because of Erich Bauer. Nevertheless, when she'd said Erich's name, Angelika couldn't help but think she sounded the way Adina from *L'elisir d'amore* did whenever she sang of Nemorino, a big-hearted labourer she wasn't supposed to love.

"You're lying," Kurt said. "If there's one thing I detest, it's being lied to by someone I care about. This is precisely the reason I didn't want you getting entangled with Erich at all. Don't you realise he and his father are Nazis? That they…"

Angelika held the receiver away from her ear,

perspiration gathering on her forehead as her face scrunched into a scowl and an idea took shape inside her head. If Kurt already considered her a liar, she might as well go to town with it.

"Kurt?" Angelika scraped her fingernails across the mouthpiece, pretending the connection had soured. "I can't understand what you're saying."

"I said Erich Bauer and his father are fascist rubbish," she heard Kurt shout. "What am I supposed to tell your father and mine? That you cast me aside during a telephone call, for God's sake?"

Angelika didn't care what he told them, or what Rudolf Eder had to say about the matter. With her life so rapidly changing and countless other concerns competing for her attention, Angelika's wits had been stretched beyond capacity.

"I can't believe you would let an ignoramus like Erich destroy what we have together," Kurt droned on. "Why, I have half a mind to..."

Angelika smacked the receiver into its cradle with more bravado than necessary, then pushed open the alcove's divider screen just in time to see the eavesdroppers duck into the den, the two of them looking about as innocent as a pair of foxes who'd raided a chicken coop. Angelika scowled behind their backs as, meanwhile, her golden-haired classmate Marta approached.

"Are you done using the telephone?" she asked, oblivious to the dramatic discussion Angelika had weathered. "I want to try ringing my family in Hollabrunn."

"Yes, I'm finished."

If only Marta realised just how true that statement was.

Angelika stepped aside and, longing for privacy and fresh air, headed outdoors. She had a feeling Kurt wouldn't try telephoning her back immediately, though she also knew he wouldn't give her up without a fight. She had no doubt she'd hear from him – the bombastic baron of business who hated taking no for an answer – before the week was over.

"Telling me I look like a peasant," she muttered to herself while venturing into the deepening dusk. "And accusing me of lying, too."

At least Kurt hadn't deigned to call her derogatory names the way her former sweetheart Paul had. Angelika winced at the memories while meandering through the quiet courtyard and perching at the edge of a still-flowing stone fountain. Several young couples snuggled in the nearby grass, their laughter drawing Angelika's attention and compelling her heart to tap out a sad serenade. How had these smitten sweethearts met, and how long had they been together? Did they respect each other? Understand one another?

"Pardon me, miss."

Angelika jumped, turning toward the sound to find an unfamiliar, copper-haired young man waiting in the shadows and leaning against a bicycle.

"Are you Fräulein Angelika Eder?" he asked, although his tone conveyed that he already knew the answer.

"Yes," she replied, standing and narrowing her eyes.

"I have a message for you." The deep-voiced, teenaged

courier reached inside his pocket. "Something I was told to place directly into your own hands and no one else's."

Even cable-obsessed Kurt couldn't have dispatched a telegram that quickly. Perhaps the message was from Andreas or Erich. But if so, why would either one of them be so particular about the way it was delivered?

"Uh, thank you," Angelika said after taking a crisp white envelope in hand and studying it in the lamplight. "I…"

But the messenger had already remounted his bicycle and began peddling away.

After watching him pass beneath the conservatory's limestone archway and into serene Schiller Park across the street, Angelika more closely examined the envelope, which had been made out to her in flawless, scrolling script. With fingers slightly shaking, she opened the flap, easing out a folded slip of thick, expensive letterhead.

Baldur von Schirach, it said at the top, alongside a printed black swastika. *Hitler Youth Leader.*

Herr von Schirach, Angelika thought with a shudder. The leader of the Hitler Youth, a close friend of Erich's father and a newly elected member of the German parliament. The man who wanted her to sing at the Nazis' concert in Munich, and who fancied her as a living reminder of Adolf Hitler's dead niece.

Dear Fräulein Eder, the handwritten letter began.

I trust that this message will find you eagerly awaiting your National Socialist concert debut in October. We are busy preparing, and look forward to announcing your performance in due time. It is our hope that the inimitable soprano Lotte Lehmann, who I understand is an acquaintance of yours, will also one day sing for the glory of Germany, in a mutually beneficial partnership with us.

Angelika gasped and held the letter at arm's length, as if afraid it might burn her. She'd had no idea the Nazis had set their sights on Lotte, as well.

In preparation for our concert, the missive continued, *I have enclosed a list of songs by respectable German composers, including Richard Wagner and Ludwig van Beethoven. You will select two songs to sing in addition to the national anthem. Given your prodigious talent and ability, which I've witnessed at Viktor Bauer's beer garden and during your music school recital last winter, I expect you will easily find several pieces that suit you.*

Another shock. If Baldur von Schirach had been secretly present during Angelika's Christmas recital, it meant he had been watching and assessing her for months. It was also a confirmation that, in spite of what Angelika considered to be her shortcomings as a singer, the Nazis considered her incredibly gifted. A compliment which, under normal circumstances, might have made her proud. Coming from Baldur von Schirach and the Nazis, the statement sickened her instead.

I anticipate receiving your selections within the next week, the letter concluded. *I also look forward to our becoming better personally acquainted upon your return to Munich next month. Heil Hitler!*

Baldur von Schirach

If only the delivered message had indeed been from Kurt. But it wasn't. This letter was from someone – a group of someones, rather – who were far more controlling than he'd ever been.

One week. Angelika sank down onto the rim of the fountain, hiding the letter in a fold of her purple-and-black plaid day dress before anyone else could join her and see it. She, Andreas and Erich wouldn't have time to devise a plan after all. Not before Baldur von Schirach expected her reply. To Angelika's revulsion, she had run out of time.

*

Her appetite having evaporated, Angelika hurried inside to seek Gretchen's advice about the concert. Not that Gretchen would have any miraculous solutions. To say no to the Nazis might have disastrous consequences, but to go through with singing for them would be unfathomable. Had Lotte Lehmann gotten wind of their intentions, too? Would she seriously consider letting the National Socialists use her talent to make a case for German superiority?

After creaking open the bedroom door, Angelika discovered that it hardly mattered about asking Gretchen's opinion, for there – a Verdi biography stretched open across her stomach as the sheet music for "O mio babbino caro" crinkled beneath an elbow – lay Gretchen Hoffmann, fast asleep. With one hand, Angelika gently removed the book and music, then covered her friend with a light cotton blanket.

Staring at the unwanted letter still clutched in her other hand, Angelika realised she hadn't yet read through the list of Nazi-approved song choices Baldur von Schirach had sent her. Truth be told, it didn't matter what they were, or whether they suited her voice. Either way, she couldn't bear to look at them. Instead, Angelika reached inside her half-unpacked travelling trunk, pushed aside a wrinkled pile of silk chemises and shoved the communiqué deep down to the bottom. If only setting it out of sight could make the dilemma disappear. If only...

Angelika stopped, the unexpected feeling of smooth, cool leather greeting her palm. She shifted away the remaining silken slips until, sure enough, she'd unearthed the culprit. Erich Bauer's jacket. Angelika had been wearing it when they'd talked in Munich's Nymphenburg Palace gardens the night of her birthday. After witnessing the Nazi-instigated newspaper office fire, she'd forgotten to give it back to him, and he'd forgotten to take it. In the housekeeper's flurry to help Angelika pack, she must have accidentally added it to the travel trunk. Either that, or the astute maid had been trying to send Angelika a subliminal message.

"Erich," Angelika whispered, as though the jacket were a transmitter through which he might be able to hear her voice.

She lifted the leather gently into her hands as a lingering scent of beer garden chicken and hops, plus smoke from the fire, rose to meet her nostrils. Erich was the person she most longed to speak with that night, but if she tried telephoning the brewery, his father might interfere and wish to talk with her about the propaganda concert. Still, Angelika wondered what Erich might say if she could tell him about the setback in Daniel's class, the letter from Baldur von Schirach and the schism with Kurt.

Ach, Kurt. An imaginary dagger pierced Angelika's heart, not because she thought she'd made the wrong decision, but because letting him go would nevertheless hurt. He was the first young man she'd opened herself up to after Paul's betrayal and the loss of her mother. The only person she could have, at the time, imagined entrusting with her shattered soul. Someone who seemed quite different now than the boy she'd met seven years prior.

Angelika lay Erich's jacket at the foot of her bed and removed her memory book from the nightstand. Whether she liked it or not, another story was itching to be told. And however reluctant she may have felt, Angelika soon gave in to its powerful pull, fingers and fountain pen flying across the pages as twilight turned to night in Vienna.

Angelika's Memory Book

July 1925 – Seven Years Ago
Lake Fuschl, Austria

I was eleven years old the first time I spoke with Kurt.

The carefree afternoon had started out like every other that week, with my cousin Christina and I racing about my family's summer estate near Salzburg while dressed in a set of too-big, well-worn opera costumes Daniel had recently given me. It was only after I darted out from behind a trellis, collided with an unexpected visitor and toppled to the ground that everything changed.

"*Ach*, please forgive my clumsiness."

A young man's voice shattered the silence, and I turned to find that he had tumbled to the cobblestones alongside me, an operatic libretto I'd been carrying having also landed squarely in his lap.

"Ah, the Scottish play," he said, flipping through its pages before rising and brushing off his pressed grey suit. "Or rather, Verdi's first interpretation of it."

I gazed up at the unexpected caller, a long-legged teenaged boy, perhaps a couple of years older than me, with wavy brown hair the colour of chestnuts and eyes even bluer than the postcard-perfect Lake Fuschl that shimmered in the background.

"As I'm sure you know," he said, "this opera isn't commonly performed anymore."

He smiled and extended a hand to me, but I remained paralysed upon the ground, an unfamiliar heat consuming my cheeks, chest and entire body, and not only because of the hot pavers that burnt my legs beneath the dress.

"This libretto is written in Italian," the young man continued, his adolescent voice in the midst of changing and deepening. "Can you read it? I mean, do you understand the language?"

At the moment, I could scarcely understand my native German.

"Yes." Christina approached and answered for me. "She speaks English and French, too. You can ask her more about it after we've finished our game. Would you like to play *Macbeth* with us? I'm one of the witches, and she's Lady Macbeth. You can be Yorick's gravedigger."

I looked to my cousin and glared, mortified.

"Yorick's gravedigger is from *Hamlet*," I said, nerve returning as I sprang up, cheeks flushing with an unaccustomed embarrassment I didn't understand. "And besides, he…" I hesitated. "I'm sorry, what is your name?"

"Kurt von Hügel," he replied, still beaming through teeth as white and straight as Andreas's piano keys.

"Well, it seems to me that Kurt von Hügel, here, is hardly suited to play the part of a commonplace gravedigger."

That elicited not only a bigger smile from Kurt, but a melodious, light-hearted laugh.

"And how about you?" he asked. "Fräulein…"

"Angelika Eder."

I lifted my chin and smoothed my sweaty hair, trying to look and sound more refined than I felt. I'd never before met anyone who made my heart beat so quickly or my stomach flutter as if there were a troupe of butterflies dancing ballet inside.

"Fräulein Angelika Eder," Kurt repeated, the sharp scent of his amber cologne tickling my nose for the very first time. "Do you believe you're well-suited to play the part of a cold-hearted Lady Macbeth?"

"Yes. I mean, no. I mean..."

"Kurt!" A man's voice boomed from the nearby terrace doorway, interrupting my ineloquent answer. "Have you finished collecting your notes from the car? Get back in here so we can begin the business meeting. Why are you wasting time?"

Kurt and his father, I realised, must have come to our estate to meet with Rudolf and discuss business opportunities. I'd been so busy playing with Christina and running all about the property that I hadn't noticed their automobile arriving.

"I'm not wasting time," Kurt answered. "I'm having the most riveting conversation with Fräulein Angelika Eder about gravediggers and ladies, librettos and literature."

I chuckled at his reply, plus the quick flicker of defiance that flashed in his eyes. Kurt's father, however, wasn't amused.

"Get in here now, and stop being impertinent," Herr von Hügel snapped. He had grey hair and sagging skin – a sign of too much work, little rest and a dreadful disposition. "We've more important things to do than while away the hours conversing with children playing dress-up. We can discuss Fräulein Eder again at a later time, once she's grown up a bit."

Humiliated by his remarks, I fled to my room, the

indignation lingering for days until, a week later, a finely wrapped, Munich-sent package arrived for me.

"Who gave you these?" Mama asked later that night as she tucked me in, leather-bound copies of *Macbeth*, *Hamlet* and *Twelfth Night* adorning my nightstand alongside two beloved porcelain-cheeked dolls.

"Kurt von Hügel." I passed her the accompanying note. "He says he's sorry for the trouble he caused last week, and that he hopes these new Spanish editions might help me master a fifth language."

"Oh." After reading the letter, Mama rose from my bed and gazed out of the window at the moonlit boat dock. "Toil and trouble indeed."

I ignored her sarcastic remark, the mysterious heat flaring as I told Mama that in spite of my embarrassing encounter, I hoped Kurt would come to think well of me. Such a naïve and insecure way of thinking, though I failed to realise it at the time.

"It doesn't matter what he thinks of you, *Liebling*," Mama insisted, the fire in her voice a fitting match for her red hair. "Only what you think of yourself."

Mama sighed and sat back down beside me. She smelled of lilac perfume and looked beautiful as ever – her skin smooth and rosy, blue eyes glittering with emotion, and a waterfall of auburn waves cascading across her shoulders. How I longed for the day I might be as lovely, curvaceous and poised as Mama.

"Listen, honeybee," she whispered. "A boy like Kurt is being groomed by his father, who has certain expectations. A certain vision of the way things must be."

"So, you won't help me, then?" My heart sank as I thought about Kurt, whose only memory of me was that of a dress-up playing little girl. "If he comes back for another meeting, I want to fix my hair a special way. Please, Mama. Please say you'll help me."

"I'll help by being here to talk and listen, my love," Mama finally whispered with a kiss, a melancholy smile taking shape. "I'm here for you. Always. No matter what."

A promise made, then later broken. Just as this wicked, wretched world had slowly broken her.

Twelve

*D*espite several spurts of refreshing mid-August rain, Angelika's first week at the conservatory seemed to pass by in a heavy haze. She attended classes, practised songs and smiled alongside her classmates, but continued to struggle, both emotionally and artistically. Angelika hardly said a word during Daniel's class each day, and when he all but begged her to speak in private Thursday afternoon, she cordially declined, overwhelmed by the sad reality that the two of them seemed destined to remain student and teacher, but little more.

I was wrong to sound hopeful in the postcard I sent you, Angelika wrote to Erich later that evening. *So many things are happening, and I don't know what to do. Please write to me as soon as you can. I miss laughing at your foolish jokes and rolling my eyes when you mention Marlene Dietrich. I miss getting doughnuts together at the Wolpertinger Kaffeehaus and hearing you call me your siren. Most of all, I just miss you.*

Erich might never let Angelika hear the end of

admitting as much, but she missed him too deeply to care. She missed Andreas, too, especially when she spoke with him on the telephone Friday night and he relayed that Kurt had become even more work-obsessed than usual, toiling around the clock and expecting everyone else to do the same.

"Ever since the two of you split, he's been swigging schnaps in the morning and smoking cigars all afternoon," Andreas told her. "Yesterday, I overheard both of our fathers shouting at him from down the hallway. I couldn't quite make out what they were saying, but your name was mentioned. Once Kurt came back, he flung a gigantic stack of old Christmas catalogues onto my desk and said that if I didn't put together a yuletide sales plan by the end of the day, he'd withhold my salary for an entire week."

"*Ach*, no," Angelika said, heart sinking.

She surprisingly hadn't yet heard from Kurt following the split, and part of her felt sorry for the man. Perhaps she'd been wrong to end things by telephone and hold his attentiveness against him. On the other hand, she also remembered the cruel things Kurt had said about disliking Erich and not wanting to let Angelika remain in Vienna. A full three days later, his thoughtless words still made her blood boil.

"I can try telephoning the office and talking with him if you think it would help," Angelika offered.

But they both knew that doing so would only make matters worse for Andreas. He seemed so demoralised, Angelika didn't have the heart to tell him about the letter she'd received from Baldur von Schirach. She had ended up not telling Gretchen, either. There was no use worrying her friend and brother when there wasn't anything they could do. Not when time was running out, and Angelika would have to send some sort of response very soon.

"Don't let Kurt's bark scare you," she told Andreas. "You're a lot more capable than you realise, and I have faith in you."

"That makes one of us," Andreas answered with a sigh. "But I have faith in you, too. Keep trying your best, and don't let Daniel Weiss crush your spirit. I still can't believe that louse is one of your professors."

Andreas had become quite upset during another telephone conversation earlier that week, when Angelika had told him that Daniel Weiss was her and Gretchen's professor. Although Angelika hadn't told her brother anything about the embarrassing experience in class, he'd seemed to sense that something was wrong.

"Daniel Weiss is not a louse," Angelika hissed, unable to mask the shock in her voice. She knew Andreas didn't care to remain in touch with Daniel, but he'd never resorted to vicious name-calling before. "Why would you say such a horrible thing? He isn't crushing my spirit, either. Daniel has been trying to lift me up. He wants to help me."

But if she believed that last part was true, why had she been avoiding Daniel's gaze the past several days? Why had she refused to talk with him after class? It was time to stop being ridiculous and make amends.

Which was precisely the reason why, on Saturday afternoon, Angelika found herself traversing Wehlistrasse near the Danube river's western bank, a cool breeze rustling her hair as she strode to a stop before a colourfully painted, four-storey brick building that housed artists' studios and flats. If Angelika shut her eyes, she could almost imagine it was the start of many a promising summer past, when she, Andreas and Clara used to leave their villa in the Hietzing district and travel through the city centre, then across the canal, for a boat ride on the river and a visit to the nearby Prater amusement park.

As if the treasured outings had happened only yesterday, she could still taste the park's savoury hot sausage and hear the delighted screams from riders who'd dared to climb aboard the alpine-inspired roller coaster. Most of all, she remembered watching with envy as other children waited in the *Riesenrad* line alongside both parents, the fathers protectively wrapping arms about their little girls' shoulders while the nearly sixty-five-metre-high Ferris wheel made its steadfast, reliable, unchanging revolutions.

I'm too busy, Rudolf Eder had snapped the one time nine-year-old Angelika dared ask him to come. It was something her governess had insisted upon after Angelika said she wanted to invite Daniel Weiss. When the governess had told Rudolf that part of the story, he'd not only sent Angelika to bed without supper, but had become angry with Clara, calling her a whore and adulteress. Never mind that he'd long since had a habit of being unfaithful himself, and not with a person he truly loved, as Clara loved Daniel, but with whichever prostitute happened to catch his eye. In any event, the eviscerating reaction had deterred Angelika from ever asking Daniel to join them.

But that conversation was in the past. Now, a decade

later, Angelika had to find a way forward. Forcing the hurtful memories aside, she tried her best to smile as young families ambled by, making their way toward the riverfront alongside tourists carrying cameras and couples strolling arm-in-arm. A train whistle sounded from the nearby station, automobiles zipped down the riverside road beneath lush linden trees, and artists filed in and out of the blue-and-yellow building before Angelika. In spite of the melee, some of the surrounding apartment buildings seemed quiet, surely because many of the Leopoldstadt district's Jewish residents were honouring the Sabbath. The person Angelika had come to see, however, wasn't known for being observant. In fact, while he had been raised in the Jewish faith, he'd never professed to believe in a higher power.

"Anni?"

Angelika arched her neck, meeting a familiar man's quizzical gaze as he peered out a third-storey window with the red-and-white striped Austrian flag dangling from its edges.

"*Hallo*," she answered, striving to sound casual.

Angelika hadn't arranged her visit ahead of time, but now that she'd arrived, she realised a little advance warning would have been wise. What if he was due at an appointment or had company? Unfortunately, it was too late to worry about any of that.

"A beautiful day along the Danube, isn't it?" Angelika called up to him. "Cool, refreshing air, and no more rain."

A mixture of confusion and warmth lined Daniel's sleepy, unshaven face. He appeared as if he'd recently awoken from a nap, and had hardly been expecting to glance out of his window and find a visitor standing on the sidewalk.

"Is that why you came all the way over here?" he asked, the teasing hint of a laugh dancing in his high, light voice. "To tell me it stopped raining? I may be forty years old, but my eyesight hasn't given out on me yet."

The corners of Daniel's mouth twitched, and Angelika felt her own lips curving upward.

"I was hoping I could speak with you," she said.

"I'm glad. If it's all right with you, though, I'd rather talk face-to-face instead of hanging halfway out of this window. Come inside and up two flights of stairs. First door on your right."

Angelika nodded and showed herself into the aging concrete building, which was vibrantly painted and charming, but a dramatic departure from the handsome limestone townhouse Daniel and his former wife, Hedwig, one of the city's preeminent female attorneys, had shared. Angelika had never visited his new artist's-studio-turned-flat before, but knew the address from letters they'd exchanged during her time in Munich.

"I didn't expect to see you again until Monday," Daniel greeted Angelika as she entered the flat's messy main room – lived in, comfortable and boasting a seemingly familiar smattering of sheet music, librettos, discarded newspapers and half-read books. The space was cluttered with furniture, too, including a sofa that had seen better days, a small kitchenette, a potbelly stove, a writing desk, a card table and, as the *pièce de résistance*, the heirloom upright piano Angelika had always adored. "Go ahead and sit down, if you can find a spot."

Daniel switched off a desktop radio and, in the process, accidentally toppled a pile of letters that had been stacked alongside it.

"Ah, *Scheisse*," he said as the envelopes fluttered about Angelika's low-heeled ebony pumps, making her chuckle. Messiness was a trait the two of them had in common. "I meant to turn off this radio programme an hour ago. But never mind all the envelopes. For now, I just want to talk. Make sure everything's all right between us after the debacle in class earlier this week."

Angelika drew a shaky breath, set aside a pile of yellowing newspapers and took a seat upon the sloppily reupholstered, paisley-patterned sofa. She also longed to talk – to tell Daniel what she'd forever felt for him deep inside her heart, even if she feared he might never love her in return, not really and truly, as a daughter.

"I'm sorry you were upset after singing 'Evening Prayer' on Tuesday," Daniel went on before she could answer. "I'm afraid I acted like an *Arschloch*. But I only want you to succeed, and I would never purposely hurt you. You understand that, right?"

"I... um... yes."

Now that Angelika was right there before him, her voice seemed to be faltering again. She looked out of the flat's larger second window, which faced the river, and drank in the familiar sight of barges on their way to Budapest, plus sailboats filled with passengers busy exploring the artistic city she and Daniel so dearly loved.

"I've been thinking more about 'Della crudele Isotta' as your new competition song," Daniel continued while leaning against his colourfully painted piano, which scarcely fit inside the cramped studio space. "I wanted to get your thoughts about the opening to see if you had any ideas about engaging the audience and drawing them in right at the start."

Angelika's heart dropped, and her confidence further diminished. As usual, they'd shifted straight back to a discussion about singing.

"Let's see your music," Daniel prompted.

Angelika gazed into her lap, empty but for her peacock-embroidered clutch purse, berry-hued beret and restless hands.

"Don't tell me you came all the way across town and didn't remember your music." Daniel was clearly teasing, but to Angelika, his words sounded harsh, much as they had during Tuesday's class. "I hope that when you meet privately with Lotte Lehmann, you'll have a songbook ready. Isn't it marvellous that she's working with us at the conservatory?"

"It's splendid," Angelika agreed in a quiet voice.

"Madame Lehmann still speaks fondly of the time we all travelled to London together six years ago. You remember it, right?"

"Of course. *Don Giovanni* at the Royal Opera House in Covent Garden."

In that particular production, directed by Daniel, Lotte had sung the role of Donna Elvira, and Clara had sung the part of Donna Anna. Angelika couldn't help but smile at the memory, a giggle burbling up from deep inside her chest.

"Do you remember opening night, when Mama was so anxious, she kept fiddling with her brooch?" Angelika said. "And she ended up tearing open the front of her costume a couple of minutes before taking the stage?"

"*Ja.*" Daniel chuckled, too. "The dressers used a ratty black shawl to hide the tear. Your mother thought she looked 'preposterous', but I told her the only preposterous part was her saying such a thing. Clara was so lovely, she could have gone onstage wearing a burlap sack, and she still would have been the most beautiful..."

He stopped himself, cheeks reddening. He needn't have felt embarrassed, though, because Angelika knew her mother had indeed looked beautiful that night. Not just because of her seventeenth-century, Spanish-style costume or pretty face, but because her radiance had shone from within.

"Anyway," Daniel said, fumbling, "when you present 'Della crudele Isotta' during the competition..."

Angelika did her best to listen, but found her gaze wandering to Daniel's writing desk, where framed photographs of his "real" children – thirteen-year-old Leah and seventeen-year-old Benjamin – resided. Angelika had met them on several occasions, years earlier, before Daniel and Hedwig had eventually parted ways. Sadly, there had always been an unspoken rift between the two sets of children – Leah and Benjamin, plus Angelika and Andreas – and they'd never become anything close to friends. Just as Angelika and Daniel had never become a real father and daughter.

"Why is it always like this?" The words flew out of Angelika's mouth as she shifted her focus back to Daniel, who was busy pouring over his files in search of an extra copy of the song. "Is this really all you care about? All that I mean to you?"

"What in Mozart's name are you talking about?" Daniel asked, face furrowing.

Angelika had nearly forgotten it was Daniel who'd first imparted that silly phrase she often used.

"I didn't forget my music," she said. "That isn't why I came here today. Not that it matters, because to you, I'm just another student, especially now that Mama is gone."

Daniel's jaw plummeted.

"That's what you think?" he asked. "That I see you as just another student?"

"Yes." Angelika stood to face him, her voice soaring to a shout as Daniel's tall, lanky frame rose high above her head. She didn't understand how he could appear so surprised, and not realise he'd been holding her at arm's length. "Or if not another student, then another... Oh, I don't know."

"I realise you're upset, but please, do you have to yell?"

"Yes, I have to." Angelika knew she must sound like a bad-tempered child, but was becoming too worked up to stop herself. "What are you going to do about it? Scold me? No, you're not. You've never scolded me, even the times I deserved it, because to you, I was never really your daughter."

Her sharp words hung in the air as grating grief filled her heart.

"Angelika, enough." Daniel's own tone had taken on

a choppier edge than usual. "Let's talk this over without resorting to raised voices and angry words."

"*Naaa*," Angelika said, lapsing into Viennese dialect as she refused. "I shouldn't have come here today."

Her defiance was gone, replaced instead with longing and pain. She started for the door while, from behind, Daniel's strained voice cut across the silence.

"So, this is the way it's going to be?" he asked. "You're going to run away, using your own pain as a vengeful weapon, without giving me a chance to explain?"

Angelika stopped, hand trembling against the tarnished brass doorknob.

"If you only knew," Daniel continued, voice cracking, "how deeply I care for you, love you and worry about you. I always have, every day of your life, ever since the first time I saw you, just a few days old, lying in a wooden cradle alongside your brother, tiny and helpless, though already carrying that mischievous twinkle in your eye. If you only knew how badly I want you to live out your dreams, be happy and never let the things bigoted people say about me hurt you or hold you back. I've always loved you, *Annichen*, even if I haven't done the finest job, especially lately, of letting it show."

Throat tight with the weight of the prickly past and its muddle of memories, Angelika remained frozen in place, her skittish fingertips lightly rattling the doorknob.

"What about Mama?" she choked out. "Did you really love her?"

"Yes, since long before you were born."

Daniel sucked in a loud, unsteady breath while

Angelika slunk back over to the sofa and sat. She couldn't tell whether there were tears glistening in Daniel's eyes, or whether it only appeared that way because of her own brimming waterworks.

"I've loved your mother ever since the day I met her at the music academy we attended together as teenagers," Daniel said, joining Angelika on the couch. "Her inner beauty and talent far surpassed that of anyone else I'd known."

"You never married her."

"I should have, but it wasn't so easy for us. My parents didn't want me marrying a Catholic girl any more than Clara's wanted her to marry me."

"That hardly seems fair," Angelika said.

"You're right. It wasn't fair. Your mother said she would have converted and married me anyway, no matter what our families believed. That still didn't satisfy my parents, and as a young man, I wasn't brave enough to take a stand with them. Even though today, I'd be the first to admit that I do not believe in a traditional God. Just as I don't believe religion should keep people who love each other apart."

Daniel sighed to himself, the pain of past regret weathering his face.

"After we turned eighteen," he continued, "I told your mother I needed some time apart, to think. It was then that she took up with Rudolf Eder and I started stepping out with Hedwig, a family friend who was, and still is, in love with someone her own family didn't fancy. I thought your mother and I could both get past it and move on, but as you know, we never could. Instead, we ended up leading dishonest lives and hurting others along the way."

Daniel's earnest and remorseful words caused Angelika's heavy, wounded heart to slowly begin softening. For unlike her and Andreas, who at least had each other, Daniel – the only other person who had loved Clara nearly as much as they did – had no one else to share in his grief.

"Have you…" The words caught, and Angelika paused to steady her breath. "Have you gone back to…" Dark memories of a too-sunny day swirled in her head as she recalled her mother's funeral at Vienna's sprawling, impersonal Central Cemetery. She'd begged Rudolf to lay Clara to rest near Salzburg, by her beloved lake, but he had refused. God only knew how or why he'd convinced the closedminded clergymen to allow a Catholic burial for a woman who had died by suicide. "Have you been back to the…"

A ragged groan left Angelika's throat, and Daniel clasped her hand before gesturing toward a bouquet of dark red tea roses that lay upon his writing desk, right alongside a photograph depicting him and several friends he'd once served with in the armed forces during the Great War.

"I visit her every week," he whispered. "I bring her flowers and tell her that all of us – me, the operagoers and even the long-lingering ghosts of Mozart and Donizetti – miss her terribly."

Angelika nodded in silent agreement, comforted by the steady weight of Daniel's hand in her own.

"Do you think it would be all right if I came with you the next time?" she asked. "And visited you again, here?"

"If anyone finds out, or sees us together at the cemetery, people will say all sorts of ignorant things about you."

"It shouldn't matter what they say," Angelika insisted.

"No, it shouldn't. But it does. Not because they're right, but because of what they're capable of doing." Daniel gave Angelika's hand a protective squeeze. "It's why I've been so careful all these years, and why I never fully opened my heart to you the way I wanted." He then drew a breath and, in spite of everything, let a small smile spread across his face. "I suppose, though, if you really want to spend your precious free time in the company of a middle-aged opera snob, I should consider it a compliment."

Angelika chortled, then coughed, the tightness in her throat easing.

"Let me fix you some warm water with lemon and honey," Daniel said, gesturing toward his kitchenette. "It'll help calm your voice."

He stood, heading past a folding card table and narrow hallway that led to the makeshift bedroom overlooking the street. While Daniel searched for a kettle, Angelika stepped over to the piano and perused a pile of sheet music that had been haphazardly stacked on top.

"'Gretchen at the Spinning Wheel,'" she called out after taking the celebrated Schubert piece in hand. "I've always dreamt that perhaps someday, if I learnt to sing it well, Andreas and I could present this song together."

"That would be marvellous." Daniel cleared old dishes off the card table while water boiled on a burner. "But why someday? Why not now? We can work on it together."

Angelika hesitated, setting the music down. She planned to refuse, but before she could, Daniel was there, beside her, offering a gentle push.

"Take it," he said. "Try."

Angelika wavered another moment, then finally agreed.

"*Gut.*" Daniel handed her back the piece, along with, unexpectedly, the heavy black stage direction textbook the pianist had brought to class the first day. "You can take this, too. In fact, before Monday, I'd like you to review the first two chapters and prepare a thousand-word report."

"A thousand words? Why?"

"Because, dear girl, I'm afraid you're too old for any conventional scolding. Even if you weren't, it wouldn't teach you much. This assignment hopefully will."

Though a bit surprised and rather embarrassed, Angelika could also feel the smallest of satisfied smiles tickling at her lips.

"You seemed a bit shaken during class these past couple of days," she said. She'd wanted to ask Daniel what was wrong, but had allowed her pride to stand in the way. "It wasn't only because of me, was it? Something else has happened?"

Daniel's face fell, and he slowly nodded.

"It's Hedwig's mother," he explained. "She's suffering from lung cancer and isn't expected to live much longer. Leah doesn't speak with me very often anymore. Not since Hedwig and I formally divorced last year. But a couple of evenings ago, the poor girl turned up at my Theater an der Wien office, heartbroken about her grandmother."

"*Ach*, how sad she must feel. I'm terribly sorry."

"Thank you." Daniel leant forward and, for the first time Angelika could remember, gave her forehead a quick, fatherly kiss. "Life is short, my Anni. Live yours well."

His heartfelt words remained with Angelika the rest of the afternoon as she and Daniel worked together, made music, laughed, cried and shared cherished stories. His message was also at the forefront of Angelika's mind when she returned to the women's residence that evening and sat before her desk to pen a long-overdue letter to Baldur von Schirach.

While I know you consider me a talented young singer, I am still learning and improving, Angelika wrote. *I do not feel ready to sing before such a large crowd, where my nerves will consume me, and I will surely make numerous mistakes.*

Supposed stage fright was one of many outrageous Nazi explanations that had circulated following the death of Adolf Hitler's niece. Angela Raubal had purportedly died by suicide because she was too nervous about an upcoming public singing appearance. And if the Nazis were so stupid as to have used that nonsensical excuse, perhaps Angelika's feigning stage fright might make them change their tune about wanting her to appear.

I must therefore decline your invitation to sing at the National Socialist concert this October, Angelika finished writing before signing her name and sealing the envelope.

And yet, even if her strategy worked, she hadn't explicitly disavowed the Nazis' twisted beliefs and abhorrent way of thinking. If she ever did, how would they retaliate? Cowardly as it might be, Angelika remained too terrified to find out.

Thirteen

In the next few days that followed, Angelika put her nose to the grindstone and poured her entire soul into singing. Although her "Della crudele Isotta" interpretation was far from perfect and she was still struggling in certain spots, the more Angelika worked with Daniel, the more she felt as if she were, for the first time in ages, learning to sing from her heart again. While her mother's legacy would forever serve as an inspiration, Angelika could also slowly feel herself becoming a singer in her own right, discovering her own unique voice and original path via every hard-fought note, well-placed breath and confident instinct.

"It's a matter of understanding and staying true to your inner voice," Daniel told her as they practised together at the conservatory on Tuesday afternoon, three days after her unexpected visit to his flat. "If you listen to yourself and trust that voice, I know you'll be unstoppable, both as a singer and a person."

A grateful smile graced Angelika's face. While she and Daniel had continued discussing music and working together on songs, something significant had shifted in their relationship. On Sunday, they had made a tearful visit to her mother's gravesite and spoken in private about the past, present and future. The beginning whispers of a genuine father-daughter relationship were gradually taking shape, even if those whispers remained private, playing out inside Angelika and Daniel's own hearts, safe from society's evil prejudices.

"I hope so," Angelika agreed. "I mean, I'll try."

She was too ashamed to tell Daniel about the National Socialist concert fiasco, which she'd tried pushing out of mind after mailing her response to Baldur von Schirach. Angelika could only hope the Nazis would accept her stage fright excuse and set their sights elsewhere. But a nagging feeling told her she was foolish to hope for such an easy outcome.

Nevertheless, by the time regular lessons let out on Wednesday afternoon, Angelika could think about little else but meeting Daniel at his Theater an der Wien office so that they could discuss one of her songs again, then have dinner at the renowned Café Frauenhuber, the oldest coffee-house in the city. That night, she planned to tell Daniel about her memory book and some of the special stories she'd been writing in it.

"Fräulein Eder!"

The housemother's gravelly voice carried up the staircase as Angelika dropped things off at the women's residence before beginning the short walk to the theatre. Gretchen wasn't back yet, and Angelika assumed she had stayed late at the conservatory, practising. They both wanted to be as prepared as possible for their upcoming private lessons with Lotte Lehmann, who had temporarily left town to sing at the Salzburg summer music festival. Once Lotte came back, Angelika would also ask her about the shocking statement Baldur von Schirach had made in his letter – the insinuation that the Nazis wanted Lotte to consider an artistic alliance with them.

"Yes, Frau Fuchs?" Angelika called back, poking her head out of the bedroom door while affixing the daisy clip to her burnt-orange day dress. She'd forgotten to add it that morning and had missed its comforting presence throughout the day.

"There's a young man here to see you. He said he'd wait outside in the courtyard, by the fountain."

Angelika's newfound joy and confidence dissipated as if someone had popped her like a prop balloon simulating the sound of a gunshot. She started toward the window to glance outside but stopped herself midway. There was little point in looking, since she already knew who the visitor must be. Someone Angelika had parted ways with over the telephone a week ago, and who had apparently decided to visit Vienna to try hassling her into restarting the relationship.

But Angelika was determined to remain strong and listen to her inner voice, as Daniel had advised. An inner voice that had told her, all the more clearly throughout the past week, that Kurt was not her proper match. That much was certain as Angelika made her way downstairs into the foyer, where the housemother was hard at work clearing the floor of dried mud that had been tracked inside during the recent rain showers.

"I told your visitor he could have a seat on one of the wooden benches out front, but he said that after straddling a motorcycle seat for hours on end, he'd rather stand." Alma Fuchs stopped sweeping and smoothed her apron, a girlish simper spreading across her face. "He even had the audacity to ask if I'd like to go for a spin in his sidecar later. Can you imagine? A woman of my age riding a motorbike?"

The housemother's usual bluster was gone, and she let loose a hearty laugh while Angelika's jaw dropped. A motorcycle? Either Kurt had gone mad, or Alma had misunderstood.

"You're certain this young man is here for me?" Angelika asked. "Not one of the other young ladies?"

"He said Fräulein Angelika Eder, then also pretended to mistake me for a conservatory student." A twinkle flickered in Alma's turquoise eyes. "A real charmer, that curly-haired imp."

At that, Angelika felt as if her jaw might plummet straight down into the floorboards. Kurt had straight, slicked-back hair – definitely not curly, unless he'd taken to wearing a wig. A jolt of electricity shot through Angelika, and her imagination began to whirl. But no, it couldn't be the curly-haired, hazel-eyed boy she'd been unwittingly thinking about the past couple of weeks. That would be impossible. Wouldn't it?

Angelika stepped outside and hurried toward the fountain, expecting to see an unfamiliar young man who would say he had come to town in the hope of visiting Marta, Ruth or one of the other young singers. Instead, she saw a boyish face, muscular arms, broad shoulders and messy blond curls. Features that belonged to one person, and one person alone.

"Erich!" A joyful shout erupted from Angelika's throat, and she broke into a run, her patent-leather pumps kicking up flecks of dampened dirt as she all but sprinted across the lawn, whizzing past couples picnicking on park benches and students biking beneath the maple trees. "It's really you."

Angelika flung her arms around Erich so forcefully, he lost his balance and almost toppled backward into the courtyard's burbling, three-tiered stone fountain.

"Well, hello to you, too," Erich said with a surprised chuckle. He managed to steady himself, then returned Angelika's hug, wrapping well-built arms around her waist. "If it's a swim you're looking for, can't we go to a public pool? A lake? Do you have to try flinging me into a fountain? When I said you were my siren, I didn't mean for you to literally drown me."

Angelika tried to conjure a witty response, but could only lean back and stare at Erich's round face and into his dancing, mischievous eyes, which seemed to have grown to a richer hazel in the couple of weeks since she'd left Munich. In spite of their levitous sparkle, Erich's eyes also conveyed strength, sincerity and understanding – three things that had always been present, but that Angelika had never fully allowed herself to appreciate.

"What are you doing here?" she asked, keeping her arms looped about his neck as a cool mist from the fountain swirled in the late afternoon breeze.

"I had to make sure you were all right after the ridiculously nice postcard and letter you sent me. What are they doing to you at this conservatory? Has all the singing deprived your brain of oxygen?"

"Oh, you're impossible." Angelika gave Erich's bicep a playful swat. "Perhaps I should fling you into the fountain after all."

"There's the saucy sarcasm I'm used to."

Erich's grin softened, and he pulled her into a tighter embrace, so close that Angelika set any inhibitions aside and rested her cheek against his. Perhaps she'd lost her mind, or perhaps she'd finally found it. All she knew for certain was how intensely she'd missed him, and how suddenly right it felt to be enveloped in his arms.

"But you also seemed upset and confused in your letter." Erich's razor stubble gently scratched Angelika's face, and an earthy smell of dirt greeted her nose. "I'm sorry I didn't write back to you yet. I was trying to, but nothing I said sounded right. I've been going out of my head without you, and after reading that letter, plus Kurt paying me a visit, I decided to take a chance and come to Vienna."

"Wait, what?" Angelika reared back, lips curving into a frown. "Kurt paid you a visit?"

"He sure did." The playful look in Erich's eyes had been replaced by pity. "Kurt came to the beer garden and accused me of trying to steal his girl. He said you called things off with him, and that I was the reason. According to Kurt, you weren't thinking straight."

Appalling. What a scoundrel Kurt was, going behind

Angelika's back and accosting Erich. Not to mention questioning her state of mind. And yet, like Erich, she also pitied the man. For all of Kurt's gaudy gold pocket watches, millions of *Reichsmarks* and overpriced silk-lined suits, he was vulnerable and desperate deep down inside.

"I told him that whatever happened between the two of you, it was your decision who you want to be with – him, me, a racecar driver or even the ringmaster over at the Circus Krone," Erich continued. "Kurt must not have liked that answer very much, because the next thing I knew, he tried throwing a punch."

Angelika's resulting gasp seemed to carry across the courtyard. Though Kurt was noticeably taller than Erich, he was also lean, and no physical match for a husky young man.

"Don't worry," Erich said. "It was a weak swing, and I ducked out of the way in plenty of time. Kurt's breath stank of schnaps, and wouldn't you know it that right after that, he threw up all over my work boots? Not the first time I've been vomited on, and probably not the last."

Erich explained that he'd brought Kurt a bucket, then helped him climb back into his chauffeured car to be ushered home before anyone else could intervene and make matters worse.

"I wanted to get him out of there before my father or the brownshirts caught wind of what was going on. If not, they'd have hurt him badly, and me, too, if I tried stopping them."

"*Ach*, how awful." Angelika sighed and stared at Erich's mud-streaked black boots, presumably a different pair than the ones Kurt had soiled. "Thank you for helping him. And I'm sorry. This is all my fault."

"Don't be sorry." Erich's velvety voice was soothing. "And don't blame yourself. I didn't come here to talk about Kurt, or to try pressuring you into anything you don't want. I just missed you. I couldn't wait until the middle of September to see you again."

Although Erich may not have been there to pressure Angelika into anything, his feelings were as clear as they had always been, especially as he eased a thumb across the daisy-shaped clip he'd chosen as Angelika's birthday present. It was such a simple yet special gift, and one Angelika had proudly worn every day since, all the while thinking about the thoughtful young man who'd given it to her. With a contented sigh, Angelika embraced Erich a second time as he, in turn, gave her an unabashed squeeze, his hot palms burning a proverbial hole through the back of her dress.

Yes, Angelika felt sorry about the difficult time Kurt was having. And yes, in hindsight, she might have handled things differently. But was Kurt really upset over losing Angelika, or simply angry that she had taken a stand, denying him of affections he'd come to believe were rightfully his? Angelika didn't know for certain. One thing she did know was that she did not wish to become Kurt's sweetheart again. She had told the man she needed time to think, and now that she had, she couldn't fathom rekindling their relationship.

"I also came here to get my leather jacket back," Erich said, a teasing tone returning. At the moment, he was dressed in a grey work jacket, plus beige motorcycling breeches streaked with dust. "I went by your house to ask Andreas, but he wasn't home. Then the housekeeper told me she must have accidentally packed it in your travelling trunk. If you ask me, she seemed a little funny about the whole thing."

So, Erich also suspected it had been intentional.

"And here I thought you'd given me the jacket to keep." Angelika taunted Erich in return, her fingertips tingling with a growing desire to knead the sweaty curls that had gathered about the nape of his neck. "Didn't you think it suited me?"

"Why don't you wear it for a ride on my new motorcycle? Then we can see for sure."

Erich gestured toward Elisabethstrasse, where a black motorcycle and sidecar were parked across from a popular park that showcased a monument honouring poet Friedrich Schiller.

"You really made a five-hour drive on a motorcycle?" Angelika asked.

Erich nodded and shrugged, as if the journey had been little more than a merry jaunt around the block.

"I got the bike a couple of months ago." Erich led the way past rainbowed beds of dahlias and over to the kerb, where the motorcycle was sandwiched between two posh blue Steyr automobiles. "It's a BMW R 52 model from a few years back. One of Doctor Hoffmann's colleagues bought it for his son, but the boy didn't take care of it. Doctor Hoffmann's friend said that if I was willing to get it working again, I could have it. I didn't say anything to you or Andreas, because I wasn't sure I'd be able to get it going. I wanted it to be a surprise."

The motorcycle was almost entirely ebony, with the exception of white trim around the wheel-housing and an unmistakable blue-and-white BMW emblem on the side. The most eye-catching part was its matching sidecar, which boasted a round, protruding front and curved silver handlebar that made it look like a rollercoaster car at the nearby Prater amusement park.

"Since this is a touring model, I could almost make it from Munich to Vienna on one tank of petrol," Erich said. "It sure is a lot speedier than a delivery truck."

Speaking of deliveries, Angelika didn't understand how Erich had come to visit her right in the middle of a work week.

"Did your father say it was all right for you to take a few days away from the brewery to come and see me?" Angelika stepped closer to Erich and made way for a group of passersby, including two leashed rottweilers dragging their owner toward the park. "How long can you stay? And how much must it have cost you to come?"

"Why, are you worried I don't have enough money left over to buy you a spin on that fancy Ferris wheel you mentioned in your postcard? I was hoping we could ride it today."

Excitement rippled through Angelika, even as she eyed Erich suspiciously. It wasn't like him to deflect, refusing to offer a straight answer to her question about his taking time away from the brewery. Before she could say anything more, however, any remaining giddiness gave way to guilt.

For there, ambling toward the dormitory with a confused expression upon his face, was Daniel.

Their study session… Dinner at the café… Angelika had been so caught up in the happy surprise of seeing Erich, everything else had slipped her mind.

"I'm sorry I lost track of time," she called out as he approached, Daniel looking every bit the free-spirited creative in a bright orange beret, wide-legged beige pants and a polka-dotted green ascot. "I was about to come to the theatre and meet you when our housemother told me I had a visitor. This is my friend Erich Bauer, from Munich. And Erich, this is Herr Daniel Weiss."

"Ah, yes, Erich Bauer." Daniel shook Erich's hand and gave a quick tip of his beret. "It's a pleasure to meet you. Angelika told me quite a bit about you the other day."

"It's nice to meet you, too, sir." Erich straightened his stance and brushed dirt from his jacket. "But uh-oh. What exactly did she say about me?"

"I'd never break Angelika's confidence," Daniel said, his tone light-hearted, "but let's just say it didn't sound as if you're ready to become a French diction adviser anytime soon."

"A smart assessment, sir."

The two of them laughed, and Angelika suggested that Erich join her and Daniel for dinner. Daniel, however, looked from Angelika to Erich with a knowing glint in his eye, then held up his hands in protest.

"As the operatic gods would have it, I was just coming over here to tell you I need to reschedule," he said. Obviously a kind-hearted lie. "My colleagues and I have been talking through some changes to the musical arrangements for our new operetta, *The Flower of Hawaii.*" Angelika knew that much was true. "And I accidentally double-booked myself tonight. I'm due at an important meeting with the maestro. But perhaps the three of us, and your friend Gretchen, can have dinner tomorrow night instead?"

"Perfect." The prospect of people she deeply cared for getting to know one another better had Angelika bouncing on her heels. "Thank you, Daniel."

He winked before shifting his focus to the motorcycle's sidecar, where a large brown knapsack lay alongside Erich's leather cycling gloves and a couple of pairs of eye goggles.

"Are these your things?" he asked Erich. "Have you found a place to stay yet?"

"*Nein.* I came straight to the conservatory after getting into town. Which was no small feat with you crazy Viennese driving on the opposite side of the road. I noticed a men's residence around the corner, though. Perhaps I can get a room there for the next few nights."

But as Angelika and Daniel knew, the influx of summer singing students meant that the nearby men's and women's residences were full.

"I have a better idea," Daniel said. "And a free one, at that. Why don't you stay at my flat? If you don't mind a lumpy sofa and a little bit of clutter, that is."

Angelika couldn't help but snicker. The clutter inside Daniel's flat would hardly be considered minimal. However, she also knew that Erich wouldn't mind.

"That's kind of you, Herr Weiss. I am a little… tight on money right now."

"It's settled, then. Anni knows where I live, so she can tell you how to get there tonight. Just as long as you understand it'll be a far cry from Hotel Sacher. Or any hotel, for that matter."

"As long as my father isn't there trying to beat me black-and-blue in the middle of the night, I'd be fine sleeping inside a cardboard box," Erich said.

A deadpan joke, but one Angelika feared held plenty of truth behind it. She scanned her friend's body, wondering what sad realities the bare skin beneath his clothing might reveal. He at least seemed fully mobile and free of significant injuries. But something awful must have happened at the brewery between Erich and his father in the past couple of days. Angelika hoped he would tell her more about it later, even as she dreaded hearing it.

"Dark humour, eh?" Daniel asked Erich, though not without a flicker of concern flashing in his caring blue eyes. "You'll fit in just fine here in Vienna."

Daniel then said his goodbyes, and Angelika went inside to gather her purse and leave a note for Gretchen.

"Ready, Marguerite Mareuse?" Erich said, referencing the famous French racer as Angelika returned with his leather jacket slung about her shoulders. He helped her into the sidecar, passed her the extra pair of goggles and shifted the knapsack so that it rested by her feet. "*Oui?*"

Though Erich looked audaciously fetching while donning cycling gloves and pushing back floppy curls, his French accent had remained ridiculous as ever.

"*Oui*," Angelika replied, because yes, she was indeed ready.

Once the bike had rumbled to life with a deafening roar, Angelika gave Erich shouted directions as he headed toward the Wienzeile thoroughfare that would carry them past the lavish Musikverein concert hall and sprawling Stadt Park, then across the Danube canal.

"Erich, watch out," she yelled, knuckles white against the sidecar's handlebar after he momentarily veered onto the wrong side of the street while rounding a corner.

Driving on the lefthand side was a major difference between Vienna and Munich, and Angelika worried it might take Erich more than a little getting used to. Still, the wind in her hair and exhilarating jolt of the motorcycle made Angelika feel as if, after more than a year in darkness, the world was slowly opening back up to her again. A world that was hers for the taking if she only allowed herself to embrace the beautiful new spring blossoming inside her soul.

The singer chooses which roles she will play.

Angelika drew in a breath, threw back her head and felt Clara's presence as surely as the sun in the summer sky, the breeze in the linden trees and the whir of the motorcycle's refurbished engine. Her mother wasn't gone, but there. Forever and always. A promise once made and, now, a promise kept.

"I love you, Mama."

Angelika breathed the words, letting them swirl into the wind and come rushing back to her in an unending cycle, an infinite loop. A long-overdue realisation that, even in death, love could never perish.

Fourteen

"**M**an alive!" Erich craned his neck upward, squinting in the late afternoon sunlight as the iconic Prater amusement park Ferris wheel soared high above his curly-topped head. "It sure didn't seem this tall in that dinky postcard picture you sent me."

Angelika paused alongside the twenty-storey-high *Riesenrad* and stared at Erich, who stood immobile amidst vendors selling balloons, families toting toys they'd won at game stalls, children snacking on *Wiener Würstel* sausage, and mothers chastising those same children for eating too quickly. The scent of sugary sweets and savoury meats intermingled in the air as peals of laughter carried on the breeze from nearby attractions, including a miniature railway and children's puppet show. Erich, however, who had seemed boisterous as ever during the motorcycle ride across town, appeared about as enthused as the time he'd misplaced a thousand-word French essay at school and had to start over from scratch.

"What's the matter?" Angelika asked her friend, half-teasing. Truth be told, she didn't know how to regard

Erich anymore – as a friend; a suitor; a young man who looked undeniably winsome with windblown hair and lips flecked with sticky sugar from the vanilla ice cream cones he and Angelika had devoured after first arriving at the amusement park. "Are you afraid to ride it?"

"Me, afraid?" He chuckled, though still without meeting Angelika's eye. "Not a chance."

But the truth was as plain as the nose on his usually fearless face. Erich was frightened, though not because he had a weak stomach or lacked a sense of adventure. Erich Bauer, Angelika realised, was afraid of heights.

"Why don't we go on something else instead?" she suggested, eschewing the tiny swelling of disappointment that cropped up inside her chest.

As much as Angelika had longed to ride the Ferris wheel with Erich, she would only have a good time if she knew he was enjoying it, as well.

"Let's try the alpine roller coaster," she said, looping her arm through Erich's. "It's fast, but the hills aren't terribly high. We could ride the spinning swings, too. And the swinging boats."

"Oh no, you don't." Erich pulled Angelika closer while wearing a sheepish smile. "I know how much you want to ride this Ferris wheel. I'll be fine."

Yet by the time they'd boarded an apple-red, boxcar-like cabin and started making a slow yet steady circle toward the top, Erich didn't appear fine at all.

"Don't look straight down." Angelika stood near one of the cabin's open-air, wire-protected windows beside her ashen-faced companion. Sidling up closer, she slipped her sticky hand into his as tiny streetcars and people swarmed the streets below. "Would it help if I pointed out a few landmarks?"

Erich nodded, and although he didn't speak, he squeezed Angelika's hand, turned it about in his own and interlaced their two sets of fingers.

"There's the Danube canal and the bridge we rode across on our way over here," Angelika said as the Ferris wheel circled higher into the sky.

The last time she'd beheld the same familiar view, she had been with her mother and Andreas two summers prior. But instead of feeling the usual underpinnings of grief creeping in, Angelika felt a surprising sense of calm and contentedness wash over her as she traced her thumb along Erich's wrist. She was glad that, busy as the amusement park seemed to be on a summer's evening, she and Erich had gotten a Ferris wheel cabin all to themselves.

"And there's St. Stephen's Cathedral. See the spire? One time, when I was seven years old, I snuck into their organ chamber after Easter Mass and tapped out the opening to the 'Queen of the Night' aria. Luckily, no one but Mama figured out it was me."

Angelika expected a laugh from Erich but heard only a strained sigh as the Ferris wheel neared the top. She'd have to come up with a better distraction, and fast. She knew what she wanted to do, and had imagined doing ever since she'd stepped outside the women's residence and saw him standing there in the courtyard. But no sooner had she prepared to lean in than the cabin rattled and Erich gasped.

"I'll bet you're wishing you really had flung me into that fountain," he mumbled with a self-deprecating snicker.

"Why didn't you tell me you were afraid of heights?"

Erich didn't answer, instead releasing Angelika's hand and turning to face her as a cool blast of wind danced between the protective wire running across the windows. She'd left Erich's leather jacket folded up inside the motorcycle's sidecar, but had nevertheless felt pleasantly warm holding his hand and standing close to him. Yet the two of them now stood at arm's length, no longer touching.

"You want the truth?" Erich observed Angelika with widened hazel eyes. "I didn't say anything because I'm scared witless about ruining whatever this is that's happening between us. Sure, before I met you, I stepped out with a few different girls, but they weren't like you. The way I feel about you is..."

Erich's cheeks turned as red as the Ferris wheel cabin, and a frustrated sound, somewhere between a grunt and a groan, arose from deep inside his throat.

"Ah, hell, I don't know what I'm saying." He looked away and out of one of the windows as the rotunda that had once housed the 1873 Vienna World's Fair sailed across his and Angelika's sightline. "We're so high up, I must be suffering from altitude sickness. The next thing you know, I'll be needing a fainting couch and smelling salts."

A child's lost blue balloon floated past the cabin then, and Erich glanced toward it with apparent pity in his eyes, the tiny object appearing so small and helpless, it was no match for the unempathetic winds that carried it farther and farther from the hand in which it had wanted to remain.

"Never in a hundred years did I think I'd get a chance like this with you," Erich went on. "I wanted it to happen, but now that it seems like it might be real, I'm afraid it'll disappear like a rabbit inside a hat. Because what do I have that a gorgeous, gifted, dynamite girl like you would want? I can't even ride a Ferris wheel without acting like a nitwit. I guess I just hoped that…" He stopped speaking and raked a hand through his messy hair. "Damn it, Anni, how much longer are you going to let me go on spouting nonsense?"

Angelika opened her mouth to respond, but at first, no words came. Because in those few stumbling sentences, Erich had given her something no other young man ever had. Not Kurt. Not Paul. Not anyone. In this unplanned and unanticipated moment, cool and unflappable Erich stood before her, utterly vulnerable and bare. His words weren't nonsense. In fact, they were the clearest, truest words any man had ever said to her.

"Nonsense?" She closed the distance so that the two of them stood face-to-face, breath-to-breath, heartbeat-to-heartbeat. "And worrying you have nothing that a 'girl like me' would want? I think you were right when you claimed to have altitude sickness. Because that's the only way you could possibly believe that statement is true."

"I just—"

Angelika cut him off, tracing two fingers across Erich's lips and feeling relieved when his clenched jaw relaxed at her touch.

"Take a good look around." She raised her other hand and brushed it across his stubbly cheek. "On second thought, don't do that, because then we might need the couch and smelling salts after all. But for God's sake, Erich, we're going around in circles on a ridiculously high Ferris wheel that petrifies you, but that you decided to ride anyway because you knew it was something I wanted to do. Because you're the most thoughtful, selfless and caring young man I've ever met. That's why you rode all the way to Vienna on a motorcycle, why you gave me this daisy clip, and why you helped convince me to fight for my dream of becoming an opera singer. Because you understand me. You see me. And I…"

Here was Angelika's chance – the chance to tell Erich how much he meant to her, too, and how spending time with him, whether as friends or something else, allowed her to feel more genuinely herself than she had with Paul, Kurt or any other young man. It was her chance to offer him the same raw vulnerability he'd just shown her.

"And I'm glad I marched up to you at school last year and said your French accent was atrocious," she blurted out.

For a couple of quick beats, Erich stared back at Angelika, silent and bearing an unreadable expression. Then he burst out laughing, and she did, too, the tension in the air easing as he snaked a solid arm around her waist and tugged on a fluttering lock of her hair.

"I'm glad, too," Erich said, his voice smoothing and its customary cadence returning.

"Because you'd have failed the course without me?"

"Because that's the day you became my siren. It's the day I fell in love with you."

Angelika's heart flip-flopped like a fish in an alpine lake, and a firecracker seemed to explode inside her chest. But Erich had said the words easily and naturally, almost as if he were telling her that *Schnitzel* was fried, or jelly doughnuts were sweet. Paul had never claimed to love her, and as for Kurt, his endearments were always of the 'set my heart aflame' variety. Not simple and sincere. Not like Erich's.

But did she dare to tell him the same in return? In spite of the sincere sentiments she'd just expressed, could she truly trust him with her heart? A heart that had been shattered before and, while slowly healing, often felt like a collection of splintered Swarovski crystal shards being held together with gloppy glue. And did she – the most important question to ask herself – love him, too?

Angelika thought back to that day at school the previous autumn, after she'd first come to Munich, and many of the other boys had seemed bitter or resentful about a girl being better than them in French class. But not Erich. From that very first day, he'd looked at her with a sense of admiration and respect. He had never once seemed threatened by her brain or talent, and that was something she loved about him.

While Kurt and Paul had never admonished Angelika's intelligence, they hadn't sought her counsel or allowed her to best them at anything, either. Instead of merely tolerating Angelika's opinions and advice, Erich relished them. And that, undoubtedly, was something else she loved about him.

Just as she also loved the way he made her laugh. The way he could give and take sarcasm. The way he was honest, steady and true. The way he hadn't run away the times she'd sank into grief or snapped at him because she was hurting inside. The way he gave encouragement without purporting to know what was best for Angelika or making her feel irrational. The way he'd always worked so hard at the brewery. The way he'd been brave enough to board the Ferris wheel, already knowing that being so high off the ground would spook him. The way he was kind and warm in spite of the pain his father had inflicted. A pain others might have used, as Daniel would say, as a vengeful weapon.

Yes, Angelika's relationship with Erich seemed to be rapidly changing, and she was still exploring the exhilarating new feelings taking root. But the answer to his declaration was as clear as the sinking sun in the sky, and Angelika owed it to Erich to tell him the truth. Just as she owed it to herself.

"I fell in love with you, too," Angelika said. "Perhaps not that day, or in that same instant, but sometime. Perhaps it was the day you climbed through the window at my music school. Or the night of my birthday, when that newspaper reporter turned up at my house. Or when I saw you kneeling on the hard marble floor in my foyer, showering sweet little Mokka with affection. I did fall in love with you. I did. Even though I didn't realise it at the time. Even though I was afraid to realise it."

The gondola shook a bit then, and Erich pulled back with a start, instinctively scrunching his eyes shut. And with that, Angelika waited no longer. While Erich stood there, body rigid and taut, she enveloped his face in her hands, and then finally, eagerly met his lips in a hungry, heady kiss.

"*Mein* Erich." His mouth tasted sugary, its corners still speckled with hints of sweet vanilla, while his lips, slightly chapped from the motorcycle ride, felt pleasantly rough. "Strong, clever, smart aleck Erich."

"Anni," he breathed, kissing Angelika back with a passion that all but knocked her off her feet. "My own siren and muse. And apparently everyone else's, too, the time you played that organ music inside the church. Such a mischievous girl."

"Mischievous, indeed. And you haven't seen the half of it yet."

The Ferris wheel ride and panoramic views forgotten, Angelika remained lost in the spectacular feeling of Erich's deepening kiss and responsive touch, the heat of their connection burning straight through her dress and infiltrating her veins. Pent-up desire inflated Angelika's heart from within as though she herself were the lost balloon that had soared past the gondola's window. Perhaps Erich needn't have felt sorry for that errant orb after all. Perhaps, like Angelika, it had temporarily escaped the bounds of an iron-fisted, grief-inducing world below. Perhaps it had finally found its freedom.

"There are so many things I need to tell you," Angelika whispered to Erich in between kisses. In spite of his fear of heights, he seemed suddenly quite content that the Ferris wheel ride included more than a single trip around. "So many things I want to say."

"Me, too."

But at the moment, all they could do was continue clinging to one another, Erich's fingers digging into Angelika's burnt-orange day dress as she, in turn, gently bit his lower lip and worked her fingers beneath his jacket. There would be countless questions to answer and endless details to iron out. And Angelika knew she and Erich would do just that, all in good time. Right then, however, soaring high in a sunlit sky above Vienna, they were welcome to do and be and feel with no regard for anything but the present instant. Angelika and Erich, just like that boundless blue balloon, were flying free.

Fifteen

Angelika and Erich's first kisses were so divine that by the time the Ferris wheel ride ended, he had the temerity to ask if she wanted to get back on again. But the line had lengthened, and Angelika's stomach was growling. So, after a quick visit to a ball-toss game stall, where he won her a stuffed baby elephant reminiscent of the one she'd loved seeing at the Munich zoo, they left the amusement park and headed into the heart of the city to eat dinner at Café Central, an iconic Viennese meeting place since 1876.

There, in a quiet corner, they filled their bellies with potato mushroom soup and pork dumplings while Angelika told Erich everything that had happened throughout the past couple of weeks, including details about her classes, the upcoming competition, her blossoming bond with Daniel and the excitement of being reacquainted with Lotte Lehmann. She also told him about Baldur von Schirach's communiqué and her subsequent response, in which she'd feigned stage fright and declined the invitation to sing at the Nazis' October propaganda concert.

"He may have received my letter by now," Angelika said with a shudder. "Who knows what the reaction will be?"

She'd hoped Erich might offer encouraging words, but he unfortunately had none. Only the grim, unhappy rehashing of the way his abusive father had, a day earlier, flown into a rage, struck him with a broomstick and told Erich he must either agree to join the National Socialists or have ten minutes to pack his things and leave the brewery forever. And leave forever, Erich had.

"I stuffed as much as I could into that knapsack you saw in the sidecar," he said while Angelika gripped his hand beneath the café's round, marble tabletop. "I tried going to your house to ask Andreas for help, but he wasn't there. So, I stayed one night at Doctor Hoffmann's, then left for Vienna first thing today. Luckily, thanks to all the times I delivered beer to Salzburg, I had my passport at the ready."

Ach, poor Erich. Angelika wished they weren't in a public café so that she could comfort and embrace him the same way she had aboard the Ferris wheel. She also wished Andreas had been available in Erich's time of need. But Kurt was still demanding that Andreas work long hours at the office.

"Thank Mozart's ghost you thought to come here," Angelika told Erich, the few remaining bites of her meal lying untouched. "And don't worry. We'll come up with some sort of plan for what you can do next."

"I have a couple of ideas, but haven't decided for sure yet. I knew this would eventually happen, though. My father's always been a monster. And big as I am, he's even bigger. He hated everything I ever did. To him, I was worthless and unwanted. He said that since my mother died right after I was born, it was my fault it happened. And he especially thought I was a fool for staying in school to give myself options in case I decided not to follow in his footsteps. Imagine that, huh? Me not wanting to be like him."

Tears welled in Angelika's eyes, and red-hot abhorrence for Viktor Bauer cascaded through her core. For every kind and caring man like Erich who existed in the world, there seemed to be a dozen other brutes and devils waiting in the wings. What she wouldn't give to smack a broomstick against Viktor's pig-headed skull and see how he liked it.

"The only way I lasted so long at the brewery, and got him to pay me something to boot, was because I knew his secret," Erich said. "That he's been swiping recipes from other brewers for years. But none of those legalities matter now. He and his friends are so powerful, they can get away with anything."

"That man is a demon." Angelika's tone was low and livid. "And none of what he said about you is true. Please tell me you know it isn't true."

"I know." Erich reached his free hand across the table and chucked Angelika beneath the chin. "And don't cry. Because you know what? I would go through it all over again, a million times, if I knew that in the end, I'd wind up here – in Vienna of all places – coming within a whisper of fainting on that blasted Ferris wheel, then overeating fancy food inside a palatial café with you."

He gave Angelika a reassuring wink and let his

fingertips graze her leg beneath the tabletop. Horrible as his experience had been, Erich was still Erich. Strong, unwavering and hopeful. Angelika glanced about at the restaurant's columned pillars and soaring vaulted ceiling, grateful that her treasured friend and newly named sweetheart was safely there with her.

"May I bring you anything else?" A tuxedoed waiter reappeared to clear away dinner plates and deliver the two tall glasses of *Einspänner* coffee Angelika had requested. In keeping with Vienna's longstanding Habsburg tradition, he also laid out palate-cleansing glasses of water with overturned coffee spoons on top. "A couple of slices of our signature torte, perhaps?"

Angelika began shaking her head, Erich's terrible story having stolen away what little remained of her appetite. Besides that, there was also the price to consider. Angelika had told Erich she could pay, having already planned to reimburse Kurt using the funds Clara had left her. But Erich, in spite of no longer having a job, had insisted that the meal was his treat.

At least let me do something right, he'd joked. *Let me take you someplace nice and buy a real dinner for my girl.*

His girl. Erich had called Angelika his girl, though hardly in the possessive way Kurt so often had, with too strong an emphasis on the "my" and too little focus on the "girl".

"The torte sounds good," Erich told the waiter while Angelika took a careful sip of her drink, its whipped cream topping helping cool the hot coffee as it travelled across her lips. "Two slices, please."

If Angelika couldn't finish the slice herself, she was certain insatiable Erich would. As Mozart's "Piano Sonata No. 11" began playing on a grand piano in the background, Angelika discretely slipped a stockinged foot out of her pump and ran her toes along Erich's pantleg, casting him a saucy little smile. She didn't blame him for desiring dessert in a place where, all around the café, coffee-lovers and sugar-seekers devoured rum punch cakes, puff pastries and, of course, the coffee-house's signature chocolate, orange and marzipan torte. Perhaps Angelika wanted dessert after all, though hardly the kind that could be served in a café.

"After this, why don't we go for a walk along the river by Daniel's flat?" she said. "We can finish what we started aboard the Ferris wheel."

Erich agreed, and the two of them, though no longer alone in their corner, continued stealing touches beneath the table, paying little mind to the nearby diners. Angelika shared tales of her favourite sights and sounds in Vienna, then surprised herself by eating every last rich morsel of her torte. It wasn't until afterward that she found herself glancing to the right, where an elderly man was attempting to stand, and an accompanying middle-aged woman helped guide him to his feet.

"There you are, Papa." The tall, greying woman handed the man his cane. "Easy, now. Nice and slow."

Angelika observed as the pair inched their way across the floor, the woman moving calmly in step beside her father and making sure he remained steady on his feet. From the affectionate way the man's daughter regarded him, Angelika could tell he must be a loving father. Not a louse like Viktor Bauer and far too many others. Angelika then returned her attention to Erich, who'd unfathomably decided to order another slice of torte.

"At this rate, I'll have to roll you into the sidecar and drive the motorcycle to Daniel's neighbourhood myself," she said, laughing. "How can you still be hungry after…"

An unexpected commotion erupted from across the room, and Angelika's head snapped around just in time to see the elderly man knock into a table – the stumble resulting in spilled mochas, a toppled chess board and thirty-two black-and-white game pieces sent scattering across the floor.

"Oh dear," the man's daughter groaned.

She grappled to catch her father as Erich, Angelika and a couple of others rushed over to help. The two university-aged chess players showed little interest in lending a hand, however. Instead of expressing any concern for the man's well-being, they squawked like hens over the coffee stains on their trousers, then skewered the gentleman with fiery glares.

"Watch where you're going, Jewish scum," one of them shouted, shoving the man and eliciting a loud gasp from his daughter, plus shocked looks from Angelika and Erich. "Worthless invalid."

"Invalid is right," his friend added. "Look what you did, you filthy old rat."

The man's daughter looked as if she might cry, and the couple of other customers who'd come to help slunk wordlessly away, whether because they were too afraid of being caught in the middle of an argument or because, like the bigoted chess players, they now believed the elderly man to be unworthy of their help. How did these stooges even know the man was Jewish? And why on earth should it matter?

Angelika prepared to say as much, but before she could, Erich squared his shoulders and strode straight up to the burly young men.

"Looks to me as if you two are the only filthy rats here," Erich said, his baritone voice all but booming. "You'd better scurry back to your hole before you get eaten by a fox."

A couple of the café's waiters had taken to cleaning the spilled coffee and gathering the chess pieces, focusing entirely on their tasks and staying out of the ensuing verbal exchange. The pianist also went right on playing, and customers continued eating, everyone pretending to be oblivious to the shameful scene that had played out before their eyes.

"We overheard this blithering buffoon talking in here the other day," one of the boys said, ignoring Erich's sarcasm and remaining fixated upon the silent septuagenarian. "Blathering on about the political discussions at his synagogue. We heard him calling Adolf Hitler an insufferable liar."

"You mean someone had the gall to speak the truth?" Breaking free from his father's abuse seemed to have emboldened Erich, and the words tumbled out fast and furious. "I'm shocked."

"You'll see," the boy spat back, shifting his attention

to Erich. "Our National Socialist wing is planning a huge rally here in Vienna next month, with Adolf Hitler himself coming to speak. You'll see just how many people turn out to support us. People who want unification and freedom from the Jewish scourge."

Angelika had been so caught up in singing and her own personal concerns, she hadn't realised a Nazi rally was to be held in Vienna during September. She imagined Hitler and his henchmen arriving in the city, swarming the streets, mounting one of their raucous rallies and spewing their sickening ideology. The mere thought of it nauseated Angelika, and the hearty meal she'd eaten threatened to come back up.

"I cannot believe this." Angelika tried interjecting herself into the argument as festering ferocity, plus two shots of espresso, coursed through her veins. "You boys are..."

A heave constricted Angelika's middle, and vomit rose into her throat. But she couldn't allow herself to be sick. Not then and there. She forced the vomit down, then tried to steady herself with diaphragmatic breathing. And still, in spite of her best efforts, another heave threatened.

"Perhaps I'd better go wait outside," Angelika murmured.

While antisemitism had long existed in Vienna, it seemed to be growing even worse. Indeed, it now appeared to encompass Nazi-inspired hatred shouted from the floor of a decades-old café Angelika loved. A place she'd long considered to be representative of Vienna's artistry and intellectual diversity.

"All right," Erich told her, keeping narrowed hazel eyes trained upon the boys, one of whom was looking Angelika up and down, assessing her physique with a fiendish smirk. "I'll be there as soon as I finish telling these two nitwits exactly what I think of them."

Head spinning and stomach roiling, Angelika returned to her and Erich's table, snatched her peacock-embroidered pocketbook and prepared to leave. She was almost to the door and ready to eschew the chess players' leering gaze when one of them jutted out a hand and grabbed her by the arm, painfully wrenching the skin and eliciting a wince.

"What's the hurry?" he asked Angelika as her purse tumbled to the floor by Erich's feet.

It was the same clutch she'd been carrying the evening of her ill-fated nineteenth birthday, the night a reporter had forced his way into her house and Johann had given her his swastika-and-sword pin.

Johann's pin... Angelika hadn't known what to do with it then, and had never again wanted to grasp its cold, bronze metal between her fingertips. Instead, she'd left it tucked away inside an interior pocket of the purse, unseen and forgotten, as if it didn't exist.

If you ever find yourself in trouble, just present this pin, and it'll prove what a proud and loyal German you are.

It wasn't until the present moment, standing in Café Central with a searing pain shooting through her left arm, that Angelika heard Johann's voice inside her head and remembered the trinket remained hidden inside her pocketbook. But no, she could never use the pin in such a way, no matter what this boy or any other might do to her. It would be hypocritical and despicable, just like her actions that wretched afternoon at the Munich streetcar stop, when she'd used her acquaintance with Viktor Bauer to get out of a bind.

"Get your hands off her," Erich cried in a forceful, virulent tone Angelika had never before heard him use. "Now."

As Angelika struggled and scratched in an attempt to free herself, Erich hurtled forward, ready to pummel the perpetrator. He didn't have the chance, however, because in one brief instant, the young man had released Angelika and, with his friend's help, heaved Erich against a pillar.

"No!" Angelika's nausea gave way to fear, and she watched in horror as Erich struggled against the boys, inadvertently knocking over a claw-footed coat stand and rack of newspapers in the process. The piano music stopped, and the café became so silent, everyone could have heard a pin far smaller than Johann's drop. While Erich surely could have taken on each of these boys one at a time, the two of them together had managed to overpower him. "Let him go."

She must use Johann's pin for Erich's sake. She must tell these boys she was a talented young singer and that Baldur von Schirach wanted her in his corner. Perhaps, in as unanticipated an instance as the one at hand, the ends might justify the means. But no, she could never do such a thing.

The tallest boy drew back his fist.

Yes, she must. It was the only way to…

"That's enough!" Two brawny waiters mercifully intervened then, blocking Angelika's view as they wrested away the chess players. "There will be no violence inside this establishment."

But as the waiters yanked the hooligans aside, Angelika realised their help had arrived a split-second too late. For there sat Erich, slumped against the pillar, a rush of blood splattering his grey motorcycling jacket, then dripping onto the pristinely polished floor.

"Erich." Angelika dropped down beside him, vaguely aware of the chess players and waitstaff arguing amongst themselves in the background. The elderly man and his daughter were fortunately nowhere to be seen, the two of them having slipped silently away in the middle of the melee. "Oh, Erich, your nose."

Angelika whipped a monogrammed handkerchief out of her purse and pressed it against the injury, hand trembling all the while.

"I'm all right," Erich said in a nasally tone while tilting his head forward. He gave Angelika's fingers a firm squeeze, then helped hold the handkerchief in place, the bleeding beginning to slow after a couple of minutes. "It's you I'm worried about. I can't believe that *Arschloch* grabbed you. Does your arm hurt?"

It did, but Angelika shook her head, not wanting to further exacerbate things.

"*Nein.*" She moved her left wrist in circles. "I'll be fine."

A fresh-faced young waiter bustled over to help, offering Erich a warm, wet cloth and handing Angelika a stack of clean napkins to use in wiping away the remaining blood. The pianist had started playing again, and nearby, to Angelika's chagrin, the chess players were rearranging their board and ordering new coffees as if nothing had happened.

"Pardon me." She rose and addressed the helpful waiter, a thick-haired, clean-shaven young man who appeared close in age to her and Erich. "Why are those fellows being permitted to stay here after assaulting an elderly man, harassing me and attacking my sweetheart?"

"I'm sorry, miss," he answered with a distressed sigh. "We tried telling the head waiter over there…" He pointed to a balding, thin-lipped man in his mid-fifties. "…that they should be forced to leave, but he refused. He said that passionate, politically minded students can be a bit rowdy at times."

A bit rowdy? Passionate and politically minded? Angelika's ears rang as if someone had blasted two large tubas directly alongside.

"Come on, Anni." Erich stood, leaving the soiled handkerchief on the floor next to the dirty napkins – the entire bloodied bundle ready to be discarded inside a rubbish bin. "Let me pay the bill, and then we can get the hell out of here."

The bleeding had stopped, and except for the redness around Erich's nose and the drying blood on his jacket, there was no sign he was in any terrible distress. Nevertheless, Angelika couldn't help but stare at the stain, which was turning darker in colour as it dried, almost as if it were a smear of melted chocolate.

Chocolate. She froze, then turned her eyes toward

the head waiter, who was sauntering up to a nearby table and checking on other customers, Erich's injury and the terrible treatment of the elderly man having been completely forgotten. But Angelika couldn't let the abhorrent behaviour stand. She couldn't let the head waiter or the chess-playing instigators get away with this. And chocolate – sweet, simple chocolate – was her answer.

"Well, sir, in that case," she said to the empathetic young waiter, speaking loudly enough that the head waiter also turned to look, "I'm afraid my family won't be able to continue selling your café any of our chocolate. You do still use Eder-family products in your recipes?"

She knew that they did. She had tasted it in the cocoa powder sprinkled atop the *Einspänner* coffee she'd drunk with dessert. Angelika was so used to the ubiquitous taste of her family's fare, and had been so focused on spending time with Erich, she'd paid it barely any attention.

"You mean…" The portly head waiter hurried right on over, eyes widening as he nervously cleared his throat. "Are you…"

"Fräulein Angelika Eder. Would you mind if I use your telephone to get in touch with our Vienna headquarters? So that I can relay how dreadfully people are being treated at this coffee-house? A coffee-house your owner, Herr Ortner, has led us to believe represents the very best of Vienna?"

She had no real intention of telephoning anyone. If she did, and Rudolf Eder or Kurt's father got wind of it, the only person they'd be angry with was Angelika. She supposed she could try telephoning Kurt instead, but he would then discover that Erich had come to town. Given the aggrieved look on the head waiter's face, Angelika had a feeling no telephone calls would be necessary, though.

"Ah, yes, Fräulein Eder," the man said, his eyes growing as big as the countless cakes filling the café's display case. "Do forgive me, miss. Won't you please have a seat?" He rushed over to an empty table and pulled out a chair. "Let me see what I can do."

And with that, everything changed. Within minutes, the chess players had been tossed out and the head waiter had continued apologising, even offering to front the money for replacing Erich's soiled jacket. An offer Erich refused.

"Don't worry about the cost of tonight's meal, either," the waiter insisted. "It's on the house."

"We neither need nor want your charity," Angelika replied. "But if you insist upon not charging us, we'll donate the money to the needy instead."

Angelika gave the man a curt nod, then gathered up her bag and, with Erich following behind, hurried out onto Herrengasse, gulping in the evening air as horse-drawn carriages, automobiles and foot traffic filed past. A number of workmen, likely heading home after another day spent constructing Vienna's first high-rise, either tipped their caps or scowled at her as they walked by. At sixteen storeys, the nearby Herrengasse skyscraper would be the tallest residential building in the city, and a modern, sophisticated one at that.

Look at the fancy rich girl, the frowning men's faces seemed to say.

A fancy rich girl whose family might procure a flat in a skyscraper while those who had built it went on living far more meagre lives. It was no secret that radical political parties like the Nazis used economic disparities to drum up nationalistic support and scapegoat others. Never mind the fact that Adolf Hitler, the supposed champion of the working man, lived and dined like a prince. And yet, a bubble of guilt surfaced as Angelika thought about those who had lost so much following the economic collapse and who had, in susceptible desperation, turned to groups like the Nazis, who made lofty promises of jobs, food and transcendent tomorrows, consequences be damned.

"Are you feeling sick, Anni?"

Erich's warm touch pulled her back into the present moment.

"Yes," she admitted, looking into his eyes as they languished outside the café's Venetian and Florentine-inspired stone building, formerly home to the national bank and stock exchange. Boasting carpeted front steps, a clock above the doorway and elegant sculptures gracing its façade, the stately sight seemed entirely at odds with the disturbance that had just occurred within its walls. "But I'll be all right. What about you, *mon beau*?" Angelika ran her index finger down the bridge of Erich's swollen nose. "Perhaps we'd better find a doctor."

"I don't need a doctor." Erich caught Angelika's hand in his and used the other arm to pull her to him. "All I need is my girl. My beautiful, talented, clever girl."

Angelika didn't feel clever, though. Not at all. Not after she'd considered using Johann's pin inside the coffee-house.

And not when her eventual solution had been to evoke the Eder family name – a name belonging to a man who wasn't genuinely her father. What about all of the mistreated people who didn't have business connections they could leverage to get their way? And really, what was Angelika doing to help others? What good did it do to have two imbeciles thrown out of a café when there were thousands of others ready to swoop in and take their place?

"Come on," she murmured, glancing toward the darkening eastern sky and clutching Erich's hand. "Let's get to Daniel's flat."

Angelika considered telling Erich that Johann's pin remained hidden inside her bag and that she'd almost used it, but in the end, she said nothing more about the matter.

"Your nose will definitely bruise and be sore for the next few days, but it doesn't feel broken," Daniel said a short while later, examining Erich's injury after he and Angelika had described the incident. "I don't like what's happening, though. Here in Vienna. Throughout Austria." A sad, dark look arose in Daniel's pensive blue eyes. "It's bad enough our own government is moving toward fascism and totalitarianism."

Totalitarianism propagated by Austrian fascists who opposed the German fascists.

"And now, we have to worry about that *Scheisskopf* coming in and gaining a foothold," Daniel said, referring to Hitler. "It makes me wonder whether I should…" He couldn't seem to continue. "Anyway, you must be exhausted, Erich."

"Not just yet," he replied, stifling a yawn.

But sure enough, within five minutes' time, Erich fell sound asleep on a small crevice of lumpy sofa Daniel had cleared of yellowing newspapers. While Daniel fetched a blanket from his makeshift bedroom, Angelika rolled the leather jacket into a ball and slipped it beneath Erich's head as a pillow, also removing his boots and leaving the stuffed elephant with a quickly scrawled note she'd slid between its feet. *Meet me by the fountain tomorrow afternoon.* She leant down to give Erich a kiss on the cheek, then felt embarrassed when she realised Daniel had re-entered the room.

He pretended not to notice, however, instead feigning great interest in the ever-growing pile of papers littering his writing desk. Daniel was another good person in a world that reeked of evil. A person whose love Angelika, at the moment, didn't feel she deserved.

"I'm sorry," Angelika whispered to him before leaving the flat. "So terribly sorry."

And she truly was. She was sorry about Johann's pin. Sorry about getting tangled up in the Nazis' plans for a propaganda concert. Sorry about the couple of drunken nights she'd spent singing at Viktor Bauer's beer garden.

"Sorry?" Daniel cocked his head, confused, while yanking a chain to turn on a floor lamp. "You mean about forgetting our dinner plans earlier? I told you it was all right, silly goose." He glanced at Erich, asleep on the couch, and then back at Angelika. "You wouldn't know it from looking at me now, but I was once young myself."

Nostalgic remembrances flickered across Daniel's face, and Angelika embraced him tightly, promising herself she would never again fathom doing anything as heinous as what she'd considered at the café. And that was why, instead of going straight to a streetcar stop and back to the conservatory, she detoured down to the riverfront and stood alongside a wrought-iron railing, gazing upon a swath of rippling water.

Thanks to the setting sun and a fluffy bank of clouds, the river's surface had been painted the loveliest shades of pink and orange – a watercolour work of art that seemed almost too pretty a sight to mar with the ugly metallic object Angelika surreptitiously extracted from her purse. Yet mar the river's beauty she must. Because the object in question belonged anywhere but glistening in the fading light of day.

"Go to the devil, Johann," Angelika murmured, quietly enough that only she and the southeastern-flowing current could hear the words as she extended her arm over the railing. "Go to the devil, all of you."

She then watched, eyes narrowed and lips pursed, as the swastika-and-sword pin plummeted downward, struck the river's surface and disappeared into the Danube's dark, unseeable depths.

Sixteen

arly the next morning, during the brightening hours before dawn and while languishing in the half-lucid stirrings of sleep, Angelika dreamt of water. Not the genteel Danube, into which she'd deposited Johann's pin, or its tributary that sliced through Munich. No, after Angelika had returned to the conservatory and stayed up far too late baring her soul to Gretchen, she dreamt of the lovely turquoise lake lapping the banks of the Eder family's summer estate outside Salzburg.

Ensconced within the fuzzy, watercolour picture reel of a dream, Angelika found herself seated alongside Andreas in their rickety old canoe, both twins laughing and teasing one another about who was doing most of the work. Just as she'd so often done in real life, Angelika soon stopped paddling altogether, preferring to stand on wobbly legs and prepare for a jubilant jump into the cold, clear water.

But no sooner had Angelika risen, rocking the boat and receiving a nagging admonishment from her brother, than she saw it – a tidal wave of biblical proportions that had appeared at the opposite end of the lake and was hurtling toward them faster than a hound chasing after a strand of sausage.

Take my hand, Angelika shouted in the midst of the dream, lunging toward Andreas at the precise moment he also reached for her. *Hold onto me, and don't let go.*

The monstrous wave crashed over the canoe, tossing the twins to and fro in a torrent of icy water. And still, no matter how fervently the lake raged, Angelika continued gripping her brother's hand, its familiar weight willing her to continue kicking, thrashing and fighting until, at last, the water receded, and the lake once again became calm.

It's over, she whispered, bobbing amidst serene surroundings as a golden sun beamed down, ducks floated past and a rainbow painted the cloudless sky. *We're all right.*

But when Angelika glanced at the hand still grasped within her own, she beheld a grizzly sight. Where her fully formed brother had been just a few short minutes earlier, only a bloodied, dismembered limb remained.

No. No.

An otherworldly scream erupted from inside Angelika's throat and echoed across the foothills as she remained trapped inside the nightmare.

Andreas, where are you?

She scanned the lake, then held her breath and searched beneath its surface, to no avail. Andreas – her twin, her other half, the music to her lyrics – was gone.

"Andreas!"

The dastardly dream falling away, Angelika bolted

upright in bed at the women's residence, her silken pyjamas damp and her forehead streaked with sweat. Her heart thudded, her breath rattled, and she flailed her arms as if treading water, all the while desperately seeking someone who wasn't there.

Anni, I'm lost. Anni, I need you.

She could hear Andreas's voice ringing inside her head. Could hear him calling to her in the darkness. A shuddering sob wracked Angelika's core, and she curled herself into a ball as Gretchen's shadowy form appeared at the edge of the bed.

"It's all right." Gretchen lay down and wrapped loving arms around Angelika. "I'm here."

While Angelika had endured a couple of jarring nightmares since arriving at the conservatory, the nightly terrors hadn't been as prevalent as they'd so often been in Munich. And they certainly hadn't been anything like the awful dream she'd just experienced.

"Something has happened to Andreas," Angelika said. "Something is wrong."

"Andreas is fine." Gretchen hugged Angelika tighter and smoothed her matted hair. "I spoke with him by telephone a few hours ago, remember? Just as you spoke with him last night. Kurt's been working him hard, but he promised me he's fine. You've just had a ghastly scare."

But Angelika couldn't manage to silence the cacophony inside her head. Despite Gretchen remaining steadfastly by her side, Angelika slept fitfully the rest of the night. As soon as the sun came up, she dressed, rushed to the telephone and tried placing a call to Munich. As luck would have it, the operator wasn't able to make a connection before Angelika had to leave the women's residence and begin her daily classes.

"Fräulein Eder!" The housemother called after Angelika as she headed out of the front door, already on the verge of being late. "A message just arrived for you."

A jolt of dread coursing through her, Angelika tore open the nondescript envelope. Was this the Nazis' response regarding her refusal to sing at the concert?

But it wasn't. Not yet. Instead of an unwanted missive from Baldur von Schirach, Angelika's eyes beheld a thick notecard with Lotte Lehmann's name imprinted at the top.

Due to a personal engagement, I've briefly returned to Vienna in between appearances at the Salzburg Festival, the message read. *As such, I'd love to meet you at the Vienna State Opera this afternoon during your scheduled practice time so that we may begin our work together.*

The message went on to suggest Angelika meet Lotte inside the opera house's historic Emperor's Room, the same place the end-of-term recital competition was to be held in roughly two weeks' time. Had Angelika known she'd be performing for a distinguished singer like Madame Lehmann that very afternoon, rather than the following week as originally planned, she'd have been studying even harder and trying to feel better rested. But as Angelika knew from her mother's experience, being a singer often necessitated rising above one's self-conceived limitations and focusing on the job at hand. The job a singer had been trained to do.

"I can't wait to hear all about it afterward during our

dinner at Café Frauenhuber," Daniel told Angelika once his movement and expression class had ended for the day. "And don't worry if your session runs long. Erich told me he was off to explore the city this morning and would meet you by the fountain the same time as yesterday. If you're not there yet, either Gretchen or I can let him know you're studying with Madame Lehmann."

Angelika thanked Daniel, gathered her materials and began the short five-minute walk to the Vienna State Opera, its iconic building serving as a physical iteration of Vienna's living, pulsing heart. In Angelika's opinion, it was the opera house, not St. Stephen's Cathedral, that served as the architectural cornerstone of the city. Since its founding as a new home for the burgeoning Vienna Court Opera in 1869, the opera house had seen the city through the tragedy of the Great War, the fall of the Habsburg monarchy and the ongoing struggle of establishing a functioning republic. Of course, the house had also played an instrumental role in Angelika's own internal battle, in which she'd witnessed the rise and fall of the divine, incomparable coloratura soprano known to the world as Madame Clara Eder, but to her simply as Mama.

The last time Angelika had entered the opera house had been in May of 1931, one month before her mother's passing. She could still hear Clara's glorious trills filling the space as she sang the role of Konstanze in *Die Entführung aus dem Serail* to jubilant cheers of "*brava*" from patrons sitting shoulder-to-shoulder amidst the house's sold-out ivory-toned tiers. Little did Angelika know it would be the final time she'd see her magnificent mother take the stage.

Oh, what she wouldn't give to go back in time and savour those fleeting, finite moments. Although Angelika, Clara and Andreas had been reeling from the scandals, there had nonetheless been pervasive moments of love, joy and hope. Or so Angelika had believed. But her mother's cold, lifeless form a mere month later had told a different story. The story of a woman so deeply hurting, she'd felt she had no other choice. If only there had been something, anything, Angelika could have done to help. Doctor Hoffmann had repeatedly insisted that Clara's death was not Angelika's fault, and yet, no matter how much time had passed or how Angelika's heart might slowly begin to heal, a piece of her would forever believe that it was.

"*Ach*, Mama," Angelika whispered.

She hesitated while approaching the Renaissance-inspired stone structure that boasted resplendent arches, spacious verandas and stately statues depicting two winged horses guided by Harmony and the Muse of Poetry. Standing at a streetcorner with the opera house locked in her sights, Angelika's throat tightened, her pulse quickened and gutting grief surged like an orchestra's crescendo. But if she wished to carry forth her mother's legacy by becoming a famous singer, she must summon the strength to cope with the horrific past while developing her voice and sharing her gift.

I'm here for you. Always. No matter what.

And so, with Clara's loving words echoing inside her head, Angelika marched into the foyer and stood before a grand staircase adorned with marble statues honouring architecture, poetry, dance, music and other celebrated forms of art. All of the old familiar sights, welcoming Angelika home.

"Good afternoon, Fräulein Eder." An elderly male caretaker approached from alongside the bifurcated staircase. "Let me show you upstairs to the Emperor's Room, where Madame Lehmann is waiting."

When Clara was still alive, Angelika had loved attending gatherings inside the ornate Emperor's Room, a historic remnant from the days of the monarchy, when members of the royal family attended the opera. Although she could have easily located the room blindfolded, Angelika thanked the gentleman and followed him up the stairs. But for a few other caretakers coming and going, the house was largely silent. A good many singers and musicians had travelled to Salzburg for the summer festival, and no rehearsals were taking place. Once the artists returned at the start of September, the moving music of Verdi's *Aida*, Wagner's *Das Rheingold* and Bizet's *Carmen* would herald the arrival of an exhilarating new opera season.

"Fräulein Eder." Lotte's enthusiastic voice rang out in greeting as Angelika entered the Emperor's Room, a spacious salon decorated in twenty-two-carat gold leaf, silken yellow tapestries bearing the initials of bygone Emperor Franz Joseph I and a colourful ceiling painting aptly entitled *Music on Eagle's Wings*. "I'm delighted to see you today."

A Bösendorfer grand piano had been moved into the salon, and Angelika saw that Oskar Huber – her accompanist from the conservatory, who had offered to assist during the practice session – was already seated before it.

"I am delighted to see you, as well, Frau *Kammersängerin*," Angelika said, addressing Lotte by her honorary title of distinguished singer. "Are you enjoying your time at the Salzburg Festival? Three more performances, correct? And you will then be singing Ariadne and Leonore here in Vienna, along with resuming the role of the Marschallin?"

Angelika stopped herself from rambling, while Lotte, poised and perfect in a chic black dress, pearls and a bejewelled hairclip, sank onto a velvet sofa and gestured for Angelika to join her. Though Lotte was in her mid-forties, she had a youthful, vibrant face and bright eyes that evoked bittersweet memories of Clara. The renowned sopranos had both exuded an energy and vivaciousness known to captivate audiences and loved ones alike.

"Herr Huber, will you kindly fetch us a couple of glasses of water?" Lotte waited while Oskar obediently left the room, and Angelika took a seat beside her. The discerning diva then launched headlong into the very question Angelika had been anticipating, and dreading, all afternoon. "How have you been getting along?"

Under normal circumstances, such a question would have served as little more than idle conversation. But in Angelika's case, it carried a far heavier weight.

"I am... all right," she replied, her heartstrings taut, though not unbearably so. "Better. Sometimes." She held Lotte's gaze, determined to make it through the conversation with nary a sniffle. "Even though I still miss her more than I can say. Even though I always will."

Lotte nodded, a sense of understanding pervading her

gaze. Although the circumstances had been different, she too had lost a parent.

"Your mother was immensely proud of you," Lotte said. "She told me so on numerous occasions. Ah, what a marvellous time Clara and I had singing together." A rush of tears flooded Lotte's eyes, and Angelika's threatened to fill, as well. "The hatred and viciousness Clara endured was horrible, as I know it was for you, too. But you have a glorious gift from God, Angelika. And no matter what, you must never let anyone, or anything, destroy your passion for singing. Promise me you'll remember that?"

Angelika nodded, grateful for the prima donna's kindness and support. Lotte had never formally weighed in about the scandals, other than to say they were a sorry distraction from Clara's career as a singer and that the gossiping busybodies ought to mind their own business. Perhaps Angelika, at the moment, ought to take Lotte's advice, mind her business and refrain from asking about Baldur von Schirach's mention of Lotte in his letter. But for better or worse, Angelika had to know where Lotte stood on the matter.

"Is it true, Madame Lehmann?" Angelika leant forward and spoke in hushed tones as she shifted toward the new topic of conversation. "The gossip I'm hearing about German National Socialists wanting to use your voice and talent for their benefit? As an example of supposed German greatness? I've heard talk that they may, at some point, wish to form an artistic alliance with you."

Lotte's eyes widened, then narrowed, boring into Angelika with unprecedented intensity.

"Where in heaven's name did you hear that? Have you been corresponding with Madame Jeritza? Is she wagging her tongue about me again?"

As Angelika knew all too well, Lotte was referring to her rivalry with Maria Jeritza, a fellow soprano who had been nicknamed "the Moravian thunderbolt". Though Maria and Clara had also butted heads on a couple of occasions, Angelika could hardly remember a time when her mother had harboured ill-will toward any of the singers she worked with, even when she had sadly received judgement and criticism from those very same people.

"It wasn't Madame Jeritza," Angelika said. "It was... someone from Munich. I can't remember who."

"That seems a rather strange thing for you to forget, does it not?"

Whether Lotte was stunned because the revelation about the Nazis was genuinely news to her or because she was simply upset others might be discussing it, Angelika wasn't certain. And Angelika dared not tell Lotte the truth about the propaganda concert debacle.

"I apologise for my forgetfulness," Angelika said. "But you would never consider entering into an agreement with the Nazis, right? You must surely despise them, just as my mother did?"

Angelika waited for Lotte's response, and a confirmation of what she so desperately wanted to believe.

"I have never concerned myself with politics," Lotte answered instead, a hint of nonchalance unfurling. "Music is a language we can all understand, and it's an honour to share my talent around the world, for all sorts of people. I make decisions based upon my love of this art form and my interest in furthering my career as a singer. Not based upon whichever political party happens to have captured people's fancy."

At that, Angelika remained silent, her mouth going dry. This was not the response she had wanted. While music could indeed be considered a transcendent form of art, couldn't it also be weaponised and used for evil? To spread hatred and hurt others? To falsely glorify a particular group of people while advocating for the downfall of another? Or, alternatively, in a positive sense, to foster acceptance and mutual understanding?

"I pay little attention to politicians like Adolf Hitler." Lotte waved her hand dismissively, as if batting away a horse fly. "Your mother was much better informed than I could ever hope to be. Politics are irrelevant to my vocation as a singer."

Angelika still didn't speak, hot kernels of frustration cropping up inside her chest. As she was witnessing more blatantly with every passing day, politics – as Lotte referred to them – affected everyone and everything. It was politics that had resulted in an innocent man's harassment at Café Central, and politics that had led to street-fighting and burning buildings in Munich. Did not politics ultimately dictate who rose or fell, lived or died?

Angelika wanted to say as much, but felt cowardice creeping in and silencing her as she stared into the eyes of a famous soprano quite her senior, and someone she had forever admired. What might Clara say if she were there?

Would she turn against Lotte or try convincing her she was wrong? Angelika could never know for certain.

"Shall we carry on with our lesson, then?" Lotte's face brightened, and a pleasant smile returned. "I didn't come here to discuss political matters, and I'm itching to hear your lovely voice again."

Whether Angelika liked it or not, the distinguished diva had spoken, and the conversation about the Nazis was over.

While Oskar re-entered the room, Angelika completed a brief warm-up exercise and sipped from a tepid glass of water the accompanist placed on a side table. She then did her best to push the prior discussion out of mind and pour all she had into singing "Della crudele Isotta" from *L'elisir d'amore*. One of her favourite comedic works, the opera told the story of a nineteenth-century landowner named Adina who had fallen in love with a peasant and rebuffed an affluent man's offer of marriage, all thanks to a supposedly magical elixir.

Along with striving to perfect her vocal technique, Angelika had been struggling interpretively. Adina's opening song, during which the character shared the timeless love story of Tristan and Isolde, was typically sung to a group of proverbial villagers onstage, to whom the singer could direct her attention and actions. Performing it solo, but with images of a chorus at the forefront of her thoughts, had thus far left Angelika feeling stiff, unnatural and unconvincing.

"You may be performing the piece alone onstage, but remember that when you sing it during the competition, you'll have an audience watching," Lotte said. "Imagine that they are the townspeople to whom Adina is telling the story. If you want to be particularly original, perhaps you might stroll out into the crowd and address the people that way. Here, let me show you what I mean."

After Lotte had demonstrated the method and encouraged Angelika to give it a try, everything seemed to begin falling into place. With a renewed sense of confidence, and while following Daniel's earlier advice to use a real book as a prop, Angelika sang the song through in its entirety, without once tripping up or stopping to look at the music.

"*E quel primiero sorso per sempre benedì…*"

The same passages Angelika had been battling the day Erich came to the music school window in Munich, she this time delivered smoothly, with proper diction and appropriate timing. Angelika carried the song to its end, snapped her prop book shut with a dramatic flourish and looked to Lotte. Though the performance hadn't been perfect, Angelika knew she'd delivered her strongest rendition to date.

"*Brava*," Lotte said. "Now, that was the performance of a singer who is well on her way to achieving wonderful things."

They both then turned toward a slightly ajar door where, unexpectedly, two familiar figures had begun applauding.

"*Brava, brava!*"

The voices of Daniel and his longtime friend, stage director Max Reinhardt, filled the cavernous Emperor's Room.

"That was marvellous, Fräulein Eder," Max said.

"I knew you could do it," Daniel added.

Angelika thanked them both and exchanged a few pleasantries with Max, a greying man in his late fifties whom she'd met on several prior occasions.

"I'm sorry to interrupt your session," Daniel said, "but after hearing that remarkable interpretation of the song, I'm glad we did. We've come to ask Madame Lehmann's advice about something."

He went on to explain that Max was in the midst of producing a semi-staged, charitable benefit performance of *Don Carlo*, to be presented two days later, on Saturday afternoon. The late-summer fundraiser, a special treat for opera fans who'd been unable to attend the Salzburg Festival that year, was to be performed at the Theater an der Wien and broadcast over the radio. An abridged adaptation of the 1884 Milan version, this *Don Carlo* would be sung in Italian, unlike the German-language rendition that had been offered by the Vienna State Opera in May.

"However, Aenne Michalsky, who was going to sing the role of the Celestial Voice, has just let us know she's sick," Daniel said. "And with so many folks away in Salzburg for the festival, we're having a tough time finding someone to take her place. Madame Lehmann, I know you'll be back in Salzburg by Saturday, but do you know a singer who might be willing to cover a small role like that, for charity and without being paid, on two days' notice?"

Lotte paused to think while Daniel and Max awaited her reply. However, it was Angelika who broke the silence.

"I can do it." She straightened her spine as four pairs of eyes pivoted toward her like spotlights. Several short weeks earlier, Angelika couldn't have imagined suggesting anything so audacious. Now, she couldn't imagine not speaking up when the opportunity presented itself. "I can cover the role."

As everyone in the room knew, the Celestial Voice was a small supporting role, which involved singing a brief solo at the conclusion of Act II during *Don Carlo*. Since the voice was intended to ring down from the sky, the singer didn't appear onstage, but was listed by name in the announcements. To Angelika, it seemed a most perfect stepping stone. Max Reinhardt, however, appeared less than enthused.

"I appreciate your willingness," he said, shaking his head. "But I'm afraid it's out of the question. You are too young and inexperienced."

"I realise I'm still a student, sir, but I also know that my mother sang this role when she was not much older. And I've practised it before with my voice teacher in Munich."

The short but powerful solo took place during an *auto-da-fé* scene in which the brutal Spanish Inquisition carried out the murder of purported heretics. As the horrors ensued, an ethereal Celestial Voice proclaimed that, in spite of the Inquisition's condemnation, all who suffered were deserving of peace and acceptance beyond the bounds of earthly existence.

"I understand the music, know the libretto and can hit a high B," Angelika said. "If I work hard between now and Saturday, I'm certain I can do this."

Max appeared to reconsider while Daniel met Angelika's eyes, a combination of surprise and pride reflected within his own.

"I don't know." Max still sounded wary. "Perhaps this is too significant a step until you've undergone more extensive training."

Angelika tried conjuring another response, but before she could do so, Lotte's strong, assertive voice filled the room.

"Just a moment, Herr Reinhardt. Under ordinary circumstances, I would agree with you. But Angelika Eder is no ordinary young singer. Why, the performance she just gave was the finest rendition of 'Della crudele Isotta' I've heard from a conservatory student, and certainly from a student her age. There are also plenty of singers who made their debuts early on. Surely, you are familiar with the American singer Marion Talley? She made her Metropolitan Opera debut as Gilda, a much larger role, at nineteen. And I made mine in my early twenties, as did Angelika's mother. Age should not be used as a means of holding back a talented singer who is capable of handling a particular role."

"I agree with *Kammersängerin* Lehmann," Daniel said. "Angelika has been extremely hardworking during our recent lessons. As a co-director at the Theater an der Wien, I say we at least give her a chance to audition for us."

"And I'll be happy to help her prepare." Oskar, the accompanist, couldn't seem to resist chiming in. "If she puts her mind to it, I believe Fräulein Eder will succeed."

Angelika's heart soared like a lark taking flight. To hear the others, including a singer of Lotte's calibre, offer such ardent praise was nothing short of a dream come true. Angelika could only hope that as time went on, Lotte would change her tune about being apathetic toward the Nazis. And yet, what was Angelika really doing to help stop them, either?

"Very well," Max at last relented. "You may come to the Theater an der Wien tomorrow afternoon and sing for us. But if Herr Weiss, Maestro Schönherr and I don't unanimously agree that you are ready, there will be no further discussion. Understood?"

"Yes, sir." Angelika forced her feet to remain flat on the floor, even as she wanted to catapult into the air. "Thank you, sir."

Perhaps nervousness would set in a short while later. Nervousness about making a mistake and, if given the role, receiving bad reviews in the papers or being jeered by patrons eager to rehash the past scandals. But for the first time in ages, Angelika felt fully confident in her ability. And one way or another, she was determined to honour her mother's memory and show the world she had what it took to become a celebrated opera singer.

Seventeen

"I'm afraid it wasn't perfect, Fräulein Eder."

In all the times Angelika had visited the Theater an der Wien – whether by stepping out to see *The Merry Widow* with former sweetheart Paul or traversing backstage passageways with Daniel after he'd become a co-director several years earlier – she'd never before stood onstage. Not until Friday afternoon, as she completed her Celestial Voice audition while gazing about the red-and-gold house, its velvet-lined seats empty but for the watchful eyes and attentive ears of producer Max Reinhardt and maestro Max Schönherr, plus Daniel, Erich and Gretchen.

"You rushed the ending," the maestro continued. A dark-haired, bespectacled man in his late twenties, he sat a few rows out, proverbially holding court alongside Daniel and Max Reinhardt. "And I also noticed you beating time on the stage."

Ach, how foolish of her. Angelika's heart sank, and she couldn't bear to meet the expectant stares of Daniel, Erich, Gretchen or audition accompanist Oskar Huber, all of whom had spent hours helping her prepare. After Lotte Lehmann had left for another engagement the previous evening, Angelika had returned to the conservatory for an urgent study session led by Daniel, facilitated by Oskar, and supported by Erich and Gretchen. Any plans of dining at Café Frauenhuber had been forgotten as the quintet buckled down and focused upon the crucial task at hand.

Though he hadn't been able to offer a thimbleful of advice about Angelika's singing, Erich had remained close at hand the entire time, listening to the song, sharing encouragement and fetching sustenance. But in spite of everyone's efforts, it now seemed as if Angelika's dream wouldn't be realised after all.

"I understand." She met the maestro's eye and tried to keep her voice from catching. "Thank you for the chance to audition today."

How naïve Angelika had been to think she was ready to make her operatic debut. She felt a few tears prickling her eyes, but wouldn't allow them to fall, at least not until she had escaped the theatre and found herself safely enveloped in Erich's arms. She took one last longing look about the house, then turned to leave the stage.

Angelika had expected to audition inside a rehearsal room, but Max Reinhardt had said he wanted to gauge her stage presence. An odd request, considering that the Celestial Voice always sang offstage. And yet, Angelika had been too excited, and admittedly nervous, to ask questions.

"Wait a minute." The maestro's call echoed about the theatre's Corinthian-inspired pediments and gilded statues. "Just where do you think you're going? We haven't finished our conversation."

With a sigh of dread, Angelika turned back around, practically colliding with short and stocky Oskar, who had risen from the onstage piano, gathered the music and started following her toward one of the wings. Since Angelika had been given permission to skip her regular classes that day, she and Oskar had studied together extensively before the audition. And still, somehow, she'd managed to bungle things.

"I wasn't asking you to leave," the maestro said. "The ending wasn't quite perfect, but with a bit more practice during tonight's dress rehearsal, I believe you'll be ready by tomorrow afternoon. Do you agree, Herr Reinhardt? Herr Weiss?"

"Certainly," Max Reinhardt said. "I'd say it was as good, if not better, than many other Celestial Voice performances I've heard, including from singers older than you. We're also out of time to make a decision, so if you'd been a disaster, I don't know what we would have done."

"Not to mention the fact that I already gave the printer the go-ahead to deliver a new poster with your name listed," Daniel added, a proud grin flooding his face.

"So… I can cover the role?" Angelika's hands flew to her chest and pressed against her pounding heart. "I can be the Celestial Voice?"

The three kingmakers enthusiastically agreed, and as Angelika suppressed a squeal of delight, a young man's whoop carried throughout the theatre.

"I apologise, sir," Erich said after the maestro had shot

him a perturbed look. "I'll remember not to do that during the play. The opera, I mean. *Juan Carlos*."

"It's *Don Carlo*, Erich," Gretchen murmured.

"That's what I said. *Juan Carlo*."

Angelika would have to set Erich straight, and celebrate with him and Gretchen, later. At the moment, she had an evening dress rehearsal to consider. She was certain that Gretchen, as promised, would get word to Andreas in the hope he could rush to Vienna in time for the big performance the following afternoon. Oh, how Angelika hoped her brother could be there. And as for Erich, he was off to meet with a tailor friend of Daniel's who had offered to lend him a morning suit.

"We haven't told you the best part yet," Max Reinhardt said several minutes later.

He and Daniel had met Angelika backstage, then waited while Oskar congratulated her and said his goodbyes.

"The best part about what?"

Angelika looked to Max, awaiting an answer, but found herself distracted by a couple of female choristers loitering behind a costume rack that held Spanish-style dresses and friars' robes.

"Did you hear the news?" One of the choristers was muttering to her friend, oblivious to anyone else's presence. "Clara Eder's daughter is supposed to cover the role of the Celestial Voice. If you ask me, it's a scheme to sell tickets and get people to tune in for the radio broadcast. Do you suppose she'll make a name for herself the same way her mother did? As both an opera singer and a whore?"

Liquid fire burnt in Angelika's veins, and she saw Daniel stiffen beside her, his face scrunching with anger as he laid a protective hand upon her shoulder. Angelika should have expected the same old hateful talk, this time delivered by a couple of cruel choristers who didn't know she was the one who had pushed to cover the role. Who also didn't know, or care, how difficult a grief-filled journey she'd endured the past year. And who especially didn't know that Angelika would no longer allow petty, odious people to destroy her dreams or hold her back.

"Getting an early start on the gossip and backstabbing this evening?" Angelika peeked around the rack to face two blonde-haired women in their early thirties. "Fortunately, before she passed away, my mother taught me decent manners. As have my other advisers."

She glanced toward Daniel, who seemed ready to deliver a similar rebuke. But Angelika could handle the likes of these sour singers just fine on her own.

"People like you speak as if you know everything about my mother and family, when you really know nothing at all. Perhaps if you'd been fortunate enough to befriend my mother, some of her kindness might have rubbed off on you, and you wouldn't be so malicious and ignorant now."

Angelika then returned her attention to Daniel and Max, watching out of the corner of her eye as the women slunk sheepishly away past a team of stagehands toting set pieces depicting a centuries-old Spanish monastery and soaring spired cathedral. Since *Don Carlo* was being performed semi-staged, rather than as a full-scale production, everything was being carried out in a more minimalist fashion. The sets and costumes, not to mention the number of musicians and singers, were being scaled back. But that didn't mean this wouldn't be every bit as moving an interpretation of Verdi's musical masterpiece about lost love and oppression.

"You were saying something about 'the best part', Herr Reinhardt?" Angelika asked after giving Daniel a reassuring nod to let him know she was all right.

"*Ja.*" Max sidestepped several other stagehands and choristers, his aging face alight with boyish excitement. "We've decided that although the Celestial Voice typically sings offstage, we'd like to make an exception this time. You have a wonderful stage presence, so why not let everyone see it?"

"You mean..."

"We've asked that a raised platform be set up centre stage and hidden behind a panel. You'll quietly take your place during an earlier scene change, and then, when it's time, two supernumeraries will remove the panel. Instead of the celestial song ringing down from the sky, it'll be sung directly in the midst of the innocent people being persecuted."

"It'll also help your voice carry for the radio microphones, and allow for a direct line of sight with the maestro," Daniel said. "But only if you'd like to." He looked Angelika squarely in the eye, and she knew there would be no pressure. "It's your decision. After all, you agreed to do this believing you'd be singing offstage."

Angelika drew a breath and considered. Being visible onstage might invite more people to heckle or whisper about the scandals, distracting her during a critical moment. It would allow anyone from her past who might decide to attend the show, from despicable former sweetheart Paul to members of her mother's family, to see Angelika face-to-face, albeit from a distance. It would also mean, however, that she would make her operatic debut while standing directly in the spotlight. One significant step closer to someday achieving her vision of fame. Singing onstage and sharing her gift were two things Angelika longed to do. And do them, she would.

"I'd love to, Herr Reinhardt! Oh yes, I'd be thrilled to appear onstage."

And with that, everything moved forward in a wonderful, whirling blur. First, Angelika perused a rack of brocades, chiffons and silks until she'd settled upon an ethereal gown of white gauzy fabric, with asymmetrical golden stripes and an accompanying beaded belt. There would be no time for alterations, but fortunately, the costume fit well enough. She paired the frock with a gilded headband decorated in a vine motif, then commandeered a make-up table and set about creating an angelic, porcelain-inspired look. Hoping to counteract the unforgiving glow of the theatre's spotlights, she applied thick layers of ivory powder and cream rouge. Angelika would also smooth on a coat of her favourite rosebud-red Coty lipstick a bit later, after eating a light meal of crackers, fruit and nuts.

Although there were a few more gossipy whispers and murmurings from amongst the gathering singers, Angelika refused to let them rattle her. Keeping a cheerful disposition, she cordially greeted everyone she encountered, including tenor Franz Völker, who would sing the role of Don Carlo, and soprano Viorica Ursuleac, who would sing the role of Elisabeth. Two characters who, though once betrothed and in love, had been driven apart when Elisabeth married Don Carlo's father, King Philip II of Spain.

"Why, Fräulein Eder, I thought you had left Vienna," Viorica said while fussing over the blue-and-silver gown she'd be wearing as Elisabeth.

"I did." Angelika took a step to the side, allowing a dresser to assist the Romanian diva with her improperly fastened costume. "But now I've come back."

Seasoned singers like Franz and Viorica didn't need to practise the entire opera. Instead, they began rehearsing a couple of key scenes while preserving their voices for the following day's performance. And still, in spite of the shortened wait, time seemed to move at a tortoise's pace as Angelika listened backstage and continued reviewing her music.

When the anticipated moment at last arrived, she ascended a carefully positioned staircase and stood hidden on the platform behind a panel, an eager readiness buzzing from deep within her core. She envisioned Daniel, Max, the maestro and all of her fellow singers awaiting the Celestial Voice's arrival. No matter what anyone else present might think about Angelika and her family, she knew they all wanted her to succeed so that the opera would in turn succeed, everyone rising or falling together, as one.

"Honour to the greatest of kings." The chorus sang in

Italian as purported heretics were led to the stake in an operatic adaptation of inhuman brutalities once carried out by the Spanish Inquisition and monarchy. Hidden behind her panel, Angelika shuddered as she thought about all of the innocent people who had met a barbaric end because a group of powerful, sick-minded men didn't like what they believed. "The world is prostrate at his feet."

Angelika's part was about to begin, and a rush of nervousness sent a second shiver down her spine. She reached for her trusted daisy clip, then remembered it wasn't a part of her costume. What if her voice didn't resonate or her Italian diction was dreadful? What if things went so horribly wrong, she'd be removed from the production and prevented from singing the next day? What if...

And then, like magic, the panel was whisked away, the spotlight found Angelika, and she felt music filling her soul and raising her voice in song. Her body knew exactly what to do, and her mind followed suit. This time, there would be no mistakes.

"Fly to the sky," Angelika sang, her sparkling soprano soaring above the stage, flying out over the orchestra and filling the house. "Fly, poor suffering people. Hasten toward peace."

Angelika delivered so strong a performance that even the two choristers who'd berated her earlier could do little more than gape in awe after it was all over. And as for Daniel, though he hadn't admitted as much, Angelika was certain she'd seen tears moistening his eyes.

"I have the most marvellous surprise for you

tomorrow," Angelika told Erich once the rehearsal had ended and he'd met her outside the theatre. "Just you wait."

"How about we skip the waiting, and you tell me now? I'll still pretend to be surprised."

"Not a chance." Angelika swung his hand in hers as they walked, her smile as big as the limestone archway they passed beneath while approaching the conservatory. She wanted both Erich and Gretchen to be astonished when they saw her standing in the limelight, onstage, during the real performance. "Patience, *mon beau*. You'll find out soon enough, once we're back at the theatre tomorrow afternoon."

They came to a stop alongside the lamplit courtyard fountain, Angelika winding her arms around Erich's muscular middle and pulling him into a kiss. She tried to avoid further injuring his nose, which had indeed bruised following the fight at the café two nights earlier.

"Fine, I'll be good and wait," he said in between kisses. "Just as long as you promise to give me your autograph after the show."

"My autograph, hmm? Are you sure that's the only thing you want?"

Angelika wove her fingers through Erich's hair, then ran them beneath his suspender straps, pressing herself against him in a way that, if the housemother happened to be spying out of one of the residence windows, would result in a disapproving smirk. Or, with the way the middle-aged woman had taken to Erich a couple of days earlier, perhaps it might be a look of jealousy instead.

"What I want is to stay with you tonight." Erich's velvety

voice came out low and husky in spite of his swollen nose. "I'm so proud of you, Anni. If I only had the money, I'd take you to the gaudiest hotel in this city and ask for the biggest room they had. I'd buy three bottles of overpriced champagne and pull you out of that pretty purple silk dress. Then, after that, I would really make you sing."

"Why, Erich, I'm shocked." Angelika ran her lips along his neck, over his ears and into his careless curls. "Is that any way to speak to an angelic celestial songstress?"

"Perhaps not. But it's absolutely the right way to speak to the sauciest siren of the sea."

How Angelika longed to strip away Erich's clothing, entangle herself in his limbs, and kiss every last spot his father and the café boys had hurt. To satisfy the powerful, ferocious desire that had been burning inside of her ever since the Ferris wheel ride.

"I've seen enough gaudiness to last a lifetime." She forced herself to pull back a bit, lest she and Erich end up toppling sideways into the fountain. "I have an idea, though. I know a place we can go. Tomorrow, after the opera. You'll see."

"So, I have two surprises to look forward to, then? Assuming I don't make a fool out of you the way I did during the audition, by getting the name of the opera wrong in front of a famous conductor?"

"You didn't make a fool out of me," Angelika said. "You've been doing everything you can to help make my dream come true."

She stared into Erich's hungry hazel eyes before continuing to speak.

"And what about you? What hopes do you have? Did you really enjoy brewing beer, or is there something else you want? Another sort of job? Attending a university? You must tell me, because I've been thinking that... Well, if I win the competition at the end of this singing programme, perhaps I could stay here in Vienna. At first, I didn't think I could bear to, but now it doesn't feel as impossible anymore. Especially not if you could be here, too. And if I could somehow convince Andreas to join us, and find a way for Gretchen to stay. Perhaps we could talk with Daniel, and he could help you find work. Something you would like, and something that would make you happy."

"I'm happy enough right now," Erich said. "But let's talk about it more tomorrow, *ja*? After the show. Because if I keep you out too late tonight, you're liable to end up singing while sleepwalking."

Angelika couldn't help but agree. And so, after a few final kisses, she went inside and straight upstairs to her bedroom.

"Are you sick, Anni?" Gretchen rushed over as Angelika dropped her bookbag, flopped upon her bed and began fanning herself with some sheet music. "You look as if you're burning up with fever."

"I'm burning up, all right, but not with fever. It's Erich. Mozart's ghost, he makes me swoon."

"Well, when I tell you this next piece of news, you might feel a bit less swoony." A deep frown overtook Gretchen's face. "Andreas isn't coming tomorrow. I telephoned Munich and spoke with your housekeeper, but she said Andreas isn't there. He skipped work today and left town for a camping trip."

"Camping?" An unsettling series of goosebumps skittered across Angelika's arms. "My brother doesn't camp. He had fun swimming and canoeing at our Salzburg estate, but sleeping outdoors? With bugs and no plumbing? Never."

"She definitely said he was camping."

The friends exchanged a disconcerted look while Angelika did her best to tamp down a surge of disappointment. It was difficult enough that Clara wouldn't be there to see Angelika's operatic debut. And now her twin wouldn't be there, either?

"But I'm here for you," Gretchen said, as if reading Angelika's thoughts. She slid close and wrapped an arm around her friend's sagging shoulders. "And so is Erich. And Herr Weiss. I know you're going to be magnificent."

Angelika hoped she would be. No, not hoped. She *must* be, come what may.

After giving Gretchen a long and grateful hug, Angelika changed into polka-dotted pyjamas and climbed into bed early, mercifully falling into a deep, restorative sleep. And yet, at some point during the night, the eerie voice inside her head returned.

Anni, I'm lost. Anni, I need you.

On and on it went, until she at last opened her eyes to find the sun shining and her debut mere hours away. And still, Angelika couldn't shake the uneasy feeling in the pit of her stomach.

Andreas, gone camping?

"I'll find you," she whispered, as if willing him to hear her message. "I can help you."

But could she? For the first time in nineteen years, Angelika wasn't certain.

Eighteen

In spite of her worsening worries about Andreas, Angelika managed to arrive at the theatre on time, her nerves held in check thanks in large part to sweet words from Gretchen and a deliciously inappropriate public kiss from Erich.

"The in-house audience is in for a marvellous treat today," Max Reinhardt said backstage as opera lovers began filling the house and radio engineers finished setting up microphones. "Just wait until everyone sees you onstage."

Other than the musicians and singers who had participated in the dress rehearsal the evening before, no one else knew Angelika would be appearing onstage. Once she had donned her costume and done her make-up, she paced throughout the backstage hallways, though not because she was nervous. Angelika could hardly wait for her momentous moment to arrive, and felt too eager to fathom sitting still. That is, until Daniel delivered terrible news right before the curtain was set to rise.

"Leah just telephoned, begging me to come and see her right away," he explained, referring to his thirteen-year-old daughter. "Remember when I told you my former wife Hedwig's mother was suffering from lung cancer? Well, she passed away this morning, and Leah is devastated. *Scheisse*, what an awful disease."

"I'm so sorry," Angelika whispered.

When Clara had died, Angelika hadn't been free to seek Daniel's comfort. Not after Rudolf Eder had insisted she not see the man rumoured to be her real father. If Rudolf discovered Angelika had been spending so much time with Daniel after returning to Vienna, he'd be furious about that, as well. But fortunately, as far as Rudolf Eder was concerned, the passage of time had bred a growing degree of indifference regarding everything Angelika did.

"Go," she said. Leah shouldn't have to suffer alone, without Daniel, just because Angelika once had. "Don't worry about me. I'll be fine."

Yet Angelika's voice had wavered as she said it, and Daniel spent a couple of quick minutes reassuring her. He then promised to try his best to listen in on the radio during the scene in which she'd be singing.

"*Toi, toi, toi, Annichen.*"

But after he'd wished her luck and left, the theatre felt empty and cold, and Angelika slunk away into a powder room, trying to gather her wits as *Don Carlo*'s first act began playing out upon the stage. There had to be something that might help settle her, but what?

Still pondering, Angelika reached around the back of her costume, where a scratchy sewn-in tag had started coming loose. Not wanting to enlist the help of a dresser for such a simple matter, Angelika did her best to adjust the errant scrap of cloth herself. But try as she might, she couldn't coax it into lying flat. At least not without taking off the costume.

With a frustrated sigh, Angelika shimmied out of the gown and glanced at the tag – a long, thin strip bearing the initials of all those who had previously worn it. After Angelika had selected the costume the previous evening, a dresser had added a flourished *AE* at the bottom, marking it as Angelika's own for the benefit performance. But it was only now that Angelika paused to examine the other sets of initials that had gone before. Including one in particular, quite faded and barely visible, imprinted at the top – *CE*.

A yelp escaped Angelika's throat, and she ran her fingers across the letters, almost as if by doing so, the previous year might fall away and she would find herself transported into the past.

CE. Clara Eder. Angelika's own beloved mother.

Perhaps Clara had worn the gown during her turn as the Celestial Voice, or perhaps she had worn it while singing another role. Either way, the dress had surely been taken in and let out countless times over the past two decades, and donned by the dozen others whose initials graced the tag. What were the odds Angelika would select that very costume to wear while making her own debut?

"Oh, thank you, Mama," she whispered.

She could do this. She could really and truly do this.

Calmness returning, Angelika's heartbeat settled into a sure and steady rhythm as she stepped back into the gown, left the powder room and allowed a dresser to verify that everything appeared intact. All Angelika's many years of admiring her mother, of studying, of losing her voice and then finding it again with the loving help of Lotte Lehmann, Daniel, Andreas, Erich and Gretchen – all of it would soon culminate in a singular, life-altering instance of operatic magic.

"Fly to the sky." Just as she had the previous evening during rehearsal, Angelika sang in flawless Italian, Verdi's score filling her soul and Clara's spirit lighting the way. "Fly, poor suffering people. Hasten toward peace."

Angelika could hear gasps carry throughout the audience as patrons beheld Clara Eder's daughter standing centre stage and pouring her heart out, just as her famous mother so often had.

"*Brava, brava!*"

The cheers erupted before Angelika had finished singing, then continued as the scene wound its way toward a conclusion, no heckling or vicious utterances to be heard. A long series of drumrolls soon resounded, and Angelika looked into the front row of the audience, able to make out the familiar forms of Erich and Gretchen seated to one side, dazed and motionless, not even clapping. But why? Hadn't she done a spectacular job? Weren't they proud?

Forcing her expression to remain untroubled, Angelika scanned the rest of the first row, everyone else appearing exuberant and boisterous. Especially one patron in particular. A man in his mid-twenties, with slicked-back hair and piercing eyes Angelika could discern even amidst the dimmed lighting. A man she could suddenly recall having seen in person a couple of times before, once during her winter recital in Munich and once in the middle of a brown-shirted crowd at the beer garden. A man whose identity she had never before acknowledged. Not until the present moment, when the man before her and the one whose likeness she'd seen in the newspapers merged to become one and the same.

Baldur von Schirach. The Nazi who had sent her the letter about appearing at the propaganda concert. A man Angelika had written back to, claiming she couldn't possibly sing in the National Socialists' show due to stage fright.

Stage fright! Already a feeble excuse at the time, and now, one that rang entirely hollow coming from a young woman who had delivered the performance of her life while standing centre stage before a significantly sized audience.

No. No!

The house, the set pieces, the theatre's exquisite ceiling fresco depicting nine Greek muses – everything seemed to close in around Angelika as she and Baldur von Schirach locked eyes, a final drumroll rumbled, a proverbial flicker of flames consumed *Don Carlo*'s heretics and the stage's heavy red curtain made its inevitable descent.

*

"What in Mozart's name was I thinking?" Still dressed in her costume, Angelika lay trembling upon the cold, hard floor of a backstage prop room, her head in Erich's lap as he wiped a steady stream of sweat from her brow. At Angelika's insistence, he and Gretchen had both been summoned to her side after the opera had ended. Not that there was much they could do. Not when Angelika had made so grave an error in judgement. "How could I go onstage like that, after I'd already sent Baldur von Schirach a letter claiming to have stage fright?"

How she'd managed making it through the rest of the engagement – curtsying, congratulating her fellow singers and politely declining interview requests from newspaper reporters and radiomen – Angelika didn't know. What she did know for certain was that as soon as she'd returned backstage after singing, she'd discovered a bouquet of crimson roses lying upon her make-up table, along with an accompanying card.

I am overjoyed to see that you have overcome your stage fright, it had read. *After you have completed your recital competition in two weeks' time, I will expect to see you back in Munich. There, along with appearing at our October concert, you will have the wonderful opportunity to begin studies with an excellent group of teachers we have hand-selected to further your progress.*

You will also have the honour to sing and perform, for the glory of Germany, at numerous future engagements. With our support, and in light of our powerful influence, you can rest assured that no one will ever again accuse you of being related to a Jew. A girl of your talent can surely see the mutual benefit in this arrangement, as well as the unfortunate consequences you would face should you attempt to refuse. Heil Hitler!

Baldur von Schirach

Baldur von Schirach's presence, as well as the card he'd obviously written ahead of time, indicated that even before the show began, he had known Angelika was set to appear onstage. If only Angelika had told Erich and Gretchen that she was planning to sing in the spotlight. While Erich could never have anticipated Schirach's turning up in Vienna, he certainly would have been concerned about the Nazis finding out. As would Gretchen, whom Angelika had a couple of nights earlier told the full story about Schirach's earlier letter and her subsequent response, in which she'd feigned stage fright.

"Someone told him," Angelika said, her melting make-up staining Erich's fingertips as they sat surrounded by piles of makeshift daggers, swords, axes and other murderous weapons. The card from Baldur von Schirach also lay discarded upon the floor, both Erich and Gretchen having read it. "Someone who was here for the dress rehearsal must have alerted Schirach. But who?"

It certainly hadn't been Daniel, Max Reinhardt or the maestro, all of whom hated and feared the Nazis. Angelika thought back to the night Baldur von Schirach's letter messenger had appeared outside the women's residence. But she had never seen that young man before or since. Could he have sneaked into the theatre during rehearsal? Had one of the disgruntled choristers spilled the secret? Or perhaps a stagehand? Angelika had no idea.

"I'm so stupid." Angelika's voice, laden with beauty and eloquence a short while earlier, now felt broken and strained. "A complete and utter *Dummkopf*."

"You are not." Erich's own voice was dangerously

quiet, and even angrier than the time he'd confronted the hateful boys at Café Central, or when a reporter had forced his way into Angelika's house in Munich. "You were a sensation out there. A goddammed goddess. And now, that monster's stolen it from you."

"We saw him walk in and sit down right before the show started," Gretchen said, her floor-length violet dress rumpled and her face splotched with tears. "Someone else was already sitting in that spot, but Schirach 'encouraged' him to move."

Angelika ran her hands across her face and into her hair, the vine-adorned headband coming loose and clattering to the floor.

"We were afraid he'd found out about the opera and had come to hear you sing," Gretchen said, "but we at least thought that since you'd be singing offstage, things might be all right. Then, all of a sudden, there you were, centre stage, standing in the spotlight."

Angelika's thus far elusive tears threatened to make an appearance.

"All I could think about these past couple of days was making my debut," she said. "I was so caught up in honouring my mother's memory and trying to become a famous singer. And now…" A blood-curdling fear arose in the pit of her stomach. "I'm afraid there's no way out. No solution. Schirach and his friends want to control me. They want to select my teachers and have a say in everything I sing. They want me to be theirs in exchange for fame and stardom, but on the Nazis' terms, in a way that helps them."

"We'll find an answer," Erich said, swiping away the couple of tears that had started to dampen Angelika's cheeks.

"What if we can't? I cannot go back to Munich, sing for the Nazis and become their protégé. But what will they do to me, and everyone I love, if I refuse?"

Erich's strong arms lifted Angelika into a sitting position, and Gretchen went to fetch her a glass of water. As far as they all knew, Baldur von Schirach had left as soon as the opera ended, Erich having watched him get into a chauffeured car and drive away. But how long would it be before his shadow once again darkened Angelika's sightline?

"I have an idea," Erich whispered into her ear after Gretchen had left the room. "I know someone who might be able to help us, and a way we can work together to help him in return. He despises the Nazis, too. But we can't talk about it here."

"Who is it you're thinking about?" Unable to resist asking, Angelika dried her eyes and stared at Erich. "Doctor Hoffmann?"

"No. Someone else."

Angelika didn't know who Erich might mean, but she did know she couldn't bear to stay inside the theatre any longer. She must change back into her teal day dress, gather some things at the women's residence and accompany Erich to Daniel's flat, where he could also change, gather his belongings and leave a note. Then, just as she'd envisioned the night before, Angelika must take Erich out of Vienna, away from everyone and everything, to her family's lakeside estate near Salzburg. Now more than ever, she needed to be alone with the young man she loved, one of the few people she knew she could trust.

"You want to ride three hours to Salzburg in a sidecar?" Erich asked after she'd told him her idea. "It'll be a rough trip."

"I don't care." Angelika rose to stand, relieved to at least have some remaining agency as far as her whereabouts were concerned. Agency the Nazis intended to take away as soon as possible. "With everything that's happened today, I would ride to Salzburg horseback if I knew it would get us there."

A rough motorcycle ride was the least of Angelika's cares. A rough motorcycle ride, she could handle, even as an uncertain future threatened to rattle her to pieces.

"Andreas, I'm lost." She whispered it into the whirling air as the ebony BMW motorbike hurtled out of the city a short while later, Erich in the driver's seat and Angelika riding in the sidecar with his leather jacket wrapped around her. "Andreas, I need you."

If only her brother could have been there to answer.

Nineteen

As if borne backward through time into the memories of her girlhood, Angelika sat perched at the end of a wide wooden dock overlooking Lake Fuschl, its ancient glacial water lapping her toes amidst a backdrop of shadowed Alpine foothills and a starry, moonless sky. Only this time, instead of her mother or Andreas helping drink in a melody of croaking frogs and rustling pines, it was Erich Bauer seated by Angelika's side.

"How about I go back inside the house and get us some blankets?" he asked, lips close to Angelika's ear as he embraced her from behind.

Though a nighttime chill filled the air, Erich had insisted, to no objection from Angelika, upon removing his shirt and shoes. Which had in turn prompted her to follow suit, stripping away her sandals and stockings, then dipping her feet into the water while Erich's hands skimmed along her curves.

"There used to be a big pile of blankets in the library." Angelika gestured toward her family's villa. "Think you can find them?"

In spite of Erich's heated touch, she couldn't help feeling cold, though hardly from the water tickling her toes or the harbingers of impending autumn that carried on the breeze. Try as she might, Angelika couldn't stop reliving the moment triumph had turned to terror as she'd stood onstage at the Theater an der Wien and locked eyes with Baldur von Schirach.

"I'll look." Erich ran a warm palm across Angelika's arm before standing and taking one of their two lanterns in hand. "Just don't decide to go swimming without me."

Angelika allowed herself a chuckle, then listened as Erich's footsteps retreated up the dock and headed in the direction of a bicycling path, glass-enclosed gazebo and back terrace staircase. It was far too dark, and the water too cold, for swimming. But the late-summer sojourn provided a most perfect opportunity for snuggling and, if Angelika had her way, perhaps something more than that.

"Oh!"

She stifled a giggle as a wayward fingerling fish nibbled at her digits. Angelika could only hope Daniel had by then discovered the note explaining that she and Erich were visiting Salzburg, and would return the following day. Despite the audacious implications of such an outing, she knew open-minded Daniel would scarcely bat an eyelash.

Unlike the middle-aged caretakers who lived near the lake and had opened up the estate for Angelika a couple of hours earlier. They'd appeared as wide-eyed as owls at the sight of an all-grown-up Fräulein Eder rematerialising unchaperoned and with a strapping young man on her arm.

"Look what I found," Erich called out as he returned several minutes later. "An old picnic basket with a bottle of expensive-looking French wine inside." He set down the wicker basket, lantern and several woollen coverlets. "I tossed in the rest of the sourdough bread and beer cheese we bought on the way here, plus the candy sticks the caretakers gave us. And some silverware and glasses I found in a hutch."

The lantern-light flickered across Erich's eager, boyish face as he uncorked the bottle, poured the wine – probably a late-1920s cabernet franc Clara had purchased in Paris – and handed Angelika a glass, along with a plate of bread, cheese and cherry-flavoured candy.

"Not exactly a feast worthy of my saucy sea siren," Erich said, "but I hope it'll hold you over until I can scrape together something better."

Angelika shook her head and took a long, luscious sip of the full-bodied wine, its blackberry afternotes tantalising her tongue. Being at the lake house without the familiar sounds of Clara's melodious laughter, Andreas's tinkling piano or even Rudolf's scolding admonitions seemed beyond bizarre, and yet, with Erich by her side, Angelika knew she could weather the bittersweet memories of the past. Memories that several months earlier might have drowned her, but now left her bobbing on the surface, occasionally buffeted and carried away in the current, yet largely in control of her heart's inner harbour.

"There's nothing better." Angelika slid closer and tipped her head against Erich's shoulder – his body solid and sure, a worthy anchor. "Nothing better than this. And no one better than you. With everything that's happened today... making my debut, seeing Schirach, coming back here for the first time since losing Mama... I couldn't imagine doing this with anyone else."

After giving Erich a grateful kiss, she sat up, took another hearty gulp of wine and filled her grumbling stomach with sustenance.

"I only wish we had more time." Angelika's voice caught as she soon set aside her empty dish and glass. "Time to be together and finish making our plans. With the Nazis trying to control my future... I mean, I don't know what's going to happen once they..."

Erich relinquished his own polished-clean plate, then pulled Angelika into his arms.

"I know things look bad." He brushed aside a lock of her wild, wind-tussled hair, a lingering effect of the three-hour motorcycle ride from Vienna. "But remember what we promised on the way out here. That we would let ourselves have this night together without thinking about any of them. Because none of those monsters are here right now. Tonight, it's just you and me. Only us."

Angelika turned so that she straddled Erich's lap, the dock beneath them creaking as she found his mouth at the same time his fingertips wove their way up her torso, grazing her breasts through the light, crepe fabric of her frock. After her teal day dress had ended up covered in dirt following the motorcycle ride, Angelika had rediscovered and changed into an old eyelet-adorned outfit she loved. From the feel of things, Erich fancied it, too.

"And I promise you that even if it kills me, I will find

a way out of this fiasco with the Nazis." Erich sounded confident as ever, and his chapped lips tasted like sugar and wine. "I won't walk away or give up. I may not have much money at the moment, or know how to tell the difference between a Wolfgang Wagner opera or a Richard Mozart aria, but I know how much I love you."

Angelika's thoughts flashed back to the prop room at the theatre, after *Don Carlo*, when Erich had vaguely referenced someone who might be able to help her evade the National Socialists. She'd planned to ask him more about it, but in the chaos of getting to the lake and arranging things with the caretakers, had held off on doing so. Because as self-assured as Erich appeared, who could he possibly know that could help? What could Erich do that might make one iota of a difference when it came to a group as brutal and powerful as the Nazis?

For the dozenth time that day, Angelika pushed the thoughts aside. Especially since it seemed she was about to become preoccupied with something else. The original something she'd longed for in the first place.

"Erich." Angelika whispered his name – a desire, a promise, a certainty. "*Mein* Erich. The only one I want. The only one I love."

Angelika deepened her kiss, then playfully pulled back, gently biting and wilfully teasing, as all the while, her fevered fingers travelled down Erich's bare chest and stomach at a speed that rivalled Rimsky-Korsakov's "Flight of the Bumblebee".

"You really were a goddess today." Erich groaned against Angelika's neck as her fingertips found his trousers.

"You've always been a goddess. A beautiful, smart, sassy, goddamned goddess. Any man would give his last *Reichsmark* to be with you, and somehow, here I am."

His adept hands made easy work of the pearl buttons adorning the front of Angelika's dress, though in Erich's haste, a handful popped loose and scattered.

"Sorry." He pulled the dress up and over Angelika's head, her chemise and brassiere next disappearing to reveal bare, goosebump-covered breasts she wanted him to touch. "Those pearls weren't real, were they?"

"No. Never mind about them."

Angelika rolled backward onto the pile of blankets, Erich hovering above her as he stroked the tips of her breasts and covered her body in kisses. Fumbling in the dim glow of the lanterns, she lowered his slacks and briefs, then cried out in delicious, giggling glee as Erich pressed his lips between her legs before sliding away silken, lace-trimmed panties.

"Did you bring something we can use?" she asked.

Angelika knew she should have enquired sooner. For if Erich hadn't come prepared, they'd be limited to an unclothed encore of what she had once carried out with Kurt while sprawled across her music room sofa. But Erich thankfully nodded. He removed a rubber from a pocket of the pants he was no longer wearing, and then effortlessly readied himself.

"What a sly devil you are, Erich Bauer." Angelika snaked her limbs around him, she and Erich at last lying skin-to-skin and soul-to-soul. "You've done this before."

"Twice," Erich admitted, manoeuvring so that he and

Angelika nestled in between two of the blankets. "Before I knew you. With a girl I met during Fasching. I was sixteen and stupid, and I didn't love her this way. I've never loved anyone the way I love you. I mean, I never—"

Angelika silenced him with another long series of kisses, her impatient body taking control and willing him forward. She had almost done it, too, and would have if not for Kurt lacking protection. But none of that mattered at the moment. None of it changed the new and exciting, yet also undeniably deep, connection Angelika felt with Erich.

"I may have been your tutor in school," she whispered, forehead pressing against his. "But tonight, I suppose you'll have to be mine."

With that, she let her head drop against the blanket, a squeal rising as their two bodies melded together as one. Angelika had feared she might experience the rush of pain other young women described, but in her own unique experience, nothing but bliss transpired.

"Erich," she gasped. "*Mon chérie. Amore mio.*"

Endearments in all four of her mastered languages rolled off Angelika's tongue as she and Erich swayed together in easy harmony.

"My goddess, my enchantress," he crooned in response. "*Je t'aime, ma chérie.* I told you I would make you sing."

Only Angelika wasn't just singing. She was sailing and soaring – the boat dock, the lake, the wine bottle that very well may have toppled over, plus any worries and fears – temporarily evaporating. In this unmatchable instance, she was invincible and unstoppable. Angelika was used to shattering from pain and sadness, not from pleasure or joy. Not from the rush of ethereal ecstasy that flooded her spirit.

Who knew what the future would hold? In the midst of such a moment, all she knew was the sound of Erich's name on her lips as she sang it, clearly and confidently, to the infinite, star-speckled sky above.

*

"I can't wait for you to see the lake in the daylight." Angelika rested her cheek against Erich's chest, both of them remaining snuggled beneath the blankets, their breathing having calmed and a pleasant afterglow setting in. "The water's the loveliest shade of turquoise, and there's even a fairytale castle in the distance."

She could hear Erich's heartbeat echoing in her ear and feel his breath rustling her hair, just like the wind off the water, which seemed to be picking up. They'd have to move inside before too long, after which time Angelika planned to spend the night enveloped in her sweetheart's arms, making love again and again between soft satin sheets. As long as he was feeling up to it, of course.

"How are your injuries?" she asked. "Are you in any pain?"

Erich sighed in response, offering a non-verbal admission. Perhaps there'd be no more lovemaking that night after all. At least not the type they'd just enjoyed. And yet, when Angelika suggested as much to Erich, he raised up onto his elbows so quickly, she feared the dock might give way.

"You think I'm going to let my father's broomstick beating stop me from being with you tonight?" As if to make his point, Erich sank back down and pulled Angelika flush against his sweat-beaded body. "Not a chance. Even though next time, I guess an actual bed wouldn't hurt. And some pillows. Definitely pillows."

"That, I can arrange." In spite of her raw and burning lips, Angelika drew him into another delightful kiss. "It's a good thing I'm not a real siren, either, because I could never bear to see you drown. Not when I'd much rather make you happy, and keep you on my island forever."

A boisterous blast of wind materialised, threatening to send their discarded clothing aloft.

"We'd better go in," Angelika said. "I think a storm might be coming."

She and Erich reluctantly reclothed, save for shoes and stockings, then set about gathering picnic items and blankets. As Angelika had anticipated, the remainder of the cabernet franc had indeed met an unceremonious end.

"Go on ahead." She knelt down, grabbed a pile of linen napkins and began blotting a blue-and-white blanket that had borne the brunt of the spill. "I'll be right behind you."

Erich set off toward the house as an even stronger gust of wind rattled the dock and sent lake water sloshing over its edge, practically toppling Angelika's lantern.

"*Ach*, no."

She hurried to steady the light source, noticing as she did that a folded slip of paper had lodged itself in between a too-close-together set of wooden dock slats. Something that had fallen from the picnic basket, perhaps? An old letter of Clara's? Angelika's heart leapt in anxious anticipation as she unfolded it. What she discovered, however, was not a letter comprised in her mother's elegant handwriting, but rather in Erich's familiar hen-scratch. The yet-to-be-mailed communiqué must have fallen from a trouser pocket in the midst of his and Angelika's fevered frenzy. Only…

Her heartbeat, having somewhat settled after the lovemaking, resumed its wild beating.

Chère Lily, the letter began.

"No." Angelika's eyes widened while skimming the page. "It can't be."

But it was.

French. Erich had written the letter in French. And not the bumbling, comically bad French he'd written and spoken the entire time Angelika had known him. No, this letter had been composed in perfect, impeccable, unimpeachable French. The French of someone who not only understood the language well, but had for quite some time. Someone whose comprehension rivalled, if not surpassed, Angelika's.

Her wavering breaths intermingled with the worsening wind as she held the parchment to the light and read in closer detail.

Dear Lily, the letter said in French. *I'm sure that by now, you've gotten my telegram letting you know I left Munich. Since I'm not there anymore, I can be less cryptic than usual. But I figured I'd keep up our usual tradition of writing these letters in French. I miss you, and hope Little Miss Dancer liked the music box I sent her. Right now, I'm in*

Vienna visiting Angelika. She's here for a singing programme and still doesn't know about our plans. She doesn't know anything about you, or us.

Us? The wind threatened to carry the letter away, but Angelika held fast to it, continuing to read against her better judgement.

A couple of weeks ago in Munich, Angelika told me her mother once knew the opera singer Rosalind von Schirach, whose brother is the National Socialists' youth leader. I haven't asked her anything else about it yet, but depending what she remembers, the information may be of use to us.

Us...

Once again, there was that simple yet significant word. Us.

I also heard something I'm afraid will devastate Angelika. I've been staying with Daniel Weiss, a Viennese opera director Angelika believes is her real father. But last night, while he was showing me some pictures in an old album, we found a couple of letters pressed between the pages. I didn't read them, but Herr Weiss said they were letters written between him and Angelika's mother. Letters saying that, based on the timing of things, neither one of them believed Herr Weiss could really be Angelika's father.

"What?"

He said that during the time Angelika and her twin brother would have been conceived, he and Clara hadn't been able to see each other that way. But the two of them always loved each other and wished they could have been a family. Clara apparently told the twins she didn't know for sure whether Daniel was their real father, because in her heart, she wanted it to be the truth. She didn't want to accept the reality that Rudolf Eder, her cold and cruel husband, was her children's father. And she wanted Angelika to hold onto that same sort of hope.

"No. This cannot be true."

Herr Weiss asked my opinion about whether he should tell Angelika the truth, especially since the two of them have been getting closer. He doesn't want to ruin the relationship, because he loves her, too. At the same time, he doesn't want to be dishonest. And with the Nazis gaining strength, he says it's probably safer and better if Angelika knows she isn't his daughter. Even though a lot of people will go on believing it anyway, for better or worse, just as they did before her mother died. And even though the Nazis' sickening beliefs are unfair to Angelika and Daniel, who both deserve each other's love.

I told him I didn't have an answer yet. Do you have any advice? You always knew what to do and say, and ever since you left three summers ago, I've been muddling through without you.

There were a couple of remaining lines, but Angelika stopped reading as the world came to a screeching halt around her. Daniel. Kind, caring, wonderful Daniel Weiss. A man Angelika loved as a father, but who wasn't really hers. After all the years she'd believed it to be so. After all the years that she had, in spite of the scandals and prejudiced people's wickedness, imagined and wanted it to be so, deep down inside.

"Oh, Daniel."

And aside from that, what of Erich Bauer? A young

man Angelika had thought she knew and could trust. A young man to whom she'd given her faith, love and body. A young man who had apparently been keeping secrets and lying to her the entire time she'd known him.

"Anni?" His voice called out from behind, the wind and Angelika's own state of panic having allowed him to approach without her hearing. "What are you still doing out here? The sky's about to open up any minute. Not that we wouldn't have fun pulling each other out of our wet clothes afterward. But…"

Erich stopped speaking and drew up beside her, stilling when he saw the letter she clutched.

"I can explain," he said without the slightest waver. "Come inside, and I promise I'll tell you everything."

But Angelika was going nowhere. Not yet, and certainly not with him.

"How could you do this to me?" She spit the words through clenched teeth while rising to stand. "After I've trusted you all this time, and after I bent over backward trying to teach you a language you already understood."

Angelika crumpled the letter, and then, before she could stop herself, flung it into the lake as a dusting of raindrops began to fall.

"I wanted to tell you." Erich offered his hand, but Angelika moved away. "All along, I wanted to tell you the truth. That yes, I really spoke French. But they told me I couldn't. Not yet, anyway."

"They? Who are 'they'?"

"Some people I know. Some people I… help. I never expected to waltz into school one morning and meet a brilliant, breathtaking new girl from Vienna who understood four languages. A girl who was an expert at French and, of all things, wanted to tutor a rascal like me."

"You could have said no," Angelika answered.

"You're right. I could have. And I probably should have. But… Damn it, Anni, I already told you that's the day I fell in love with you. How could I have guessed you'd love me, too, and that we'd end up being together like this?"

"And you were never going to tell me the truth?"

"I was going to," Erich said. "Tonight. I was going to tell you everything."

"Why should I believe you?"

Raindrops streaked across Angelika's cheeks like frigid tears. Erich again attempted to reach for her, but she flung his hand away. He'd also slipped up while they were making love, she realised, having spoken a line in French then, too. But she'd felt too euphoric to focus on it at the time.

"Why should I believe that you are anything but a scoundrel?" she said. "An insufferable liar who speaks French and writes mysterious letters to a woman named Lily? She's the girl you met during Fasching, isn't she? The one you were with before you knew me?" A steady, punishing rain continued battering the dock as Angelika fired off questions like an archer shooting arrows. "What about this 'Little Miss Dancer' you mentioned? Is she your and Lily's daughter?"

"Man alive, no. Lily, as we call her, is my older sister. And there's a good reason we started writing our letters in French."

"Your sister?" Now Angelika had heard everything. "You expect me to believe that after all this time, you have a secret sister you've never once talked about?"

"I know it sounds ridiculous." The storm had doused the lanterns, leaving Angelika and Erich bathed only in a faint glow of light from the house. "But you're asking me question after question, as if you were a professor drilling students in multiplication tables. And then you're not giving me a chance to explain. Come here, all right? Please."

Erich opened his arms, and for a split second, Angelika considered rushing into them. But then she thought about Paul and Kurt, two young men she had trusted, and who had later let her down. Two beaus who had played her like a fiddle, then taken hammers to her heart.

"Don't touch me," she choked out, rain drenching her mostly buttonless dress and dishevelled hair. "We shouldn't have done this tonight. I made a terrible mistake."

Erich's calm face faltered, crumpling in such a way that Angelika couldn't tell whether the streaks of water soaking his own cheeks were raindrops or tears. Perhaps he was right, and she ought to at least give him the chance to explain. However, unfair as it might be, Angelika wasn't about to allow him to get the best of her again. Instead of giving Erich the chance he desired, she turned on her bare heel and began storming up the dock, hastening toward the house in the middle of a deluge.

"If you want to explain yourself so badly, why don't you go back to Vienna and speak to Daniel?" she called over her shoulder. "Seeing how you two had such a grand time talking about me behind my back, when he told you he isn't really my father."

"Anni, wait." Erich's footsteps raced after her. "This isn't the way I wanted you to find out. And neither did Herr Weiss. He loves you. In his heart and in his head, he wants to be your father just as much as you want to be his daughter."

Angelika spun to face Erich, his mangled curls lying flat against his face as the rain tumbled off them in rivulets.

"All this time, I believed Daniel was the one," she said. "My real father. And now I know he's not."

"Isn't he, though? Look, there's more to love and family than whose bodies we come from, or what it says on some lousy birth record, or what sorts of rumours people spread. Doctor Hoffmann told me a long time ago that he thinks family is something we can choose. And that goes for me, too. Viktor Bauer may be the man who created me, but he isn't a father. Not like Stefan Hoffmann, who's helped support me my entire life. He's been more of a father than Viktor ever was."

Coursing adrenaline and the enduring rain made Angelika's eyes go blurry. She wanted to believe Erich was right, but it was all too much to bear. How could her mother and Daniel have kept this from her? How could Daniel claim to have loved her since the first time he'd laid eyes upon her as a newborn baby, if even then, he'd known she wasn't his?

"Don't run away." Erich laid a cold, wet hand against Angelika's arm. "Herr Weiss loves you, and so do I. I'm sorry I lied about speaking French, but I've never lied to you about anything else. And I never will."

Angelika paused to reconsider, then banished the possibility. She'd thought she was ready to choose a new role for herself by returning to Vienna, deepening her relationship with Daniel, making her operatic debut and opening her heart to Erich. Yet it had all been a dreadful mistake. She should never have taken the risk. Should never have thought she had the inner strength. Angelika had lost her mother, and now she was losing Erich and Daniel, too. In the end, loving others only resulted in hurt and loss.

"Take your explanation to the devil," she said, eschewing Erich's grasp and resuming her steady march up the dock. "Or Lily. Or…"

Angelika had made it only a couple of quick strides before a small object scuttled beneath the sole of her bare foot. Something circular and smooth.

One of the wayward pearl buttons that had taken leave of her dress a short while earlier.

"Anni, watch out." Erich reached for her as she wobbled, but even his quick reflexes proved inadequate. "*Nein!*"

Angelika's shriek merged with Erich's as she flew backward off the edge of the dock, plummeted into the cold lake with a resounding splash, and then – before she could so much as suck in a breath – disappeared beneath its inky black, rain-spattered surface.

Twenty

azy visions flashed before Angelika's eyes as a rainstorm raged above her head and cold water enveloped her body in a cloak of blinding black.

So, this is the way it's going to be? Daniel's words, spoken when she'd visited his flat a week earlier, rippled across Angelika's psyche. *You're going to run away, using your own pain as a vengeful weapon, without giving me a chance to explain?*

And now, she'd done precisely the same thing to Erich.

"Angelika! If you can hear me, say something."

She could hear his voice crying out as she briefly resurfaced, then dipped back underwater, the dress weighing her down while she panicked and drifted in darkness. Bobbing her head above the waterline, Angelika tried swimming toward the dock, but the driving rain and windblown waves made it impossible.

"*Hilfe!*"

She screamed into the night, wincing as an unwanted slosh of rain and lake water entered her mouth. Angelika spat it back out, but feared she'd soon succumb to the storm's power, disappearing amidst the dank depths until her drowned corpse was discovered the following morning.

"Lean against my back, Anni." A voice more powerful than Poseidon's materialised beside her, and a muscular arm encircled her waist. "And wrap your arms around my neck. Hold on tight, and let me do the rest."

She did as Erich instructed, clinging to him while his resilient body, as strong and certain as the medieval fortress overlooking Salzburg, hauled her safely to the rain-soaked dock and hoisted her over the side.

"*Scheisse*, are you all right?" Erich said after he, too, had scrambled onto not-so-dry land. "For a scintillating sea siren, you're not the strongest swimmer." The rain continued to fall in heavy, drenching sheets. "Let's get inside before the entire dock floods."

Remnants of their picnic, including a couple of blankets, the empty wine bottle and both lanterns, were already gone.

"Erich, I..."

Though still upset about his understanding French and keeping it a secret, Angelika knew she should indeed give him a chance to explain. Could Erich really have a sister? And was there some sort of connection between the letter he'd written to a woman called Lily and what he'd told Angelika after the opera? That someone might be able to help her elude the Nazis, while at the same time giving her a chance to do something in return? But the battering wind and rain negated any hope of having a conversation until they were indoors.

"Come on," she said, gesturing toward the villa, its lamplit windows ready to guide the way. "Let's hurry."

No sooner had they started for the house, however, than Angelika spotted two ghostly pinpoints of light, as if a mirage in the darkness, easing their way up the drive. But alas, it wasn't a mirage, for several moments later, a cream-coloured Rolls-Royce Phantom pulled to a stop and a familiar young man emerged from the backseat. A young man wearing a rumpled tuxedo, toting a large black umbrella and bearing a telltale look in his eyes.

"Oh no." Angelika rushed to meet her former sweetheart alongside the idling automobile, its chauffeur still seated behind the wheel. "What's happened? You look as if someone has died."

A fresh wave of terror gripped Angelika as she and Kurt von Hügel stood frozen upon the very spot they'd first met – the stone pavers, once so hot beneath her dress, now feeling cold and damp against her stockingless feet.

Was it Andreas? Was he dead, just as in the foreboding dream she'd had? And yet, had it been Andreas, Angelika would have surely sensed that her beloved twin's heart had stilled. It couldn't be him. It simply couldn't.

"Good heavens," Kurt said, shouting to be heard above the roar of the rain. He looked Angelika up and down, taking in her soaked, practically buttonless dress. "You look a fright." Kurt pulled her beneath the shelter of his open umbrella and eyed Erich more warily than Little Red Riding Hood when she realised there was a wolf in her grandmother's bed. "What on earth have you done to her, Erich?"

But Angelika cared nothing about Kurt's jealousy or his concern for her well-being. Not when she feared the curtain had fallen upon another friend or loved one's life.

"Never mind any of that," she demanded. "Has something awful happened?"

"*Ja*." Kurt gripped Angelika's sopping shoulder with his free hand and drew her closer. "I was able to telephone Gretchen in Vienna, and given the circumstances, I convinced her to tell me you'd come here. She said you made the trip by riding in the sidecar of a motorbike."

He scowled in the direction of a vehicle shed where, as he correctly seemed to assume, the motorcycle had been parked.

"There was a business banquet in Munich tonight," Kurt continued, face twisting in despair. "Toward the end of it, Rudolf sounded winded and seemed uncomfortable. My father wanted to send for a physician, but Rudolf refused the help. He was giving a toast before dessert, and just as the servers brought out the strudel, he keeled over."

"So, you're saying…"

"It was a heart attack. He's dead. I'm so sorry, Angelika. We can ride into Munich tomorrow morning, so that you can pay your respects."

At that, the glare from the vehicle's headlamps faded from view, and the black of night overtook Angelika. As her knees wobbled and her body teetered, she glanced toward Erich, who stood several paces away in the rain and rushed forward at the same time Kurt moved to block his path.

A litany of shouting and cursing ensued, although

Angelika couldn't fully make out the words, her vision beginning to explode with stars as her knees continued to buckle. If she fainted and hit the pavers, she might break her bones and crack her skull.

"Help…" But she was already collapsing. "No…"

A pair of sturdy arms, just in the nick of time.

"Erich?"

Angelika passed out, certain that once again, he had continued to stand steadfastly by her side, breaking her fall.

*

Rudolf Eder, dead.

Angelika turned the words over in her head as she stared out of the backseat window of Kurt's chauffeured automobile, the heart of Munich coming into view across the Isar River amidst an array of late-morning sunlight.

"Won't you please speak to me, Angelika?"

Kurt's question, and his subsequent attempt to grasp her hand, prompted Angelika to shift closer to the window, yanking away as if flicked by a flame rather than the cuffed sleeve of his suit jacket. While Angelika's hair was barely kempt and she wore a simple polka-dotted day dress she'd brought to the lake in her knapsack, Kurt had brought along his own fully stocked emergency suitcase. Indeed, he appeared more well-suited for attending Sunday Mass than for enduring an awkward two-hour automobile ride to Munich.

"I've nothing to say." Angelika scowled at the sight of

happy families picnicking in a park and strolling alongside the river as sunbeams reflected off its northward-flowing waters. A deceptively perfect Sunday unfolding before her jaded eyes. "Not after you sent Erich away from the lake house this morning before I'd woken up."

Angelika had a vague memory of coming to, being helped out of her wet dress – to the sound of more cacophonous arguing amongst the two young men – and then falling into a deep, dreamless sleep the night before. When she'd next awoken, the storm clouds had vanished, the sun was shining and the lake appeared as calm as a turquoise-blue sheet of ice. Erich, however, had already departed.

"For the final time, I did not send him away," Kurt said, his frown reflected in the car's spotlessly polished window. "Erich told me he needed to return to Munich in order to take care of something urgent this morning. I simply encouraged him to be on his way sooner rather than later."

"You insulted and badgered him, you mean. Honestly, Kurt, you could drive a hibernating bear from its den in the depths of winter."

"I showed you the note he left, didn't I?"

Yes, he had. And its words had been gutting.

I'll try finding you in Munich later today so that I can explain myself, Erich had written. *But everything you said to me last night, I deserved for lying. And even if you don't love me anymore or want to see me again, I'll never stop loving you. The past few days we've had together have been the best days of my life. Every time I have terrible Odyssey recollections, or almost pass out at the top of a Ferris wheel,*

*or see fields of daisies growing in the summertime, or read a
review for the opera Juan Carlo, I'll think of you.*

*I hope that someday, when you're a famous singer who's
free of the Nazis, just like I promised you would be, I'll get to
hear you sing again, too. Perhaps by then, if I'm lucky, you'd
at least be willing to give me your autograph. Because I still
want it. Just like I still want you.*

Angelika had memorised Erich's message, but
nevertheless felt the real letter burning a proverbial hole
in her dress pocket while the daisy clip and her other
belongings remained tucked away inside her knapsack.
Erich had left his leather jacket in her possession, too.
A certain indication that it still belonged to her. As,
apparently, did his heart.

"I knew Erich Bauer wasn't to be trusted," Kurt
muttered while Angelika's nose curled at the cloying smell
of his amber cologne. A scent she'd once relished, but
now, could scarcely stand. "I don't know everything that
transpired last night, but I can see that he's hurt you."

A lump formed in Angelika's throat, and her chin
began to wobble. If Kurt hadn't arrived, and Angelika
hadn't fainted, she would have given Erich a chance to
explain things after all. Yes, he had hurt her. Yes, she had
every right to be upset, and she didn't know whether,
explanation or not, she could bear to reopen her heart
again.

But there also had to be more to Erich's mysteriously
speaking French and conversing with Lily than Angelika
had given him credit for. In the note he'd written Angelika
that very morning, Erich had reiterated his promise to free

her from the Nazis. What did he mean, and why had he come back to Munich?

"I noticed the buttons torn from your dress, and saw that Erich's nose was black-and-blue, as if you had struggled against him." Kurt again reached for Angelika, and this time, she felt too tired and broken to bother pushing away his hand. "I wish you would let me take you to see Doctor Hoffmann."

Angelika sighed, and then, at long last, turned to face her former sweetheart.

"Erich didn't physically harm me," she said. "I swear it."

"But he let you down, then? Gave you cause to doubt him?"

Leave it to Kurt, the suave businessman, to cut to the heart of the matter, whether Angelika liked it or not.

"Yes," she whispered. "I'm terribly confused, and I don't know what to think or believe anymore. Perhaps I made a mistake in trusting Erich. Or perhaps I made a mistake in pushing him away. There are so many things troubling me right now."

Including the Nazis' grand plan for her future. Something Kurt knew nothing about. He didn't even know about her debut in *Don Carlo* as of yet. Nor the critical reviews that had appeared in the Vienna newspapers the caretakers had delivered to the lake that morning before she'd awoken, and which Kurt obviously hadn't read. Reviews penned by vile critics who had in the past disparaged Clara, and who now said Angelika had sung off-key, which she hadn't, and that she'd only gotten the role because of Daniel Weiss's supposed obsession with her. While she'd certainly also received positive reviews, the malicious ones had been heartrending.

"I promise to do whatever I can to help alleviate your worries," Kurt said. "Because whatever mistakes you've made, Anni, I have undoubtedly made a good many more. You were right to renounce me and end our courtship. I was overbearing and carried everything too far. I was trying to be the sort of man I thought I should be. The sort of man my father is, and the man he's groomed me to be. But I now see that I was wrong."

Angelika sucked in a shaky breath, her weary eyes widening as Kurt continued speaking.

"Before you cast me aside during that wretched telephone call, I had been planning to ask for your hand as soon as the young singers programme concluded. Surely, you must have known I was contemplating it. It's what my father and Rudolf wanted. It's what I wanted."

Kurt sighed like a schoolboy and squeezed Angelika's fingertips. Fingertips which, mere hours earlier, had blissfully held Erich Bauer close.

"And..." Kurt hesitated, clearing his throat as if to smooth over the uncharacteristic waver that had rattled his voice. "If you'd be willing to reconsider, I'd still love for us to become husband and wife."

For the hundredth time in the past couple of days, Angelika felt as if she were living out the plot of a convoluted Mozartian opera.

"You're proposing marriage to me?" she asked. "Right here and now?"

Unable to bear Kurt's imploring gaze, Angelika stared over his shoulder and out of the opposite window as the car wove its way through the city's centre, heading past the dual-domed Frauenkirche cathedral and the Rathaus-Glockenspiel clock with its imaginative dancing figurines that entertained onlookers each morning.

"I realise this isn't the ideal moment. However, I've thought of little else since our parting." Kurt's fingerhold was firm, but his voice sounded gentle as a newborn lamb's *baa*. "And if you aren't yet ready for marriage, perhaps you'd at least be willing to give me a second chance. A chance to show you that I can be the type of sweetheart you want and deserve. Especially now that... Well, now that you'll have to make some unexpected decisions about the future in light of Rudolf's death."

The death of a man Angelika hadn't loved and who had never loved her, either. Though Rudolf had always provided for her and Andreas at Clara's behest, everything in their lives following her death – from Clara's art collection, to her jewellery, to the money she had set aside for her children – had officially belonged to him. Angelika had known she couldn't count on his financial support forever, and nor had she wanted to.

But his sudden death left her uncertain as to what might happen going forward. It hardly seemed as if Andreas were blazing a magnificent trail toward managing the family business, and Angelika had a feeling Rudolf may have willed it and everything else to Kurt. The man who now wished to marry her.

"I hadn't mentioned this yet," Kurt said, "but I've

been in talks about a potential business opportunity in New York City. The government here is collapsing, and if we were married, we could go overseas together. Make a bold new start. And, if things went well with the business venture, we could provide opportunities for others to come and join us in…"

"…America."

Angelika whispered the name of a place she and her mother had always dreamt of visiting together. A place that now stood out as an overseas haven far away from the National Socialists. A place where others, including Andreas; Gretchen and her parents; Daniel and his children; and even Erich might someday be able to pursue a safer, better life. But would Baldur von Schirach and his men accept Angelika's marriage as a reason to release her from singing for them? Would the Nazis threaten Kurt, as well?

"You don't have to give me an answer right away." Kurt kissed her hand and continued speaking, oblivious to the dire thoughts running through Angelika's head. "But oh please, my dearest, won't you at least consider it? I know Erich caught your attention, but it doesn't sound as if you two are meant to be. You and I, on the other hand, have been acquainted for seven years. You know me well, and can trust there will be no unwelcome surprises. Especially now that I've realised what a louse I was. To you, and also to your brother."

In Kurt's hopeful eyes, Angelika saw glimmers of the inquisitive, defiant boy she'd first spoken with at Lake Fuschl so long ago. Perhaps she had indeed gone too far, too fast with Erich. And yet, being with him had felt effortless and easy, certain and sure.

"Please, Anni. Please say you'll think about it."

Angelika's exhausted mind didn't want to think about anything. Not after all that had happened, and not when she hardly knew who she was anymore, let alone who, if anyone, she wished to marry. And yet, what if Kurt was correct? What if she and Erich truly weren't meant to be?

"All right," Angelika heard herself mumble. "I'll think about it."

No sooner had she said it than the car screeched to a sudden halt, Angelika lurching forward and bracing herself against the dark leather seat in front.

"It's another march, sir." Otto, the forty-year-old chauffeur, cursed beneath his breath and adjusted his askew black uniform cap. "The *Sturmabteilung*."

Sure enough, a cadre of brown-shirted men goose-stepped in and around Rotkreuzplatz as scores of civilians, many on their way home from church, no less, lined the plaza, cheering and saluting in a fanatical frenzy.

"I'll find a different way around." Otto began manoeuvring the car toward Schulstrasse, the same street where Johann and his friends had several weeks earlier looted and burnt a newspaper office in a misguided attempt at defending Angelika's honour. "Have no fear, Fräulein Eder. We'll be safely on our way and at your house faster than you can say 'blast these bloodthirsty Nazis.'"

But Angelika hardly heard him. Not when all she could do was stare in disbelief at the throng of bystanders –

teenagers, young couples, parents with children, labourers and students – egging on the muddy parade of men before them.

"For freedom and bread, blood and soil!" the people cried as the National Socialist paramilitary force stomped past. "Arise, good Germans, arise!"

Their shouts filled the surrounding streets, echoing so loudly that, even through the closed windows of the automobile, Angelika could parse every ugly word.

"The Jews have taken everything and left hardworking Germans with nothing!" A middle-aged housewife screamed from the balcony of a flat overlooking the mayhem. "Now, we'll take it back. Death to the Jews! We'll end their global conspiracy once and for all."

More diabolical cheering ensued as Angelika clutched Kurt, their two hands entwined in a messy tangle, while inside her head, a familiar refrain began to play.

Anni, I'm lost. Anni, I need you.

Andreas?

From within the confines of the posh automobile, Angelika scanned the crowd, searching and dreading, until there, standing directly in front of the seven-storey Eder, von Hügel and Sons office building, with anger on his lips and his arm in the air, stood the sapphire-eyed, auburn-haired young man who had been an unwavering presence, and the melody to her harmony, all nineteen years of her life.

"Perhaps Winthirstrasse would be better," Otto said, backing up the vehicle.

"*Nein*, wait."

Angelika tore her hand from Kurt's, flung open the door and catapulted from the car, all the while keeping her eyes trained upon the familiar young man, his own face shifting as if he could suddenly sense his twin sister's proximity.

"Where are you going?" Kurt asked in alarm, neither he nor Otto having seemed to notice the young man in question. "Angelika, no, come back."

But she was already tearing across the plaza, dodging the marching storm troopers and pushing her way through a boisterous crowd.

"Andreas!"

Angelika needn't have screamed his name, because he had already fixed her in his gaze, watching agape as his sister accosted him on the sidewalk, yanking him backward and away from the throng.

"Anni?" A combination of horror and shock swam in Andreas's eyes while he and Angelika came to a halt alongside their family's business headquarters. "What are you doing here?"

Angelika didn't answer, she and her wayward twin standing face-to-face, eye-to-eye, and yet also worlds apart.

Too late. She had been too late. Too late to save her mother, and too late to save Andreas. For while his heart still beat, the rhythm it kept seemed forever changed. And now, she would lose him, too.

"Adolf Hitler will end our suffering," the people cried. "He'll fill our bellies and give us work. He alone can restore German greatness!"

Angelika stared at Andreas's shirt collar, where a burnished swastika pin sat poised like a black tarantula.

No, it wasn't that she would lose her brother.

The terrible truth was that she already had.

Twenty-One

"**W**hat are you doing here?"

Andreas repeated his question, cheeks burning a deeper shade of crimson than the turreted red-brick building beside which he and Angelika stood. The same familiar family business headquarters she had once regarded as romantic and castle-like, but which now seemed garish and grotesque.

"I'd like to ask you the same thing." Angelika shouted to be heard over an ever-increasing roar of the crowd, plus echoing thumps of the brownshirts' heavy black boots tramping in and around Rotkreuzplatz. "I've only been away two weeks, and this is what I come back to? And after just finding out that Rudolf is dead."

"What?" Andreas gripped Angelika's shoulders, his eyes widening and his face going ashen. "Father died? When? How?"

"Last night." Angelika tore the swastika pin from her brother's sport shirt and flung the ugly metal object against the pavement. "It was a heart attack. I'll explain everything, but not until you tell me what in the name of

Mozart, Mahler and Mendelssohn you are doing out here, cheering on this disgusting display."

"I just came back from a camping trip with some new friends." So, it was true. Andreas had gone camping. A statement confirmed by the bulging beige knapsack he wore and the lingering scent of sweat on his skin. "We're meeting at Viktor Bauer's brewery this afternoon, and I'm supposed to bring along some pamphlets I left in my desk at the office."

Pamphlets... New friends... Brewery... Angelika's fears had come to fruition, and all at once, her brother's behaviour made shocking, sickening sense.

"New friends? You mean Johann Schmitt and the others?" Angelika spit the words as if ejecting poison. "The Hitler Youth and *Sturmabteilung* boys? No wonder I've been having such horrific dreams about you."

She stopped speaking and turned her head toward the sound of deranged singing coming from the Rotkreuzplatz streetcar station.

"*Deutschland, Deutschland über alles!*" A band of Nazi supporters all but shrieked the German national anthem. "*Über alles in der Welt!*"

From the corner of Donnersbergerstrasse, there also came a sound of smashing glass, and Angelika peered through the crowd to see Hitler Youth hooligans swarming like red-arm-banded ants, shattering the windows of several brazen businesses that still had opposing political parties' campaign posters on display.

"I had a terrible dream about you last night, too." Andreas's hands remained planted upon Angelika's shoulders, even as she tried shrugging them away. "I dreamt you'd drowned in Lake Fuschl."

Lake Fuschl seemed as far away as the moon right then.

"Why are you supporting this?" Angelika gestured about at the chaos and cacophony, viciousness and violence. "How did you become friends with the likes of those boys?"

"A few days ago, I went by the beer garden looking for Erich. I was sick to death of Kurt and everyone at the office browbeating me, and I didn't realise Erich had left town. I wanted to do something to help get you released from singing at the National Socialists' concert."

There it was again – the concert. The damning, indoctrinating concert. A concert that promised nothing but unspeakable damage for Angelika, the people she cared about and all of the gullible folks who'd have the misfortune of being subjected to its propaganda.

"Once I got there, I happened upon Johann and his friends," Andreas said. "They asked me to come sit with them, and I did. I was still hoping I'd somehow find a way to get you released from the concert. But the more I got to know Johann and the others, the more I realised they aren't so bad. For one thing, they actually listen. They actually care what I have to say."

"They do not care. They're manipulating you, the same way they manipulate others."

By preying upon struggling, desperate people's weaknesses and vulnerabilities, then exploiting their naivety for personal gain. Just as they pitted people against one another in order to serve a sinister purpose.

"They aren't manipulating me." Andreas's eyes narrowed, a galvanising gleam flickering from within. The same festering flicker she'd noticed several weeks earlier, when she'd told him about the Nazis' attack on a Russian immigrant in Sendling. "And look, I don't agree with the National Socialists about everything, but perhaps there's some truth to the things they say, like the part about immigrants taking jobs away from Germans."

"Immigrants? You mean immigrants like us? Because that's what we are – Austrian immigrants. And so is Adolf Hitler, whether he acknowledges it or not."

A faint scent of smoke prickled Angelika's nose, and she glanced toward the nearby newsstand where, paces away in the street, a pile of anti-Nazi *Munich Post* newspapers had formed, and a bonfire was being lit.

"Herr Hitler believes Aryan Germans and Austrians are one people." Andreas was squeezing Angelika's shoulders so tightly, a physical ache had started setting in. "The immigrants he's talking about are parasites like the war-profiteering foreign Jews who overran Vienna during our childhood. The Jews are orchestrating a global conspiracy. They're taking over the entire world."

"They are not. How can you repeat that derogatory nonsense?"

Reading such awful statements in the press or hearing them escape the mouths of Nazi officials was horrifying enough. But hearing the same ignorance and hatred parroted by a brother she'd forever loved threatened to suck every last iota of music from Angelika's soul. Especially when, up until then, she had considered him the calmer, more level-headed twin. Someone thoughtful, kind-hearted, talented and gentle. Not the indoctrinated stranger standing before her.

"Besides, even if Herr Hitler is wrong," Andreas said, "perhaps it's worth supporting him anyway if it will make enough people's lives better. Not everyone is wealthy and comfortable like us. People are struggling. And Adolf Hitler wants to help."

"You believe Hitler is doing all of this out of the goodness of his heart?" Angelika's fingers curled into furious fists. As if Adolf Hitler even had a heart. "Because he cares about workers and the poor?"

Yes, there were serious economic problems afoot, and no, as she acknowledged with a guilty pang, everyone did not enjoy the stability she and her family typically had. But Hitler's vendetta to falsely blame the Jewish community and make lofty promises that he alone held all the answers was nothing short of ludicrous.

"He's lying to benefit himself," Angelika said. "To gain power. There's nothing remarkable about him or any of the preposterous things he says. It's the anger and hatred in people's own hearts and minds that makes it seem that way."

"You can't tell me what to believe."

The smoke from the bonfire grew thicker, and its flames climbed higher. The fanatical crowd, however, did not disperse.

"To hell with the Poison Kitchen," a group of teenagers screamed while Angelika watched, the perpetrators using one of the Nazis' several disparaging names for the *Munich Post*. "Down with the Munich Plague!"

Angelika coughed and sputtered as smoke roiled within her throat. She wanted to rush into the street and tell the perpetrators exactly what she thought of them. But Angelika was only one person in a sea of hundreds. If she couldn't make her own twin listen to reason, how could she hope to convince anyone else? How could her voice possibly be heard?

"What would Mama say if she could see you now?" Angelika extricated herself from Andreas's grasp, anger and grief raging inside like the bonfire in the street. "This is not what she taught us, and not what she believed. She'd be heartbroken. Unbelievably ashamed."

"If Mama would be ashamed of anyone, she ought to be ashamed of herself." Tears appeared in Andreas's eyes, and Angelika instinctively reached for him. But this time, it was he who pulled away. "Mama's the one who left us here without her, isn't she? Who left us alone with Father, whose stone-cold heart finally killed him? Mama abandoned us. And all because of the scandals caused by her affair with Daniel Weiss, the Jew. Our enemy and misfortune."

Enemy? Misfortune? Perhaps, as Erich's letter had revealed, Daniel wasn't really the twins' father after all. But Angelika loved him with her entire heart, and always would. No one – not Hitler, his henchmen, Andreas nor anyone else – would ever change that.

"Daniel Weiss is no one's enemy." Angelika teetered, bracing herself against the building as a group of frightened children jostled her while racing toward a nearby park. "Nor is anyone else in the Jewish community. You are spreading lies and fanning flames."

Andreas's tears evaporated, and were replaced instead by a look of obstinance. How could he be so blind? So malicious? How could he spout the same abhorrent bigotry as the prejudiced people whose judgement had destroyed Clara?

"Angelika." Kurt, breathless, appeared by her side and fixed Andreas with a hardened glare. He, it seemed, had also feared the worst about her brother. "Thank God I found you. The storm troopers were blocking my path, and I couldn't get through. But we have to leave. We can't be out here right now."

They glanced toward the entrance to the Eder, von Hügel and Sons office building, only to discover that a group of bystanders were blocking the door. With the police nowhere in sight, members of the crowd continued cheering as a couple of storm troopers who weren't officially part of the march, but had nevertheless joined the melee, wrested a bearded man to the ground alongside the newsstand.

"We have to get to that man." Angelika locked eyes with her brother, who stared back with a look of shame. Whether shame because he felt guilty or shame because he'd been caught egging on the instigators, she didn't know. "We have to help him."

Angelika started forward, but Andreas held her back in an unusual demonstration of force, his lean arms stronger than she remembered. He had obviously been exercising and training during the camping trip, his body strengthening while his mind weakened.

"*Nein*," he said. "The brownshirts will kill you."

Andreas was probably right. Angelika's beauty, her singing voice, her familial connections… none of it would matter in the midst of a riot. But she couldn't simply stand there and do nothing. There had to be something she could—

"Well, well, look what we have here." Two other stinking, sweaty brownshirts materialised in front of them, staring not at Angelika, but over her head at Kurt. Their crisp uniforms appeared exactly like those worn by the storm troopers she'd once encountered at the streetcar stop in Sendling – tan shirts and slacks, black boots, swastika armbands and ice-blue collars. "A filthy rich, pompous money grubber. How much do you think one of his cufflinks is worth?"

And then, before Kurt could so much as make a move, one of the two blond-haired men had sidestepped Angelika and socked him in the ribs so hard that even above the roar of the crowd, she heard a resounding crack. A scream fell from her lips, and she tried reaching for Kurt, but he had already collapsed to his knees against the pavement.

"Go to hell, *Arschloch*," the storm trooper said to him.

The sound of more shattering glass rent the air, and the young men, distracted, sauntered off, laughing. Meanwhile, the bearded man who had been assaulted mercifully managed to stumble away and seek refuge inside one of the vandalised businesses.

"Kurt." Angelika sank down beside him, wrapping an arm around his middle while Andreas stared open-mouthed, yet made no attempt to assist. "You were right. We'd better go."

"The car is around the corner, sir." Otto strode up to them and began easing a groaning Kurt to his feet. "Fräulein Eder and I will find you some help."

"Andreas, come with us," Angelika begged, standing and pulling at his wrist. "Don't do this. Don't be a part of this."

His face clouded, and just as in the refrain that had so many times played itself out in Angelika's head, he appeared lost. But then, any semblance of uncertainty vanished.

"I have a better idea," Andreas said. "Forget all about Daniel Weiss, Vienna and the conservatory. Stay here in Munich, sing at the concert and support the National Socialists. Once you give them a chance, I know you'll see the truth. You could sing at their events, and I could be your accompanist. We could perform together, just like we used to dream."

In the hands of the Nazis, that dream would become a nightmare.

"Angelika, now," Kurt croaked, having regained his voice after staggering to his feet.

She knew he needed a doctor, and that she was powerless to prevent the dreadful scene playing out before her eyes. Yet as Otto and Kurt began tugging her away from Andreas, Angelika felt another piece of her heart go up in flames alongside the burning newspapers.

"Forward, comrades!"

Yet another group of angry voices echoed from behind, and the next thing Angelika knew, she was lying flat on the pavement, her raw palms burning as a group of young men dressed in black tore through the crowd and entered the plaza, heading straight for the demonstrating brownshirts. Angelika had little doubt that before this rioting ended, many people would be seriously injured. And some of those people could die.

"Goddamned communists," Andreas shouted.

He pulled Angelika to her feet as a scrap of paper fluttered from her dress pocket like a lost butterfly in a burning forest. Erich's note. *Ach*, Erich. If only unassailable, unflappable Erich were still by her side. And if only she had continued supporting him, too, rather than telling him off the night before. Why had he come back to Munich? And where was he right then? In the midst of the turmoil surrounding her, Angelika knew she had to find him, and quickly.

"Anni, please."

Kurt's terrified, pleading voice resounded in Angelika's ears, and in that moment, it all became clear. As much as she cared about Kurt, the affection she felt for him was different. She couldn't marry him. It was Angelika and Kurt who were not meant to be. She and Erich, however, were.

She had to make sure he was safe. Had to make sure he knew that, mysterious letter or no mysterious letter, French or no French, she still trusted him. She still loved him.

"Go," Andreas said. He also pivoted as if to flee, albeit in the opposite direction. "I have to get to the brewery and make sure my friends are all right. God only knows what these communists are planning to do, or what they've already done."

It was hopeless. There was nothing Angelika could say to stop him.

"Go," Andreas repeated, all but shoving her into Otto's arms after she'd snatched up Erich's letter. "We'll talk again later."

But what else was there to be said? Nothing that would change things, and nothing that could erase the damage that had already been done.

"Here we go, Fräulein Eder." Otto's voice was calm yet firm, the man's dedication humbling Angelika. For there he remained, standing at attention in the middle of a riot, selflessly risking life and limb in order to help her and Kurt. "Back to the car, and quickly."

Perhaps it was the emotion of the moment catching up with her, or perhaps it was the reminder that goodness and kindness still existed. Whatever the true reason, Angelika spun up onto her tiptoes and gave the underappreciated employee an unabashed kiss on the cheek.

"Yes, Otto," Angelika said as the man blushed, and Andreas's auburn head of hair vanished into the smoke. "Let's go find a physician."

Twenty-Two

A smell of burning newsprint lingered upon Angelika's skin as Otto drove toward Doctor Hoffmann's house, the revolting Rotkreuzplatz riot and Nazi-instigated destruction disappearing in the automobile's rearview mirror. Destruction Andreas, or rather the stranger he'd become, had helped bolster.

"Are we almost there?" Kurt asked, groaning. He lay stretched across the backseat of the Rolls-Royce Phantom with his head in Angelika's lap and his face wrinkling in pain. "God, my ribs."

"We're getting closer." Angelika strived, albeit in vain, to keep him from jostling about. "Try to keep still."

But Kurt continued writhing like a restless schoolboy.

"Turn right," Angelika told Otto as they approached Pilarstrasse, a mere stone's throw from the Nymphenburg Palace gardens where Erich had gifted her the daisy clip. "That's it up ahead. The first house on the left."

Otto slowed to a stop in front of a charming two-storey green-and-white dwelling with chestnut trees in the yard and a lovely view of the Nymphenburger Kanal.

"Wait here," Angelika said.

She eased Kurt's head off her lap, exited the vehicle and raced across a manicured lawn accented with beds of blushing roses. She hoped Gretchen's parents would be home after attending their usual Sunday morning Mass at Herz Jesu, the neighbourhood parish.

"Angelika, is that you?"

The whispered greeting caused Angelika's breath to catch as she rounded a towering tree trunk and, to her horror, discovered a uniformed Hitler Youth boy crouching in the shadows. Someone whom, if she had her way, she'd have never again cared to lay eyes upon as long as she lived.

"Johann Schmitt." Angelika's shock lasted mere seconds before her hands flew to her hips and a sneer ensnared her lips. "Just what do you think you're doing here? Corrupting my brother wasn't satisfying enough? You have to harass Doctor Hoffmann, too?"

Come what may, Angelika was done appeasing Johann.

"I'm not here to harass anyone," he said, keeping his voice low. Johann tried pulling Angelika nearer, but she pushed away as though fending off a wild boar. "I'm trying to help."

"Help whom?"

Hitler? The Nazis? Himself? It wasn't as if he could possibly be talking about...

"Erich Bauer." Johann's expression darkened, his face lacking its usual motley combination of naivety and arrogance. "He's badly hurt, and he asked me to come here to get Doctor Hoffmann."

"What?" Just like Johann's pin when she'd flung it into the Danube, Angelika's heart plummeted. "No!"

Forgetting her prior protestations, Angelika moved in closer and steadied herself against the tree. It couldn't be true. Not Erich. Perhaps she'd heard Johann incorrectly. Perhaps if she squeezed her eyes shut tightly enough, she could transport herself back to Lake Fuschl and erase everything that had happened after she'd discovered the letter to Lily.

"Erich was injured in a motorcycling accident." Johann looked around as if afraid someone might be watching, even though the tree trunk kept both him and Angelika hidden from street view. Given the angle, Kurt and Otto wouldn't be able to see them, nor have a clear line of sight to the Hoffmanns' front door. "It happened an hour ago, over by the brewery."

An animalistic yelp rattled Angelika's vocal cords. How could such a thing happen to the adept driver and seemingly invincible young man who'd bent but not broken after confronting antisemitic teenagers at Café Central in Vienna? Who, in spite of the injuries his father and those very teenagers had inflicted, had made effortless love to Angelika beneath a star-speckled sky at Lake Fuschl, then rescued her from the water in the midst of a storm? Who'd done nothing but listen and love, encourage and support? And who would never in a hundred years have broken her heart the way she had shattered his?

"Erich came back to Munich to find his father and convince him to tell Baldur von Schirach he should release you from singing at the October concert," Johann said. "I heard the entire thing while I was at the brewery, waiting to meet some friends from a camping trip. My cousin and I got back into town a couple of hours earlier than everyone else."

Trembling and unable to speak, Angelika listened as Johann continued explaining.

"Erich had brought along a couple of Vienna newspaper articles to help make his point. He said the stories prove that important critics don't like your singing, that you're not ready for the stage and that you would ruin the performance."

The newspapers. The ones the caregivers had delivered to the lake house earlier that morning. Kurt hadn't read the reviews, but Erich clearly had. And he'd taken the copies with him when he'd departed, not realising there had been extras left behind for Angelika to discover.

"Erich said that even though Herr von Schirach saw and liked you in *Don Carlo*, you'd be too much of a liability." Johann's clammy palms came to rest against Angelika's quavering arms. "Erich told his father he'd heard you practising in Vienna and that you're not so talented a singer. He pretended he was saying all of this out of concern for Herr Bauer, and to try rebuilding their relationship as father and son. But Herr Bauer didn't believe a word."

Angelika didn't believe it, either. She knew Erich enjoyed her singing. She also knew that he would rather memorise Homer's *Odyssey* than rekindle his relationship with abusive Viktor Bauer.

"Herr Bauer said Baldur von Schirach has his own

informant in Vienna who's been telling him good things about your progress," Johann added. "He also said that any German critics who dare to disparage you after the concert will be appropriately dealt with. And as for Erich, he was never supposed to return to Munich at all, let alone step foot inside Bauerbräu."

So, that was the full story. Much worse than Erich had admitted to Angelika after he'd arrived in Vienna. He must have downplayed the severity of the situation so as not to worry her. Because he'd always thought of others before himself.

"Herr Bauer was so angry, he forced Erich out of the brewery, then had his motorbike chased down and run off the road. He wanted his own son dead, but Erich managed to survive the wreck and run."

Thank God he hadn't perished in the crash. But what had happened next? Where was Erich?

"By then, a few other Hitler Youth boys had started arriving at the brewery, so Herr Bauer told us to fan out and look for Erich." Johann's curious hands slithered down to Angelika's waist, but she remained too stunned by his story to pull away. "We were supposed to take advantage of Erich being injured, and either finish him off ourselves or tell Herr Bauer where he was hiding."

Her fault. This was all Angelika's fault. Erich would never have returned to Munich that morning if not for his argument with her at the lake, plus her accidentally agreeing to sing at the concert in the first place. And now, he was not only badly injured, but the Nazis were calling for his death.

"And you found him?" she asked.

Hope and fear swirled inside as Angelika choked on the stream of salty tears that had begun a sad, steady march down her cheeks. She was the one who deserved to be battered and broken. Not Erich. Not the selfless young man she loved.

"*Ja.*" Johann swiped a bony thumb across Angelika's dampened face. "I saw him sneaking into that dilapidated little hovel of a café on Leonrodstrasse."

Angelika knew precisely which café Johann meant. Only in her eyes, the eatery was an eclectic enclave rather than a dilapidated hovel. Johann was talking about the very café where Angelika had teased Erich about devouring his weight in jelly doughnuts. The café where he'd practically fallen out of his chair in stitches after hearing her sing "They Call Me Naughty Lola".

Erich had hidden inside the Wolpertinger Kaffeehaus. And, for whatever reason, Johann hadn't reported his whereabouts to Viktor Bauer and the others. Or so it seemed, and so she hoped.

"I couldn't bring myself to hurt him." Johann hung his head as if ashamed, while Angelika exhaled in relief. "I've known Erich my entire life. He was always confident and strong. I wanted to be like him. And… I don't know. Some of the things Herr Bauer and his friends say and do are…"

For the first time since Angelika had met him the previous year, Johann sounded as if he might actually be thinking for himself.

"So, even though I slipped into the café right on his

heels and was ready to telephone Herr Bauer," he said, "I ended up promising Erich I'd help."

At that, Angelika wiped her eyes, focused on her breathing and tried her best to squelch her tears. Perhaps, thanks to Johann's decision, there was still time, and still hope. Still a chance to save Erich. This was a time for action, not paralysing panic.

"What types of injuries does he have?" she asked, dreading the answer.

"It looked like his left arm and shoulder were broken. He was limping on his left leg, and the entire left side of his body is covered in cuts. I think metal from the motorcycle must have punctured his skin. It's a good thing Erich was at least wearing a helmet and goggles."

Angelika bit her lip to stop the tears from resuming. If only she and Stefan Hoffmann could reach Erich before the Nazis did.

"We tried ringing Doctor Hoffmann from the café, but the call didn't connect," Johann said. "The Hoffmanns' telephone must be out of order. I don't think he's home, either. I've knocked twice."

Perhaps Stefan wasn't home. Or perhaps he was smart enough to have avoided answering the door with the likes of Johann Schmitt standing on the opposite side. He and his wife had likely taken refuge upstairs, in the back of the house, praying Johann would go away.

"Stay here," Angelika said.

Moving with the speed of a relay runner, she hurried to the back courtyard, lifted a pebble and plinked it against a window that led to Gretchen's parents' bedroom. She hoped Otto and Kurt would continue to wait in the car without coming to see what was taking so long. When the bedroom curtains remained drawn, she removed her heels and began climbing a vine-adorned trellis that reached the second storey. Once at the top, Angelika rapped the windowpane and sang a musical scale close to the glass.

"Doctor Hoffmann, it's Anni Eder." She repeated the musical notes. "Are you in there? Please, I need your help."

The curtains were flung apart, and the window opened, Stefan and Adelheid gasping as they helped Angelika inside. No sooner had her feet hit the rug than she began conveying all that had happened. She explained that she'd come back to Munich following Rudolf's death, that Kurt was lying in the automobile with broken ribs, that an injured Erich was hiding at the coffee-house following a confrontation with Viktor, and that Johann had come to fetch a doctor.

"You're sure it's not a trick?" Stefan asked. "What if this Johann Schmitt is lying?"

Angelika didn't know for certain. Perhaps it *was* all some sort of trick. Perhaps her beloved Erich was already dead and Stefan soon would be, too, if they dared go to the café. Angelika knew that Johann fancied her, and always had. On the one hand, getting rid of Erich might, in Johann's muddled mind, give him a chance at winning Angelika's heart. On the other hand, throughout all of her nineteen years, Angelika had met quite a few talented actors. As far as she could tell, Johann Schmitt was not among them.

"I don't think Johann is lying. Not about this."

Stefan nodded in agreement, then snatched a hulking medical bag off his bureau. In his caring green eyes, Angelika could discern a deep love for Erich. A father's love. Erich had been correct when he'd told Angelika that love and family were about more than biology. One's family could be chosen and found.

"We'll ride in Kurt's automobile, and I'll see what I can do for his ribs on the way to the coffee-house," Stefan said.

They headed downstairs and outside, where Angelika grabbed her shoes. She was about to assume Johann had left when an arm jutted out from behind the chestnut tree and caught her.

"Before you go, there's one other thing you should know." Johann fired the words off rapidly, as Stefan, meanwhile, ran to the car. "When I got to the café and was planning to blow the whistle on Erich, he tried convincing me not to. Erich said that everything he's doing, he's doing to help you. He said he has to find a way to get you released from singing at the concert and working with the National Socialists, because you'd be better off staying in Vienna. I don't agree with him about that, but it's the reason he's doing all of this. He said this wasn't his only idea, either."

No, of course it wasn't. Just as, after the opera, Erich had said he knew people who might be able to help.

"If Erich stays here in Munich, or ever comes back again, Viktor Bauer and his men will kill him." In this awful instance, Angelika was certain that Johann was speaking the truth. "If you want Erich to survive, you have to convince him to leave once and for all, now, before they find him."

Yes, Angelika would. She must. Yet even if she took

Erich back to Salzburg or Vienna, he might not stay there. As long as he knew Angelika was expected to perform at the concert and study under the Nazis' tutelage, he'd continue risking his life to find her a way out of it.

"You have to convince him to stop helping you," Johann said.

There was only one tactic Angelika could think to try. One horrible, hurtful thing. In order to save Erich, she'd have to break his heart completely, thoroughly and beyond repair, far worse than she already had.

"Erich has an older sister who's rumoured to live in London," Johann added. "I don't know what she does there, but Herr Bauer despises her and doesn't allow anyone to talk about her. She left Munich three years ago. If Erich goes to England, I'll bet she can help him."

So, this was the sister Erich had tried telling Angelika about at the lake. The one whose *Dirndl*, she suddenly realised, he must have given her to wear the night she'd sung at the beer garden earlier that month. Why hadn't she listened to him? Why had she been so cruel?

"All right." Angelika sounded more confident than she felt. "I know what I have to do."

She must assume a role she didn't want to play, but which, given the circumstances, might be the only hope.

"Come along, Angelika," Stefan said, reappearing by her side. "We need to hurry."

And hurry, they did, Angelika taking one last departing look at Johann and wondering, when all was said and done, what would become of him, and who he would choose to become.

Twenty-Three

A ngelika's heart thudded with the power of a bass drum as the Wolpertinger Kaffeehaus owners ushered her, Stefan, Kurt and Otto inside through a back-alley doorway, then led them toward the storage room where Erich was hiding. If the Nazis found out the kindly husband-and-wife team were helping Erich, the two of them would most assuredly be attacked.

"Whatever you need Otto and me to do, just say the word," Kurt told Angelika as they made their way through the quiet hallways of the café, which was closed to customers on a Sunday afternoon.

As promised, Stefan had done his best to bandage Kurt's ribs in the car, discovering that only a couple of them were fractured. But despite Stefan's recommendation that Kurt take things slow, he had insisted upon soldiering through. As much as Kurt disliked Erich, he was disgusted by Viktor Bauer's viciousness. Had Kurt known the full story – that Erich had been in Munich trying to help Angelika – he'd have certainly needed smelling salts.

"*Danke.*" Angelika offered a steadying arm to Kurt, who was hobbling along with Otto's assistance. "The first thing I must do is find a way to get Erich safely to London. It sounds as if he has relatives there who can help him."

But there was nothing Angelika could fathom for Kurt to assist with at the moment. Not when all she could focus on was the opening storage room door, and then – lying upon a pile of grey woollen blankets behind a towering pile of packing crates – the strong, sarcastic, altruistic young man whose dreams she'd wanted to share and whose heart she wished she could mend.

"Anni." Erich winced while propping himself against the wall in a semi-seated position. "I was afraid they were going to kill me before I got a chance to see you again."

He appeared battered, bruised and bloody, but also, to Angelika's relief, vigorously alive. Unlike her mother, whose cold, lifeless body she'd discovered silenced upon the bathroom floor in Vienna, sorrow forever etched in her dim blue eyes as a bottle of pills sat empty upon the countertop.

"What is it you might say?" Erich muttered. "Thank Richard Mozart's ghost?"

Erich Bauer, still cracking jokes and very much himself, in spite of every awful thing that had happened.

"I know I'm the spitting image of Frankenstein's monster, but come over here, *ja*?" As usual, his stare penetrated straight into Angelika's soul, the love in his eyes shining through as though he weren't hurt, the Nazis weren't looking for him, and the two of them were back at Lake Fuschl, floating and flying. "I need to tell you I'm sorry."

"Later."

Angelika tried keeping her voice level and emotionless, even though she really wanted to envelop Erich in her arms and never let go. To tell him she was the one who was sorry and that she would never doubt him again. But Angelika couldn't do that. For she'd determined that the only way to get Erich to escape to London and stop endangering himself was for her to pretend that his plan of getting her released from the concert had worked. And, worst of all, by pretending she hadn't forgiven him and no longer loved him.

"First, you must let Doctor Hoffmann help you," she said.

Stefan was already removing Erich's soiled clothing, and Angelika turned away, planning to wait in the hallway with Kurt and Otto. But when Erich again summoned her to his side and begged her to stay, she couldn't help but sink down beside him, squeezing Erich's uninjured right hand as he interlaced their two sets of quivering fingers.

"*Scheisse!*" he screamed as Stefan, with the help of a topical antiseptic, removed tiny bits of gravel from his skin, then set the bones in his shoulder and arm. "No more. Stop."

Tears cascaded down Erich's cheeks, and Angelika, unable to restrain herself, used her free hand to wipe them away before the salt could sting the shallow cuts on his face.

"I'm sorry, my boy." Stefan's voice was comforting and steady. As a young physician, he'd undoubtedly seen worse on and off battlefields during the Great War. "But I can't stop. I have to get you fixed up, and quickly. I don't know what you and your father argued about today, but it isn't safe for you here in Munich any longer. When you told me a few days ago that you'd fought with your father and were going to visit Angelika in Vienna, I had no idea it would be this dangerous for you to return."

Stefan sadly shook his head, and appeared to be blinking back his own batch of tears.

"Do you still have your passport?" he asked. Erich's blood-stained knapsack was lying nearby. "Can you go to London and be with Liesl?"

Liesl. Likely also known as Lily. Erich's sister, whom Stefan had surely met.

"I… can't." Erich hiccupped through his tears. "Not… yet."

And then, to Angelika's surprise, he began speaking in flawless, fluent French so that Stefan wouldn't understand.

"I thought I could get you released from singing in the concert," Erich said, his gaze fixed upon Angelika. "After Baldur von Schirach turned up at *Juan Carlos* and left you that note, I thought perhaps we could both run away to London together. I thought my sister and her husband could help us. But that would have meant you'd have to leave Daniel, Andreas and Gretchen. And that the Nazis might retaliate against them. I wanted to talk to you about it, and tell you everything about my sister and her family. But then we had that stupid argument at the lake, and I was afraid you wouldn't forgive me. So, I came back here and—"

"I know," Angelika answered, also in French, and more

gently than she should have. "Johann told me. I happened upon him at Doctor Hoffmann's house. Kurt got hurt this afternoon, and I was trying to find him a doctor."

Erich nodded as Stefan fashioned a sling for his arm, which would have to do until a proper cast could be applied.

"I don't want to leave you here." Erich continued speaking as Stefan examined his leg and determined it wasn't broken. "I can't go. Not when they're planning to force you to sing at the concert and work with them. We could still try running away to London, but…"

But they both knew that if Angelika did so, especially with the Nazis now calling for Erich's death, they would retaliate against other people she loved. Angelika didn't want to sing for the National Socialists or partner with them. And if it ended up costing her own life, so be it.

But what about Kurt, Stefan, Gretchen and even Andreas? Would the Nazis turn on him if Angelika refused to do their bidding? The Nazis were planning rallies in Austria and gaining a foothold in the country, so Daniel might find himself in danger, as well, especially in light of his Jewish heritage. Would singing for the Nazis be justified if it were the only way to protect the people Angelika loved?

No. Not when it would bolster the Nazis' cause and bring harm upon fellow human beings who were every bit as important as Angelika's family and friends. She must continue trying to find a way to refuse the Nazis while also protecting the people she cared about. But first, Angelika must convince Erich to leave.

"I'm not going to London." She hardened her voice and pulled her hand away. "But you are."

"Like hell I am." Erich shook his head so hard, Angelika was certain he must feel it in his fractured shoulder. "I'm not leaving." He retook her hand and pressed it to his lips. "I love you, damn it."

Damn it, indeed. How could Angelika destroy him this way?

"Erich, listen…" Her voice wavered. She must pull herself together and play the role. She must, just like a real sea siren, drown him with her deceptive song. "When I saw Johann at Doctor Hoffmann's house, he told me your plan to get me out of the concert ended up working after all. The Nazis have decided I'm too much of a liability, and that they don't want me to sing for them. I can go back to Vienna and trust that they won't bother me."

She awaited Erich's response, but found he didn't say anything, her forsaken sweetheart staring back with discerning, narrowed eyes.

"I also need to tell you that…" The words skittered away, and Angelika sent up a silent plea to Clara, begging her mother to give her strength. "…I cannot forgive you. You lied to me, and after today, I don't wish to see you again."

If Stefan sensed what she was doing, in spite of his not understanding French, he didn't show it. Erich didn't react, either, other than to continue assessing, his lips pursed and a single eyebrow cocked.

"I don't love you anymore." Angelika released the words as if she were expelling fire like the dragon in

Wagner's *Siegfried*. "Kurt and I have reconciled, and we're going to be married."

Something resembling a lopsided simper flashed across Erich's face, followed by a grimace as Stefan treated and bandaged his lacerations with the help of soap, water and rags the coffee-house's owners had provided.

"*Zut*," Erich at last replied, cursing in French. The initial shock of pain seemed to be subsiding, and his tears had begun to dry. "You aren't telling me the truth. About the concert or about us." The accident hadn't impacted Erich's brain, that was for certain. "I'm not saying you aren't a good actress. You're great, in fact. Better than Marlene Dietrich. But I know what you're trying to do, and it isn't going to work."

It had to work. Angelika must make it work.

"How dare you accuse me of being dishonest? Unlike you, I am not a liar."

She reached into the pocket of her polka-dotted day dress, fingers closing around a small metallic object she'd moved out of her knapsack on the way to the café, but had hoped she wouldn't have to relinquish.

"Take this." With a steady, determined hand, she held out the daisy clip she adored. "I don't want it anymore. Kurt was right when he told me it's nothing more than a worthless chunk of metal. A girl like me deserves better."

Angelika waited, hoping Erich would take the clip. When he didn't, she stuffed it into his filthy knapsack with a frustrated grunt.

"You were a sorry excuse for a sweetheart, Erich." She stood and, sidestepping hefty sacks of flour and sugar, moved to the opposite side of the room. "You may have seduced me for a while, but it won't happen again. Because I am far too good for the likes of you."

Erich's bemused expression had vanished, confusion appearing in its place as, somehow, Angelika managed to avoid imploding. How she was still standing, she didn't know. Not when she'd said the most vicious and vile things – all lies – to a person she truly did love.

"Angelika?" An anxious rapping sounded at the door, and she creaked it open to find Kurt gazing back with terror in his eyes. "Otto's been monitoring the front of the shop. There's a mysterious man knocking on the door."

"Is he wearing a Nazi uniform?"

"No. But why would he come sniffing around here on a Sunday, when he knows they're closed? The owners are going to speak with him and see what he wants. He might be looking for Erich, so we need to move him out of here this instant."

Yes. Erich needed to leave for London, and swiftly. But how? The Nazis would surely be keeping an eye on the train station.

"After we got here, I took the liberty of telephoning a friend who has a two-seater sport plane at the Munich airfield." Kurt continued to whisper as Angelika and Stefan helped Erich reclothe in a hurry. "He can have a pilot there in half an hour to fly Erich to Holland."

And in Holland, Erich could visit a doctor before taking a steamer to England. Two things Kurt also offered to telephone ahead and arrange. Though Angelika hated relying upon Kurt's money and influence, there was no denying that her well-connected, fast-thinking accomplice was saving Erich's life.

"Oh, Kurt, thank you," Angelika said, her heart racing as Stefan and Otto lifted Erich and, after verifying the coast was clear, ran toward the back-alley doorway. "An aeroplane is a brilliant idea."

While Angelika spoke, she snatched Erich's knapsack and used empty crates to hide all evidence that they had been there, even as an unmistakable scent of blood and medical treatment lingered. Doing her best to help Kurt walk with broken ribs, she then led him out back, where all five figures squeezed into the automobile – Otto and Kurt in front, and Erich sandwiched in between Stefan and Angelika in back.

"What's all this talk about an aeroplane?" Erich piped up in protest as Otto manoeuvred the car out of the alleyway and began the few-minute drive to the airfield. The chauffeur promised to remain on inconspicuous roads and avoid going anywhere near Rotkreuzplatz. "If Anni thinks I'm getting into an aeroplane, she's even loopier than the time I watched her down three cups of coffee in a single sitting. Who do you think I am? The Red Baron?"

Angelika could understand his fear. Not only would a bumpy plane ride hurt Erich's shoulder and arm, but he was also afraid of heights.

"I'm afraid we'll have to try it, son." Stefan wrapped a bolstering arm around the young man he loved as his own. "You can travel to England with your passport, and once you're there, Liesl and her husband can help you figure out the rest. I only wish there were a way I could go with you."

Angelika wished she could go, too, and that she didn't have to keep up the charade that she wanted nothing more to do with Erich. But keep it up, she must.

"Curse you, Erich, just leave." If the others realised what Angelika was doing, they didn't let on, nor question her method. "I want you out of my life forever."

Erich's shuddering sigh echoed throughout the automobile, and Angelika dared a glance as the final flickers of defiance seemed to fade from his eyes.

"Fine," he said, brows furrowing. "I'll go."

The rest of the ride went by quickly, and before Angelika could let the finality of her words sink in, the car had arrived at the airport, located northeast of Nymphenburg Palace, and consisting of a grassy field with a hangar and windsock. The field seemed quiet on a Sunday, with several hobbyists taking flight, plus a dozen passengers boarding a gleaming black-and-silver Lufthansa aircraft. A globular Zeppelin, though not currently in use, sat at the far end of the field as a threatening series of thunderstorm clouds loomed in the distance.

"There's the plane." Kurt pointed to a single-engine, two-seat, silver-and-white Messerschmitt 23, a model popular with wealthy, sporting aviators. "And that must be the pilot." A light-haired man in his twenties stood alongside the aircraft with goggles on his head and an extra tan flight suit in hand. "I told my friend the faster he could have a pilot here to get Erich off the ground, the more I would pay. Just as I'll also wire money ahead for a physician and steamer ticket to England."

At that, Erich harrumphed, mumbling something about reimbursing Kurt at a later time.

"This plane is safe, though?" Angelika asked. "It's been inspected?" Drat. She'd shown more concern than she should. But under the circumstances, she couldn't help it. They were trying to get Erich safely out of Munich, not watch him perish in a flying accident. "I mean, I hope it's already been inspected so that Erich can leave right away. Because as I said on the way out here, I never want to see him again."

"Angelika, I know this is—"

Erich had started speaking, only to be cut off by Kurt.

"That's the man who came to the coffee-house." Kurt squinted in the direction of a delivery truck pulling in nearby, and from which a bespectacled man in a black fedora emerged. "He must have followed us here by commandeering the coffee-house's truck. Erich, you have to leave this instant."

"What man are you talking about?" Erich asked, leaning around Angelika in an attempt to see.

"We can't let him spot you." She moved to block the window. "Now, hurry up and go. You'll have to walk on your own, so as not to attract attention, but Otto and Doctor Hoffmann will shield you on your way to the plane." Which was thankfully located in the opposite direction of the suspicious fedora-clad man – tall, lean and in his early thirties – who stood surveying the airfield. "Goodbye, Erich."

She fixated upon the auto's leather seating as she said it, unable to bear his hazel-eyed gaze. She hoped he would indeed go quickly, both for his own safety and because she didn't know how long she could hold back the crescendo of emotion building inside.

"I won't forget this, Anni." Erich seemed to have regained some of his fire, and she could feel his eyes boring into her. "So long, siren."

A lump formed in Angelika's throat, and she watched nervously as Erich, toting the knapsack that held her relinquished daisy clip, limped to the readily positioned aeroplane while Otto and Stefan did their best to block him from the man in the fedora's view. With Stefan's help, Erich then donned a cap, goggles and the one-piece flight suit, its left sleeve draping about his arm sling. Angelika was certain that this time, Erich hadn't called her his siren as a sign of affection. This time, he'd been telling her off, as she rightfully deserved for hurting him.

"*Ach*, his leather jacket." The realisation dawned as Angelika's stockinged leg brushed against her own knapsack. She should have pretended she didn't want the jacket, either, but it was too late. For the next thing Angelika knew, Erich had boarded the aircraft and, more quickly than the swish of a maestro's baton, was hurtling into the sky.

Would she ever see him again? Even if she did, after the dreadful things she'd said, and how far she'd gone in convincing him she didn't love him, their relationship could never be the same.

"The pilot will send me a telegram once they arrive in Holland this evening," Kurt said as Stefan and Otto walked back toward the automobile, Gretchen's father dabbing at his eyes with a handkerchief. Without letting on about the propaganda concert, Angelika would have to tell Stefan she hadn't meant it when she'd claimed to want Erich out of her life forever. "The flight should last four hours."

Angelika turned her head to look for the man in the fedora, but he and the delivery truck were gone. She breathed a shaky sigh of relief as Kurt, groaning, got out of the car and moved into the backseat, which would allow him to stretch out and relieve the pressure on his ribs.

"Good grief," he muttered. It appeared as if Otto and Stefan had gotten ensnared in a conversation with a hobbyist pilot interested in purchasing his own Rolls-Royce Phantom. "We need to leave. The Nazis might still be looking for Erich, and we can't let them know we were the ones who helped him escape."

"He wouldn't have escaped at all if it weren't for you." Angelika slid closer to Kurt and took his hand. "I can never repay you for everything you did today."

"You don't have to."

His blue eyes shone, and he gave Angelika a caring smile she earnestly returned. And yet, there was something important she needed to tell him. Something that could wait no longer, and that she hoped he would understand.

"You mean the world to me, Kurt, and you always will. But as much as I do care for you, I can't—"

He cut Angelika off with soft fingers against her cheek, his other hand lifting her chin.

"I know."

And in Kurt's eyes, she could see that he did. Kurt knew she couldn't marry him. He knew she still loved Erich. Erich, whom she'd wounded, belittled and insulted. And who was careening through the skies above Germany, headed for a brand-new life without her.

Angelika's Memory Book

July 1932 – One Month Ago
Lake Ammer

I was a couple of weeks shy of turning nineteen the day Erich, Andreas, Gretchen and I spent the day at Lake Ammer, one of our favourite summer swimming spots.

"Jump in, Anni." Erich pointed to a rope swing hanging from an ash tree. "Swing on out, and I promise I'll catch you."

But I was having none of that. The last time I'd been there and tried using the swing, my jump had ended in a painful, embarrassing belly flop. Something I was hardly eager to repeat. Not even if, this time, Erich had vowed to catch me.

"I'm fine jumping in the regular way," I told him.

"You don't think I'll keep my word?"

And so, relenting, I gripped the rope and slipped my foot into the holster, then looked out to see Erich bobbing to-and-fro in the aquamarine water, bare-chested and at the ready.

"Right here." He stretched his arms out wide. "I'll catch you."

I swung out over the water only to panic, my foot slipping from the holster, and the rope burning my skin.

"*Ach*, Erich!"

I screamed, wobbled and let go, landing belly-first in the cold, clear lake.

Of course, he swam straight over, scooped me up as if

I were weightless and cared for my burn using a medical kit he'd remembered to bring. After the minor aching had stopped, Erich removed the compress and suggested I try leaping again. But I didn't want to. In fact, it wasn't only my foot that hurt.

"You said you would catch me." Instead of meeting his gaze, I picked at a snag in my green-and-black wool-knit swimsuit. "You tricked me."

"No," he said. "I promised to catch you if you jumped to me. But you didn't. You let go too soon."

I stalked back over to my blanket and remained there the rest of the afternoon, all the while watching Erich jump again and again, always so far out, never afraid to make the leap.

I promised to catch you if you jumped to me. But you didn't. You let go too soon.

At the time, I figured it was all Erich's fault, and that he could have caught me if he'd truly wanted to. I now realise I was wrong.

Erich had wanted to catch me, and surely would have. It was me who hadn't trusted him to do it.

Twenty-Four

*A*ngelika had adored summertime ever since she was a young girl, when the dark curtain of the Great War had lifted, Clara's notoriety had grown, and a seemingly hopeful future had beckoned. From strolling with Clara near Vienna's historic Schönbrunn Palace to playing tag in the *Burggarten* with Andreas, her childhood summers had wrought warmth and freedom, beauty and bounty. After her mother died in June of 1931, Angelika had known summer could never be the same.

And yet, in the weeks preceding Erich's attack at the hands of the Nazis, a semblance of magic had woven its way back into her heart, its battered void expanding like a linden blossom. In the midst of summer's steady grasp, Angelika had returned to Vienna, pursued her dreams and opened herself to love. Summer's breeze had seen her gliding atop the Prater *Riesenrad* with Erich, making music with Daniel and singing her operatic debut at the Theater an der Wien.

But summer, of course, could never last. September

arrived right on schedule, a nip dancing in the evening air as Angelika made her way to Daniel's flat the Friday after Erich's escape and her subsequent journey back to the conservatory. Autumn was barrelling toward her at the speed of sound, and with it, the end of the young singers programme. Not to mention a dreaded runup to the Nazis' October concert in Munich.

Change was imminent, and just as Angelika was powerless to stop nature's timeless turning, she felt incapable of controlling her own destiny. While Daniel still knew nothing about the concert, he'd seemed to sense that Angelika was struggling. As a result, he had clearly been doing everything he could to help. Efforts that had thus far proven fruitless.

"*Crudele?*" Angelika's voice carried throughout his flat as she sang along with one of her mother's recordings, Clara's magnificent soprano soaring while her daughter's faltered. "*Ah no, mio bene!*"

The exercise was meant to offer a cathartic release and help Angelika refocus on preparing for the end-of-term singing competition. But try as she might, her vocals were subpar, and the libretto's lyrics weighed upon her.

Cruel? Oh no, my dearest! Operatic heroine Donna Anna's ardent plea to her sweetheart, a man she had inadvertently hurt, accosted Angelika's psyche. *Don't say that I am cruel to you. You know how much I love you.*

After sneaking Erich out of Munich a week earlier, Angelika had returned to Vienna and tried her best to concentrate on her studies. But her singing had been abominable, and her temperament worse. Although Kurt had confirmed with the pilot that Erich made it safely to Holland, saw a doctor and secured his ticket for sailing to England, Angelika knew nothing more. Whether Erich didn't think it was safe to contact her following the close call with the Nazis, or whether he despised her for her cruelty, or perhaps both, she could only hope he was healing alongside his sister and establishing a new life in London. A life that would eventually include a new love.

"I'm sorry, Daniel." Angelika lifted the gramophone needle and stopped the turntable, silencing her mother. "My voice is rubbish today."

She flopped down upon the lumpy paisley-print sofa, discarded newspapers crinkling and crackling beneath her rump. All week long, the news had been abuzz with word of the Austrian Nazis' upcoming September rallies. Events that were expected to attract crowds of thousands.

"It's your state of mind, *Liebling*." Daniel sat beside Angelika and twiddled his thumbs, a certain sign that he wanted to say more. His clothing boasted its usual cheery rainbow of colour, while Angelika, a glutton for punishment, had worn a daisy-dotted skirt that reminded her of Erich. "You probably don't think a middle-aged geezer like me could understand, but I'm no stranger to that look in your eyes. The look of loneliness and heartbreak. And it breaks my own heart to see it there."

Sunset's golden reflections cast shadows about the cozy, cluttered room, a place that in merely a couple of weeks' time had come to feel more like home than the Eders' gaudy Munich mansion ever had. Daniel's flat was special not because of its outer elegance or the material possessions it contained, but because of the memories Angelika was making there with someone she loved.

"Have you ever tried to help someone…" She trailed off as Mokka, her beloved dachshund from Munich, leapt onto the sofa and nuzzled her hand. Angelika had brought her along when she'd returned from Germany, and unlike her human owner, the pup was having a ball. "But by helping, you ended up hurting the person instead?"

Hardly the full story about what had happened with Erich, but at least a start.

"*Scheisse*, what a question. You can bet your boots I have." A sweet scent of *Kaiserschmarrn* – the scrambled, raisin-rich pancakes Daniel unconventionally enjoyed eating for dinner – lingered upon his clothing and in the air. "And it should come as no surprise, either. Because you, my Anni, are one of the people I hurt. First, by keeping it a secret that even though I've always loved you and wished you were my daughter, it isn't true as far as biology is concerned. And secondly, by sharing that secret with Erich. I imagine he told you all about it, *ja*?"

No, he hadn't. Angelika had discovered it on her own by reading Erich's letter at the lake.

"I'm not angry if he did." Daniel stroked Mokka's silky brown fur while slipping her savoury bits of *Bergkäse* he'd stored in a paper sack. "From the way you've been looking at me this past week, I had a sneaking suspicion you knew. That story was our private business, and I should have had the gumption to tell you myself. I never should have talked it over with Erich. He was just…"

"I know." Mozart's ghost, did Angelika know. "He

was easy to talk to. A good listener. Funny. Thoughtful." Someone wonderful who, although Angelika didn't need a man to lead a fulfilling life, had helped her glimpse the immense joy that came from having a trusted partner by one's side. "And now, he's gone away to London, and I'm certain he never wants to see me again."

"I wouldn't be so sure of that." An enduring glimmer of hope shone in Daniel's eyes. "I don't know what went wrong between you and Erich, and I'd never expect you to tell me. But when you're my age, you've seen a thing or two. And I saw the way he cared for you, and you for him. Some dimwits might say it doesn't matter, and that you're young and will find another love, but I know better."

"Because of your love for Mama?"

"Yes." Daniel raked a hand through his thick walnut-brown hair. "What I wouldn't give to have more time with your mother. If I only had that chance, I'd fight as long and hard as I could to be with her. Because love is always worth fighting for."

"Including the love between a father and daughter?"

Angelika hadn't meant to say it aloud, but nevertheless, the words felt fitting. Such a love had never existed between her and Rudolf Eder, whose burial had taken place in Vienna earlier that week, when a small crowd of relatives, friends and business associates had descended upon the expansive Central Cemetery where Clara also rested. There in the *Zentralfriedhof*, amongst serene avenues lined with oak and chestnut trees, they'd bid farewell to a man who had been revered for his business acumen, but little more.

"I'm sorry you've lost your father." Daniel slid closer and wrapped an arm around Angelika's shoulders, Mokka bounding away in search of old envelopes to sniff, plus Daniel's well-worn green felt slippers to gnaw. "I wish he'd been a better man while he was alive."

Angelika wished Rudolf had been a better man, too. A man who'd have treated her mother with respect and shown the twins a parent's love. But Daniel was wrong when he said Angelika had lost her father. For she hadn't. Her father – her found and chosen father – had always been right there before her eyes.

"Rudolf wasn't my father," she said, the words as sure and certain as the turning of beech leaves every autumn in the nearby Vienna Woods. "His name might be noted in my birth records, but that doesn't matter. Because he isn't the one who gave me jam-filled cookies on my birthday or bought me special trinkets at the toy shop. He didn't show me a world of music and art, or let me be a part of his work. He didn't make me laugh, or listen to me sing, or push me to challenge myself. He didn't teach me about other nations or respecting people's differences."

Rudolf Eder had done none of those things. It was Daniel Weiss, along with Angelika's marvellous mother, who had.

"I wasn't a real father to you, love." Daniel leant back to look at her, teardrops glistening and clinging to his lashes as, meanwhile, boats drifted past the window on their way down the river – its waters, like time, flowing endlessly onward. "I wanted to be, but I fell flat. With you, and especially with your brother."

Angelika's heart lurched at the mention of Andreas. While she, Gretchen and Kurt had attended Rudolf's funeral services, Andreas had not. As anticipated, Rudolf had left the majority of his assets to Kurt, while Angelika retained her mother's jewellery, art collection and remaining money. Rudolf had also, in an unexpected showing of pity, willed her the lakeside estate in Salzburg. Andreas, whom Rudolf had long disparaged for having been born a musician rather than a burgeoning businessman, received nothing.

"I cannot believe Andreas joined the Nazis," Daniel said.

Angelika could hardly believe it, either, her mind remaining ensconced in a purgatorial state of shock she knew preceded full-fledged grief. Although she had promised to share Clara's money and belongings with her brother, he had refused the offer, saying he didn't need his sister's charity. While she and Kurt had discussed working together to launch a philanthropic and humanitarian branch of the company, Andreas wanted no part of it. The last Angelika had heard from Kurt, Andreas had left the business, taken up residence with Johann's family and been spotted working at Viktor Bauer's brewery.

He had chosen the Nazis over Angelika, their lies overriding Andreas's love for the twin sister with whom he had walked through life. Angelika could no longer hear his voice inside her head, and every night, she wished with all her might that their connection might someday return. Yet even if it did, and even if he found his way back to her, things would never be the same. She could never forgive him for supporting monsters like Adolf Hitler, Viktor Bauer and all the rest.

Even though, admittedly, her own behaviour had been far from admirable.

"Andreas isn't the only one who's done something awful." If Daniel learnt what Angelika had done by singing at the beer garden and getting roped into the Nazis' concert plans, she feared his love for her might evaporate. But if Angelika truly loved Daniel as a father, she owed him her honesty and trust. "I have, too."

And so, sucking in a breath deeper than the Danube, Angelika told him. She told Daniel all about the upcoming concert, her grave mistake at the beer garden and the way Baldur von Schirach had turned up during *Don Carlo*. And when she was done, she studied Daniel's face, expecting to find well-deserved anger and hatred awaiting her. What she found instead was sadness.

"Why didn't you say something sooner?" he asked, the hurt apparent in every word.

Angelika averted her eyes, staring at the checkered chenille rug below, only to feel Daniel's fingertips against her chin as he lifted it and forced her to face him.

"I was too ashamed, and also afraid of what they might do to you if you got involved. Daniel…" No, not Daniel. Not anymore. "*Vati*, I know I made a wretched mistake by singing at the beer garden, but I do not support the Nazis."

"You think I don't know that?" Daniel released Angelika's chin and gripped her gently by the shoulders. "You thought I would believe you willingly agreed to sing at a Nazi concert? After everything you just told me about believing in the values your mother and I taught you? You and Andreas may be twins, but you are vastly different. And now those…" He cursed while crumpling the empty paper bag that had held Mokka's cheese treats. "And now those despicable tyrants want to waltz in and control your every movement? To hell with Hitler, to hell with Germany, and to hell with fascism!"

In all of Angelika's life, it was the first time she had ever heard Daniel shout.

"Yes, you made a terrible decision to sing at the beer garden, but those men tricked you. I'm sure they've known all along that you only agreed to appear at the concert by accident. You are not the monster, my Anni. They are. And we will find an answer. I've already lost your mother. I will not lose you, too."

He pulled Angelika close while she, in turn, considered her future. For so long, she'd believed that becoming a famous opera singer was the epitome of success for which she should strive. Yet famous as her mother had been, Clara's notoriety hadn't brought her happiness. If anything, becoming famous had damaged and destroyed her.

Fame didn't matter after all. What mattered was that Angelika would use her voice to make people feel, think and learn. That she would be known as a singer, famous or not, who celebrated open-mindedness and remained true to herself. Angelika refused to become the Nazis' puppet, or anyone's puppet, no matter how famous it might make her.

"The Nazis are trying to get their hooks into other singers, too." Angelika told Daniel about the National Socialists' growing interest in Lotte Lehmann, who seemed to believe that politics, as she referred to them, were irrelevant. "I don't know what the Nazis might have in mind for her."

Only that they would seek to use Lotte's name and personage to their advantage.

"I tried bringing it up with Madame Lehmann during our practice session at the opera house, but she wouldn't listen to me," Angelika said. "I must try again and do everything I can to stop her from being complicit toward the Nazis. Madame Lehmann is such a tremendous star, they surely want her a lot more than they want me."

And then Angelika stopped, a gasp escaping her throat as she stared into Daniel's eyes, a sudden realisation dawning.

"I don't know how the Nazis are planning to worm their way into Madame Lehmann's life," Angelika said. "Perhaps my words won't be enough to convince her to stay away from them, but I do know for certain that she cared about Mama, and she cares about me. And if the Nazis try making me sing against my will, Madame Lehmann will not be happy."

Angelika hoped Lotte would never support the Nazis, and that she would refuse to buy into whatever sorts of promises they might make. But Lotte, unlike Angelika, was an international star. Someone the Nazis couldn't as easily make disappear in a back alley if she refused to do their bidding. Perhaps Lotte would go along with them, or perhaps she would not. Angelika hoped it would be the latter, and she vowed to use her voice and influence to compel Lotte to disavow the Nazis.

But if the Nazis forced Angelika to sing under duress, or if they harmed any of the people she cared about, Lotte would be furious. In the Nazis' twisted minds, the hope of bringing Lotte into their fold would certainly matter more than Angelika's participation at their concerts or events. At long last, Angelika had the answer she needed. She knew how to get herself released from the concert and eschew the Nazis' grand plan for her future. By reminding them of her friendship with Lotte Lehmann and then, both behind their backs and publicly, urging Lotte to reject their awful ideas.

"Promise me you'll be careful, *Annichen*," Daniel said. "And that you will never publicly say you're my daughter. It's too dangerous for you."

Dangerous or not, Angelika wasn't backing down. For she was Daniel's daughter. She would always be his daughter.

Angelika embraced him, then stood and went to the piano, where the songbook containing her competition song, "Della crudele Isotta", lay waiting. Rudolf Eder's natural-born daughter was struggling. She had lost her mother, Erich and Andreas. Perhaps she wouldn't win the competition. It didn't matter. Because there in Daniel Weiss's flat, his own chosen daughter would sing from her heart, not to win contests or to become famous, but for the love of music and artistry. Daniel's daughter would carry forth the legacy of Clara Eder. A legacy that rested not upon fame or notoriety, but in championing love, acceptance and kindness.

It was Daniel's daughter who would fight for what was right. Daniel's daughter who understood that while Clara's aria may have indeed been silenced, her voice lived on, clear as always. It was also Daniel's daughter who later that evening, after leaving Mokka in his loving care, tore down and disposed of every ugly poster she could find that had been advertising the Nazis' Vienna rallies.

"These posters have the wrong dates on them," she lied when several people asked her what she was doing or tried to intervene. "This month's rallies have been cancelled. And for good reason, since the Nazis have no business peddling their propaganda here in Vienna."

The people appeared too dumfounded to argue.

As soon as she could find an address, Angelika would write to Erich, too. Even if there was no hope for the two of them romantically, she wanted to know what he had meant about the people he helped. Including, surely, the person he'd mentioned in the prop room after *Don Carlo*. Someone who also despised the Nazis. Whatever mysterious things Erich was involved in, Angelika could do them, as well. Daniel's daughter vowed to fight hatred and ignorance with every ounce of her being.

"Good evening, Fräulein."

Angelika turned at the sound of her accompanist's voice, Oskar Huber exiting the conservatory as she made her way toward the women's residence while bathed in a familiar glow of lamplight. The omnipresent pianist must have stayed late helping other students prepare for the competition. Even though Angelika, ever since she'd arrived in Vienna, had been his primary focus, for reasons that suddenly seemed as clear as one of Clara's ethereal high notes.

"Get a message to your friends," Angelika said, without returning his greeting.

For she knew it must have been Oskar. Oskar who had been there the evening of the *Don Carlo* audition. Oskar who must have hung about spying during the dress rehearsal, after everyone assumed he'd left. Oskar who had told Baldur von Schirach Angelika would be appearing onstage. Oskar who had given the Nazis updates on her progress, and who had wanted her to succeed. Oskar, an apparent Nazi supporter, who had betrayed her.

"Tell Baldur von Schirach I need to talk with him about the October concert." Angelika straightened her berry-hued beret and smoothed her belted overcoat. "No more letters or behind-my-back discussions. If Schirach wants to hear how I'm doing, he can speak with me directly by telephone. Preferably as soon as possible."

Leaving Oskar slack-jawed and speechless, Angelika continued making her way to the dormitory, striding past a man wearing a black fedora, who sat by the fountain, smoking a cigarette.

"Pardon me, miss. I need to..."

She didn't turn to see whether he was addressing her or someone else. Angelika had made her decisions about the future and could focus on little more. If only her plan to refute the National Socialists might work. And if it didn't? She must then come up with some other way to refuse the Nazis while protecting those she loved. Because one way or another, come what may, Daniel Weiss and Clara Eder's daughter was not giving in.

Twenty-Five

"Twenty minutes until the competition."

Daniel's announcement filled Angelika's ears as she perfected her make-up backstage at the Vienna State Opera, the familiar hallways once again reminding her of the distant day she'd run away from her governess, and Daniel had rushed to the rescue. The first day she'd ever seen her mother die. Tonight, however, there were no scheduled performances or rehearsals gracing the main stage. No sophisticated Clara Eder regaling Richard Strauss and Franz Schalk with her vibrant voice. No immortal soprano bounding back to life after a gruesome onstage demise.

"Finish getting ready, and then make your way upstairs to the Emperor's Room," Daniel told the young singers. "Madame Lehmann and the other judges are gathering there now, along with the audience."

Would Baldur von Schirach be in the audience, the same way he had turned up during *Don Carlo*? Angelika had expected him to telephone her as requested, but throughout the past week, no such call had come. The man must have been too busy indoctrinating Germany's youth and licking Adolf Hitler's boots to find the time. Either that, or he had something else sinister up his swastika-stamped sleeve.

With tremulous fingers, Angelika dabbed on a splash of her mother's leftover lilac *L'Orange Variée* perfume, its eclectic bottle fashioned in the shape of an orange slice. She then set about affixing a sparkling amethyst brooch that had also belonged to Clara. Even Angelika's white silk gown, complete with frog fasteners and a gauzy overlay featuring hand-embroidered swallows, was an item the two of them had purchased together in France. If only Clara could have been present to share this momentous evening with her daughter and Daniel.

"Anni, watch out." Gretchen appeared alongside the vanity table and steadied Angelika's hand. "You were about to prick yourself with the pin."

Gretchen, clad in a violet gown and matching earrings, calmly completed the job herself. If the poor girl was still reeling from Andreas's decision to join the Nazis, she didn't let it show. His decision had, of course, compelled Gretchen to nip their blossoming relationship squarely in the bud. Yet instead of sulking, Gretchen had thrown herself into her studies and encouraged Angelika to do the same.

"I know you're nervous." Gretchen's rose-pink lips curved into a caring smile. "But you'll be perfect. You're the best singer here. You deserve to win the competition."

Angelika shook her head and took her friend's arm. She didn't feel as if she were the best, nor that she deserved to win any more than the other hardworking students. There was one thing, though, that Angelika did know with absolute certainty.

"If it weren't for you, I wouldn't have gotten through this programme at all," she said. "Let alone weathered the past year without my mother."

There were many other things Angelika wished to add. She wanted to explain how much Gretchen's friendship meant, and how she hoped their bond would last forever, come what may. However, as she looked upon her companion, Angelika realised she didn't have to explain anything. Because Gretchen, the dearest friend one could ever hope for, already knew.

"Angelika?" Fellow student Georg Schneider rounded a corner while pushing spectacles up the bridge of his nose and fiddling with his tuxedo buttons. "There's someone here asking for you. I believe he said his last name is Bauer."

"Bauer?" Angelika exchanged a hopeful glance with Gretchen. "Are you certain?"

"*Ja*. He said he'd wait upstairs on the loggia overlooking the Ringstrasse. But…"

Before he could finish, Angelika leapt to her feet and all but sprinted away, leaving behind the Vienna State Opera's backstage hallways and ascending its sculpture-flanked grand staircase. Could it really be Erich? The original set of nerves left Angelika's body and gave way to an entirely different sort, anxiousness and eagerness blending as she imagined snatching him in her arms and trying to set things right. Especially since her plan to write him a letter hadn't yet come to fruition. Stefan Hoffmann, the one person she'd hoped might have an address for Erich's sister in London, had told her that he unfortunately did not.

"Pardon me, miss, but I really must speak with you."

A man carrying a black fedora appeared in front of Angelika as she reached the top of the staircase. The same mysterious, bespectacled man – tall, lean and in his early thirties – she'd seen at the airfield in Munich while helping Erich escape. The same man, she'd realised, who had been sitting by the fountain the night she'd confronted Oskar outside the conservatory. The man who had been turning up in various places throughout the past week, asking if he could speak with her. He was obviously a Nazi – another of Baldur von Schirach's confidants, no doubt – who had been tasked with spying on her and coercing her into supporting them.

"*Nein.*" Angelika put the man off as usual, then burst out onto a dimly lit covered balcony. She felt too anxious to bother glancing upward at the fanciful *Magic Flute* frescos that adorned the vaulted ceiling, nor all around her at the loggia's leaf-inspired wall sconces, towering marble columns and artful depictions of a symphony's four movements. "Erich, are you here?"

But he wasn't. Instead, Angelika found herself face-to-face with a hulking, brawny man whose features mirrored Erich's, but whose heart was non-existent.

"Viktor Bauer." Angelika stopped short, spitting the name with venom in her voice. "What the devil are you doing here? The Vienna State Opera is a place of music, art and humanity. Murderers like yourself are not welcome."

While Viktor and his cronies might control the violent streets of Munich, the majestic Vienna State Opera belonged to not only Angelika and her fellow singers, but to everyone who loved and celebrated music. This narrow-minded wretch had no business stalking its hallowed hallways.

"Murder, you say?" Erich's father – a father on paper, perhaps, but hardly in practice – appeared causally at ease. "*Ach*, my lovely girl, must you speak so harshly?" Viktor smiled and winked, his blond hair, blue eyes and athletic physique blatantly exemplifying the Nazi ideal. "To the man who gave you your start by allowing you to sing at his beer garden? Who put you on the path to becoming a darling of our National Socialist cause? Whose friends can make you a bigger star than your dearly departed mother could have ever hoped to become?"

"Leave my mother out of this. Prejudiced people like you, who spend all of their time spouting hatred, are the reason she's dead."

Viktor pursed his lips and shook his beefy head while tugging at taut suspender straps. He looked as if he were dressed for a long day of working at his Munich brewery, not for coming within a hundred metres of a luxurious opera house.

"You are a saucy thing, aren't you, Angelika?" he said, a smirk taking shape. "After growing up under the thumb of your mother and that Jew who worshiped her, I can't say I'm surprised. And then of course, there was Erich, who couldn't teach a woman obedience if his life depended upon it. But fear not."

Viktor's eyes travelled up and down Angelika's hourglass frame as if assessing a sack of barley. She was used to men, whether young or old, staring at her body. But this was a different, more calculating, gaze.

"My friends and I will tame that wickedness," Viktor said. "Once you return to Munich and are taken under our wing, you'll learn how to properly behave. We'll find a suitable man who can offer the guidance and discipline you need."

A shudder cascaded through Angelika's core as she gazed beyond Viktor to the outward-facing bronze statues that stood on either side of him – symbols of heroism and tragedy, plus fantasy, comedy and love. How close together they all seemed, the journey from heroism to tragedy easily traversable in just a few short steps.

"No man, whether you or anyone else, will be 'guiding' me." Angelika scowled and prepared to flee. "Now or ever."

"I wouldn't be so certain of that."

Viktor gestured to his left as a second man stepped out from behind a decorative folding divider. The very man who had haunted Angelika's dreams ever since she'd received his first letter, then noticed him leering in the audience during *Don Carlo*.

"That'll do, Viktor." Baldur von Schirach, a plump-faced man in his mid-twenties with piercing eyes and a festering pimple on his cheek, approached Angelika. Just as he had while attending *Don Carlo*, Baldur wore a pristinely pressed grey suit with a swastika pin at his collar. "Fräulein Eder, I apologise for my friend's forthrightness."

So, that was their intention. Have Viktor rile Angelika up, so that she would then find Baldur von Schirach less vile. Well, it wasn't going to work.

"The last thing I want is for you and I to get off on a bad footing," he said, voice oozing with a false sincerity that might have easily won over a more gullible young woman. "Unlike Herr Bauer, I was born into a well-cultured family like yours. I am a tremendous opera supporter, and I do believe your mother had the pleasure of making my sister Rosalind's acquaintance. As I'm sure you know, Rosalind is also a talented soprano."

Angelika knew quite well who Baldur von Schirach's sister was. Just as she knew quite well who he was.

"And my new bride, Henriette, is a woman your age." The Nazi youth leader and Reichstag politician continued his spiel while Angelika's scowl deepened. "I'm certain you'll become wonderful friends once you return to Munich, begin your work with us and have the distinct honour of singing for Adolf Hitler at our concert."

Angelika didn't know what was more nauseating – the fact that Baldur von Schirach had married a woman her own age, or the fact that he could ever imagine Angelika befriending her. At the moment, however, Henriette von Schirach was the least of Angelika's cares.

"I've no interest in singing for Hitler, or in support of his cause," she said, all the while hearing Clara's voice echoing inside her head. *The singer chooses which roles she will play.* "You and Hitler may fancy yourselves opera afficionados, but you couldn't be farther from it. As my mother always said, music and opera help people come together, understand one another and celebrate our shared humanity. Opera isn't meant to falsely trumpet one nation's dominance or superiority. Or to perpetuate discrimination, hatred and fear, which are the only things your party represents. Performing for Hitler would also fly directly in the face of something else my mother once taught me."

"And what is that?"

Baldur's eyes narrowed while Viktor glowered in the background.

"Never act dumb to impress a man."

"Why, you vicious..." Viktor strode forward, pushed Baldur aside, drew back his hand and, with a crack that seemed to carry all the way to Munich, slapped Angelika so hard, she stumbled backward and saw flashes of light play across her vision. "Honestly, girl, what is the matter with you? Adolf Hitler has the foresight to make all of our lives better. To make you a star of the stage. You don't need this competition, or Daniel Weiss, or my idiotic son. The only thing you need to do is trust in Herr Hitler."

Tears welled in Angelika's eyes as Viktor grabbed the collar of her dress, its delicate fabric tearing in the process.

"You mean the same way another young singer once trusted in Hitler?" Angelika raised her chin, refusing to cry. "The young singer we all read about in the papers last year? The one who's lying dead in Vienna's Central Cemetery, not too far from my mother, because Hitler or one of his henchmen murdered her?"

"Those are rumours and lies. Herr Hitler's beloved niece Geli died by suicide."

"However Angela Raubal may have died, it was Hitler who destroyed her."

Viktor whacked Angelika harder across the other cheek, eliciting a yelp. Yet still, Angelika refused to scream, fearful that if she did, or if anyone happened to walk past the loggia and see what was going on, they too might experience Viktor's wrath. She hoped the rest of the young singers were still backstage and downstairs, and felt glad that the Emperor's Room was located on the opposite side of the stairwell.

"Have you no pride?" Viktor asked, the growl bouncing off the loggia's arches before being swallowed up by sounds of the bustling street below.

"I have a great deal of pride." The sun had finished setting in the evening sky, and Angelika shivered as a chilly wind flooded the loggia. "Viennese pride."

"Oh, really? And I suppose it's a fine showing of 'Viennese pride' to help Erich escape to London, as I assume he has, and cavort with the very Brits who helped kill more than a million Austro-Hungarians during the Great War? Who nearly finished me off in the Battle of Arras? I suppose you couldn't care a bit that Herr von Schirach lost his own brother to suicide, after the poor young man was devastated by our defeat in the war."

Angelika's eyes flickered over to Baldur, who stood watching with a sickening mixture of frustration and fanaticism on his face. Her own face, meanwhile, burnt like fire, and she was certain her cheeks must be as red as a storm trooper's armband.

"Unlike your own departed Rudolf Eder, a snivelling coward who bought his way into a health exemption, I actually fought in the war," Viktor continued. "That experience made me the man I am today. Just as doing what my friends ask of you will make you the singer and woman we expect you to be." He tightened his grip upon her collar, lengthening its tear. "Though if you continue arguing with me, that gorgeous face of yours might not be so pretty for our concert."

But Angelika wasn't about to acquiesce. She couldn't. Wouldn't.

"You can yell at me, beat me or even kill me." Angelika kneed Viktor between the legs, then watched him crumple at her feet like a rag doll, moaning and groaning as Erich surely had the countless times his father had struck him. "But I am not singing at your concert or studying with your advisers." Angelika shifted her gaze back to Baldur. "You should also know that if you continue to mistreat me or anyone I care about, you'll have little chance of making your case to Madame Lehmann. Even though I intend to do everything in my power to stop her from partnering with you."

"I'm going to wring your neck," Viktor said. "*Hündin*! We'll see how well you sing once I'm finished."

He stumbled to his feet, and Angelika turned to run, only to feel Viktor's hand catch hold of her slender wrist. She was certain he was about to twist and break it, when suddenly, as if summoning all of his might, Baldur extricated Angelika from Viktor's grasp and heaved him to the side.

"That is enough, Viktor." The men wrangled like rabid dogs before coming to a halt alongside one of the loggia's marble columns. "What is the matter with you? Are you too foolish to realise that, whether we like it or not, this conniving little witch is right?" Angelika remained too stunned to remember to retreat. "Our new Reichstag President Hermann Göring is even fonder of Lotte Lehmann than he is of the goddamned lions at the Berlin Zoo. Do you know what he'll do if he finds out we hurt his chances of bringing her into our circle?"

Viktor stopped fighting against Baldur, then turned to face Angelika, his expression so scrunched, she could scarcely see his eyes.

"You're making a terrible mistake by turning down this opportunity," he said. "We are growing more powerful every day. This week's rally here in Vienna attracted thousands. Your own brother has seen the light and wisely joined us. Why can't you do the same?"

Angelika reared back as if Viktor had slapped her a third time. Andreas. Why was he following these people? Why had he abandoned her?

"How dare you speak of my brother!" Angelika choked on the words. "He…"

A familiar pair of gentle hands landed upon the backs of her shoulders before she could finish.

"Here you are, silly goose." Though Daniel's fingertips trembled, his voice had remained steady while repeating the same several words he'd once spoken when rescuing Angelika from her disgruntled governess. "Georg said you'd come to meet someone on the loggia. He said he had an uneasy feeling about it."

Angelika turned and met Daniel's eyes, which flashed with pain as he noticed the redness marring her cheeks.

"What have these monsters done to you?" he asked.

"Monsters?" Viktor laughed, and Angelika wrapped

an arm around Daniel, as if she might somehow be able to protect him. "A peculiar accusation coming from a subhuman Jew."

"The only subhuman creatures here are you two Nazi pigs." Angelika quivered as Viktor took one step, then another, closer to her and Daniel. "*Vati*, would you ask Madame Lehmann to come out here? Perhaps she'd like to see the horrible way these Germans are treating us."

This was Angelika's last chance. If her appeal didn't work, she'd have no other recourse but to try, however fruitlessly, to fight back physically if Viktor attacked.

"That won't be necessary," Baldur said. His false cordiality had vanished, and he'd sneered upon hearing Angelika address Daniel as her father. Nevertheless, her request for Lotte to come and join the conversation seemed to reignite a spark of concern, and Angelika allowed herself a tentative sigh of relief as both he and Viktor edged toward the exit. "We are leaving. You're lucky for your friendship with Madame Lehmann, Fräulein Eder. And you may be safe for today, but your victory is fleeting. Lotte Lehmann and other proud German singers will someday form an alliance with us, and there will be no one left for you to turn to for help. When that day comes, we will most assuredly meet again."

Then they were gone, and Angelika told Daniel everything that had happened.

"Oh, my dear girl," he said, holding her tightly. "If you don't want to sing tonight, you don't have to."

Angelika drew a breath and thought about all of the people in her life who loved and believed in her. People who wanted her to sing. Just as she also, now more than ever, wanted to raise her voice in celebration of music, artistry and the freedom of expression.

"I'll sing," Angelika told Daniel. "Those men rattled me, but I refuse to come undone on their account."

"You've come so far, *Liebling.*" He tucked a loose strand of hair behind Angelika's ear and kissed her sore cheeks. "Such a long way from the frightened little girl who cried during her mother's *Rigoletto* rehearsal twelve years ago. Back when you needed me to comfort you."

"I suppose you're right." Angelika leant up and kissed his own cheek in return. "I still want you here with me, though. I love you, *Vati.* I always have."

"I love you, too, my Anni."

Angelika kept Daniel's words, and her mother's, close as she slathered soothing cream onto her stinging face and used a crepe scarf to hide the rips in her collar. Once ready, she then joined her fellow singers inside the gold-leafed, silk-adorned Emperor's Room, Clara's presence guiding her thoughts, heart and soul, just as they always would.

The Nazis wouldn't stop or silence Angelika. They wouldn't win. Not tonight, at least.

"Good evening," she said in a steady, confident voice after taking the stage. "I am Fräulein Angelika Eder, and tonight, I had intended to sing 'Della crudele Isotta' from *L'elisir d'amore.*"

She drew a breath and gazed upon an audience of several dozen people, including other young singers, their families, the judges, newspapermen and opera fans.

"However, in light of recent events, I've decided I

would rather share a different song instead. A song my mother used to sing to me and with me, and a song that, by my interpretation, helps remind us precisely who we are as artists, friends and people."

Daniel and Lotte, plus the new accompanist Angelika had selected after eschewing Oskar, appeared flabbergasted, and with rightful reason. Angelika hadn't been prepared to sing a different song in the competition. Her performance would have to be given *a cappella*, and the piece she'd decided upon wasn't written for her voice type. She would have to improvise as she went, making the necessary adjustments and conveying what she felt in her heart. There was little question that Angelika would lose the competition. But that didn't matter. Tonight, she was determined to take a stand and use her voice to relay what she believed.

"I dedicate this performance to my remarkable mother, Madame Clara Eder," she said. "And also to my loving father, Herr Daniel Weiss."

A series of gasps rippled through the audience, but Angelika paid them no mind. Instead, she raised her voice in song, the rousing words to "Viva la libertà" from Mozart's *Don Giovanni* pouring forth and filling the salon.

"All are welcome," Angelika sang, her passion and sincerity encapsulated in every note. "Long live freedom!"

After singing the song once through, Angelika invited the audience to join in for a second round, many of them obliging and coming together in glorious harmony, while others sat stoically silent with disapproval burning in their eyes.

But still, Angelika continued to sing with all the strength and power she could summon, a message larger and greater than herself propelling her forward.

All are welcome. Long live freedom.

Today, tomorrow and always.

Twenty-Six

hird place. That was the pronouncement awaiting Angelika after her song had been sung and the competition had come to a climactic close. Not that she was upset about it. Given her audacious eleventh-hour decision to sing "Viva la libertà" instead of her original piece, she hadn't expected to place at all. While Angelika may not have won, she had used her voice to convey a meaningful message. She had made the audience think and feel. That was the power of music. That was what mattered most.

"Can you believe it, Anni?" Gretchen embraced her friend amidst the post-recital chaos. "Me, winning the competition and scholarship? And Georg finishing second?"

"I can believe it." Angelika bounced on her heels, her face breaking into its biggest smile since she'd snuggled beneath the stars with Erich, right before everything imploded and he'd hurtled away in a silver-winged Messerschmitt 23. "Just wait until your folks hear. They'll be as proud as I am."

Although Stefan and Adelheid had wanted to visit Vienna for the competition, Gretchen had convinced them to remain in Germany and continue tending to those in need.

"Georg says he's coming back to the conservatory this autumn as a paying student," Gretchen said. She and Angelika lingered alongside the grand piano as a couple of reporters milled about; Daniel and Lotte congratulated everyone; and the entire group of thirty-five students prepared to descend upon nearby Café Sacher for celebratory chocolate-and-apricot torte. "If only you could do that, too. Then all three of us could be together. But the Nazis… Their concert… Whatever are you going to do about it?"

Jarring visions of Viktor Bauer and Baldur von Schirach flashed before Angelika's eyes, and a dull ache lingered upon her cheeks.

"As it turns out, I've mercifully managed to circumvent the Nazis." Angelika exhaled a heavy breath as Gretchen's eyes widened with relief and hopefulness. "For now, anyway. I'll explain more later. And as for attending the conservatory this autumn…"

As the competition's third-place finisher, Angelika was welcome to pay tuition and enrol as a Tonkunst Conservatory student when the autumn term began in a couple of weeks. She wanted to remain in Vienna and be close to Daniel, as well as do everything she could to convince Lotte to disavow the Nazis. The chance to be with Gretchen and Georg would be like the delightful whipped cream topping on *Einspänner* coffee. She wished things could have been different, and the Andreas she'd grown up with could join them, too.

And Erich, of course. *Ach*, Erich. While Angelika may have convinced Viktor Bauer and Baldur von Schirach to stay away from her family and friends for the time being, there was no denying that Erich would be safest living in London. For Viktor had been correct when he said the Nazis were growing more powerful. Their Vienna rallies were attracting thousands, and during the past week, there had been violent clashes between National Socialists and communists in the southern city of Graz. Like Germany, Austria was devolving into a powder keg of political tensions that some might say made music and art seem frivolous. And yet, to Angelika, artistic expression remained more important than ever.

"I think I'll be able to enrol," Angelika told Gretchen, a plan having begun solidifying in her mind. While there were certain sentimental pieces from her mother's artwork and jewellery collections that Angelika hoped to keep, her memories could live on without material possessions. She could sell some of the items and, as she'd already begun arranging with Kurt's assistance, donate most of them to charity. She could also seek paid singing engagements and tutor less experienced singers as a way to earn money. "Isn't Frau Fuchs going to be tickled when we tell her we'd like to stay on at the dormitory?"

Angelika expected Gretchen to laugh, but found that her friend's face had turned serious.

"Are you coming down sick?" Gretchen rested a palm against one of Angelika's cheeks. "You're awfully flushed, and your voice seems strained."

Later that night, Angelika would tell Gretchen all

that had happened with Viktor Bauer and Baldur von Schirach. She would explain that if her cheeks were red, it was because Viktor had slammed his meaty hand across them. She couldn't say anything yet, though. Not in the midst of her friend's winning moment. And not when nosy newspapermen with competing loyalties were afoot. Already, one of them had been badgering Angelika, asking why she'd called Daniel her father during the recital.

I called him my father because he is my father, she'd matter-of-factly told the reporter, as well as several other questioning members of the audience. *And I am incredibly lucky to be his daughter.*

Daniel would probably tell Angelika she shouldn't have done what she had. That she was endangering herself. But no matter what he said, Angelika had seen the love in Daniel's eyes as she'd dedicated the song to him and Clara. She had noticed proud tears glistening as she'd sung "Viva la libertà" and been announced the third-place finisher. She loved Daniel, and he loved her. That true, simple fact would never change.

"Congratulations, ladies." Lotte, appearing ever regal with carefully coifed brown hair and a rose-inspired barrette that matched the pattern on her dress, grinned as she approached Angelika and Gretchen. "You should both be quite proud of yourselves. Your performances, whether planned or not, were marvellous."

"Thank you, Madame Lehmann," Angelika said.

She felt honoured that Lotte, along with soprano Elisabeth Schumann and a couple of faculty judges, had given her the third-place title. She'd also been overjoyed to see Lotte singing along during her "Viva la libertà" performance. Perhaps Angelika might eventually succeed in convincing Lotte to stand against the Nazis.

"I've decided to stay here in Vienna and enrol for the autumn term." Angelika linked arms with Gretchen while giving Lotte the news. "We both have."

She then shifted her attention toward the salon's ivory-handled double doors, where the man with the black fedora loitered, a small bouquet of flowers clutched in his hand. She excused herself and made her way over to him, befuddled as to why he was still there when Viktor Bauer and Baldur von Schirach had long since left. Angelika hadn't noticed him during her performance or throughout the remainder of the recital, but he'd apparently been lingering.

"Pardon me, sir." Angelika crossed the plush red carpet and marched up to the fedora-toting man. His light brown hair, bespectacled caramel-coloured eyes and slim build made him appear somewhat like an older, taller version of Georg Schneider, who'd finished second in the competition. "If you don't mind my asking, why are you still here? Your friends left quite some time ago."

"My friends?" The man spoke quietly, and his lips curled in amusement as he stepped out into a private corner of the hallway and beckoned for Angelika to follow. "If you're referring to the two National Socialist beasts who accosted you on the loggia, you should know that I was never here with them in the first place. I also apologise for not intervening. Had Viktor Bauer gone farther than a couple of cruel slaps, I certainly would have." Although the man's German seemed impeccable, if Angelika listened closely, she could discern a hint of an accent buried beneath the surface. An accent she couldn't quite put her finger on. "However, I had good reason for not wanting those men to realise I was here."

"You mean, you haven't been spying on me for the Nazis?"

"Good heavens, no. I'd like to think I haven't been spying on you at all. I've been trying to speak with you and give you a message from an admirer." He leant in closer and whispered in Angelika's ear. "I also wanted to ensure that if anyone tried seriously harming you, I could quickly find you a way out of the country."

Angelika's head spun, not only in confusion, but in ever-rising trepidation about the Nazis. The more powerful they and groups like them became, the more destruction they would bring about. The more innocent people's lives they would seek to destroy.

"Finally, I wanted to give you these." The man extended a petite bouquet of dried daisies. "A gift from your admirer."

"My admirer?" Angelika asked while accepting the arrangement.

She scarcely knew this mysterious man. Why in Mozart's name would an admirer have asked him to give her flowers?

"Yes," he said, "though I'd rather not divulge too many details here." He looked around as if to verify that no one was listening. "I can see you're in the middle of a celebration, so perhaps we can speak a bit more tomorrow. I'm staying at Hotel Sacher if you wish to find me. Just give the staff your name, and ask for James Webber. I'll be in the country a few more days."

He headed toward the stairs, and Angelika stared at the bouquet in her hand. Of all the things to give her, why dried daisies? Just like the ones she and Clara used to create. Just like the one Erich had placed in her hair the day he'd turned up outside the Munich music school. Just like...

Angelika gasped, then took off at a hasty clip, flying past silent statues as she descended the grand marble staircase.

"Sir, wait." She panted to a stop beside him, her Louis-heeled patent-leather pumps skidding across the foyer's polished floor. "Did you say that... an admirer... sent you here? That he's the one who asked you to give me these daisies?"

"Yes," the man named James replied. "He told me you'd be wary, and understandably so, if I tried speaking with you. He said you aren't a young woman to be trifled with. He also told me you'd be clever enough to eventually figure out who I was. It appears he was right."

Angelika sucked in a shuddering breath and held the dried daisies close to her heart. Daisies from a young man she dearly loved. Daisies that served as a sign it wasn't too late to make amends.

"You're his sister's husband," Angelika said.

"Correct. And I should probably share a few other important details. Is there somewhere private we can speak?"

Angelika led James through a labyrinth of hallways

to a storage room filled with boxes for an upcoming production of *Fidelio*. Once he had launched into his explanation, a good many things started making sense. Angelika learnt that after she'd toppled into Lake Fuschl and passed out for the night, Erich had telephoned his sister in London to say that he was planning to return to Munich to try getting Angelika released from singing at the National Socialist concert. His sister had then telephoned James, who was away on a business assignment in Berlin, obtaining beer and goods for his London hotels and nightclubs – establishments that catered primarily to German or French travellers and immigrants.

"My newest club is called the Silver Whisker," he said. "It's become quite the sensation since we opened its doors a year ago."

Based on Erich's letter at the lake, as well as her own suspicions, Angelika assumed that James's business ventures and travels were some sort of cover for gathering information about the political situations in Germany and elsewhere.

"Perhaps you'd like to visit the club sometime," James said. "We're always hiring talented singers. But we can discuss that later."

"Along with other potential ways I can help you?" Angelika couldn't resist asking the forthright question. "Can we discuss that, as well?"

James didn't answer straightaway, his eyes assessing and studying her expression, until at last, he nodded.

"All in good time," he replied.

He next explained that Erich's sister – whom James had

met while conducting business in Munich several years earlier – had warned her husband by telephone about Erich's plan to help Angelika. James had then hurried to Munich, hoping to stop him from doing something foolish. But James had been too late. When he'd arrived at the Wolpertinger Kaffeehaus, whose owners were his well-informed friends, he had learnt of the motorcycle accident. The owners had overheard Kurt making the aeroplane arrangements and had allowed James to use their truck to travel to the airfield and make sure Erich safely left.

"When I saw you there in the car, helping Erich escape," James said, "I knew you must be his brilliant French tutor, Angelika. The vivacious young woman he'd written to his sister about. A young woman who is well-connected within artistic communities and is also quite the talented linguist."

James had travelled to Holland the following morning, where he'd met Erich dockside and prepared to see him safely to London. Erich, however, had implored James to visit Vienna and deliver a message to Angelika, help find a solution to the Nazi concert fiasco and, if need be, help her leave the country. As it turned out, Angelika hadn't needed James's help regarding the concert. Nevertheless, being in Austria had surely helped him obtain useful information about the Nazi rallies and menacing violence.

"Thank you for looking out for me, sir," Angelika said once he had finished. "And I'd like nothing better than to visit London and see Erich again. But perhaps it could be a surprise?"

Something to show him how much she cared. How much she would always care.

"In that case, you're in luck, my lady." James smiled and gave Angelika an exaggerated bow. "Arranging surprises happens to be my specialty."

Twenty-Seven

*A*ngelika had never expected to find herself appearing at a London nightclub. She hadn't expected to spend mid-September of 1932 in England at all. And yet, there she stood, an Austrian opera singer wearing a slinky, open-backed evening gown reminiscent of Marlene Dietrich, Greta Garbo or another alluring Hollywood starlet.

The first time she'd visited London with Clara and Daniel six years prior, the trip had become a whirlwind of sights and shows, monuments and museums. Clara had told her that as impressive as it was to gaze upon such iconic sights as London Bridge and Buckingham Palace, the real joy came in sharing the experiences, whether grand or commonplace, with those who meant the most. As always, she was right.

For ever since Angelika had arrived with James Webber several hours earlier, she'd cared precious little about anything but pulling off her grand surprise and reuniting with Erich. In the few days that had passed since the singing competition, James had sent Erich a telegram from Vienna, discretely letting him know the Nazi concert debacle had been resolved and that Angelika was safe. The telegram had also promised she would write to him soon. Little did Erich know she had travelled to London with James and that, this very evening, she would be appearing as a special guest at Piccadilly's Silver Whisker Nightclub and Hotel.

"And now, please join me in welcoming to the stage..."

A master of ceremonies' deep voice carried into the wings as Angelika prepared to make her appearance. She was more nervous than she'd ever been before a performance, not because she doubted her ability, but because James had promised to make sure an unsuspecting Erich would be there to watch. Tonight, Angelika would be singing not for herself, nor the countless other patrons present. Tonight, she would be singing especially for Erich.

"...a talented singer who has come all the way from the illustrious city of Vienna."

Mutterings in English, German and French floated from the audience as Angelika straightened her pearls and smoothed her black silk gown. In her hotel room upstairs, she'd fashioned her hair into finger waves and applied shimmery purple eyeshadow. Quite a different look from that of the ethereal Celestial Voice she'd portrayed in Vienna. This time, Angelika's feet would remain firmly grounded on earth, even as her hopeful spirit soared high.

"It is my pleasure to introduce the lovely, the talented, the marvellous... Miss Angelika Eder!"

Adrenaline coursing through her veins, Angelika strode into the spotlight, the club's small orchestra seated at the side of the stage, ready to accompany her. Throughout the art deco-inspired house, chandeliers glistened from the ceiling, a couple of dozen round-top tables filled the floor, and the walls boasted bold geometric patterns and glimmering gilt. In the back, a long crystal bar also displayed a sparkling array of beer mugs, wine goblets and champagne flutes.

"Good evening." Greeting the audience in English, Angelika stepped up to the microphone and stared into the crowd, her eyes beholding patrons young and old. Some folks were sitting, and others standing. Some were busy drinking, smoking or dining while others waited on the dance floor, eager to swing and sway. "I'm pleased to be here with you tonight, and to sing a couple of special songs."

Seated at a table up front were James and his wife, a woman who appeared to be the spitting image of Erich. He, however, to Angelika's disappointment, was not sitting with them.

"Including this first number," she said, "which is dedicated to someone I love. Someone who happens to be Marlene Dietrich's biggest fan. Yes, I know. I don't have a top hat or scintillating knee-high stockings like the divine Miss Dietrich." A chuckle rippled through the crowd. "But I hope this Chanel evening gown, long though it may be…" Several whistles rang out. "…and my voice, will be suitable substitutes."

Still scanning the club for signs of the sweetheart she'd forsaken, Angelika launched into a rousing rendition of "Give Me The Man" from Marlene's American film

Morocco. One of Erich's favourites. But although Angelika's singing was smooth and saucy, and the jubilant audience hung upon every last note, the lyrics felt dry in her mouth. For Erich had yet to appear. Had he found out she was singing and changed his mind about coming? Had he decided that the things Angelika said in Munich were too heinous after all?

By the time she'd started her second number, "Falling In Love Again" from *The Blue Angel*, she felt certain that must be the case. Perhaps he was at James's Mayfair residence helping a kind, thoughtful and pretty nanny look after "Little Miss Dancer", the two-year-old niece Erich had alluded to in his letter at the lake. Perhaps he'd already found a new sweetheart and taken her out on the town. Wherever he might be, the second chance Angelika had hoped she'd have seemed to evaporate like the tendrils of cigarette smoke curling in the air.

"Thank you for such a warm and wonderful welcome," Angelika told the audience once she'd finished singing. "I suppose I did all right, hmm?" She forced herself to remain outwardly jovial as a triumphant chorus of cheers met her ears. "Perhaps I'll come back on with more numbers a little later."

The clubgoers finished applauding, and Angelika headed to her backstage dressing room as a group of can-can dancers flounced into the limelight to perform their act. A fluffy orange cat she'd learnt was the club's namesake rubbed against her leg, and Angelika leant down to give the feline a pet, all the while trying to keep her heart from caving in. Erich wasn't there. He hadn't heard her sing.

Perhaps he regretted asking James to give her the daisies after the Vienna recital. She ought to have sent him a letter from Vienna and accepted the outcome, whatever it might have been. So much for her grandiose plans.

"You never did give me that autograph I wanted."

A young man's voice resounded, the cat meowing and zipping toward it as Angelika also rose and turned. Her breath caught in her throat, and her knees couldn't help but wobble. For there, leaning against the doorjamb, stood a well-built, curly-haired, hazel-eyed miscreant. His left arm was in a cast, and a smattering of cuts and bruises lingered upon his boyish, grinning face.

"Erich." Angelika whispered his name, even as her feet remained frozen in place. Angelika had wanted to surprise him, but Erich, as usual, had ended up surprising her instead. "I didn't see you out there. I mean, I didn't notice you in the audience."

"I wasn't in the audience." He moved nearer, closing the distance until he and Angelika stood face-to-face. Erich was still walking with a slight limp, but his injured left leg seemed markedly better than it had two weeks earlier, the last time she'd seen him. "I was operating the spotlight from a platform behind the bar. With my decent arm, that is. An arm I almost busted after falling off my step-stool when I realised it was you coming onstage. No wonder James sent me out running errands this afternoon and wouldn't let me watch the rehearsals."

Angelika managed a small smile, gazing into Erich's rich eyes and then down at his clothing – pin-striped suspenders, fitted beige slacks and a white sport shirt.

"I suppose you're working here, then?" she asked, palms clammy and heart thudding.

Angelika hadn't expected to be so jittery.

"You suppose right. And I'm lucky. Not everyone has well-connected relatives in England. Not everyone has a way to evade murderers like the Nazis." Erich stood close enough that Angelika could smell his woodsy aftershave and the faint scent of peppermints on his breath. "My friend took over with the spotlight so that I could come find you. He's a German immigrant, too. And just like me, he wants to go to university someday. We both want to become physicians."

So, that was Erich's dream. A dream that filled Angelika with pride and admiration.

"I'm living here at the Silver Whisker," he added. "In the hotel workers' quarters, that is. Not the regular, fancier guest rooms. I guess James set you up in one of those?"

Angelika nodded. She wanted to tell Erich that as nice as the room was, it would be empty and lonely without him by her side. More than anything, she longed for the two of them to reconnect that night – laughing, talking and lying in each other's arms until the sun peeked out over Piccadilly. If only they could find a way to bridge the lingering emotional distance. If only Angelika could regain her wits and find a way forward.

"I had a feeling you might mention the autograph." She lifted her peacock-embroidered pocketbook and extracted a photograph Gretchen had recently developed, its frozen image depicting Angelika and Erich bantering in the music room at her former house in Munich. "Here."

Angelika handed Erich the picture, watching as he drank it in, then flipped it over to read the inscription.

Lontano dagli occhi, vicino al cuore, she had written on the back. *Tanti baci, Anni.*

"I speak German and French, remember?" Erich teased. "Plus, a decent amount of English, which I'm getting better at every day. I hid those last two languages from Viktor, because he didn't want me knowing them. It made secretly writing to James and my sister easier, too. But I never did study Italian."

"It means, 'Far from the eyes, close to the heart. Many kisses, Anni.'" Gently, tentatively, Angelika raised a tremulous hand to Erich's clean-shaven cheek. "Even though, the last time I saw you, I said…"

Erich's spotlight-warmed fingertips captured her hand, pressed it against his chest and stopped it from shaking.

"I remember what you said. Every last word. Especially this part…" Erich cleared his throat, and when he spoke, it was in an exaggerated, sardonic tone. "'Curse you, Erich, just leave. I want you out of my life forever.' Perhaps I should have a talk with Daniel and the other advisers you've been studying with in Vienna. Because I'm sorry to be the bearer of bad news, but your performance on the way to the airfield that day was atrocious."

"That's because everything I said was rubbish." Angelika rested her free hand against Erich's unbroken shoulder, his solid body settling her. "It was worse than rubbish. Worse than the time I told my governess I hadn't been eating raspberries, even though I had the red juice smeared across my mouth. I was afraid you'd never agree to leave Germany unless I laid it on as thick as honey on a black bear's paw."

"I know."

Erich's voice was steady and sincere, even as Angelika's broke.

"I thought you were going to die." Her eyes blurred with tears. "I thought I was going to lose you, just like I lost Mama. So, I did the only thing I believed might…"

The tears spilled over at the precise moment Erich's mouth met Angelika's in a kiss that was long and lasting, sure and certain, with no remaining room for doubt.

"I'm sorry, *mio bene*," she said after their lips had parted. "I love you. I never wanted to hurt you."

"No, I'm sorry." Erich kicked the dressing room door closed with his boot, then continued kissing Angelika's neck, her eyes, her hair. "I made a mess of everything, but I love you, too. Richard Mozart's ghost, do I love you."

"Thank you for the daisies, darling."

"Thank you for saving my life. Terrible performance or not, if you hadn't said all the things you did, I never would have left. I knew that for you to go so far, you really must care. I knew you'd forgiven me after what happened at the lake."

Memories of that night came flooding back. Memories of Erich's mouth, his skin, his body entwined with Angelika's. She had thought that if a London encore happened, it would be upstairs in her hotel room, but now that she and Erich were together, she couldn't stop herself from pressing her hungry, impatient body against his.

"I want to know everything that's happened," he said, holding her to him with his uninjured right arm. "Every last thing that happened after I escaped."

"I'll tell you." Angelika eased herself backward onto a vanity table as Erich's fingertips traced the smooth silk of her dress, then travelled across her bare-skinned back and the tender skin around her collarbone. "You must tell me everything, too. Just not quite yet."

She reached again for her bag and showed him what she had brought.

"You had this all perfectly planned out, didn't you?" Erich said.

"Not perfectly planned. Hoped for, though."

Fortunately, Angelika didn't have to hope any longer. Just as they had at the lake, the two of them came easily together, Erich moving more slowly on account of his heightened injuries, but still as sturdily and strongly as Angelika remembered. All the while, the two of them whispered in each other's ears, their voices remaining soft, not only because they were behaving scandalously backstage at a club, but because they were focused on the blissful feeling of each other's bodies, every give and take conveying acceptance and forgiveness. This time, Angelika hadn't been too late. This time, love had won.

"You must come and see my room tonight," she said after it was over, her breathing slowing and a contented sense of calm setting in. "For the sake of the hotel. You can make sure it's comfortable enough for guests. It's what any responsible employee would do."

"There's my sassy siren." Erich rested his forehead

against Angelika's and gave her a squeeze. "What's the saying? The customer knows best?"

Angelika kissed him, then set about fixing her hair and make-up. She knew there would be pain and sadness conveyed during their later conversations, including awful news concerning Andreas, Viktor Bauer, Baldur von Schirach and the Nazis. Yet she also knew that she and Erich would weather the future together – her in Vienna and him in London, but a team nevertheless – come what may, for as long as fate allowed. Together, they could support James's work and help keep watch over the worsening threat of fascism. Together, and individually, they would stand for what was right.

"There you are, miss." The master of ceremonies, a slight man with a disproportionately deep voice and a silly circus hat perched atop his head, beckoned to Angelika as she and Erich made their way through the backstage area several minutes later on their way to the dance floor. "The audience would like to know if you'll sing another song for us. Is this a good time?"

Angelika looked to Erich, who gave her an encouraging wink. This time, she knew he would be watching from the audience. Just as he would, once again, be waiting for her when she was finished.

"Yes." Angelika removed her strand of pearls and tucked them into Erich's breast pocket before making her way toward the stage. "This is the perfect time to sing my next song."

Angelika's Memory Book

September 1932 – Tonight
London

If the real ghost of Mozart had descended from the heavens to tell me that at nineteen years of age, I would make my operatic debut in Vienna and become a runaway sensation at a sophisticated nightclub in Piccadilly, I'd have never believed a word. But the erstwhile maestro's absurd prediction would have been correct.

For as luck would have it, the Silver Whisker's audience liked my sultry singing so much that James Webber has already invited me to come back during my breaks from the Tonkunst Conservatory. I know *Vati* will get a thrill out of hearing the news, and I know that if Mama were here, she'd be happy for me, too. Some finicky folks in the Vienna opera circles might not consider this respectable work, but Mama believed all forms of artistry matter.

I wish I could tell her about Erich, and the plan we've made to continue our romance while living apart, as difficult as that may be. I'd tell her about my plans to return to the conservatory in Vienna, spend precious time with *Vati* and use my voice to stand up for what is right. I'd also tell her about my plan to support what I suspect to be James's clandestine information network while at the same time compelling Lotte Lehmann to denounce the Nazis. Most of all, I'd tell Mama how much I love her and always will – how the pain of losing her has brought me here, to a new love and a new hope, even in the face of lingering uncertainty.

Don't be afraid, Angelika, mein Liebling. Everything's going to be all right.

I can still hear her saying it, both in my memories and in the recurring nightmare I've been having since the night of the singing competition. The vision starts out pleasantly enough, with Mama and I singing the "Sull'aria" duet from *Le Nozze di Figaro* onstage at the Salzburg Festival. But then, the image shifts, and suddenly, we're racing through the city streets, trying to lead other people to safety amidst shattered glass and smoke while Viktor Bauer and Baldur von Schirach chase after us, the two of them throwing rocks and screaming, "Adulteress! Traitor!" I try helping our group evade them as Mama reassures me, but still, they progress. Still, they spew their odious words.

And then, before us, another figure appears from out of the haze. At first, I think I must be gazing at a reflection, but I'm not. It's Andreas. I cry out for help and shout his name while stumbling toward him. I reach out my hand, but that's when it all ends. I wake up, never truly knowing whether he's there to help us or…

*

"Anni?"

Angelika lowered the pen as Erich appeared by her side.

"I woke up and reached for you, but you were gone," he said. "For a minute, I was afraid I'd imagined everything that happened between us tonight."

Angelika drew in a steadying breath while glancing about the hotel room, which contained a double bed, oaken bureau and hand-carved writing desk she'd already cluttered with items, including the beloved daisy clip Erich had returned to her.

"Silly man." Angelika stood, playfully tussling her sweetheart's sloppy hair while flicking off the floor lamp. "No one's imagination is that extraordinary."

Despite having one workable arm, Erich lifted a pyjama-clad Angelika and carried her over his shoulder, back to bed, by the gleam of streetlight from a nearby window.

"All these stories you told me you write about in your memory book…" Erich eased Angelika onto the mattress and slid down beside her, both of their eyelids heavy after hours spent talking and reconnecting earlier. "Will you read me some of them tomorrow?"

Though Angelika hadn't yet told Erich about the dream, she knew he shared her feelings – the intermingling trepidation and hope, fear and puzzlement over what the future might hold, not only for them, but the world as a whole.

"Of course." Angelika kissed him, still astonished that the very person she'd once doubted was the only one she wanted. "I'll tell you my stories. Especially since, no matter what might happen next, you'll always be a part of them."

Angelika brought her head to rest against Erich's chest and closed her eyes, ready for whatever dreams or nightmares sleep might hold, and for whatever the following day might bring.

*H*eather Walrath is an author crafting new stories while celebrating the release of her debut historical novel, *The Diva's Daughter*. Whether they are standing against evil in fractious 1930s Europe or solving a sticky bootlegging mystery in Prohibition-era America, Heather's relatable heroines make the past accessible and engaging for modern readers. She holds a master's degree in publishing and a bachelor's degree in journalism.